Elemental
Forgotten Heritage

C.G. Macington

Publisher: Rivera Publishing
Editor: Alex Gogoulis

ISBN: 978-1-7389180-3-4

Table of Contents

Dedication

To my brave editor Alex: thank you for your bold edits, and stalwart advice. I gave you a rough version of this story, and you turned this novel into a gem!

To Moss: thank you for your encouragement and suggestions along the way. Without your guidance, this book would have turned out quite differently(and much less spicy).

To Tyler: On the off chance you read this, do you want me to rescue you from a tower?

Maps

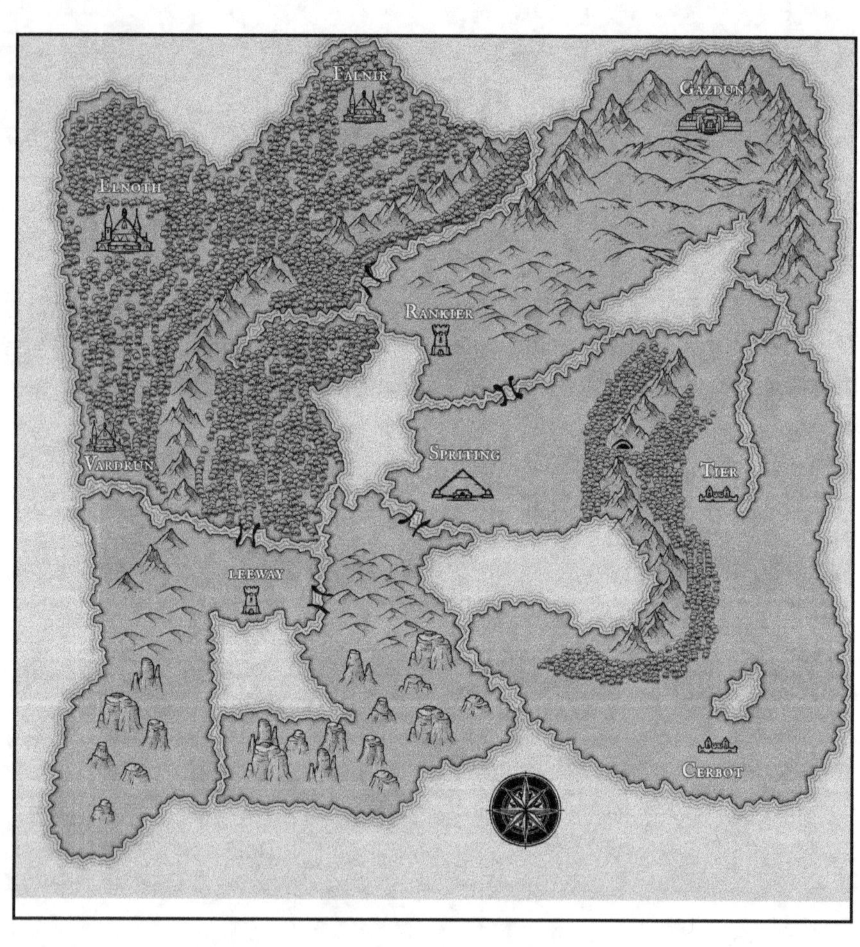

Falnir
Gazdun
Elnoth
Rankier
Spriting
Vardrun
Tier
Leeway
Cerbot

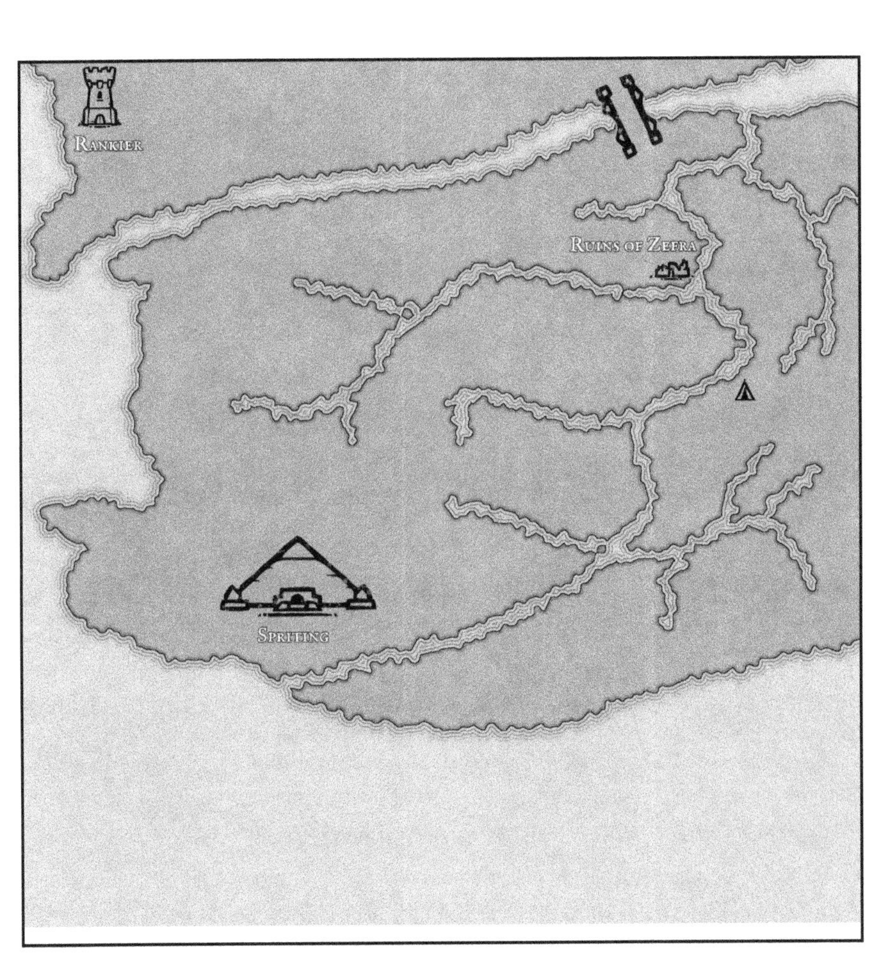

Rankier
Ruins of Zefra
Spriting

Part 1

C.G. Macington

Prologue:
Demonic Pact

As the sun dipped below the horizon, darkness enveloped the sprawling city of Nova. Nestled at the base of a large mountain, the city's heart pulsated life. Homes and businesses bustled with activity while the vibrant citizenry moved through the labyrinthine streets but amidst the bustling life, a sinister presence lurked high above them all.

At the pinnacle of the mountain, piercing the night sky like a malevolent monolith, loomed a foreboding black palace. Its grand columns soared into the heavens, while spires adorned with jagged peaks and crenelations clawed at the stars. With every gust of wind, a dark and eerie essence seemed to seep from the very stone, casting an aura of dread upon the entire city.

Beneath the darkened heavens, the contrast between the city's life and the haunting presence of the black palace created an electrifying tension, as if a cosmic battle between good and evil played out on this very hilltop. Nova's citizens may have gone about their lives, but deep down, they could feel the malicious gaze of the sinister palace, as if it were a cursed sentinel watching their every move.

Within the brooding confines of the palace, the dark King, a figure of enigmatic power, made his way to his bed chamber, ready to surrender to the embrace of slumber. As he settled into his opulent bed, his eyes drifted shut, and darkness consumed him. Little did he know that his dreamscape would transform into a nightmarish reality.

In the realm of his dreams, an unsettling presence coalesced, shrouded in an aura of mystery. Step by step, this entity drew near to the Dark King's incorporeal form, taking on the shape of a man. Unimposing yet unsettling this man had eyes hidden behind round spectacles that emphasized the minuscule nature of his being. But despite his unassuming appearance, an overwhelming wickedness radiated from his very core.

The man's facial features appeared muddled, as if contorted by some unearthly force to conform to the body they adorned—a twisted facade concealing the truth beneath. It was as though his identity itself was a veil, a disguise to deceive and confound all who dared to peer into the depths of his soul.

In this surreal dream realm, the lines between reality and illusion blurred, and the King found himself trapped in a sinister dance with this otherworldly intruder. Each moment in this strange encounter carried an intensity that threatened to shatter the fabric of the King's sanity. The figure tormented the Dark King, hunting him through his dreams, turning them into nightmares.

As the night wore on, the bedchamber became a battleground of dark forces, and the King's nightmares grasped him firmly, where the evil presence taunted him with cryptic whispers, pushing the boundaries of his fears.

Little did he realize that what transpired in this surreal realm might have repercussions in the waking world. The veil between dreams and reality had been torn asunder, and the fate of the King now hung precariously in the balance between the palpable darkness and the uncertain dawn.

In the dimly lit confines of the palace settings in his dreamscape, having found nowhere else to run within his own mind, the King stood face to face with the man, their encounter fraught with foreboding. The air seemed to thicken as the man's words hung heavy, portending an impending cataclysm that could reshape the very fabric of the world and bring the King's own life to a harrowing end.

As the man spoke, his voice took on an eerie quality, akin to that of a serpent with a forked tongue. Its words slithering forth like oily tendrils, laced with evil. Every syllable seemed to gnaw at the King's soul, leaving a trail of unease in its wake.

Then, with a deliberate and unsettling motion, the figure extended a hand adorned with long, sharp nails honed to lethal points. With a touch as cold as ice, the hand settled upon the King's forehead, unleashing a torrent of visions that tore through his mind like a tempest.

The specter of a courageous young hero materialized, radiating with righteous fury. His palms ablaze with a searing fire of retribution, a sword hewn from obsidian materialized in his grasp. It was a weapon of justice that resonated like a tolling bell, heralding the reckoning to come.

The young avenger drew closer, a harbinger of doom marching inexorably towards the King. The vision beheld the impending clash, where great blasts of fire erupted and the obsidian blade carved a path of vengeance, piercing through flesh with chilling clarity.

The gut-wrenching scenes unfolded before the King with agonizing clarity, evoking a terror that gripped his very soul. Yet, as swiftly as the visions came, they vanished when the figure retracted his hand from the King's forehead, leaving him disoriented and trembling with an overwhelming sense of dread.

The warning had been delivered, and the chilling specter of doom now lingered in his mind like a dark omen. He could feel the weight of destiny bearing down upon him, as the portents of his own demise and a world in turmoil haunted his every thought. The stage had been set for an impending clash of cosmic proportions, and he knew he had been marked by the touch of an enigmatic harbinger of fate.

With a voice as harsh and slithery as a serpent's hiss, the imposing figure laid bare a chilling prophecy before the King. The vision of an impending doom, the end of his rule, and the hollowness of a life unfulfilled echoed in the dark chamber, leaving the King paralyzed by fear and desperation.

In a quivering and hasty response, devoid of rational thought, the King surrendered, offering anything in exchange for the power to confront and vanquish the looming threat. It was a pact sealed in desperation, the price paid without hesitation, unaware of the sinister machinations at play.

Exuding an aura of diabolic delight, the figure wickedly grinned as he once again placed his razor-sharp talons on each side of the King's face. In that moment, the very fabric of the man's mind was torn asunder, and the torment of unimaginable agony enveloped him. His consciousness splintered into fragments, as a foreign entity invaded his innermost thoughts.

"We are one now," the slithery voice taunted, as the invasive presence delved deeper, entwining with the King's very essence. Like a serpent burrowing into fertile soil, this sinister being insidiously coiled around his consciousness, shrouding him in an intoxicating blend of power and rage.

In a disoriented frenzy, his mind lost all semblance of order, drowned out by the overwhelming sensation of malevolent might coursing through his veins. Within the chaos, a haunting laughter reverberated, drowning any last traces of rationality, and a new force emerged—the amalgamation of his own self and the serpentine malevolence now bound together.

The pact had been struck, but the price exacted was far more than King had ever imagined. He now wielded formidable power; a lethal gift laced with a venomous curse. And as the dust of the night settled, the once-sound mind of the King had been forever usurped, lost in the maelstrom of a relentless, discordant power—one that would shape his fate and the destiny of the world.

Chapter 1:
The Dream

As the first rays of dawn pierced the horizon, Noah jolted awake, his mind entangled in the clutches of a haunting nightmare. A soft moan escaped his lips, betraying the distress that lingered from the troubled slumber. Beads of sweat glistened on his forehead like tear drops, remnants of the unsettling visions that had plagued him throughout the night.

With a heavy sigh, Noah released himself from the grip of tangled sheets and rose from his modest bed in the humble cottage he shared with his grandmother. The worn floorboards creaked beneath his feet as he stumbled toward the window and entrance, seeking solace in the embrace of the early morning sunlight.

Emerging into the golden rays that painted the world, Noah gazed upon the farm they called home, a place where toil and love mingled to form the fabric of their lives. The vast fields of wheat swayed, like an ocean of gold, undulating in response to a gentle breeze that whispered across their secluded valley.

But as his eyes turned back to the cottage, reality confronted him with its stark and unforgiving presence. The quaint two-bedroom thatch cottage that was once a sanctuary, now bore the marks of time's relentless march. The time-weathered walls begged for fresh coats of whitewash to mask their scars. The thatched roof, a thin barrier between the outside world and the shelter within, tattered and fragilely transparent in places.

Each year, the need for repairs grew more pressing, yet the resources remained forever elusive. Noah and his grandmother struggled to make ends meet. Their livelihood depended on the ebb and flow of each harvest and the meager earnings from occasional side jobs in the nearby village of Tier. Yet, these side jobs often demanded more than just time; they required a compromise of precious moments that could have been spent nurturing the home and fields they held dear.

Amidst the fields of plenty, they wrestled with scarcity. Each day was a dance between hope and uncertainty, where determination clashed with the harsh realities of a world that offered no reprieve. Despite the hardship, their bond of love and resilience kept them steadfast, forging ahead on this unpredictable journey called life.

Noah's breath steadied as the gentle wind cooled his perspiring skin, almost chasing away the remnants of the haunting nightmares. Yet, as the tranquility of the morning wrapped around him, his mind stubbornly clung to the fragments of the unsettling dreams. The anguished cries of the woman in his dreams echoed in the corridors of his mind, tugging at his heartstrings with a haunting call from a realm he couldn't comprehend. The remnants of the violent sound of clashing iron and steel reverberated through his senses, as though ancient battles were waging within him.

And then there was that manic and frenzied laugh, an eerie echo that resounded in the depths of his soul. It was a chilling laughter, one that seemed to know the darkest secrets of the universe, like a wicked jester taunting Noah with enigmatic riddles.

The vision of a burning city ignited his mind with a sense of apocalyptic urgency, as if the flames held the key to an impending catastrophe. But try as he might, the dream remained elusive, disjointed, as if the threads of memory had been torn asunder and crudely stitched back together.

A gnawing feeling in the pit of his stomach warned him that this was more than a mere dream. It bore the weight of portentous revelation, a glimpse into a reality that transcended the boundaries of his waking world. Though Noah could not fully grasp its meaning, an undeniable foreboding and dread clung to the edges of his consciousness, like the shadows of an impending storm.

Noah was left grappling with a torrent of emotions and questions, each one threatening to consume him like the flames that had scorched the city in his dreams. The fragile balance of his tranquil life now teetered on the edge of uncertainty. He could feel an unseen force gathering at the horizon, an intangible danger threatening to shatter the fragile peace he had known.

In the midst of this enigmatic storm, Noah yearned for answers, for clarity to pierce through the veil of confusion and fear. He knew that to navigate the treacherous currents of his destiny, he would need to delve deeper into the enigma that was his dream. He felt a sense of driving desire to uncover the truth that lurked beneath the surface, this thing waiting to emerge and reshape his very existence.

In the village of Tier, boys of Noah's age reveled in the simplicity of their existence, their days devoted to toil and their nights to revelry and camaraderie. They knew little of the world beyond their immediate surroundings, for they saw no need to explore the realms of knowledge that beckoned him.

Safely tucked in their tranquil valley, Noah and his grandmother were shielded from the world's clamor and intrusion. Strangers were rare visitors, and the solitude they cherished was only occasionally interrupted by traders or travelers from the nearby village of Tier. But it was within these serene surroundings that Noah's grandmother wielded an intriguing air of mystery.

His grandmother Serena's past was shrouded in secrecy and mystery, leaving Noah to wonder about the origins of her profound knowledge and wisdom. From the very moment he began to articulate words, she initiated him into the realm of knowledge, imparting the arts of reading, writing, and mathematics. Even when Noah questioned the unconventional nature of his education, his grandmother remained resolute, her eyes holding an enigmatic glimmer that spoke of profound truths yet to be unveiled.

But his grandmother saw beyond the confines of the village, recognizing a destiny of greatness in her grandson. She steadfastly believed that Noah's path diverged from the ordinary, and that he was destined for something more profound. For her, being special meant embracing a different journey, one that transcended the ordinary rhythms of life.

The old woman spoke of a purpose far greater than the cultivation of crops or idle pastimes. She urged Noah to rise above the mundane and strive for intellectual and spiritual growth, encouraging him to hone his mind and elevate himself beyond the common lot.

And so, Noah acquiesced to her wishes, dedicating his precious spare time to the pursuit of knowledge, embracing the tomes that held the wisdom of ages past. He delved into the depths of his grandmother's library of old texts, each one a gateway to realms of understanding and insight that beckoned him like a siren's call.

As the village boys frolicked under the moonlight, Noah sat with parchment and quill, absorbing the teachings that his grandmother had bestowed upon him. He grappled with ideas that expanded his horizons, nourishing the spark of potential she had ignited within him.

Though he often felt like an outsider among his peers, Noah couldn't help but be drawn to the allure of his unique path. In the stillness of the valley, his grandmother's words echoed in his mind. He sensed that beneath the facade of an ordinary life lay the seed of greatness—his destiny waiting to unfold.

Noah's bond with Serena ran deep and unyielding, a testament to the love and care his grandmother had bestowed upon him since his earliest days. Despite the hardships they had faced, their lives had been marked by a profound contentment and a steadfast devotion to one another.

As Noah immersed himself in the sea of memories, Serena stood silently by the entryway to their cottage. Her gaze was unwavering as she regarded her grandson, her demeanor a reflection of the formidable strength she possessed. At six feet tall, her commanding presence demanded respect and her eyes, a piercing steel gray, seemed to possess an almost supernatural intensity.

Her once pale and smooth skin bore the weathered and toughened marks of a life spent toiling under the relentless sun. Time had left its mark in the form of wrinkles, etched like the lines of wisdom on her face. But despite the passing years, her indomitable spirit remained unchanged, a resolute resolve shining through her eyes.

The transformation of her once brilliant blonde hair, now a radiant white, symbolized the passage of time and the wisdom accumulated over the years. It was a mane that had witnessed the joys and struggles of a life well-lived, tied back with practicality, yet exuding an unyielding pride.

To Noah, Serena had been more than just a caretaker; she had been a guide, a mentor, and a pillar of strength. The sacrifices his grandmother made for him had been immeasurable, ensuring that he never went without even if it meant foregoing her own needs. Though they had known no opulence, their bond had been enriched by the wealth of love and resilience that had sustained them through the trials of life.

In contrast to Serena, Noah's physical demeanor exuded warmth and approachability, a stark juxtaposition to his grandmother's imposing stature. Standing at six feet two inches, he carried himself with a sense of ease and gentleness, his broad shoulders bearing the evidence of hard work in the farm's fields.

Unlike Serena's steely gray eyes that could intimidate with a single glance, Noah's were chocolate brown, holding a softness that could melt even the sternest of hearts. There was an inherent charm in his gaze, a way of coaxing agreement and understanding from others, especially his grandmother, whom he held in the highest regard.

The legacy of their family lineage remained apparent in Noah's shining blond hair. But beyond the external resemblances, his character was distinct, a blend of compassion, humility, and an unwavering determination to face life with an unworried smile.

Yet, on this particular morning, Serena couldn't help but sense that something troubled her grandson. She had keenly observed his departure from the cottage at such an unusual hour. The tension in his shoulders and the distant look in his eyes were not characteristics she associated with the normally carefree and contented young man.

Noah's mind seemed to wander beyond the confines of the tranquil valley, preoccupied with thoughts that eluded his grandmother's understanding. As she studied him, Serena felt a welling of maternal concern for her beloved grandson, her affection for him grounding her in the reality of their bond.

Approaching him, she gently laid a hand of comfort and reassurance on his shoulder. Her eyes softened, searching for answers in the depths of his gaze, but she knew that he would speak in his own time.

"Noah," she said in her steady and gentle voice, "Is there something on your mind, my dear? You know you can share anything with me, don't you? You've always been a beacon of joy and warmth, but I can sense something has unsettled you this morning."

Noah's eyes met Serena's; gratitude evident in his gaze as he confided to her about the unsettling dream that had shaken him to his core. The dream had left a lingering residue of confusion and foreboding, and he struggled to put the fragments into coherent words.

"It was unlike anything I've ever experienced, Grandmother," he began, his voice tinged with uncertainty. "I saw a woman screaming my name, as if she was calling out for help. And there was a clash of weapons, iron and steel smashing together amidst the chaos of battle. It felt so vivid, as if I was there in the midst of it all."

His hands fidgeted with each other, his mind still grappling with the haunting images. "There was laughter too," he continued, his brow furrowing. "A manic, frenzied laugh that seemed to mock the very essence of life. And then, the city burning—it was as if the world itself was unraveling, consumed by some unknown darkness."

Serena listened carefully, her expression a mix of concern and a hint of knowing. Though she waited patiently for his explanation, she felt that she already knew what this dream might signify.

As Noah paused, searching for the right words, Serena's mind raced with thoughts she had long wrestled with in secret. As the matriarch of their lineage, she understood the weight of their family's legacy and the unique birthright that often revealed itself around the age of eighteen.

She had hoped that Noah might be spared from this burden, but the tendrils of fate seemed to be closing around him, ensnaring him in a destiny that she had long dreaded. It was a gift, yes, but one that came with a price—a price that she had feared Noah might have to pay. As she looked at her grandson, she couldn't bear the thought of him being burdened with the responsibilities and consequences of this gift, for she knew firsthand the sacrifices it demanded.

Gathering her resolve, Serena spoke with a mixture of love and a solemn acceptance of what was to come. "Noah, my dear, there are things I've kept from you for reasons that will now become clear. Our lineage carries a unique birthright, one that awakens around the age you're approaching. It bestows gifts and powers upon us, but with it comes challenges and dangers that we must face."

Her voice softened as she continued, "I had hoped that you might be spared from this, but it seems the time has come for you to understand the truth about our family's legacy. It is not something to be taken lightly, and the path ahead may be filled with trials that will test your strength and resolve."

Pausing for a moment, Serena looked into Noah's eyes, her love for him shining through. "But remember, my dear, you are not alone in this journey. I will be here to guide you and support you every step of the way. Our family's strength lies in the unity we share. Together we will face whatever challenges the future may hold."

Serena's heart ached for her grandson as he struggled to make sense of the haunting visions that had consumed his sleep. She led him back into the cottage and gently guided him to the rough table where they had shared countless meals and memories.

Taking a deep breath, Serena began revealing the long-guarded truth, knowing that once the words were spoken, there would be no turning back.

"Noah, what you saw in your dream is not a mere figment of your imagination," she said, her voice steady but filled with a mixture of love and sorrow. "It is a glimpse into a part of our family's legacy—a birthright that has been passed down through generations."

She hesitated for a moment, gathering her thoughts before

continuing. "You see, our family possesses unique abilities, gifts that grant us extraordinary powers. But with these powers come great responsibilities, and the weight of this burden can be overwhelming."

"Noah, you are not just an ordinary boy. You are a part of a line of individuals who have been blessed—or some might say cursed—with incredible abilities," she explained. "The woman screaming your name, the injured man fighting another, and the city burning behind them—it is as if you were witnessing fragments of a past, present, or future event, connected to this birthright."

Her eyes locked with his, unwavering and filled with maternal love. "As for the laughter you heard, that may be a clue to the darker side of this legacy—the temptation to use these powers for personal gain, to lose oneself in the pursuit of dominance and control. It is the allure of such darkness that fills you with dread, for you fear what you might become. It can also be a harbinger of what we oppose, for these powers have a use and an opponent that must be defied."

"You have inherited this legacy, Noah, and the dreams you experience are glimpses into a world of both immense potential and unfathomable danger," she confessed. "But you are not alone in this journey. I will stand by your side, guiding you through the challenges that lie ahead."

Serena paused, giving Noah a moment to process the weight of her words. "I wanted to shield you from this burden, but fate has chosen otherwise. Now that you know the truth, it is up to you to decide how you will embrace this birthright and wield these powers. You have the strength and goodness within you to resist the allure of darkness and use your gifts for the greater good."

Her voice softened as she reached out to hold Noah's hands, conveying her unwavering support. "You are still the same kind-hearted and compassionate young man I have raised, and that will never change. Together, we will face whatever challenges come our way."

Chapter 2:
The Truth

N oah, to understand the meaning of your dream, I must share a story about our family," Serena's voice held both solemnity and love. "For seventeen years, we have lived in quiet peace here, and you've never asked about your parents. It's time you knew what happened to them."

She closed the cottage door behind her and returned with a small ornate wooden box, placing it on the table between them. Opening it, she revealed its dazzling contents—rubies, emeralds, diamonds, gold rings, and pearl necklaces. Noah's disbelief was evident as he tried to reconcile this wealth with the humble life they had led. Emotions warred across his face, leaving him frozen with uncertainty.

Taking his hand in hers, Serena began her tale. "Our family's history spans nearly nine centuries, with a proud legacy that has defined us. While you and I have lived in Tier, our family's roots lie in Spriting, the capital city of the Empire of Kirenth. I was born to Empress Caelia and

Emperor Cassius, of the Earpa dynasty."

"Our lineage has been the legitimate rulers of our country for generations," Serena continued. "Your parents, Elizabeth and David, were the last monarchs to rule before a rebellion erupted seventeen years ago. Your father, my son, was a noble and courageous man. He trusted Vladimir, a distant cousin, and granted him control of the palace guards for his loyalty. Little did he know that Vladimir's ambitions went far beyond his assigned position."

The weight of the revelation settled on Noah's shoulders as he listened intently to his grandmother's words. "When the rebellion struck, your mother smuggled you out of the palace to my country residence, where I was staying at the time. She fought valiantly to protect your father, but in her desperation, she unleashed a long-hidden secret power within our family."

Noah's curiosity piqued, and he asked, "What secret power?"

Serena's eyes held a mix of pride and sadness. "Our family possesses a unique connection to ancient elemental powers. Your mother had the ability to control fire, a power she had kept hidden until that moment of dire need. Your father could control the earth, and with it would make the ground tremble and split open if enraged."

Noah's mind raced, trying to grasp the enormity of what he was learning. "So, I have these powers too?" he questioned.

"Yes," Serena confirmed. "You carry the same elemental abilities as your parents and the generations before them. The dreams you've had are glimpses into this awakening power within you."

"But why was I hidden away, Grandmother?" Noah asked, his heart yearning for answers.

"Your parents knew that the palace was lost," Serena explained, "and they wanted to ensure your safety. They believed that beyond the palace walls, you could have a chance at a life free from the turmoil brought on by Vladimir's treachery."

As the weight of his royal heritage settled on his young shoulders, Noah felt a both awe and apprehension. "I'm part of all this? A part of a royal family?" he asked, trying to comprehend the new reality before him.

Serena nodded, her eyes filled with pride. "Yes, my dear. But remember, the true strength of our family lies in our hearts, not in titles or power. You have the potential to use these abilities for good, just as your parents would have wanted."

In hushed tones, Serena continued to recount the extraordinary powers wielded by members of their royal lineage. "These supernatural abilities, granted by the royal blood's lineage, connect us to the natural elements in various ways. While not all-knowing or invincible, they provide a significant advantage in critical situations if used wisely."

"For your father, his affinity lay with the earth," Serena explained. "He possessed the power to make the ground tremble and, when pushed to the edge, he could part the earth itself, swallowing up anything in his path. But he rarely unleashed this power, for he feared frightening others and preferred to be known for his kind heart, generosity, and mercy. Unfortunately, this very kindness may have contributed to his downfall."

Noah listened intently, captivated by the tales of his parents' remarkable abilities. Serena's gaze softened as she continued, "Your mother, on the other hand, had a remarkable affinity with fire. She had a unique mastery over this element and would often conjure small fireballs above your crib, bringing you joy as you watched them dance.But then came the fateful day when the rebellion struck their palace, and everything changed." Serena's voice grew somber as she recounted the tragic events that unfolded.

"When your mother saw your father fall to the treachery of his cousin, her grief and loss consumed her," Serena said. "In a moment of despair, she tapped into an unimaginable power. She transformed into a being of flame, wielding fire with an unprecedented intensity. The palace and the surrounding city were engulfed in flames, leaving a path of destruction in her wake."

"As she fought, her humanity slipped away, and she became a force of fiery vengeance," Serena continued. "Her fiery touch turned everything she encountered to flame, and even the men who had attacked her were filled with terror at her power."

"The treacherous cousin Vladimir, realizing the peril he was in, sought help from loyal witches he had been secretly preparing for such an eventuality. A fierce battle ensued, and while the witches managed to overpower and kill your mother, the cost was great. She had defeated all but one of them and left Vladimir scarred with an indelible mark—a blackened imprint of her hand that could never be healed."

Serena's eyes glistened with sorrow as she concluded her tale. "Your mother's immense power and sacrifice in her final moments will be remembered in our family's history. Her love for you, her son, was boundless, and it was that love that guided her actions even in her darkest hours."

Noah listened intently to his grandmother's words, his mind swirling with newfound revelations and the weight of their family's history. The truth about his royal heritage, the incredible powers that lay within him, and the danger posed by the usurper King Vladimir left him both amazed and fearful.

As Serena continued, her steady voice tinged with concern, she explained, "The dread you feel in your dream, is a sign of your instincts warning you about the evil that surrounds the usurper. He is a ruthless ruler, hungry for power, and his wicked laughter echoes with malice and cruelty."

Noah's brow furrowed with confusion and apprehension. "But why am I seeing these visions now? Why did I dream of that man, and the city burning? Is it a glimpse of the past, or a warning of the future?"

Serena took a deep breath, her eyes filled with loving concern for her grandson. "It is likely a combination of both, Noah. Your connection to our family's elemental powers may have awakened something within you, allowing you to witness glimpses of events from the past and the future. These visions tend to make themselves known when one turns eighteen, and today is your name-day."

Her hand gently squeezed his, offering comfort and reassurance. "Your dreams may be guiding you, preparing you for what lies ahead. With great power comes great responsibility, and it is clear that you possess the potential to be a force for good in this world."

Noah's mind raced with the weight of the knowledge he now carried. He felt awe and heart-pounding trepidation, realizing that he held the key to a legacy that spanned centuries and a responsibility that he had never imagined.

"Grandmother, what do we do now?" Noah asked, looking to her for guidance.

Serena's gaze softened; her determination clear. "We must continue to evade the usurper's grasp and use this time to hone and understand your powers. You are not alone in this journey, my dear. We have allies scattered throughout the country who oppose Vladimir's tyranny."

She leaned in closer, her voice barely above a whisper. "But remember, we must be cautious and discreet. The witches and sorcerers under his command are dangerous, and they can track our family's elemental magic. We cannot afford to expose ourselves prematurely."

Noah nodded, absorbing every word with a sense of newfound determination.

"I won't let you down, Grandmother," he said, his voice filled with resolve. "I'll do whatever it takes to protect you."

Chapter 3:
The Warning

As Serena listened to her grandson's resolute words, she was torn between her desire for revenge against Vladimir and her fear of involving Noah in this dangerous feud. For eighteen years, she had protected and raised him as if he were her own son, and the thought of endangering him now sent waves of fear through her body.

A small smile graced Serena's lips, proud of the strength and courage she saw in her grandson. "I know you will protect us, Noah. With your heart and your powers, you have the potential to change the course of our family's history. Together, we will face whatever comes our way, and we will overcome."

Her love for her grandson was immeasurable. However, she also recognized that he was on the cusp of adulthood, and the burden of his heritage would soon fall upon his shoulders. She would support him in whatever decision he made. If he chose to confront Vladimir and reclaim what was rightfully his, Noah needed to be prepared. He needed training to master his powers, learn how to wield a sword, and understand the art of war. These were skills she was ill-equipped to teach, having been an empress dowager whose responsibilities lay in diplomatic affairs and navigating the intricate webs of noble politics. She knew how to wield a weapon, of course, but her control of the elements was not formidable.

Although she feared the path he might tread, she also knew that he would not turn away from his destiny. The power within him, coupled with his family's history, made it inevitable that he would face King Vladimir.

After a moment of contemplation, Serena looked into Noah's eyes, her resolve firm. "My dearest heart, I will support you in your journey, whatever choice you make. You have the right to reclaim your birthright, and I will stand by your side every step of the way. However, it is essential that you receive proper training to harness your powers and prepare for the challenges that lie ahead."

She paused then made her decision. "I will seek out what remains of our family's allies, those who oppose the usurper's tyranny. They will help train you in the ways of combat and strategy. But remember, my precious grandson, this path is perilous, and you must tread with caution. King Vladimir's sorcerers are formidable, and we must remain hidden until the time is right."

Noah nodded, determination in his eyes. "I understand, Grandmother. I won't let you down."

Serena smiled, pride and love shining in her gaze. "I know you won't, my brave Noah. If you are to learn to master your powers, we will need to leave this valley immediately. There is a safe place for us where you can learn how to use these powers, and some of our family's allies there that can help you master them sooner than I could by just teaching you on my own. While I have my own powers, I was never the best teacher. For me, my powers came instinctually, and I do not actively control them."

Noah looked curiously at his grandmother and asked, "What is your power grandmother?"

"I possess the power to harness the air and the wind. While I do not actively control it, this may also be that in some ways I feel the temptations of the wind itself. It does not like to be controlled; it wants to be free as a wild stallion roaming the plains. The wind has been my constant companion and friend, but it has not been something I can freely command unlike your parent's powers" Serena responded.

As she said this, Noah felt the wind violently stirring outside the house, howling like a vengeful spirit. The door crashed open, propelled by an unseen force, and he cautiously followed his grandmother outside as she rose in alarm. His heart pounded in his chest as he witnessed the unnaturally straight path the wind had carved through the fields, leading straight toward their home. The sand and dirt swirled menacingly in front of them, kicked up by the wind's sinister rage.

Serena shaded her eyes, but her expression was one of dread. "Something is not right; the wind would not act this way unless something unspeakable has disturbed or angered it."

The wind grew even more frenzied, creating a large dark cloud of sand and dirt that obscured the light. Within its twisted whirlpool, dark and haunting images began to take shape. Noah and Serena could make out two sinister figures – a man with a twisted crown and another in the form of a snake, its forked tongue a symbol of deceit.

The sand shifted and transformed, revealing a nightmarish scene. The snakelike figure sunk its venomous fangs into the man with the twisted crown, transforming him into a monstrous being with scales and glowing, malevolent red eyes. The sense of danger emanating from this new creature was overwhelming, sending chills down their spines.

As the nightmarish images evolved, and Noah and Serena were horrified to witness the snakelike man leading a vile army of wretched creatures. In a ravine, they cornered two valiant figures – a proud woman and a tall man armed with a sword. The woman's attempt to strike the snakelike man only resulted in her impalement on his dark sword.

Noah's heart sank as he saw the young man's desperate attempt to fight back, only to be overpowered and brought to his knees over the lifeless body of the woman. The snakelike man's dark sword shattered the young man's own weapon, leaving him defenseless and vulnerable.

A terrifying force seemed to emanate from the snakelike man, connecting with the young man. It drained him of something vital, and he writhed in agonized torment. As seconds stretched into what seemed like eternity, the young man's struggles ceased, and the flow of energy ceased with him.

The serpentine man reveled in his newfound power, his glowing red eyes reflecting a sinister glee. Cracks of crimson light spread across his twisted form, intensifying the wickedness within him. He raised his sword and severed the young man's head from his body in an act of coldblooded brutality.

As the wind abruptly subsided around them, the images vanished, leaving Noah and Serena in an eerie silence. Noah's heart pounded in his chest as he looked at his grandmother, searching for the familiar strength and reassurance he had always found in her. But the woman before him was no longer the unshakable figure he knew; instead, she wore an expression of pure terror that sent shivers down his spine.

In a voice filled with urgency, Serena gathered her composure and declared, "We must leave, now! Pack only what you can carry in one bag. We have less than an hour before we must flee. Noah, please, no more questions. There's no time, and I promise I'll tell you everything once we reach safety."

Without waiting for a response, she turned and hurried into the house, her footsteps echoing with haste. Noah followed suit, quickly collecting his few meager belongings. In that moment he realized how little he truly possessed, a stark reminder of the hardships they had endured.

Within a mere half hour, they abandoned their once-humble home. Serena's face bore a determined resolve, her eyes gleaming with an unsettling intensity. She led them towards the dense and foreboding forest that loomed immensely before them.

The forest was no ordinary one; it concealed secrets and dangers unknown to most. It led towards a vast mountain range that guarded their valley, its dense foliage offering little hope for safe passage unless one knew the elusive paths that hid within.

As they ventured deeper into the shadowy woods, the trees seemed to close in on them, their gnarled branches reaching out like ghostly hands. The silence was only broken by the rustling of leaves and the occasional hoot of a distant owl, as if the forest itself held its breath, watching their every move.

Noah felt a chilling presence, an intangible malevolence lurking just beyond the tree line. His senses became heightened, every fiber of his being on edge and alert to the lurking dangers. Perhaps it was just his mind playing tricks, but he felt as if they were being watched and followed. His grandmother, however, moved with unwavering determination, leading them onward.

As they pressed on, the absence of light engulfed them, and the veil of uncertainty grew thicker. Every step took them deeper into the heart of darkness and towards a fate they couldn't yet fathom. The fear of the unknown clawed at Noah's mind, but he knew he had to trust his grandmother, for she was the only anchor he had left in this harrowing journey.

The forest held secrets that neither of them was prepared to confront, and as they journeyed on, Noah's sense of disorientation deepened. The familiar world he once knew now seemed like a distant memory, replaced by an unsettling reality he had never imagined.

"To reach our ally's sanctuary, we must move swiftly and silently," Serena whispered urgently, glancing back at Noah who trailed hesitantly behind her, unsure of their path.

"Here, on the outskirts of Tier, we've been overlooked, deemed insignificant by the rest of the country. Forgotten like a faded mark on old maps. That's to our advantage, but we can't risk drawing attention now," she continued, her voice barely audible as if the forest itself were listening.

Her eyes darted around, scanning for any sign of danger or prying eyes. "We head west, straight through that mountain range. Though treacherous, it's the fastest way."

Noah nodded, trying to quell his unease as he fell in line behind his grandmother. The immense canopy of trees cast a dappled gloom over the forest floor. The air felt cool and damp, carrying both an inviting allure and an ominous chill.

As they ventured deeper, it was as if the forest possessed a dual nature – part welcoming embrace, and part dark force. The very air seemed charged with a mysterious energy, whispering of ancient secrets and hidden perils.

Noah took a deep breath, trying to steady himself as he stepped further through the darkly mottled light beneath the canopy. Shadows danced around him, and the forest seemed to watch with unseen eyes. The foliage rustled, every snap of a twig sending shivers down his spine.

His grandmother's warning echoed in his mind, urging him to be vigilant and cautious. The forest was home to a vast array of creatures, some harmless and others potentially deadly. In normal circumstances, people traveled in large groups for safety, but their situation demanded discretion.

As he followed Serena's lead, Noah trusted in her powers and her connection to the wind to navigate them through the unknown. Each step felt like treading a path between two worlds – the familiar life they left behind and the uncertain darkness that lay ahead.

With every footfall, the forest seemed to tighten its grip, embracing them with both an allure of shelter but also a sense of lurking danger that hid in its depths. There was no turning back now; they had chosen this perilous path, and they had to find strength in one another to endure.

Chapter 4:
The Forest

Treading along a narrow game trail that seemed abandoned by all but the creatures that called the woods home, Noah and Serena moved through the forest with hushed steps. The air gradually enlivened with the chorus of songbirds, the scampering of chipmunks, and the chattering of squirrels. A small creek meandered alongside their path, and the unmistakable hoof and paw prints of deer and other wild game crisscrossed the trail.

As they continued onward, Noah's initial nervousness waned, replaced by a profound sense of belonging. The trees embraced him like old friends, and the foliage whispered shy secrets in the breeze. He felt an unspoken kinship with the natural world surrounding him, as if he were a part of this intricate tapestry of life.

His grandmother's wisdom had led them westward, guiding them away from potential danger. In this forest, they found solitude and a rare kind of peace. Having had no contact with other humans for days before their journey into the forest, they shared an intimate connection with nature, weaving their own path within the ancient sanctuary. The sense of unease he'd previously felt faded the further they advanced into the forest and away from their farmstead.

Noah couldn't help but smile as he noticed the mirrored peace in his grandmother's eyes. They both sensed the vibrant melody of the forest, a song that resonated deep within their souls. Each step seemed to harmonize with the rhythm of the woods to a song that only they could hear, a dance only they could feel.

As they walked, the forest invited them further into its heart with an unspoken trust, creating a bond of kindred spirits. They were no longer mere strangers in this realm; they were welcomed guests, embraced by the very essence of the wilderness. The forest subtly whispered to them, sharing stories of ancient times and hidden wonders. Noah's heart swelled with gratitude and wonder, grateful for this rare connection with the natural world.

His grandmother's reticence over the past days had been palpable, and the unsettling message from the wind had clearly left a lasting impact on her. Noah's thoughts kept revisiting the haunting images he had witnessed in the swirling sands, the sinister figures intertwined in a tale of treachery and bloodshed. It was painfully obvious to him that the hunted figures represented himself and his grandmother, and the snakelike man was undoubtedly the ruthless usurper Vladimir, the same man who had orchestrated his parents' tragic demise.

But what truly chilled Noah's bones was the sight of the man draining his vital essences with a power that seemed otherworldly and abhorrent. His grandmother had described Vladimir as a cunning mortal but had not mentioned him possessing such demonic abilities. The thought that a person could willingly invite such dark powers into their soul was unfathomable to Noah. It would require a wickedness beyond comprehension, a willingness to sacrifice one's very humanity for unfathomable power.

Fear and doubt gnawed at Noah's heart, leaving him hesitant and uncertain. How could they possibly stand against a man so steeped in darkness? The prospect of confronting a sorcerer possessed by demons was beyond daunting, and it cast a shadow of doubt in Noah's mind over their chances of success.

He found himself torn between hope and despair. He yearned to protect his family's legacy, to reclaim what was rightfully theirs, but the horrifying image of the young man's demise reminded him of the immense stakes. Could he truly face such evil and emerge victorious? Steeped in his thoughts, the burden of responsibility pressed heavily on his young shoulders.

Noah glanced at his grandmother, searching for answers in her wise eyes. He saw the weight of determination etched on her face. She had seen the darkness, but she had also seen hope. The wind had delivered a grave warning, but it had also guided them thus far. Her unwavering resolve offered a glimmer of reassurance in the encroaching shadows.

The realization that their journey was far from over sank into Noah's mind as they continued on their quest. The road ahead was perilous, and the darkness they faced was unlike anything he could have imagined. But he also knew that his grandmother's courage and the ancient power of the wind would guide them. They may be confronting unnatural evil beyond comprehension, but they were not alone in their fight.

Contemplating his thoughts, Noah recalled that he'd had an experience of this snakelike man as a young ten-year-old boy. It was during one of the few years that their farm had done incredibly well, and they had funds to spare after paying off their debts from the growing year and preparing for the next year's harvests. His grandmother had taken him to purchase new clothes, which he sorely needed as he had been growing as fast as a bean stalk that year. After purchasing the clothing, she had given him several coins and told him to go enjoy himself while she attended to other personal matters in the village. As this was harvest time, the village held a two-week festival to celebrate the harvest and thank the Gods for their support with the crops. It was also a chance for the residents of Tier to celebrate and come together before a harsh winter arrived and they would again be forced to endure.

The harvest festival was wonderful for young boys as there were games and contests of strength. It also brought outsiders into their small insular community. During this particular harvest festival, a circus troupe had come to their village, with all the expected acts including a show of bizarre freaks of nature. Noah had been entertained by the bearded ladies, and the dwarves that were paraded in front of them. Although they were all smiles when he had paid to enter the show, he did note the tinge of sadness in their demeanor.

Leaving the freak show feeling somewhat guilty for reveling in the misfortune of those who could not have chosen to be born the way they were, Noah noticed a smaller purple tent to the side of the freak show that was not busy and that no one else appeared to have noticed. Deciding to take a look, he slowly walked over and looked above the entrance to the tent. Where before he had not seen anything, he now saw a small sign flash into existence above the tent's entrance. The sign read "Enter all who dare and be your fortune read, know though that once told it cannot be undone, for good or bad".

While somewhat scared by the fact that this sign had magically appeared from nowhere, young Noah was not a coward, nor was he easily perturbed. He felt drawn to the tent and whatever lay within. Taking a deep breath to steady himself, he pulled open the tent flap and walked inside.

The interior of the tent the was thick with incense and smoke. A metal brazier filled with coals hung from the center at the top of the tent, dimly illuminating the interior. As smoke lazily unfurled from the coals, it released a heady scent which Noah could not identify. The flooring consisted of rugs laid upon the grass, while large ornate tapestries hung on the tent walls. These tapestries depicted enormous battles betwixt men and demons, the deaths of the men shown graphically and in various ways.

On one of the tapestries, a man could be seen driving the demons back to the underworld from whence they came. In his hand he bore a large black sword which appeared almost glass-like. Taking a step closer to study it, Noah found himself entranced by this man and the sword. Something in the picture spoke to him, and he felt something indescribable stirring in his chest, a familiarity with the image that he could not place.

Sensing movement behind him, Noah swiftly turned around and found that he was not alone. From behind a curtain at the back of the tent, a hunched woman dragged herself out on her hands and knees. She appeared to be ancient, garbed in long filthy robes and unseeing eyes glazed with quicksilver. Her face was creased with a myriad of wrinkles. Her matted and knotted hair, a lackluster gray, had the appearance of dried out straw. Neglect and the tolls of long hard years of life had made their indelible mark upon her. With toothless mouth gaping and sightless eyes eerily glowing, she slowly pulled herself across the floor onto a smaller rug located directly beneath the coal brazier.

The woman turned intuitively toward Noah and unerringly beckoned him to come closer and sit across from her. As Noah hesitated, some unseen force pulled him to her, his body moving against his own volition. Once he settled across from her, she pulled out a set of cards from within the folds of her worn robes.

In a low rasp, the woman began to speak. "These cards tell a great many things about a young man. They can foretell the future, and what will happen to you. They also speak about the past and reveal truths which you cannot otherwise know. To consult the cards is to consult the Gods, and for this there is always a price. What is told cannot be untold, for good or bad. The gods have drawn you to me today and what I tell you now must be remembered, for it may prove your undoing if you forget. Do you understand?"

Realizing he had nodded dumbly to the blind woman, Noah nervously stammered out his acceptance. The woman set the cards down and began to pull out individual cards, shuffling through the deck randomly while mumbling to herself. The words she spoke did not make sense nor seem coherent, yet they seemed to have power. As she uttered them, Noah felt the air thicken with an energy he could not see. He felt the oppressive pressure of something intangible bearing down upon him, invisible claws caressing his face. Terrified, Noah sat stock still as the claws withdrew and the unknown force released him. Looking at the old crone, he saw that she had placed one card down in front of him.

"The first card I show to you is of family. The family you know is not the family that you think you know. Cherish the one that you have and protect her against all else, for there will be a day that you will lose her cruelly. The angel Azriel has told me this, and he has judged you worthy to hear this information. He advises me to warn you this: One day there will be an enemy you cannot defeat, and you will feel helpless as you see everything you love crumble in front of your eyes. When this day comes, reach for the stars, and call upon his name and aid will be given."

The woman then stretched her hand toward the deck and began shuffling through the cards again. Once more, Noah felt a pressure bear down upon him. This time he felt something warm and wholesome trickling over his body, something akin to love and belonging. Soon the sensation left him, and he looked at the cards again to see that the woman had drawn another card for him.

"The Mother looks favorably upon you, child. This card is one of significance and represents the power you hold within you. With this power, you can mold and change the world as you see fit. Use this power well, and people will love you. Use it selfishly and they will turn upon you. The Mother also has another word of advice: when you find the man with red hair, trust in your feelings. Do not let others dissuade you from your path, lest you risk his betrayal and heartbreak. A lover scorned will be your downfall, while a lover cherished shall be your savior. Only together shall you be whole."

Again, the woman shuffled the cards, and this time he felt a presence unlike anything he had felt previously. Noah was forcefully pushed to the floor spread eagled; his shirt pulled roughly up from his forearms. He heard the old woman gasp in pain at the same time as an agonizing cut appeared slowly across his right arm. He felt something hot and rough and barbed lap up the blood that ran down his arm. Noah wanted to scream in terror, but dread sealed his throat, prohibiting him from uttering a sound. The thing that held him down chuckled, taking pleasure from his pain and fear. Just as suddenly as it began, Noah's young body was released from its prone position. Cradling his right arm, Noah watched transfixed as a long-ragged slash began to heal itself rapidly before his eyes.

The woman sat motionless; her eyes closed as if listening to something in the distance. Her mouth twitched in pain and the color leached from her face as whatever she was listening to clearly gripped her to impart its message. Across her weathered cheeks, he could see the bloody grooves that the sharp talons had left. With a deep sigh, her body relaxed and fell back slightly before she caught herself and tilted forward instead. From her hand, a card fell before him.

"The third card I give to you is war. Your life will be filled with many battles and because of it you will lose those you love throughout your life. Even as the child you are, you have seen war and have lost loved ones. Train well for your future for will be rife with conflict, and how well you fight will mean the difference between saving your loved ones or losing everything and everyone you love. The demon Soneillon chose this card for you and wishes you to know that there is glory in killing others. He has tasted your blood and senses the violence within you, and the propensity for death you possess. He urges you to embrace this violence and use it to channel your hatred into all methods of aggression. He looks forward to seeing you in battle, and to welcoming the souls you send to his domain."

One last time, the woman reached for her cards even as blood dripped from her cheek. Noah sat with trepidation pounding in his 10-year-old heart as the power built once again. Noah felt his face being pulled forward, and a dazzling light emerged from the coal brazier. This light was blinding and clean and pure. He felt the heat of it pressing against his skin, burning him as was unable to pull away. From the light he sensed no malice, just serene judgment, and a faint sense of approval.

The light swooped away and then plunged rapidly into his chest and his heart. Noah could feel the intense heat inside him, a burning sensation in his heart as if the light searched for something. He felt the moment it found what it was looking for as a radiant sense of joy, accomplishment, and pride filled him. As he felt this joy fill his soul, the light exited his chest and slipped back into the brazier.

As the glowing light disappeared, he felt the weight of something solid materialize in his hands. Looking down, he saw a beautiful shining crown had appeared in his grip. The crown was unlike anything Noah had ever seen or dreamed of. Made of platinum and gold, inset with beautiful diamonds adorning the circlets, it gave the appearance of airiness and light. The diamonds themselves seemed to enhance and reflect the luminous light emanating from a central gem of dazzling brilliance. The gem shone like the light that had entered his chest, vibrating with a sentient sense of justice.

The old woman cleared her throat, and looking up Noah was shocked to see that the same woman who had been stooped and shriveled was now young and beautiful with soft and supple skin. Her blind quicksilver eyes had become a clear emerald green, and her scraggly gray hair had become a glossy and brilliant red.

The woman's hearty and a breathless laughter sent joy streaking up Noah's spine. She proclaimed "The father finds you perfect. He is the most important of our gods, and he has judged you worthy of his name and his banner. He gifts you his allegiance in your upcoming battles and grants you the card of righteousness. He will support your stand and his supporters will follow you into battle. One day, when you are ready, he will reveal the mighty weapon you will use to defeat his enemies. He grants you this crown made from his own essence and entrusts me to safeguard it until the time that you are ready to accept it. He has healed me and returned my youth to me, charging me with returning the crown and serving you when it is time. Until that time comes, you shall not see me again. Goodbye Noah and may our paths cross again in the future."

As the words were spoken, the crown was lifted from Noah's hands and he fell back to the ground knocking his head softly as he fell. Shaking his head slightly, he found that he was no longer in the tent with the woman but was instead outside of the freak show tent he had left earlier. There was no evidence of the old woman's tent; it had vanished completely.

Walking away, Noah asked one of the handlers standing outside of the freak show tent where the old woman's tent had gone and was met with a blank stare. Anyone he asked had no knowledge of a fortune teller's tent and insisted that there was no such woman with the troop. From that moment on, Noah gathered that he had experienced something supernatural and kept the words he had been given to himself. He did not know if they would prove significant but knew that he must have been told them for a reason. He did not even share them with his grandmother, and when she saw his clothing had been muddied from his fall to the ground, she was cross with him for soiling his new clothes.

Regardless of her displeasure, Noah took this knowledge of the supernatural with him and had not forgotten it.

Since that day, he had taken any spare minute he had to ask for tales around the village at carnivals, festivals, and whenever he met an old spinster willing to tell him stories. They told him tales of demons and the dalliances they had with men. He learned that the demon Soneillon, who had encouraged him to engage in violence and to kill, was the demon of hate. This demon was known to encourage men to hate one another and fight for his enjoyment and pleasure. Everything he learned about the supernatural he cataloged in his mind, as he was both fascinated and repelled by some of the myths and folktales he was told.

Leaving his absent-minded reverie and recollections, Noah could hear his grandmother muttering under her breath, and he felt the wind puff by him to stir around her. It seemed that she was communing with the wind as if it were an old long-lost friend, conversing with it even though he could not detect a discernible response. The wind appeared to be guiding them through the forest, as they had not encountered anything remotely dangerous. While they had seen paw prints from a bear and scat from a badger, the most dangerous animal they had seen thus far was merely a skunk. Thankfully neither of them had experienced the tail end of the skunk or the less than pleasant odor it created, as it had quickly scurried off into the underbrush as they approached it.

As they reached a critical juncture in their journey, Serena came to a halt, her keen instincts guiding her decision. The path ahead diverged into two separate directions, offering distinct choices for their next move. One path followed the gentle meander of a small creek, leading northward before vanishing around a bend. It held a certain allure, promising a serene route through the wilderness. The other trail headed westward, the direction they had intended to pursue, but an ominous aura seemed to shroud it, creating an uneasy feeling in her heart. A sense of darkness lurked further along that route, and she worried about the unknown perils that lay ahead.

Noting the approaching dusk and their weary state from marching relentlessly since dawn, Serena wisely decided that they would make camp for the night. With the veil of darkness soon to descend, setting up camp was a practical and necessary measure to ensure their safety and rest.

Serena shared her decision her grandson. "Noah, it's time to rest for the night. We've been marching without pause since sunrise and we must gather our strength. This fork in the road demands careful consideration to face whatever lies ahead with renewed vigor come morning."

Noah, trusting in his grandmother's wisdom, nodded in agreement. The forest had grown darker with the fading light, and the sounds of nocturnal creatures slowly filled the air. As they found a suitable spot to pitch their tent, Serena couldn't shake the feeling that their journey was about to take a turn further into the unknown.

Under the canopy of trees, they lit a small fire, its crackling warmth bringing a sense of comfort amid the wilderness. As they shared a modest meal of dried provisions, Serena spoke carefully about the choices that lay before them.

"We've come a long way and the road ahead won't be easy. That westerly path holds a foreboding energy that must be tread carefully. Whatever lies in that direction, we can't ignore the signs of danger that surround it. We'll rest tonight, and in the light of day, we'll decide our next move with clarity and determination."

Noah listened attentively, the words of the mysterious woman's fortune-telling still echoing in his mind. He knew that their journey was far from over, and the trials they were about to face could define their destiny. In the flickering light of the campfire, he found solace in his grandmother's strength and the bond they shared.

As the night deepened, they settled into their sleeping bags, Serena keeping a watchful eye on their surroundings. The forest held its secrets, and they were but travelers in its vast expanse. Yet, with the morning light on the horizon, hope glimmered in the distance, guiding them onward to face the shadows that awaited them on the path ahead. Together, they would embrace whatever challenges came their way.

Chapter 5:
Family

Noah and Serena decided that the tranquil clearing they had chosen, not far from the gently babbling stream, was a perfect place to rest for the night. Noah took up the task of clearing weeds and brush from the immediate area around their tents, creating a secure perimeter for their sanctuary.

Childhood memories of hunting trips with the village men had left a lasting impression on Noah, emphasizing the importance of a secure campsite. He had learned the hard way that dangers lurked in the wilderness. In the predawn hours of one such excursion, while the men slumbered, a stealthy mountain lion infiltrated their camp and taken one of the smaller boys from a nearby tent. The gruesome discovery in the morning had forever etched in Noah's mind the necessity of vigilance.

With the area sufficiently cleared, Serena began to prepare a fire pit for cooking their dinner. Noah set out in search of small twigs and moss to help ignite the flames. As he returned to the camp with a bundle of firewood, he was met with the sight of his grandmother skillfully tending to a merry fire she had already started.

Her expertise didn't end there, he noted with pride; she had managed to snare a plump hare that had unknowingly stumbled into their encampment, and it now roasted above the crackling fire on a spit.

As darkness descended upon their camp, Noah stretched out before the warming flames, finding solace in the gentle sounds of the forest night. The nocturnal world was just as alive as the day had been, with the soft rustling of tiny creatures scurrying amidst the underbrush, and distant calls of birds and owls echoing through the night. The firelight danced, casting playful shadows around the camp, creating an atmosphere of homey comfort amid the wilderness.

Under the stars and to the sounds of the forest, Noah and Serena dined on the delicious roasted hare. As they spoke in hushed tones about the journey ahead, Noah couldn't help but marvel at his grandmother's strength and resilience. He knew he was fortunate to have her as his guide and protector.

Tentatively, Noah found the courage to voice the question that had been gnawing at him throughout their journey through the forest. "Grandmother, could you tell me more about my parents and our family? I can see that you hold fond memories of them, and I want to know who they were."

A warm smile illuminated Serena's face, and her eyes sparkled with happiness as she reminisced about her son and daughter-in-law. "Your father was a kind and compassionate soul. Helping others brought him great joy, and he never hesitated to lend a hand to those in need. His dedication and strong work ethic were evident in all that he did. You are truly a reflection of him, with the exception of your nose and chin, which you inherited from your mother. The similarities between you two go beyond just physical appearances; your kindness and willingness to help others mirror his spirit."

Leaning back, Serena's expression turned contemplative as she delved further into her memories. "Your mother was an extraordinary woman, a perfect match for your father. Intelligent and forthright, she had no qualms about speaking her mind to anyone she believed was acting foolishly. She was strong-willed and provided the support your father needed to stand firm against his adversaries at court. Yet, your mother was also a curious and joyful soul. She cherished her time in a laboratory your father had built for her in the palace, where she conducted inventive experiments, sometimes with a touch of danger. When you were born, your father asked her to keep the laboratory locked to ensure your safety. He worried that you might wander in and cause explosions that could potentially burn down the palace. This caused a few playful arguments between them, as your mother felt it implied she couldn't take care of you while indulging in her experiments. Truth be told, she sometimes got so absorbed in her work that things could get a bit chaotic."

Serena couldn't help but chuckle as she recalled their endearing spats. Their relationship had bloomed naturally, and she had played no role in orchestrating their union. Unlike past royal marriages, which were arranged for political gains and prestige, her son David had been adamant about finding his own wife when the time was right.

She vividly remembered the day, with a mix of shock and delight, when David had returned to the palace with Elizabeth by his side. The scandal was amplified because Elizabeth was the daughter of a prominent merchant in the capital and not of noble lineage. Her husband, a traditionalist, had resisted David's choice, but the young prince stood his ground, threatening to abandon his claim to the throne if he couldn't marry Elizabeth. Standing his ground as the sole heir, David's determination had eventually swayed his father, who reluctantly welcomed Elizabeth into their family. Serena had quietly supported David throughout, wielding influence behind the scenes, as it was often said that real power lay with those behind the throne – and she was a firm believer in that adage.

With a sense of fulfillment, Serena cherished the memories of her family, and she knew that through the echo of their love, Noah carried a legacy of kindness, strength, and curiosity that would continue to shape his own journey through life.

Noah contentedly watched his grandmother, listening to her tales of his mother and father. Despite not remembering them and never really thinking of them as a child, he was still happy to now get a chance to learn more about these people who bore him and brought him into this world from their love. From the sounds of it, his parents had been a couple to be reckoned with. Even more-so his mother, who seemed to be a power unto herself that no foolish man would ever dare confront or reckon with unprepared. His father sounded like a gentle man, someone kind and friendly to speak with. Noah wistfully thought to himself that had he known his father growing up, he was certain that he would have been his best friend and closest confidant.

Looking up and disrupting Serena from her silent reveries, Noah raised another question to his grandmother. "Is there anyone else left in our family that we can look to for help or support?"

Serena sadly motioned no in response. "When your father died, the kingdom was thrown into chaos. Into this chaos, Vladimir emerged with a troop of sorcerers that he had been training in the background unnoticed. These sorcerers began to execute any who resisted his claim to the throne. The vast majority of our family was killed in the first week after your father was murdered, as they immediately rebelled and raised their men against Vladimir. Some men died in open battle against forces he supplemented with foreign mercenaries, bribed with promises of baronies and riches beyond their greatest dreams. Others were found dead in their beds, supposedly dying from infirmity, disease, or old age. This of course was not the truth, as Vladimir dispatched his sorcerers and their assassins to eliminate those who resisted him and quietly fomented rebellion against him. Our family all fought him, and every single one of them was unsuccessful in defeating him.

The closest one to defeating him was your great uncle, Albert. He raised a grand army of men loyal to our family and marched on the capital. He laid siege to the city, and after several weeks of hard battle and backbreaking labor his army broke down the solid oak gates which guarded the city. When he and his men marched into the city, they expected a proper welcome from loyal citizens happy to be liberated from the tyranny of Vladimir. Instead, they found a populace maddened and armed. Vladimir and his sorcerers had poisoned the citizenry's minds. They made the people of the city believe that our family were the usurpers and that it was we who had been relying on black sorcery and magic to sustain our rule. The city turned against Albert, and he and his men were slaughtered in the streets as they fought their way to the black palace." Serena looked sadly into the fire, as she thought of her brother-in-law Albert and the death he encountered at the hands of the crazed masses.

Serena turned back to her grandson looking solemnly at him. "We are the last that remain of our family. Over the past seventeen years, the people have been told that we were evil, corrupt, and that we were the cause of the famines and economic free fall that occurred after your father was murdered by Vladimir. They believe that we are to blame for their misfortune, and Vladimir's sorcerers have encouraged this belief. The truth is that Vladimir's machinations caused the near bankruptcy of the nation, as the mercenaries he enlisted took baronies and much of the kingdom's wealth for their own after he defeated our family. They became the ruling class, and the kingdom suffered greatly as they took the reins of power from the hereditary ruling class.

In the capital, Vladimir's sorcerers have created a religion with Vladimir as their central god-king. They attract followers with the promise of food, gold, and advancement in life. Once they enter the temple, the followers are given a 'holy' rite which rids them of their free will and makes them manic firebrand preachers of his divinity. These men are called priors, and they are clothed in robes of purest white and are granted large gnarled white wooden staffs which contain an emerald at the very top of the shaft. They are sent to walk through the lands of this kingdom and to preach of his 'holiness' to the people living in the countryside. Twice now the priors have come to Tier over these past seventeen years, and we have been lucky to have been missed by them and their detection."

Silence lingered between the two as the fire flickered and crackled. Both Noah and Serena were caught in their own thoughts. Serena remembering the anguish of her lost family and friends, and Noah thinking of the threats they now faced. Noah's mind shifted to the powers that his grandmother had said his family possessed. A part of him was curious as to where these powers came from, as it was highly unlikely they could have just manifested on their own. Surely something must have caused them to occur in their family's lineage.

Tentatively Noah asked his grandmother "You mentioned that our family possesses supernatural powers and the control of select elements. I've seen you commune with the winds and know that you are telling the truth. It is a wonder but for the life of me I cannot think of a way that we could have acquired these skills. Can you explain this to me?"

Serena stared pensively at the crackling fire as she thought of how to explain their family's powers and their origin to Noah. "While none in our family truly know when these powers first manifested themselves, we have long passed down a story from parent to child which tells of how we gained this intimate power with the elements. The story begins with one of our long distant ancestors, who journeyed across the plains of Drun with his family.

One night his family set camp near a river, and they lay sleeping deeply and recovering from the arduous journey they were undertaking. A group of bandits came across their campsite, and in the darkness of night snuck into it with poor intentions. The bandits entered the tent where our ancestor and his family were sleeping, and roughly seized his wife and daughters. They pulled the women out from the tent, while one of the men had bound him and forced him to his knees to watch what they did. The bandits threw our ancestor's wife and daughters to the ground and began to tear at their clothes with the intentions of violating them, forcing him to watch before killing them all. The man struggled against his captors, and loudly pled to the Father of all gods to save his family from these men.

Suddenly, in response to his prayers a brilliant white star streaked down from the sky and shot straight into the man's chest, and he began to glow with a white light that chased the darkness from the night. The light grew so bright that it temporarily blinded those around him. it could be seen from miles away. Upon opening his eyes, where they had been gray before, our ancestor's eyes glowed red and burned with a fire deep inside them. His bonds burned away as fire erupted from his hands. With a sweep of his hands the bandits were blown into the river as the very ground itself trembled beneath them and threatened to open up and swallow them whole. Our ancestor then raised his fisted hands and pushed down violently, the river water itself formed a great fist and smashed into the bandits, holding them down. The bandits slowly drowned as they tried to breathe beneath the water." Serena's voice was hushed as she recounted the tale to Noah.

"As soon as the thieves perished, the great white light left the man's chest, the star traveling back to the heavens. His eyes became their usual gray color and he appeared diminished, as though he had lost a large part of the power that had entered him. The brilliant star left a message for the whole family, imparted as a booming voice in all their minds, saying, 'use this gift well, for one day your ancestor will serve my needs on this earth and will take up my banner'. As the voice echoed in their minds, the wife and daughter found their hands alight with flame, their bonds also burned away with the unearthly fire.

Thoughtfully stroking the ends of her braid, Serena said softly, "Since this event, our family has always had these powers. While the first ancestor to possess the light inside his chest was powerful, he quickly found that of all the elements, he had an affinity with water. The water spoke to him, and he found that he could do wondrous things with it, and even walked across it from time to time. His daughters each had their own kinship with the powers as one influenced fire and the other earth, while his wife could guide the winds like me.

As our family has grown throughout the years, this gift has been passed down from generation to generation. All those who marry into our family have gained powers of their own as well. It appears that whatever light entered our ancestor must still bless us, for our spouses gain these powers after our marriage rites are consummated. Our children inherit these powers upon their birth, though they do not manifest until their eighteenth birthday."

With a tired grunt, his grandmother raised herself from where she sat. "It is late, and I am weary from our travels today. I sense that we will have a great many obstacles tomorrow, and we will need our rest for them. Goodnight Noah, rest well." Serena stiffly walked off into her tent and soon her lamp was extinguished for sleep.

Noah stood and stretched from the pack he had been lounging on and went to the roll in his tent. Settling on the hard mattress, his mind drifted to the story his grandmother had told him of their ancestor. The great light intrigued him, as did the mention of the father. He remembered the feeling of the light that entered his chest in the tent of that fortune teller and sensed that this light was most likely the same one that had visited his ancestor so many generations ago. It must be true that his family was blessed by the father of all Gods, as the old woman in the tent had said that he would take up the banner of this god. In some ways, this worried Noah immensely. If this was true, he would be the subject of a prophecy involving powers that had not yet manifested in him, powers that he could not even fully comprehend yet.

Sighing to himself, Noah turned over and slowly drifted to sleep. As his mind spiraled away, thoughts of his parents swirled. With a soft smile on his lips, he slipped into dreams of a life with parents that he had never known and a brave great uncle who had been willing to fight to the death for what he believed in.

Chapter 6:
The Dark Path

Waking early the next morning, Noah and Serena broke camp and continued on the path they had followed the previous day. At the same fork in the road, Serena paused and reached out for the wind with a flourish of her hand.

The wind came rushing forth like a puppy eager to please its owner, and then stopped abruptly at the fork in the trail. It hovered for a moment, swirling the grasses surrounding the path before rushing past them and down the dark trail that headed in a westerly direction.

Hesitant with the outcome, Noah spoke quickly "Grandmother, something feels off about this path. I know the wind is saying we must follow this trail to reach our destination, but the air on the path feels corrupted. I cannot describe why I feel this way, I just do."

Nodding, Serena responded "I agree, something wicked lays down that path. I sense evil hanging in the air. However, we do not have a choice in the matter. There is only one westerly path that heads in the direction we must take. We are lucky in that we have the wind with us, and we can use it as a weapon if need be."

Serena withdrew a small glittering blade from her pack and placed it in a specially designed sheath at her belt. Once more, she reached into her bag for a compact bow and quiver of arrows which she handed to Noah. "I know that you can use these from your hunts with the men of the village. While hunting an animal is very different than fighting a man, ultimately the act of using the bow and arrow remains the same. Do not let your worries of hurting another being get in the way of defending us. If we are attacked, it will simply be us against them. Either they or we will die, if given no other choice."

The steely resolve in her eyes held Noah's until he nodded and accepted the weapons. He laid the bow across his shoulders for easy accessibility and swung the quiver behind his back in a manner that allowed for a swift reload if necessary.

As they managed their way down the path and through the foul air, Noah began to feel a sickness spreading through him. His stomach felt weak, and his head began to spin as the air became thin. Gasping for breath, he motioned to his grandmother to stop. They both struggled to breathe and felt sick to their stomach as they rested.

As they stopped to rest, Noah observed that the forest fauna had tinges of blackness to it, almost as if it were diseased or sick. The leaves were crispy to the touch, their veins corrupted with a blackened sickness. One of the trees had an open wound in the trunk and a thick black liquid resembling tar oozed slowly from it. Pointing to it, he showed his grandmother the liquid.

"Do not touch the liquid!" Serena exclaimed, as Noah went to reach toward it. As she said this, a globule of it broke away from the slowly descending larger mass and hit the ground with a great hiss. As they watched, it bubbled and boiled, infecting the surrounding area with some sort of disease.

"I don't want to know what would have happened had I put that on my skin" Noah said to his grandmother, as they both backed away from the slowly spreading black patch not the ground.

"Nor I. I think it's best that we move on from here. This area is dangerous, and I do not want to meet whatever or whomever is spreading that black corruption among the trees. Have you noticed that the forest has been silent since we began down this path? It's as if the life has left the forest or the animals have died from whatever is invading it" Serena said, as she continued onward.

Noah nodded to her and began to listen more closely for forests sounds. Where before the forest had been full of life, he now heard nothing. The trees did not rustle, no sounds of growth or life could be heard, and there had been no evidence of animals the entire day. They had not seen any animal tracks along the trail, nor had they seen field mice in the underbrush or small robins among the trees. The forest was dead, and the spreading blackness was eating away at the very vitality of it.

Ahead of them, a rock face emerged from the side of the forest. It appeared that they had finally reached the start of the mountain range itself. There was no valley between the mountains, simply trails and narrow passes. Crafty, well-armed merchants and adventurous travelers used these paths to traverse the mountain range directly, rather than taking the more circuitous path around the forest and mountains that added a month to the journey.

Recessed in the rock face was a small dark cave that held evidence of recent life and habitation. A travel pack belonging to someone, and the desiccated remains of a horse laid alongside a campfire that had long since burned cold. Slowly Noah and his grandmother approached the cave, warily looking for signs of life or an enemy. As they came closer to the cave, it seemed deeper than the initial impression it presented. A wispy wind could be heard rattling through the cave, and temperature quickly dropped as they approached the entrance.

Heart pounding in his chest like a drum signaling impending doom, Noah ventured further into the gloom. The weak murmur from within grew louder, a haunting and sinister chant lurking in the shadows. A rustling sound echoed through the cavern, like hunter closing in on its prey.

Suddenly a voice cried out from the depths, desperate and pleading for help, only to be choked off by a juicy, heart-wrenching gurgle that sent icy fingers of dread down Noah's spine. He and Serena tightened their grip on their weapons, bracing for the unknown terror that awaited them.

From the depths of darkness emerged a nightmarish figure—a soldier clad in tattered armor, pulled from the horrors of a long-ago battlefield. The face, a grotesque canvas of scars and decay, bore witness to the atrocities of war. But it was the eyes that froze Noah's blood in his veins. Silvery-gray and lifeless, they mirrored the soullessness of the damned.

A darkness infected the soldier's flesh, transforming it into a twisted mockery of humanity. Thick black veins snaked across the forehead, pulsating like hungry worms. Decaying skin seemed on the verge of peeling away, revealing the horror beneath.

The soldier staggered forward, hunched over like a marionette controlled by a malevolent puppeteer. A deafening shriek pierced the air as he lunged at Serena with inhuman ferocity. Mouth foaming with putrid saliva, a trembling hand gripped a rusted sword dripping with the evidence of recent violence.

Serena's heart raced as she dodged his feeble attack, her instincts propelling her to safety. She called out to Noah, urging him to ready his bow and prepare for the impending fight. But the dead soldier's deranged gaze fixated on Serena, and with a primal scream, it pounced on her like a rabid beast.

It clawed at her face with dirt-ridden nails, desperate to share the same malevolent infection. Broken and jagged teeth snapped at her throat, as if yearning to tear the life from her. With a surge of strength and the aid of her pack, Serena pushed away, struggling to keep the demonic creature at bay.

As the dead man lunged at his grandmother, Noah's mind froze in shock, paralyzed by the horrifying scene unfolding before him. But the sound of Serena's desperate screams jolted him back to reality and he sprang into action, reaching for his bow and arrow. With trembling hands, he notched the arrow and let it fly, solidly piercing the creature's back. To Noah's dismay, the undead being did not react to the arrow at all, as if it was impervious to mortal wounds.

Fear gripped Noah as he hastily reached for another arrow, this time aiming for the neck. He released the arrow, and it found its mark with deadly accuracy, impaling the soldier through the neck. But instead of halting the monstrous assailant, the arrow seemed to fuel its relentless aggression. Shrugging away the pack that separated it from Serena the creature attacked her with renewed ferocity.

Serena's terrified screams echoed through the cavern. Despite her brave efforts to push the soldier away, she was no match for his unholy strength. Noah watched in horror as the creature's poisoned blood spread and corrupted the ground beneath them, his grandmother's life hanging in the balance.

Desperation consumed Noah, and he reached for the last arrow in his quiver. A surge of determination and protectiveness coursed through him, as he imbued the arrow with his unwavering will to defend his beloved grandmother. He tapped into every last ounce of strength he had, unaware of the mysterious powers stirring within him.

Noah's eyes blazed with an unnatural crimson light as he pulled back the bowstring, the arrow's tip igniting in a fiery blaze. With a resolute breath, he released the arrow, and it flew true, piercing the being's heart with a searing heat. But in that moment of triumph, Noah felt his soul ebb, as if his very essence was draining from him.

Struggling against the weakness consuming him, Noah watched the soldier's body convulsing and stiffening, flames erupted from the arrowhead engulfing him in an inferno. Shrieking in torment and flailing wildly as the fire consumed him from within, the once lifeless silvery-grey eyes of the soldier now flickered with life as color returned to them.

In a last, desperate gesture, the man flung himself from Serena's presence, attempting to stagger away from the flames that engulfed him. His body succumbed to the ravaging fire, every inch of his corrupted form eaten by the flames and reduced to charred remains. The fire finally reached his eyes, completely erasing the haunting silver and replacing it with the vivid hues of life.

The man collapsed to the ground, his fiery ordeal coming to an end. With a fleeting moment of consciousness, the man met Noah's gaze, silently mouthing a thank-you before the light faded from his eyes forever. As the flames extinguished, a strange calm settled over the cavern. Noah watched in awe and terror as the blackness that had infected the man's veins seeped out from every orifice, strangely nonthreatening now that its host was vanquished.

As Noah rushed to his grandmother's side, he carefully avoided the puddles of black liquid that spread like a sinister stain on the ground. He reached out and quickly pulled her up from the wretched scene, enfolding her trembling form in the solace of his embrace. With a shaky grip, Noah guided them away from the remnants of the tormented man, Serena's sobs echoing in the air as they both grappled with the terror they had just witnessed.

Serena clung tightly to Noah, seeking comfort and support from the only family she had left. The fear in her eyes mirrored the terror that Noah felt. Slowly, as the adrenaline began to wane, Serena managed to calm herself, albeit still trembling with shock. She looked up at Noah, her eyes filled with both gratitude and concern for her grandson.

A dreadful weakness washed over Noah, and his mind drifted into an unsettling haze. The edges of his vision darkened, the eerie blackness encroaching like a cloud. The drain to his life force continuing from the moment after he had unleashed the fiery arrow. He tried to shake it off, but his body wouldn't obey. Struggling to remain upright, he felt his legs falter beneath him, betraying his desperate efforts to stay on his feet.

He felt utterly drained, and his muscles refused to respond to his will, even the act of lifting his head proved to be a daunting challenge. With a lurch, his body gave in to the overwhelming weakness, and he tumbled forward, landing on his face.

Through the haze of darkness, Noah heard his grandmother's voice, crying out his name. But it was distant and faded away into oblivion as world around him receded. The darkness consumed his vision, leaving him sinking into an abyss of nothingness.

Time seemed to stop as Noah lost all sense of awareness, his mind swallowed by the void of unconsciousness. Serena's desperate cries for her grandson echoed in the cavern, a haunting reminder of the peril they had faced and the heavy price they had paid. The fate of their journey, and indeed the destiny of their ancient family, now hung precariously in the balance.

Chapter 7:
Vision

Noah's heart raced as he felt himself plummeting into an endless void, his long golden hair whipping in an unseen wind. In this dark abyss, he strained to see a glimpse of something, anything, to give him a sense of direction. But all he encountered was the impenetrable absence of light.

The sensation of falling persisted, and the sound of rushing wind filled his ears, emphasizing the maddening descent. With no idea how deeply into the abyss he fell or what awaited at its bottom, he pushed his fear back and tried to keep his mind focused, attempting to make sense of this eerie nightmare.

As his eyes slowly adjusted to the darkness, a faint glimmer of hope sparked. In the distance, a joyous trilling sound echoed through the abyss, like a siren's song calling out to him. And there it was, a distant speck of light, almost imperceptible against the inky blackness.

With each passing moment, the light grew stronger and larger, illuminating the void around him. Noah's heart skipped a beat as he recognized the light—the same brilliant star he had seen as a young boy in the old woman's tent. That captivating star that had always stayed in his thoughts, a mysterious presence hovering at the edge of his memories.

The radiant glow of the star cast ethereal shadows on the darkness the closer Noah fell towards it. Noah contemplated what this celestial entity wanted with him. The closer they came together, the more intense its light became, bathing him in a warm, otherworldly radiance.

Suddenly, the star surged forward with a burst of searing heat, causing Noah's heart to pound even harder. Before he could react, it collided with his chest, enfolding him in a blaze of blinding light. His body felt infused by an all-encompassing power.

In that moment, Noah felt a profound connection to the star, as if it were probing the depths of his very soul. The experience was both exhilarating and terrifying, a whirlwind of emotions he couldn't comprehend. Was this a gift or a curse?

As the brilliant star settled within him, Noah's vision swirled as if he were being pulled in a myriad of directions at once. The boundaries between reality and illusion blurred, his dream and the waking world melding together.

With a flash Noah he found himself standing on the balcony of a grand palace adorned with majestic granite and marble columns. Overlooking a bustling city below, a vibrant scene unfolded before him: the city gently cascaded down a hilltop, leading to the riverbanks where boats and merchants bustled with their wares. The joyful laughter of children echoed in the air as they played on the sandy shores.

Pulled from the city's mesmerizing panorama by the sound of laughter and playful screams emanating from within the palace, Noah turned toward the interior. Curiosity guided him through the corridors of the palace until he entered a room where the sounds appeared to have originated. There, his eyes locked onto a tall, broad-shouldered man with luminous blonde hair, much like his own. It struck him that this man had to be his father.

And there, beside his father, stood a petite yet commanding woman with warm chocolate hair. Her features mirrored Noah's own—his grandmother's words now evident in front of him. As he beheld her beautiful eyes filled with love and happiness, he realized the depth of the connection he had never had the chance to experience with a mother and father. He had known his grandmother's love, yet seeing his parents filled a part of his heart that he hadn't known was empty.

Noah watched as his parents engaged in playful banter, their love for each other radiating in their every glance and gesture. His mother placed her hand gently on her stomach, and Noah's heart skipped a beat as he understood the profound truth—he was witnessing a snippet of time before his birth.

His father leaned in with affection, placing a tender kiss on his wife's belly, and then rested his ear against it, intently listening to the sounds within. A rush of emotion surged through Noah, realizing that he had missed his mother's loving embrace and the unwavering support of his father.

A bittersweet feeling swept over him, filling him with a deep sense of loss. Although his grandmother had been a staunch supporter in his life and had raised him with unconditional love, he had never truly grasped the impact of not having his parents in his life—until this moment. He had missed out on the wisdom, playfulness, and total love a mother and father would have given him. His mother's nurturing guidance, her scientific curiosities, and his father's unwavering support—these were treasures he had been denied.

Grief intertwined with joy as he witnessed the loving bond between his parents. In that brief glimpse of the past, he felt an intense longing for the parents he never had the chance to know. A wave of emotions made tears well slip down his cheeks as he mourned the life that could have been—a life with his loving mother and devoted father by his side.

Hesitantly, Noah extended a hand to touch his mother's shoulder, yearning to initiate a conversation with them. He desperately wanted to warn them of the impending betrayal, to prevent the future from ever taking place. But just as he reached out, the haunting trilling noise of the white star filled his ears once more.

In an instant, the scene morphed before his eyes. The once joyful room now became a nightmarish hellscape, engulfed in flames and covered in blood. The clashing of steel resonated from an adjoining room, and Noah instinctively rushed towards the great hall, where the sounds of battle intensified.

Entering the room, a horrifying sight unfolded before him. His father, flanked by two weary palace guards, found themselves cornered by a sinister group of men and women clad in dark cloaks. The air crackled with an awful power as the cloaked figures chanted incantations, brandishing staffs that glowed a sinister red.

At the head of this evil faction stood a man that Noah instinctively knew was Vladimir—a figure with an ordinary appearance yet exuding an unsettling aura. With short blonde hair and murky gray eyes, his unassuming demeanor hid the darkness that lay within.

Suddenly and without hesitation, Vladimir lunged forward, striking down one of the guards defending Noah's father. Enraged, his father retaliated, engaging Vladimir in a fierce and deadly duel. But despite his skills, Noah's father was gradually overwhelmed by Vladimir's dark magic and the sheer number of attackers.

In the chaos, the remaining palace guard valiantly fought, but succumbed to the onslaught, falling to the floor with multiple blades piercing his chest.

As the battle raged on, the sorcerers surrounding Noah's father and Vladimir chanted rhythmically, ensnaring them in a malevolent spell. The ground turned into treacherous quicksand, holding Noah's father in place, while Vladimir's swordsmanship seemed to gain supernatural strength.

In one swift move, Vladimir disarmed Noah's father, driving his sword deep into his heart. The spiteful man pulled the blade free with a wicked smirk and an insane laugh, kicking Noah's father to the ground to watch the life rapidly leave his own cousin's eyes.

Amidst the tragic scene, an unearthly scream echoed behind Noah. He turned to see his mother, her eyes glowing with white light, consumed by rage and despair at the sight of her beloved husband dead in their own home. Her grief turned to fury as she connected the dots, realizing that the man standing over her husband's lifeless body was the orchestrator of this unspeakable act.

Noah's heart pounded with terror and sorrow, knowing that the dreadful future he had witnessed was now in motion. The weight of his powerlessness crushed him as he could only watch helplessly while tragedy unfolded before his eyes.

In an instant, Noah's mother transformed into a being of searing flame. Her entire form was enveloped in intense, bright red fire. The scorching heat emanating from her was palpable even from a distance. The sorcerers, realizing the danger, launched an attack, but with a mere gesture of her hand, Noah's mother conjured massive balls of fire that engulfed several of the sorcerers, their agonized screams filling the air as they met their blazing end.

She continued her relentless advance, systematically striking down the remaining sorcerers while closing in on Vladimir. A grim smile adorned her face as the last sorcerer fell unconscious under an unseen force, and she focused her attention on the terrified Vladimir.

In a desperate attempt to defend himself, Vladimir brandished his sword and struck at Noah's mother, just as he had done with his brother. But she effortlessly caught the blade and reduced it to molten metal that spilled onto the floor, surrounding Vladimir in a pool of liquid steel. She grasped his face, leaving a scorching imprint of a hand on his cheek. As he shrieked in agony, she reached for his heart, intending to end his wicked existence. However, before she could deliver the final blow, a sharp pike suddenly pushed out through her midsection.

Noah's heart sank as he saw the sorcerer, whom his mother had previously knocked unconscious, had revived, and crept behind her with the deadly weapon. His grief-stricken cries filled his ears as he watched his mother crumple to the floor, her flames extinguishing as her life slowly slipped away.

Amidst the chaos, the spreading fire had set the entire building ablaze, and the sounds of alarms and terrified cries echoed throughout the city levels. As Noah witnessed the painful demise of his mother, the haunting trilling sound resurfaced.

Once again, Noah's world flickered, and when his vision steadied, he found himself in a different place. This time, he stood within the confines of a towering castle, several hundred feet above the ground. The window he approached offered a breathtaking view of the sky and the sprawling landscape below. Perplexed, he searched the room for any familiar items, but it appeared to be a plain bedroom devoid of any distinctive signs of wealth or extravagance.

As he attempted to leave and explore further, frustration welled within him when he realized the door was locked from the outside, secured by a sturdy wooden bar. Noah's determination to uncover the purpose of this vision intensified, as this vision seemed unrelated to his family's history.

With a heavy sigh, he sat on the bed, its cushions offering a comfort he hadn't experienced since he and his grandmother had been forced to leave their home and venture through the unforgiving mountains. Suddenly, a very human sounding chuff emanated from beneath the bed frame, startling Noah. Before he could react, two strong hands grabbed his ankles and pulled, causing him to fall onto the floor. A lithe male figure sprang out from under the bed, pinning Noah down with powerful arms, using with his body weight to hold Noah's torso firmly to the ground.

The man's fierce blue eyes locked onto Noah's and he felt an intrusion into his mind, as if a foreign presence was attempting to enter. Reacting instinctively, Noah pushed back with all his physical strength, breaking free and successfully wrestling to pin him down.

Noah sized up the panting young man beneath him, his red hair contrasting sharply with his striking blue eyes. Despite his slender frame, the man's well-defined muscles were evident beneath his attire, which, though not overly opulent, hinted at a certain level of comfort.

The man asked, "Who are you, and why are you in these chambers?" His entrancing voice announced, "You know that I am not 18 yet, and your sick little ritual won't work until I've reached my majority."

Perplexed, Noah responded, "Ritual? I do not know what you are talking about. The light brought me here and showed me things, but you're the first person I've encountered who seems to know about my existence." Leaning back slightly, he said, "Where are we, and why are we locked in this room? What have you done to deserve being confined?"

To his surprise, the young man's eyes widened with excitement. "A light brought you here? Could it be the bright star that has been appearing in my dreams?" he eagerly inquired.

As Noah listened to the young man's words, he felt a mix of confusion and concern. Realizing the threat had passed, he lifted himself up after awkwardly noting that their bodies were aligned a little too perfectly and allowed him to scamper away. "I don't know if your star and my bright white light are the same. All I recall is saving my grandmother from a diseased creature and then being flooded with memories of my family's history after the light entered my chest.

Now, here I am with you. I don't have all the answers, but there must be a reason the light brought me to see you," he explained, trying to make sense of the situation.

The young man nodded, acknowledging Noah's words. "Yes, your light and my star must be one and the same. As for the ritual, my father is a sorcerer who serves King Vladimir. He plans to offer me as a tribute to the King once I reach my majority, which is in a little less than three weeks. I will either be forced to serve the King as a sorcerer like my father, or he might have me serve him in more… undesirable, base ways," he admitted, a hint of mortification coloring his cheeks.

Noah blushed as he realized what the man meant when he said baser ways. Evaluating the man in front of him, he found that he was quite attractive in many ways. From the gorgeous blue eyes which appeared to have great depths, the full pouty lips which were currently being gnawed on nervously by their owner. With the muscular physique the other man possessed he could clearly see why he would be worried that the King may desire him as more than a sorcerer. Ignoring his sudden unexpected attraction to the man and attempting to hide his blush from earlier, Noah moved slowly toward the other man and cautiously reached his hand out in greeting.

"My name is Noah, and I don't mean to harm you. What is your name?"

"My name is Liam" the man hesitantly replied, grasping Noah's hand in a firm grip.

"Liam, if you do not want to serve the King, do you have any other choices to prevent this? Do you have anyone who can help you escape?" Noah asked, attempting to see if he had any way of getting out of the predicament he was in.

"No, I already tried to persuade my father otherwise, but he is convinced that giving me to the King will gain him prominence and power." Liam stated, looking both frustrated and disgusted by the thought of his father selling him out to such a revolting creature as the King. "It's all a bunch of idiocy as the King doesn't care who serves him; he is selfish and power hungry. So long as his needs are met, he doesn't care."

Noah decided to offer his help when he heard the distant trilling of the star. As the song of the star grew louder, Noah's sense of urgency intensified. With a determined look in his eyes, he rushed his words out quickly, asking one last question. "Liam, where are you? I can try and help, but I need to know where to find you. Tell me how I can reach you."

Liam's eyes widened, surprised by Noah's sudden resolve. "I'm in the city of Rankier, being held in the house of the Priors," he replied. "They have me under lock and key in the northern tower. If you can help me, I would be extremely grateful to you. Regardless, thank you for the company. It has been a long while since I have spoken to someone other than the sorcerers or one of the fanatical Priors."

As the words left Liam's lips, the trilling of the star reached a crescendo, and Noah felt himself fading away from the room. Liam watched in astonishment as the space Noah had occupied just moments ago was consumed by the brilliant light, and then nothing.

Liam slowly reclined on his bed, his mind occupied with thoughts of the mysterious man he had just met. There was an undeniable aura of authenticity surrounding Noah, one that made him feel secure and safe. Liam couldn't deny the intense physical attraction he felt towards Noah—his strong, muscular physique and the warmth in his gaze ignited a spark deep within. The moment they were entangled, with Noah pinning him, was both exhilarating and surprising. As Noah disappeared,he couldn't help but notice the unexpected physical response —the undeniable arousal from their brief but electrifying contact.

For the first time since his imprisonment, Liam fell asleep feeling a glimmer of hope. In his dreams, he saw warm brown eyes and felt the strong, protective embrace of Noah's muscular arms around him.

Chapter 8:
Awakening

Serena sat restlessly by the crackling fire she had carefully built in a secluded clearing, anxiously awaiting her grandson's awakening from the mysterious stasis that had befallen him. Once they had escaped the horrifying encounter with the infected man, she had managed to compose herself and move Noah to a safer area, far away from the malevolent presence that had attacked them. Struggling with her exhaustion, she had carried him along the path to a small, untainted clearing. Then she put ingredients for their supper into a pot to hang over the fire. They both needed a well-deserved respite and some solid nourishment.

With Noah secured, she braved a return to the encampment where they had been accosted with the intention to salvage anything useful from the attacker's belongings, all the while avoiding contact with the spreading black corruption. Surprisingly, the once-infected man's lifeless body lay motionless, and the black matter seemed strangely quiescent, no longer possessing its malevolent power.

After taking only items that might aid them on their journey, Serena hurried back to Noah's side, hoping he had regained consciousness. Though his eyes remained closed, he stirred occasionally, faintly whispered names escaping his lips. In his dreams, he called out for his parents, a heart-wrenching revelation that left Serena troubled and wondering what had prompted such deep emotions in him.

As she gazed at her grandson, Serena's heart swelled with love and concern. The journey they had embarked upon was fraught with peril and uncertainty, but she knew she had to protect and guide him, for he was all that remained of their cherished family. With unwavering resolve, she stayed by his side, waiting for him to awaken from the mysterious slumber, praying that whatever haunted him in his dreams would be soothed and that he would find the strength to face the challenges ahead.

As Serena stirred the simmering broth in the pot over the fire, her mind continued to dwell on the extraordinary display of power she had witnessed in her grandson earlier. She knew that their family possessed unique abilities, but what Noah had shown was beyond anything she had encountered before. It was exceedingly rare for a family member to manifest their powers before reaching their majority, and those who did usually exhibited minor talents. But Noah's flames were unlike anything she had ever seen – they held a strength and purity that defied explanation.

The flames had responded not just to Noah's will but also to some deeper force within him. Serena couldn't shake the feeling that there was something divine about the power he had wielded. She blushed at the thought, chiding herself for entertaining such a notion. Yet, the sensation lingered, a whisper in the back of her mind that this power was more than just natural talent.

Noah's abilities had surpassed even his parents, and she knew they were both powerful in their own right. His mother's control over elements was impressive, but it didn't compare to the raw intensity of Noah's flames. There was a missing piece to the puzzle, and Serena was determined to uncover it. She couldn't help but wonder if there was a hidden legacy within their family, a lineage of power that had been dormant until now.

Her musings were interrupted by a gasp and rustling sound behind her. She swiftly turned to find Noah rousing from his trance. Concerned, she leaned over him, placing a gentle hand on his shoulder.

"Noah, are you alright?" she asked, her voice filled with worry.

Breathing quickly, Noah opened his eyes and raised himself up on his elbows, then to a sitting position on the pallet his grandmother had laid him out on. Groaning he felt his head pound as a wave of physical exhaustion hit him hard. He began to rub his temples with weary fingers, even as the memories of his dreams assailed him. With a loud gasp, he looked to his grandmother. "I saw them! I saw my parents."

Taken aback, his grandmother gaped at Noah. "What do you mean you saw your parents?"

Noah sighed thoughtfully and pieced his words together before responding. "After we fought whatever that thing was, I passed out. I remember falling into darkness and this light found me. It showed me things. It showed me my parents together. It also showed me when my mother and father died. I watched my father get stabbed through the heart and my mother be impaled on a pike by a cowardly witch who stabbed her from behind."

Leaning back with a gasp, Serena was astonished at what he described. "What could possibly have shown you this? You couldn't remember these things; you weren't even there when your parents died. Your mother took you safely away from the palace before going back to fight alongside your father!"

Nodding, Noah replied "I don't know if I can explain it properly, but it was this light. It made this shrill yet beautiful trilling noise in the darkness I was in. The light was hot, and it felt like it would burn the world around it if it got too near. When it got close to me, I felt it slam into my chest, and then it showed me these memories. I was there, I could walk around the palace. I saw them laughing and smiling together when mother was pregnant with me, but I couldn't speak to them." Gasping, Noah recalled, "I tried to reach out and touch her, but when I did the light just took me away."

With a rough inhale, Noah remembered another facet of his dreams. "It showed me someone else! His name was Liam, and I don't think he was a memory. He told me he was being held against his will by the Priors, so it can't be possible for that to be a memory."

Slowly Serena sat back and contemplated what Noah had said. This light sounded like a powerful entity and made her suspect that there was more to this story than first met the eye. Noah was special and this light intervening just reinforced how important he was. The memories that he described of his parents were most likely true; she couldn't see any reason to doubt what he had been shown. The story about the man being held by the Priors was interesting and intriguing, however she could not see why he would have been shown to Noah.

Bracing herself, Serena looked back at Noah and asked "Noah, I realize that this may sound odd, but have you ever had visions like this before? Have you ever seen this light in your dreams, or ever had someone speak to you about it?"

"I did have one experience when I was ten; the year we'd done well on the farm, and you sent me to the harvest festival to enjoy myself. When a strange fortune teller told me my fortune, something similar happened" Noah replied hesitantly, continuing to explain what had occurred that day. As he recounted the tale his grandmother's visage became both more apprehensive yet awestruck.

Settling herself more comfortably on the ground across from Noah, Serena took a moment to contemplate Noah's experience as a child. Absentmindedly she gestured to Noah to serve himself dinner, from the fragrant pot of food. Noah raised himself up and went to the fire, serving a bowl for himself and one for his grandmother before returning to settle down.

"I don't know that I have an answer for all of this, but it seems clear that divine intervention is at hand here" Serena breathed thoughtfully. Her thoughts spoken out loud rather than to Noah directly. Turning her eyes away from the fire, which she had been gazing at with glazed eyes, she continued to ponder what her grandson had revealed. She looked at Noah as he began to eat the dinner she'd prepared for them.

"It seems based on what you've experienced, there is more to our journey than I had initially thought. If there is a divine intervention at play here, which there must be based on your visions, our mission becomes even more important. Evidently the gods have something planned for you, and I can guess that it is in relation to Vladimir. The signs have been warning us of his dark dalliances, and it may be that he has gone too far and lost control of himself with his experiments and power mongering." Serena mused, pondering the words as she spoke them.

"If that is the case, do we change our plans?" Noah nervously asked, voice tight with tension.

Serena deliberated for a moment, before shaking her head negatively. "While we need to take this into advisement, we cannot alter our course at this moment. Our plan remains the same; seek shelter with our allies and focus on your training. Only once we have had a chance to regroup and gather our strength, and you are ready, will we be able to strike against Vladimir."

Serena turned back to face Noah, lovingly caressing his cheek. "For now, you need to sleep, Noah. Lay back and get some rest, the battle with that monster took a lot out of you. I'll stand guard for tonight while you sleep." Noah nodded, eyelids already heavy with exhaustion from the simple tasks he had just completed and lay down on his pallet. Quickly he drifted off to slumber as Serena stood watch over him.

Part 2

Chapter 9:

Journey

As the sun rose above the trees nestled into the mountain pass, a renewed sense of vitality embraced the landscape, with the once absent animal life returning in full force. The canopy came alive with the melodious sounds of birdsong, accompanied by the playful banter of chipmunks and squirrels vying for precious acorns. Rising early, Noah and Serena seized the morning, dousing the remnants of their campfire and methodically packing their belongings.

Serena beckoned Noah to join her, and as he approached, she unfurled a timeworn parchment map. With care, she spread it out on the ground before them, allowing both of them to examine its markings.

"We are right here," Serena stated, indicating a spot on the map with a confident gesture. "Having just traversed the Ceredor Pass, we'll soon emerge from the forest and find ourselves on the plains. Spriting, the capital, lies due west of our current position. However, we must steer clear of it since Vladimir's forces heavily patrol the vicinity."

Concern etched in his voice, Noah inquired, "What about Liam? He mentioned being imprisoned in a tower in Rankier. Can we locate it on this map?"

Nodding, Serena pointed to a city positioned north of the capital, situated across a meandering river. "Rankier is situated here. Vladimir has placed the city firmly under the control of his sorcerers, making infiltration challenging. Fortunately, it's not as intensely guarded as the capital itself. You see, Vladimir is only possessive of what he values most, and he has little regard for his sorcerers. Consequently, they are left to their own devices, vying for whatever little scraps of power he tosses their way," Serena explained, her distaste for the sorcerers evident as her lip curled in disgust.

"And where are we ultimately heading? Who are these allies we're seeking?" Noah inquired, tactfully avoiding any further mention of the sorcerers, at least for the time being.

"Our allies are the Wood-Elves of Elnoth, the main Elven stronghold, located northwest of Rankier. It is across the Androth River, deep within the vast Elven woods. Their domain is well fortified, offering us safety once we reach there," Serena reaffirmed her focus on the mission ahead.

Noah's expression reflected his troubled thoughts. "If these allies were so powerful, why didn't we seek their help when I was just a baby? Perhaps they could have assisted us in reclaiming the kingdom."

Serena's gaze softened as she explained, "The Wood-Elves, though strong, do not form a single unified nation. Instead, they consist of three competing Elven cities: Elnoth being the most prominent, followed by Falnir and Vardrun. These cities often vie with each other, and during the time of the insurrection, it was uncertain which one could be trusted. All three experienced their own internal conflicts. Any attempted mediation did not succeed, making it unsafe for us to seek refuge with any of them at that time. Elnoth and Vardrun have historically been our allies, but Falnir sought independence from the others, making them opportunistic and, in my personal experience, untrustworthy," Serena replied, her eyes distant as she recollected past failed negotiations with Falnir.

Noah found himself even more uncertain about their chosen path.

"If they were untrustworthy in the past, what has changed that now we would consider approaching them?" he questioned, seeking clarity.

Serena's response was candid, "To be truthful, very little has changed. The conflicts between the Elven cities persist, and they remain unresolved to this day. The last news I'd heard, Elnoth and Vardrun have relentlessly besieged Falnir for years, employing both land and sea forces, yet the city's walls remain unyielding. It's somewhat admirable, their resilience, but it seems foolish, for eventually, they must succumb."

With a deep sigh, Serena rose from her kneeling position and began carefully rolling up the aged parchment. "What has changed is our circumstances," she explained. "When you were just a child, I believed it was wiser to stay concealed in a quiet hamlet, far from any major city or royal court. The danger of Vladimir having either of us assassinated was ever-present. We couldn't be sure whom to trust, so it was safer to trust no one and live an unassuming life until I deemed it safe to resurface. But now, you have grown into a capable defender, and the messages and warnings we've received indicate that it's time to abandon hiding."

Noah acknowledged his grandmother's response with a nod, feeling content with her realistic explanation. "Alright then, first, we avoid the capital, then make our way stealthily into the sorcerer's stronghold, and finally navigate through a labyrinthine forest to reach Elnoth's fortress."

Serena couldn't help but chuckle at Noah's straightforward portrayal of their plan. "Indeed, that's one way to put it – a rather simplified version of our elaborate strategy, which involves evading Vladimir's relentless forces, evading the clutches of his sorcerers, and surviving the perilous creatures lurking in the depths of the Elven woods."

Having finalized their plan, the duo completed their preparations to set off on their journey. Serena took the lead as they followed the trail, making their way down from the mountain pass that was rife with treacherous sections and unstable ground, hindering their pace. As the day's sunlight reached its zenith, the terrain finally began to level out, and they stepped onto the plains that led towards the capital, Spriting.

After a morning spent in friendly silence following their initial planning, Serena glanced back at Noah. "We've arrived at the plains of Ergos. We need to be extremely discreet while we're here. The capital lies directly west of us, and although military patrols rarely venture this far from the city, there's still a chance we might come across some on our way."

Noah agreed, taking his grandmother's advice to heart. "If we do encounter them, what's our plan? I still don't have full control over my powers; what happened earlier with that monster was a lucky accident, and I really don't want us in such a dire situation again."

Letting out a sigh, Serena nodded. "You're right; our priority should be honing your powers as we cross these plains. While I may not be the most skilled instructor in this regard, I'll have to do for now."

Serena unslung her bag from her back and carefully rummaged through its contents until she pulled out a time-worn book. She handed it over to Noah, making sure not to cause any damage to its delicate pages. "This book has been handed down through our family for generations. It contains the experiences and knowledge of each family member who came into their powers. Every new generation has added to it, hoping to aid the next in mastering their abilities and control. I'd like you to read it thoroughly, and once you're finished, we'll start your practical elemental training.

During our evenings, we'll also work on your swordsmanship," Serena explained, pointing to two swords she had retrieved from the cave while Noah was unconscious. "You've shown proficiency with a bow and arrow, due in part to your hunting, but your close combat skills with a blade need to be practiced. It's crucial that we address this gap in your training, as it could put you in serious danger if we're not careful."

Noah reverently accepted the book from his grandmother, handling it as a cherished family heirloom. "Thank you, grandmother. I'll begin reading it as we journey through the plains," he replied earnestly.

Serena's eyes remained sharp as she nodded firmly. "Excellent. Tonight, over dinner, you'll summarize what you've read today," she instructed with resolve.

The vast golden fields of wheat stretched endlessly as they continued their journey, the plains occasionally dotted with modest farmer's huts and barns. Rough dirt roads deeply rutted from wagon wheels had been carved through the fields, providing them with a discreet path to traverse for the remainder of the day. As the day's light waned, they carefully navigated these roads, steadily advancing towards Rankier. Noah remained engrossed in the book he had received, absorbing its contents, while Serena stayed vigilant, keeping a sharp eye out for any potential soldiers who might interfere.

✳ ✳ ✳ ✳ ✳

Weary and sore after such a long day's journey along the rugged land, Noah and Serena settled themselves around their carefully arranged campfire safely nestled within a small copse of trees and concealed from the view of passersby. Although the roads had been relatively calm and quiet, they both agreed it was better to err on the side of caution and choose a discreet location to rest.

The fire crackled and a savory aroma wafted through the camp as a stew made from the preserved hare Serena had snared during their mountain pass journey cooked over the flames. The broth had been enhanced with local herbs foraged along the roadside, infusing it with delicious flavors. Hungry from their travels and exertions, Serena and Noah both eagerly devoured their meal, savoring the nourishing energy it provided.

Once the food had been consumed, Noah and Serena engaged in a deep discussion about the contents of the book he had been reading. Demonstrating that he had devoted ample mental effort to understanding its teachings, Noah answered questions asked of him in great detail. Serena listened attentively, nodding in satisfaction with each of his answers.

Serena rose from her seat and determinedly fetched the two swords she had been carrying. Tossing one towards Noah, she announced "It's time to practice your sword skills." Swishing her sword to get a feel of the balance, she continued, "I was once trained in the deadly arts of battle, even as a woman, and though I may be a bit rusty, you'll find that I can hold my own against most men." Her smile held a hint of lethal confidence as she readied herself for the sparring session.

Noah leaped willingly to his feet, eager to engage in sword practice with his grandmother. Snatching up the sword, he made an enthusiastic but somewhat clumsy advance towards Serena, swinging his blade. However, he was taken aback as he found himself swiftly disarmed and knocked to the ground. The wind was knocked out of him, leaving him momentarily stunned by his grandmother's skill and agility.

"Oh dear, far too eager," Serena taunted with a grim smile on her face. "Try again."

Noah flushed with embarrassment at being taken down so easily. Quickly regaining his composure, he jumped back up and adopted a more cautious and defensive stance. Circling his grandmother, he carefully approached, taking his time to assess the situation. Serena mirrored his movements, her approval evident at his new approach.

With newfound focus, Noah attempted another strike, but this time he didn't throw himself into it recklessly. Instead, he swung the sword carefully, aiming to disarm his grandmother. However, Serena effortlessly parried his thrust, knocking his blade out of his hands in the process.

Noah's eyes widened in surprise, impressed by his grandmother's skill and speed. He retrieved his fallen sword and returned to his stance, determined to learn from the experience and improve his technique. Serena nodded, encouraging him to try again, as they continued their sword practice under the moonlit sky.

Training continued for another hour, the clash of steel against steel echoing in the dark, the flickering firelight gradually dimming as the coals burned down. Finally, Serena gave a signal to stop, and she lowered her blade, settling down to rest by the fire's fading embers to drink thirstily from a flask of cool water that she passed to Noah.

"I can see we have our work cut out for us. Your sword skills are almost non-existent, but I'm pleased to see that you approach it with the right attitude," she remarked. "We'll need to practice every night and review different stances as well. Your current stance is too aggressive, leaving you vulnerable to attacks. I noticed several openings in your defense where I could have easily struck and incapacitated you. Even less experienced fighters than me could exploit those vulnerabilities."

Noah nodded, acknowledging the seriousness of his shortcomings. He knew he had much to learn, but he was determined to improve and become proficient in swordsmanship under his grandmother's guidance. With renewed resolve, he looked forward to each night's training, eager to refine his skills and strengthen his defenses.

With their practice concluded, both Serena and Noah settled into their bedding, ready to rest for the night. Despite being tired from the day's travels, Serena's body was accustomed to such exertions, and she knew she would wake up feeling fine the next morning. On the other hand, Noah's body was not used to the physical strain of their training, and he could already feel muscles he had never used before protesting.

As he lay down, he couldn't help but anticipate the challenge of the next morning. "Fun" might be one way to describe it, he thought to himself wryly, knowing that it would undoubtedly be a test of his physical limits. However, he was determined to persevere, to grow stronger with each passing day of their journey. With that thought in mind, he closed his eyes and settled into the embrace of a restorative sleep.

Chapter 10:

Dream

As Noah drifted into slumber, he found himself back in Liam's tower bedroom. The room remained largely unchanged from his previous visit—comfortable and opulent enough to satisfy someone of a wealthier class, yet devoid of personal belongings. Despite the signs of habitation, there was no sign of its occupant; the room stood empty.

On a nearby table, a small wooden tray held a slice of stale bread and the remains of a bowl of cold soup, suggesting that someone had been there recently. A few scant pieces of clothing were neatly folded and arranged on the bed, offering further clues of recent activity in the room.

Noah looked around, trying to make sense of the mystery of Liam's whereabouts. A sense of worried curiosity washed over him, a concern that something had happened to Liam.

A scuffling noise echoed through the nearby corridor, catching Noah's attention, and he instinctively moved toward the sound to investigate. Through a small gap in the barred door, he peered into the hall to witness a distressing scene: Liam, head hanging to his chest and feet dragging along the floor, was being roughly hauled down the hallway by two armed guards. Noah's heart pounded forcefully as he observed the alarming sight.

Thinking quickly, he withdrew from the vicinity of the door and sought cover behind a wardrobe at the far side of the room, his mind racing with concern for his friend's safety. From his hidden vantage point, he watched as the guards callously heaved Liam's unresisting form face down onto the bed, and with a loud, jarring clang, they threw the lock on the door as they withdrew, leaving Liam incapacitated and defenseless inside the room.

Noah's heart sank as he approached his friend and saw the grim state he was in. Liam lay motionless on the bed, emitting faint whimpers of pain. As Noah looked closer at the young man, his heart broke at the sight before him. Liam's shirtless form revealed his pale and battered skin was covered in numerous bloody lash marks. Dozens of wounds marred his back in an awful crisscross pattern, the torn flesh oozing blood as his body struggled to deal with the physical trauma.

Noah fought back tears as he tried to process the brutal beating that Liam had endured. He now realized that he had to act swiftly to save his friend and put an end to this senseless suffering. The sight of Liam's pain and vulnerability only fueled Noah's determination to confront those responsible for this unimaginable cruelty.

Noah moved to place a hand on Liam's shoulder tenderly. His heart ached as he gently asked, "Liam, can you speak? Are you okay?"

Liam tensed and recoiled suddenly; the movement making pain evident on his face as he let out an agonized cry. He fell hard to the floor, flinching and gasping a tortured breath, but soon recognized the figure before him. Relief washed over him as he realized it was Noah.

"Noah, you're back!" Liam groaned, his eyes lighting up with trust. "Have you come to break me out of this hellish prison?" he asked hopefully. The longing for freedom from his tormentors clearly evident in his exhausted gaze. This glimmer of hope spurred Noah's determination with sharp teeth.

"I am so sorry Liam, we are still a distance away from you. We have to bypass the capital undetected before we can find a way into Rankier. Stay strong, we are coming to save you." Noah responded, trying to sound positive in spite of Liam's defeated expression.

Noah's heart dropped as he watched sadness sink its claws into Liam's expression. Rescue was coming but not soon enough for the poor young man. "Please don't worry, Liam. I will save you" Noah's voice rang with resolution. "I swear we will find a way to reach Rankier as quickly as possible. Just promise me that you will hang on a little longer." His words were filled with hope and conviction, a determined effort to bolster Liam's spirits despite the horrific circumstances.

Liam nodded his head tiredly, a myriad of emotions flickering across his face, but he trusted Noah's promise. "I'll hold onto the hope. Every day it gets more difficult; my refusal to bow down is tolerated less and less the closer we get to my birthday. Oh God Noah, once I turn 18, they will take me to the King, and I won't ever be able to escape."

Noah's mouth contorted with distress as he was reminded of the dire situation. "How did you get these wounds?" he asked with sadness, lightly placing his hand against the small area of unblemished bare skin of Liam's shoulder.

Leaning into Noah's touch, Liam painfully recounted the terrible events that led to his current state. "They've been torturing me, trying to get me to submit and accept my fate," he ground out, his voice hoarse with the weight of his ordeal. "They want me to submit and serve the King in any way he desires. I've refused everything, but…the torture, it's been unbearable." His voice trailed off, the pain of his experience clearly evident.

Noah's fists clenched in anger and frustration, a deep sense of helplessness at not being able to protect his friend overwhelming him. He silently vowed that he would do whatever it took to rescue Liam. "Hang on, please," he murmured encouragingly. "I'm coming for you, and I won't let them hurt you any longer. Stay strong for me, I will get you out of here."

Noah instinctively moved to tenderly support Liam and guide him back onto the bed, mindful of the wretched wounds, he made sure not to cause any further discomfort. As Noah gently put his arm around him,

Liam found comfort in Noah's physical presence, finding solace in his support.

They settled onto the bed, Liam rested his head on Noah's shoulder, the warmth of Noah's body against his offered a brief respite from the hardships he had endured. The two sat together in silence, sharing in the cherished peaceful moment. With that intimate connection, words were unnecessary; their unspoken bond spoke volumes, conveying their mutual attraction and determination.

Time seemed to stand still, and the world around them faded away. It was just the two of them, finding strength in each other's presence, and offering support in the face of adversity. In that quiet embrace, their budding friendship grew deeper, each knowing that they would face whatever obstacles came their way together until Liam drifted to sleep.

Noah looked down, his heart melting at the sight of Liam peacefully slumbering against him. With the utmost care, he gently laid Liam back onto the bed, thoughtfully arranging pillows to ensure his comfort. As he brushed a lock of hair away from Liam's face, Noah couldn't help but be captivated by the man's exquisite beauty. His delicate complexion, enticing lips, and strikingly handsome features left Noah in awe.

Emotions washed over Noah and he felt a deep sense of responsibility to protect his friend and ensure his safety. The gravity of the situation weighed heavily on his sturdy shoulders, but a newfound determination settled into his heart to see this through. He also found himself grappling with his attraction to another man. Growing up, he had been quite isolated, rarely interacting regularly with anyone other than his grandmother. The absence of strong male figures in his life had led him to assume that he would naturally be attracted to women.

Yet, his attraction to Liam came as a surprise, stirring deep feelings he had never experienced before. Matters of the heart were already confusing enough, and now he had to come to terms with feelings he hadn't anticipated. Noah couldn't deny that he found Liam incredibly attractive, yet he was uncertain about how to navigate this new development.

Noah knew that the world in general might not be accepting of such feelings, considering the prevailing norms he had grown up with. He worried about the potential judgment and societal rejection if he were to acknowledge his attraction to another man. A male taking a male lover was something that was murmured about, juicy gossip on the lips of many. Tales of noblemen from the larger cities taking male lovers as escorts inevitably made their way to smaller towns. But these noblemen rarely fell in love with their paramours and even fewer married them for it was scandalous for a man to openly take a male lover. It was an expectation that men and women wed to produce children and continue their line.

Despite these concerns, Noah couldn't dismiss his feelings for Liam. He cherished their recently discovered bond and understood that in spite of its newness their connection ran deep, transcending societal expectations. As he watched over the sleeping Liam, Noah couldn't fathom how this had happened, but he did know that he was enamored of this quietly strong young man.

With a determined breath, he tucked the blankets in around Liam, resolving to set aside his inner emotional turmoil to focus on saving his friend from his captors. The priority at this moment was to free Liam from his prison and everything else, including his own confounding feelings, could wait until later.

Besides, the idea that Liam would reciprocate his feelings seemed like a distant dream. Noah was aware that few men would share his same-sex attraction, or at least it wasn't commonly acknowledged in the world he knew. He reckoned that his feelings were one-sided, which made him all the more apprehensive about exploring them further. He was certain that, if he dared express his feelings out loud, Liam would reject him.

With Liam settled and looking as comfortable as possible, Noah silently made his way towards the room's expansive window to gaze out across the bustling streets below. The city was alive with the activity of people going about their daily routines. Amidst the crowd, he spotted the distinct red uniforms of the city guards, adorned with heraldic symbols. The sorcerers' red capes could also be seen, their presence quite prominent throughout the city. It was evident that they wielded considerable influence and authority within the metropolis as almost every street corner teemed with red.

With a keener eye, Noah noted that formidable defenses surrounded the city. High stone walls encircled the perimeter, guarded by vigilant armed men. The city's main and sole entrance was a large gatehouse with a well-maintained cobblestone road leading through it.

The sight of the heavily guarded entrance heightened Noah's apprehension. It was evident that getting into the city unnoticed would be a daunting challenge. The presence of the well-armed guards and the imposing walls painted a clear picture of the city's fortified defenses.

Noah knew he and his grandmother had to devise a clever and stealthy approach to infiltrate the city in order to reach Liam's location undetected. Everything needed to be planned and carefully executed. The stakes were high, and any misstep could jeopardize their entire mission. It was highly possible that if they failed to rescue Liam, they could also be caught and that would be disastrous.

With this newfound knowledge of the city's defenses, Noah retreated from the window, his mind racing with thoughts of how they could best navigate their way into the heart of the city and carry out their daring rescue operation.

As Noah contemplated the city's defenses, he felt a peculiar tugging sensation pulling at his consciousness. He recognized this sensation as his mind being called back to his physical body, and the pull grew stronger, making it increasingly difficult to resist.

Abruptly, his mind's eye went black, and he knew that he was being drawn away from Liam, He disappeared from the tower as if he had never been there at all, leaving no trace of his visit behind.

Chapter 11:

Attack

A sense of disorientation and confusion swamped Noah as he returned to his physical body at the campsite. He tried to recall all the information he had gathered from the tower but found that the details were fading quickly, slipping away like a fleeting dream upon waking.

Despite the sudden end to his astral exploration, Noah knew that he had obtained valuable insights into the city's defenses, and he was determined to share this information with his grandmother to devise a solid plan.

In the pre-dawn darkness, Noah knew that he couldn't waste any time, so he swiftly rose from his pallet and approached his grandmother. Gently shaking her awake, he urgently whispered, "Grandmother, wake up! We need to talk. I've had another vision!"

Serena stirred, slowly waking, and rubbing her eyes as she identified the urgency in Noah's voice. Knowing the importance of his visions, she looked at him intently. "What did you see?" she asked, fully alert and ready to listen to the details of his encounter.

Excitedly, Noah began recounting everything he had learned of the city's defenses from his astral exploration. He tried to keep the details as fresh as possible, sharing his insights and observations about the guarded entrance, the walls, and the patrolling armed men.

As he spoke, Serena listened intently, absorbing the information, and considering the implications of their newfound knowledge. Together, they brainstormed strategies, discussing how to navigate the city and successfully execute their rescue mission. Time was indeed of the essence, and they had to act swiftly and wisely to save Liam and accomplish their mission.

As Noah recounted the details of Liam's torture, Serena's heart ached with empathy and concern. Though she hadn't personally met Liam, she could understand why Noah felt such a strong connection to him and was determined to save him. The bond between the two friends was evident, and she could sense the depth of their attachment. However, Serena also couldn't shake the feeling that there might be more than chivalry or camaraderie in Noah's determination to save Liam. There seemed to be a deeper connection between them, something she couldn't quite put her finger on. If there was more to this story, she trusted that Noah would confide in her when the time was right.

For now, their focus was to rescue Liam and carry out their mission. Serena was fully committed to supporting Noah in any way she could, and she vowed to stand by his side through the challenges that lay ahead. As such, she sprang into action, swiftly rolling up her pack and efficiently gathering their meager belongings. "We must hurry if we are to make it before the three weeks are up," she declared, urgency evident in her voice. "Rankier is at least a two-week journey by foot, and we can't afford any further delays."

She gestured for Noah to hasten his preparations as well, knowing that every moment counted, and they needed to set out without delay. Her determination was palpable, and she was ready to lead the way towards their destination.

Noah moved quickly, fully grasping the significance of their quest to rescue Liam and reach Elnoth. He gathered his belongings, efficiently packing up the camp and within moments, everything was ready.

They returned to the road, pushing forward with great resolve, choosing not to take any breaks in favor of prioritizing speed and progress. Despite the icy rain pelting them, they endured, marching ahead undeterred, the chill seeping into their bones but failing to break their spirit.

*****

Their journey had been grueling, a week of trudging through relentless rain on muddy roads had left Noah and Serena utterly worn out and drained. They pushed themselves to the brink, taking brief rests only when absolutely necessary.

Despite the hectic pace, Serena continued Noah's training. While their reading exercises were delayed due to the demands of their journey, their evening training sessions intensified significantly. Noah displayed a growing proficiency in blade fighting, and Serena pushed him even harder, honing his abilities and adopting a more aggressive approach in their sparring sessions. Noah's skills improved steadily, and the short half-minute bouts transformed into five-minute-long engagements before he would be bested or forced to concede.

Though proud of her grandson's progress, Serena understood that his sword craft education needed to be taken further. Their mission to infiltrate the sorcerer's stronghold was far from straightforward, and they hadn't yet devised a plan to enter the city, let alone the fortress itself. Serena's mind raced with thoughts, exploring various solutions to find the best way forward.

As she pondered their next move, Serena considered two potential paths that might lead them forward. The first idea was to assume the roles of sorcerers, using deception to gain entry into the city. This bore great risk though, as she was uncertain whether the city had magical safeguards to prevent access to interlopers or impersonators.

Amidst her thoughts, another intriguing idea emerged. Serena began contemplating the possibility of uncovering a hidden passage that could provide them access beneath the imposing walls. She recalled that the city was constructed above a complex network of naturally formed caverns, some of which her late husband had ordered sealed off during his reign. It occurred to her that there might be a forgotten cavern that led directly into the heart of the city, an entrance that had been overlooked.

As she delved into these possibilities, Serena felt a glimmer of hope. Finding a secret entrance could potentially offer them a covert and less risky way to infiltrate the city's stronghold. However, despite the potential paths she had envisioned, Serena remained aware that nothing was guaranteed until they actually reached the city and assessed the situation firsthand. The true feasibility of each option would only become apparent once they stood at the city's gates.

Serena understood the importance of ongoing preparation for the inevitable challenges that lay ahead. She couldn't help but be anxious about the possibility of having to split away from Noah during their mission into Rankier. The thought of them being separated, her grandson facing potential dangers alone, weighed heavily on her mind. Noah was still young and inexperienced, and she questioned whether he was truly ready to fend for himself in such perilous circumstances.

The love she held for her grandson was immeasurable, and the idea of leaving him behind if something went awry was a painful prospect. Serena was determined to protect him with all her might, but she also knew that their journey could carry unforeseen dangers. She couldn't shake the worry that she might have to make an unimaginable sacrifice to keep him safe if the worst were to happen. Bracing herself for the trials ahead, she cherished their time together on the journey, hoping that their strength and bond would see them through whatever challenges they encountered in Rankier.

*****

With their camp finally set up for the night, Noah settled down beside Serena, noticing the distant look in her eyes. Trying to break her reverie, he reached into his bag and pulled out a packet of dried meat. Offering a piece to Serena, she accepted it with a small smile. Following her lead, he tore off a portion of the dried meat and began to eat, hoping the simple act would bring a moment of comfort in the midst of their taxing journey.

As they rested, Noah began to reflect on the surreal circumstances they found themselves in. Turning to his grandmother, he spoke thoughtfully, "Did you ever think that we would be here at this point in life, grandmother? I can't say I had imagined I would be turning 18 and fleeing the forces of the King at the same time."

Myriad emotions crossing face, Serena looked at her grandson and in a gentle tone, she responded, "Life has its own way of unfolding, my dear. While I could never have predicted these exact events, I always knew that one day we would have to step into the world and confront the challenges that awaited us. When you were just a child, I did my best to prepare you, providing you with the education and skills you needed to navigate this path."

She rested a comforting hand on Noah's shoulder, "I understand that it all feels overwhelming and frightening, but remember, as long as we have each other, we'll find our way through. There's a greater plan at play, and it appears that destiny has marked a unique path for you."

With a glimmer in her eyes, Serena encouraged her grandson to embrace whatever lay ahead. She had faith that the gods had a purpose for him, guiding their journey to an ultimate destination, and protecting them along the way. She only hoped that her place would remain by his side, protecting and guiding him.

"I think I'm going to get some rest," Noah eventually declared, settling down onto his bedding and turning away from the crackling fire.

"Sleep well; I'll stay up for a while longer," Serena whispered softly, her gaze fixed on the dancing flames.

*****

"Noah, wake up!" Serena urgently whispered, shaking him from his deep slumber.

Groggily Noah swiftly scanned their surroundings and became fully alert when he noticed four armed men silently advancing towards the camp. Thanks to Serena's quick observation, the intruders had lost the

83

advantage of surprise and the attackers were unaware that their presence had been detected.

Reacting swiftly, both Noah and Serena sprang to their feet, sleep quickly fading from their eyes. They snatched up their weapons and positioned themselves back-to-back, ready to defend against the intruders. The men, abandoning any stealth, charged at them, undeterred by their preparedness. Both sides clashed together in fierce combat.

Noah found himself fending off two assailants, maintaining a defensive stance due to their numerical advantage. Serena engaged in a fierce struggle with the other two adversaries behind him. The once peaceful campsite became a battleground, with the sound of weapons ringing out into the night, crackling embers of the fire serving as a backdrop to the intense skirmish.

Seizing the opportunity presented by a momentary gap in one of the intruder's defenses, Noah lunged forward. His blade found its mark, piercing the side of the man. Collapsing to the ground with an agonized scream, his threat neutralized, leaving Noah facing the remaining foe who stared in shock at his comrade's death.

With adrenaline pumping through his veins, Noah squared off against the second attacker who had now redoubled his efforts. The fight intensified as their blades collided, each vying for the upper hand. Despite the odds stacked against him, Noah remained resolute, his instincts and training guiding him through the life-and-death struggle. The night air was filled with the sounds of desperate grunts, the clashing of metal, and the haunting echoes of pain and determination in the heat of the battle.

Serena faced her own daunting challenge against the other two more experienced attackers. These men had seen their share of battles, and their combined efforts worked against her, making it difficult for her to gain the upper hand even with her skill and prowess. With precision and coordination, they managed to evade and counter her strikes effectively, skillfully creating a formidable barrier against her attempts to land a decisive blow.

The minutes dragged on as she deftly thrust and parried, searching for any opening that could give her an advantage in the intense struggle. The battle reached a tense stalemate as Serena's determination to break through their defenses matched the attackers' determination to overpower her. The air was thick with the intensity of the fight, each moment carrying the weight of potential victory or defeat.

Seizing a crucial moment, Serena acted with lightning speed, driving her blade through the chest plate of one of her opponents, ending his life swiftly. However, as she committed to her attack, the remaining assailant saw an opening in her defense and lunged forward with deadly intent.

Time seemed to slow down for Serena as she noticed the incoming blade, realizing that she wouldn't be able to evade its course in time. With a desperate twist of her body, she tried to maneuver out of harm's way, but it was too late. The enemy's weapon found its mark, slicing across her side with searing pain, bringing her to the ground with a cry wrenched from her lips.

Gasping in agony, Serena fought through the pain, refusing to succumb to her injuries. Despite the crimson stain spreading across her linen tunic, she clutched her side and mustered all her determination. With unwavering resolve, she struggled to rise from the ground, intent on facing her opponent once more.

As the man's blade descended once more, intent on ending her fight, Serena summoned every ounce of strength left in her body. Swinging her own blade from the ground beside her, she mustered a desperate parry, trying to halt the lethal strike with all her might. Looking toward Noah, still locked in battle with the other assailant, she met his gaze and managed to whisper, "I'm sorry,"

Again and again, her assailant swung down, relentlessly attempting to overpower her defenses. Though Serena fought valiantly, her energy waned and the next blow proved too forceful. With a powerful strike, the man knocked her blade from her grasp, sending it flying and leaving Serena defenseless.

Helplessly sprawled on the ground, Serena refused to waver. Though the odds were stacked against her, she clung to her unyielding determination. Her eyes burned with a steadfast will to keep fighting despite the overwhelming danger that surrounded her. Every fiber of her being was devoted to pushing forward. Yet, even in her unwavering spirit,

Serena knew deep down that this might be the end. before closing her eyes, accepting her fate as the man's blade down swung down towards her once more.

In that moment of surrender, Serena made peace with her final stand. Her heart was heavy with regret for leaving Noah, but she trusted in his strength and resilience to carry on without her. With a deep breath, she released the tension from her body, ready to face whatever awaited her in the afterlife.

*****

Noah fought with determination despite facing a more skilled opponent. However, amidst the fierce clash of blades, he heard the cry of someone falling behind him. Instinctively, he risked a quick glance toward his grandmother and was met with a shocking sight. Serena had been struck down by her assailant and now lay defenseless on the ground, unable to fend off the attack.

As their gazes locked, and his grandmother said her silent goodbye, a surge of apprehension washed over Noah. The gravity of Serena's dire situation ignited an overwhelming urgency to protect her.

Torn between defending himself and coming to Serena's rescue, Noah fought with even greater determination. He engaged his opponent with renewed ferocity, seeking to swiftly overcome the threat before rushing to his grandmother's aid. The battle became a desperate race against time, every second counted in saving the last surviving member of his family, the woman who had raised him.

Noah launched a relentless assault fueled by both fury and desperation, attempting to breach his opponent's defenses by any means necessary. He swung recklessly, momentarily forgetting to protect himself as he tried to overpower his opponent and force him into submission. However, his wild strikes were deftly parried, and a sense of panic began to creep into Noah's heart.

Amidst the chaos of the battle, he became acutely aware of the dangerous situation his grandmother was facing. The sound of her opponent raising his blade against his grandmother's echoed in his ears, serving as a chilling reminder of the imminent threat to her.

Noah's vision blurred, and a surge of intense emotion washed over him. The seething anger from inside him seemed to take on a tangible form, wavering with the heat rising from his body. The overwhelming intensity of his feelings caused a visible rippling effect of the air around him so that even the assailants felt the vibrations of the air surrounding him and Serena.

In that moment, Noah lost himself, his eyes turning red as he surrendered to the overwhelming emotions coursing through him. His connection to the elements grew more pronounced, as if the very forces of nature were responding to the turmoil he was experiencing. The wind whipped up, swirling sand into vortexes that encircled the men, causing panic to grip their hearts as they realized they were facing a formidable, magical adversary.

In the throes of this unexpected manifestation, Noah's own power surprised even him, and he felt himself getting lost within it. The elements not only bent to his will, becoming both a weapon and a shield against their attackers, but they overwhelmed him as an otherworldly power possessed his body. The air crackled with sparks and tension as the battlefield transformed into a surreal scene. Noah had apparently tapped into a hidden reservoir of power to protect himself and his grandmother. The assailants now faced not only a skilled fighter but the forces of nature itself, leaving them trembling with terror at the prospect of a being imbued with such incredible abilities.

With a swift motion, Noah raised his right hand, summoning a ball of fire that ignited with an unyielding intensity. The flames danced and flickered above his palm, eager to be set free. Determination etched on his face, he pivoted towards the assailant threatening his grandmother, and with a mere flick of his hand, Noah unleashed the searing fireball to hurtle towards the man. Panic overtook the attacker as the deadly projectile closed in on him, frantically he attempted to escape his fiery fate, his screams of terror echoing through the night. The fireball pursued its target relentlessly, closing the distance with blistering speed. It engulfed the man and scorching everything in its path. Flames consumed the air around Noah and the attackers, creating an awe-inspiring spectacle of power and destruction.

Seizing upon Noah's distraction, the other assailant lunged toward Noah with deadly intent, aiming to strike him down with a swift slash of his blade. To his astonishment, his weapon collided with an invisible barrier created by the elemental forces of wind, sending him stumbling to the ground with force.

In response to this attack, Noah's very essence underwent a dramatic metamorphosis. His corporal form dissolved, becoming an ethereal being wreathed in mesmerizing flames. As if driven by an unseen force, he ascended upwards, lifted effortlessly by the power of the wind itself.

In this otherworldly state, Noah's left hand stretched forth with an upward motion, and from the very earth beneath him, a javelin formed of rock materialized and flew toward the attacker with breathtaking speed. With a thunderous impact, the spike effortlessly pierced through the man's armor like a knife through paper, leaving him impaled and suspended in the air. Noah's powers had reached a zenith, merging nature's elements in a mesmerizing display beauty and might.

In this extraordinary moment, Noah embodied the sheer force of the wrath of nature, a celestial being empowered by the elements themselves. His actions were no longer solely his own, but rather an intricate dance with the primal forces that surrounded him. The battlefield had become a canvas for an otherworldly spectacle, and the outcome displayed Noah's potential.

Having vanquished both adversaries, Noah's potent powers waned, no longer needed to defeat the immediate threat. As he returned to his mortal self, weakness washed over him, causing him to stumble unsteadily towards his grandmother.

The world around him swayed and blurred, his legs gave way beneath him. Noah sank to his knees, vaguely noting that his clothing had burned away leaving him naked as a newborn. He struggled to remain upright as the strength that had surged through him moments ago now drained away rapidly. He reached out for his grandmother, desperate to ensure her safety, but his body refused to obey his commands.

As the world around him faded to darkness, Noah felt his consciousness slipping away like a distant tide. The dissolution of his formidable powers leaving him vulnerable and defenseless, his vision blurred around the edges. The sound of his grandmother's voice calling his name became a distant echo. He fought to hold on, to stay present, but the pull of oblivion was too strong.

With a final effort, he whispered her name before succumbing to the enveloping blackness.

Chapter 12:
Naked and Aroused

Liam jolted awake, still recovering from his harsh treatment at his captors' hands, startled by the sudden sensation of a weight falling onto the bed beside him. Quickly pulling back the covers, he leapt out of bed, his heart racing with alarm. To his astonishment, he found Noah lying unconscious and completely naked, face down on the bed. Blushing furiously, Liam averted his gaze, wanting to respect Noah's privacy. But he couldn't help stealing glances, unable to resist the magnetic pull of Noah's perfectly proportioned body, with his broad muscular shoulders and back tapering down to a narrow waist and rounded buttocks which lay before him like a work of art, captivating and alluring.

Pushing aside the stirring of attraction, Liam approached the bed with concern and softly said, "Noah? Can you hear me?" When Noah remained unresponsive, Liam gently rolled Noah onto his back, to inspect him for any possible injuries.

Liam's hands traced Noah's body with a tender touch, his fingers exploring every inch with meticulous care. Looking for any signs of harm, he pressed his fingertips gently against Noah's temples to feel for any head injuries, then slid them through his thick hair to check his scalp. As his hands moved further, they glided over Noah's muscular shoulders and chest, his touch both cautious and intimately tender. The well-developed muscles and skin he touched were flawless, Liam couldn't find any sign of injury there.

Moving further down across Noah's ridged abdomen and the deep vee of his Adonis belt, Liam's eyes darkened as his hands traced the fascinating dips and valleys. He inspected Noah's solid flanks, strong thighs and calves to confirm no injury before moving upward again and hesitating as he reached Noah's groin. Though flaccid, Liam saw that Noah was certainly gifted in this area. He found himself tempted by the large appendage that dangled enticingly between deliciously thick thighs.

In this intimate moment of vulnerability and closeness, Liam felt the sparks of his burgeoning desire for Noah grow, though he didn't know if his feelings would be reciprocated. The simple touch of his fingertips on the other man's bare flesh ignited a passionate flame in his chest, making it challenging to keep his emotions in check. Despite the distracting allure of Noah's exposed form, Liam tried to focus on the task at hand.

Standing tall and breathing deeply to regain his composure, Liam gently brushed the back of his hand against Noah's forehead to check his temperature. The coolness of his skin was most likely a result of exhaustion from an arduous journey. A shiver wracked Noah's frame, unable to find warmth in his body's fatigue. The sight filled Liam with concern, compelling his heart to provide comfort and care to the one he was quickly developing feelings for.

As he noted Noah's fluctuating temperature, Liam began to worry. Without hesitation, he gathered whatever meager supplies of blankets and furs he could find in his prison. Swiftly, he wrapped them around Noah, hoping the added warmth would soothe the shivers and bring some relief. However, to his dismay, Noah's condition seemed to worsen. His once rosy complexion began to fade, and his shivering intensified, leaving Liam feeling even more desperate to help.

As Noah's shivering invited teeth chattering, Liam realized that urgent action was necessary. Without hesitation, he swiftly stripped off his own clothing, letting them fall to the floor beside the bed and slipped under the covers to gently wrap his warm body as much as he could around Noah's naked torso.

Liam spooned himself tightly against Noah, seeking every opportunity to transfer his body heat to the shivering man. The skin-to-skin contact was intimate as Liam held him close, their bodies pressing in private places. Talking sternly to himself, he tried to ignore the attraction he felt in an attempt to remain clinical while chasing away the cold that leached into Noah's flesh.

Slowly, the sound of Noah's chattering teeth lessened as Liam's body heat began to have the desired effect. Color began to return to his cheeks, and Liam felt the shivers abate beneath the blankets. Making himself comfortable, Liam settled into Noah's chest relishing the feeling of his bare skin against Noah's. The warm blankets and furs he had draped over them created a warm cocoon with the relaxing sensation of the rise and fall of Noah's chest. Liam felt himself drifting off, lulled into sleep with the soothing physical presence of Noah beneath him.

*****

Noah stirred awake, feeling the gentle pressure of another body wrapped around him. His heart skipped a beat as he tried to comprehend the situation while blinking away sleep-induced confusion. His last memory had been of the battle with the men who had invaded their camp, and he vaguely recalled dispatching the last one with the stone spike he had conjured. He glanced down to see who was resting with him. He discovered Liam snuggled up against his chest, soundly asleep. With a glance around his vicinity, he recognized the tower prison cell.

Relief washed over Noah as he recognized his bed mate, and the tension in his muscles slowly eased. Cautiously, he drew Liam closer, wrapping his arm around him, cherishing the warmth that enveloped them both. Liam's peaceful slumber brought a serene calm to the moment, and Noah couldn't help but admire the beauty of the man before him.

Liam's lips were slightly parted, and his steady breaths brushed across Noah's chest, creating an intimate and tender connection between them. In the soft light filtering through the room's window, Noah noticed the delicate hairs on Liam's chest, causing his fingers to tingle with the desire to touch and explore.

Feeling Liam's skin pressed against his, Noah realized that they were both naked in the bed. Certain parts of their bodies touched intimately with Liam's thigh stretched across Noah's legs and Noah couldn't help but feel aroused as he felt Liam's semi-hard erection brush against his own. Peeking under the blankets, Noah snuck a look at Liam's firm naked torso. His form was not overly muscled but firmly toned though exercise. His lean body accentuated curves in the most delicious places, and the rise of his rounded and perfectly proportioned buttocks made Noah bite his lip in temptation. He was sorely tempted to reach down and knead them with his hands, to play with Liam's body in a way he hadn't ever done with another man. He resisted however, knowing that he wanted his first time with Liam to be when they were both conscious and engaged in each other.

As Noah's heart pounded in his chest, he felt an exhilarating rush of emotions coursing through him. The intense adrenaline of the battle had given way to a different kind of excitement, a tender vulnerability that made him feel alive in a whole new way. With Liam resting peacefully in his arms, Noah couldn't deny the truth any longer — he was undeniably infatuated with the man.

In that confined space, surrounded by the dim light of the prison cell, Noah found comfort in Liam's arms. It was as if a missing piece of his heart, an elusive fragment he had never known he needed, had miraculously found its way back to him, completing the puzzle inside his soul.

With each passing second, the warmth emanating from Liam's body filled Noah with a profound sense of contentment. Gone were the haunting shadows of loneliness that had plagued him for as long as he could remember. In Liam's presence, all of those feelings faded into the distance, replaced by the joy of connection and affection.

Noah felt an irresistible attraction towards Liam, not just physically but on a deeper, emotional level. His heart swelled with tenderness, and he marveled at the way their lives had intersected in his dreams. It was as if fate had conspired to bring them together in that very moment, in that cramped locked room, where they could discover one another.

Liam began to stir and tentatively lifted his face from Noah's bare chest, eyes brightening as he saw that Noah was awake.

"You're awake! I was so worried you weren't going to wake up!" he cried, sliding his arms around Noah's neck, and pulling him in close.

Noah didn't resist and let Liam pull him closer, his eyes focused on Liam's perfect lips.

"I'm sorry I didn't mean to wake you" Noah replied. "You were sleeping peacefully, when I woke up and I thought I'd let you rest some more."

"That's thoughtful, but not necessary. I was more worried about you; when you got here stark naked you frightened me. You were hypothermic and shivering violently so I wrapped you up in blankets and when that didn't help, I got in bed with you to warm you back up." Liam said, eyes filled with concern and shy desire.

Noah smiled back, eyes flashing teasingly, he decided to take a chance. "Oh, so that's how I ended up naked in bed with you then? You didn't just want to be in bed with me?"

Liam blushed, surprised by Noah's bold statement and stammered over his words. "I…what… yes I admit getting into bed with you had its appeal, but you were genuinely freezing, and it was the only thing I could do to warm you up."

"It's fine, I was only teasing you. I think the next time we end up in bed, I'd like to be conscious for it, if that's fine with you?" Noah laughed, hoping his suggestive comment hit the right note.

Liam nodded back, suddenly feeling shy after Noah's teasing. Noah sensed Liam withdrawing into himself and sat up. He pulled Liam into his lap, facing towards him, still ignoring the sensations caused by the friction of their erections rubbing against one another for the moment.

With a tender gesture, Noah leaned in and softly pressed his lips against Liam's, surprising them both. Liam jerked in surprise but quickly responded to the kiss. Noah coaxed Liam's lips apart, his tongue gently slipped into Liam's mouth. The sensation made Liam's head spin with an overwhelming rush of emotions as he surrendered to the enchanting moment.

Both men eagerly pressed into each other, fueled by their desire for one another. Their bodies moved closer, Liam shifted to straddle Noah's heavy thighs, his legs wrapping around Noah's hips. They were insatiable as their passion ignited. Sparks flew between them, and neither wanted this moment to end. Noah's hands roamed Liam's body, moving from his shoulders down his lithe back and further to knead and cup those deliciously perfect ass cheeks. Liam moaned in pleasure and responded by bucking up against Noah, rubbing his erection against Noah's firm abdomen and rock-hard cock.

Twisting his mouth away from Noah to gasp a breath, Liam licked his palm and reached down between them to grasp Noah's cock. His fingers barely encircled its girth, and he began to slide his hand along Noah's long veiny shaft. Noah sighed in pleasure and began placing hot open-mouthed kisses along Liam's neck, moving down to his chest. He tongued Liam's sensitive nipples, and when they hardened to little nubs, he suckled them. Liam threw his head back, lost in the pleasurable feeling of his nipples being played with while his ass was being massaged.

"Oh gods, that feels so good. Your tongue feels so hot against my nipples. Your hands on my ass make me so hard." Liam murmured.

Noah redoubled his efforts at Liam's words, sucking harder, nipping gently at the reddened man-teats with his teeth and kneading and massaging at his ass cheeks more firmly. Pulling Liam's cheeks apart, Noah teased the tight little hole he found there with the tip of his finger. A loud moan slid from Liam's mouth as he relinquished control of himself to Noah's mouth and deft hands.

As Noah opened his mouth to say something, he felt the now-familiar sensation of being drawn away from Liam's cell. With a frustrated breath, he reluctantly leaned back from Liam.

"Damn it all, I feel myself being pulled away again. As much as I want to stay and finish what we started, I think we're going to have to resume this another time."

Liam couldn't hide his disappointment even as he nodded in

understanding. "It's alright," he reassured, "You'll rescue me, and then we can pick up right where we left off."

"Oh, we definitely will, though it's a shame. I was looking forward to what was going to happen next to that perfect ass of yours." Noah replied with pained arousal.

"Me too" Liam replied, just as Noah faded away. Without Noah's body there to hold him up, he found himself falling to the bed. He glanced down at himself, his thighs spread wide and his solidly erect cock bobbing with every heartbeat while the flush of arousal stained his cheeks and body. He had been eager for more, ready for fingers and tongue and for Noah to take him entirely. Now he would be forced to wait until their next meeting if that ever occurred.

"Shit."

Chapter 13:
Consequences

Noah materialized back at the remnants of the campsite, his heart pounding in his chest with a dizzying combination of excitement from his interaction with Liam and smothering fear for his grandmother. The once lively fire was reduced to smoky embers, the bodies of the marauders strewn about the area and the stink of death hung oppressively over the vicinity. Dread washed over him as he scanned the area frantically, desperately searching for his grandmother.

Rushing to the spot he had last seen her; he found a trail of blood leading away from the camp and toward a nearby creek. Anxiety gnawed at his insides as he moved to follow the trail but the chilly air swiftly reminded of his vulnerable nudity. Quickly donning trousers from his bag, set out on his search for her.

When he reached the creek, his innards clenched in a visceral response to his worst fears. There, against a boulder by the riverbed, he found his grandmother. She was slumped back against a large rock. It bore the smears of her bloody handprints, testimony of her efforts to rise to her feet. Her clothing was torn and dirty, a large dark bloodstain trailing down her side in a grizzly display. Most alarmingly, her eyes remained closed as he approached her side.

Terrified that she left this world, Noah reached a trembling hand toward Serena, his heart pounding with both dread and hope. Pleading with the gods for a miracle, he placed his fingers on his grandmother's wrist, searching for any sign of life. To his intense relief, he felt a pulse beneath his fingertips, a weak yet undeniable throb of life. Leaning in closer, he felt the faint puff of her breaths caressing his cheek.

Unfathomable relief washed over him like a tidal wave. She was still alive, clinging to the fragile thread of existence. Grateful tears of joy streamed unchecked from Noah's eyes as he gathered her fragile form in his strong arms. Cradling her with utmost care, he carried her back to the campsite and gently laid her down on her bedding.

He then sprang to add wood to the smoldering fire, causing the flames to roar back to life. They cast a warm glow over the surroundings and provided the much-needed light and heat for his urgent task. Sacrificing his grandmother's modesty in light of medical need, Noah efficiently removed her clothing to clearly assess her injuries. Once her bare flesh was exposed, the grim reality of her injuries assaulted his eyes. His heart sank at the sight of a large, deep gash stretching the length of her side, the wound oozed blood that had somewhat coagulated about the edges.

Having completed his assessment, he dreaded the action he knew was necessary for her survival and placed the blade of a short dagger pulled from his bag into the hottest part of the fire. He then filled a pot with water and set it to boil, tore strips of linen from his last remaining clean shirt and washed his hands thoroughly. His mind raced, running through his knowledge of what needed to be done. Holding his fear at bay with stalwart determination, he gently cleaned the wound with a strip of clean cloth dipped in the hot water. Satisfied that it was as clean as possible, he removed the heated blade from the fire and with a deep breath to steady himself, carefully pressed the red-hot blade against her flesh. The sound of sizzling meat filled his ears and scent of burned flesh lodged itself in his nose. Serena's weak, pained cry pierced his heart, and he felt a wave of anguish wash over him. But he held the blade steady, allowing it to sear the wound and burn off any infectious contaminants.

As the cauterization sealed the injury, the bleeding gradually stopped, and Noah knew he had more work to do, he needed to finish dressing the wound with a healing poultice. In an instant, he was in the nearby clearing gathering the plants he needed, guided by the medicinal knowledge that had been passed down his family through generations. His grandmother's well-being depended on his ability to find the right elements for the poultice, so he carefully searched for each herb, mindful of their unique properties and benefits.

When he had gathered what he needed, he rushed back to the campsite and there, by the flickering fire, he meticulously prepared the healing poultice as quickly as he could. The scent of nature's restorative powers filled the air around them as he worked and with a tender touch, he began to dress the wound, applying the poultice over and around the cauterized area. With the poultice carefully applied, Noah breathed a sigh of relief as he watched it take effect. He finally reached for the bandages he had prepared, his hands steady and gentle as he began to wrap them around his grandmother's torso.

Taking utmost care, he ensured the bandages covered the wound completely with just the right amount of pressure to hold the poultice and to ensure the least amount of discomfort was felt. Time seemed to stand still as Noah focused solely on his task, his heart full of love and concern for the woman who had been a guiding light in his life.

She had calmed whilst the healing poultice drew the pain away and she lay still on the bedding, breathing shallowly. In time and with care, the ugly wound would heal, but his grandmother would forever carry the scar as a reminder of this fight for her life.

Noah's eyes never left her face, watching for any signs of pain or distress. Though he couldn't bear to see her suffer, he found strength in the knowledge that this sacrifice would give her the best possible chance at survival. He knew that the proper dressing of the wound was crucial to her recovery, and he wouldn't leave anything to chance. Having accomplished the task he set out to do, his hands trembled with exhaustion. Anxiety washed over him, but he knew he couldn't rest just yet. There was still much to do to ensure her safety and recovery.

Noah set about removing the dead marauders from the campsite. He unceremoniously dumped the cold and stiffened bodies over the edge of a ravine, watching with satisfied eyes as they tumbled far enough away that scavenging beasts would not come near his grandmother's resting spot. He then grasped his blade firmly, feeling its weight and reassurance, to settle down by the crackling fire. A steely determination lit his eyes as he set himself in position to guard his grandmother, ready to face any potential intruders that might approach.

He knew that this night would be a test of his strength and endurance, but he was willing to endure the sleeplessness to ensure their safety. With every flicker of the flames, he kept a vigilant eye on their surroundings, alert to any movement or sound. The unexpected intrusion earlier had left him on edge, and he couldn't shake the feeling of vulnerability.

The hours passed slowly and as fire cast dancing shadows in the waning darkness around him, the first light of dawn poked its pale fingers through the distant horizon. But Noah's vigil did not waver. He remained alert, memories of his grandmother, the moments they had shared, and the bond they had forged fueled his determination to safeguard the woman who had always been there for him.

Chapter 14:
Forging a New Path

Despite the slim likelihood of another attack, Noah spent the entire night on watch, alert for any potential intruders or assailants returning to their camp. He refused to let his guard down until the sun's rays had finally pierced through the predawn clouds and appeared on the horizon. He remained seated alongside the cold embers of the campfire, exhaustion visible in his haggard expression, the dark circles under his eyes resembling coal smudges.

Throughout the night, Serena had slept uneasily, muttering fitfully and occasionally groaning in pain. Witnessing his grandmother's suffering was agonizing, as Noah could do nothing but sit, wait, and worry. He had already done everything in his power to help her heal, yet he still felt helpless. Knowing there was nothing more he could do for her, he relit the fire and put together the ingredients for a nourishing broth that would help to heal her.

As Noah stirred the bone broth filled with mushrooms and herbs, he heard movement beside him. Turning, he saw Serena struggling to sit up. He sprang swiftly to her side, offering support as she gasped in pain. With his assistance, she managed to settle into an upright position. Taking a moment, Noah brought her a bowl of the delicious broth he had made.

Serena murmured a quick thank you and drank the broth in silence, leaving Noah anxiously assessing her and happily finding that she had miraculously avoided a fever. Now all he wanted was to hear her voice ring out true and clear. After draining the bowl, she set it down and looked wearily at him.

"Where were you last night?" she asked, confusion in her eyes. "You used your powers, and then you vanished completely. Oh Noah, I thought I was going to die alone, so I dragged myself to the riverbank to at least pass away somewhere peaceful."

Noah felt both guilt and relief roll through his chest. "I'm so sorry, Grandmother. I never intended to leave you alone like that," he confessed. "My powers did drain me, and I lost control. I can't even remember what happened after I killed those men. I was trying to come to your side, but then I lost consciousness. The next thing I knew, I woke up in the tower with Liam," he admitted, feeling a bit embarrassed as he recalled Liam's warm welcome.

His grandmother took a moment to collect her thoughts. "I understand," she said steadily. "There's no use dwelling on what has happened. What matters is that we are still together. However, I am worried about our ability to reach Rankier now. My injury will undoubtedly slow us down, and I can't see how we'll manage to reach Rankier in time to aid your friend."

"I've thought of a solution to the situation while I stood watch through the night, actually," Noah said earnestly, as he pulled out the map they had been using throughout their journey. "Considering your injury, it's crucial for you to rest and recover properly. Traveling on the road would only worsen your condition and hinder your healing. What if we use the river instead of the land? I can make us a small raft from the nearby trees, and we can follow the river all the way up to Rankier. This route would be less taxing for you, and it would also get us there faster than if we had gone on foot."

Serena nodded thoughtfully but then raised a concern. "It's a very good suggestion, Noah, but there's one problem. Our original route would have avoided the ruins of Zefra altogether. If we follow the river, it will lead us straight through the heart of those ruins."

Noah was baffled by Serena's words. "What's wrong with the city's ruins? If it's abandoned, I can't imagine there would be anything dangerous apart from vagabonds who might try to stop us," he asked, seeking to understand.

"Unfortunately, it is far worse than just vagabonds," Serena replied. "Zefra was once a thriving city in our kingdom, the center of trade and commerce in the region. But something sinister took root there. Rogue sorcerers began to wield dark magic, corrupting their bodies and souls in a relentless pursuit of power, wealth, and influence. They delved into deals with demons, forging twisted alliances that defiled their very essence."

A chill ran down Noah's spine as he listened to his grandmother's tale. Serena continued heavily, "These sorcerers, consumed by evil, bred with the demons they allied with, giving rise to abhorrent offspring—foul creations that defied the laws of nature. They traded their very souls for eternal power, embracing darkness and madness in equal measure."

The eerie image Serena painted unsettled Noah, his imagination conjuring grotesque scenes of depravity and horror. As he considered the prospect of venturing through the ruins, he thought of the malevolent forces lurking within, waiting to ensnare any unsuspecting intruders. The idea of crossing paths with these demonic remnants filled him with dread, casting an ominous shadow over his seemingly straightforward solution.

Serena's voice took on an eerie tone as she continued. "These sorcerers lost all control, and their unholy offspring spread like a foul pestilence. Maddened by demonic influence, they violently overtook the once-thriving city and our brave soldiers who were stationed there to protect it. The innocent residents fled in terror from the rampage, while our men bravely sacrificed themselves to save as many lives as possible."

Her words painted a grim picture of the chaos that had consumed Zefra—the relentless spread of the demon offspring and their merciless assault on the city and its defenders. "Those creatures multiplied rapidly, their saliva carrying a deadly contagion that turned their victims into one of them. Our soldiers fought valiantly, but the demonic forces overwhelmed them, leaving only a few survivors."

Serena's voice trembled with sorrow as she recounted the valiant effort of Noah's ancestral grandfather and his men. "In a desperate attempt to regain control, your many times great grandfather led an enormous legion to confront the horrors that had befallen the city. They engaged in a fierce battle, one that resulted in heavy losses on both sides. Eventually, they managed to contain the remaining monsters within the ruins."

Noah's heart sank as he grasped the severity of the situation. He could only imagine the horrors his ancestors had faced and the sacrifices they had made to protect the kingdom. Serena's voice lowered to a whisper as she revealed the final measures taken to ensure the demons' containment. "Loyal mages of the court worked together to cast a binding spell, which kept the few remaining monsters confined within the ruins. To safeguard the kingdom further, an aversion spell was cast, deterring anyone from entering the accursed city."

Noah's shocked silence lingered for a moment as he processed the grim tale. "So, the question is, are the monsters still there?" he finally spoke, his voice laced with uncertainty. "It has been hundreds of years since then. Surely they would have wasted away in the meantime, without food or sustenance."

Serena sighed heavily. "I wish we could be certain but the truth is, we don't know what supernatural forces may have sustained them over the centuries. These creatures are products of dark magic and demonic influence. Their existence defies natural laws. It is possible that they have found a way to endure, hidden away in the ruins, feeding on something we cannot comprehend."

Noah uneasily considered the possibility that the malevolent entities from the past might still linger in the shadows, awaiting unsuspecting travelers like themselves. "And the binding and aversion spell?" he asked, hoping for some reassurance.

Serena nodded, but her expression remained somber. "The spells were cast by powerful mages, and they have proven effective all these years. The aversion spell deters ordinary people from entering the city, but we must be cautious. Our bloodline is linked to these protections, so we are able to bypass them. Those same protections and their link to our bloodline may attract the monsters. Their hunger for power would make us a temptation too great to ignore."

It was clear that their ancestral connection might not protect them from the horrors that awaited within Zefra. "What should we do then?" he asked, dread mingling with determination in his heart.

"We must tread carefully," Serena advised, her exhausted gaze unwavering. "If we decide to venture through the ruins, we must stay vigilant and cautious at all times. And if we sense any danger or malevolence, we must turn back immediately. Our safety must come first, even if it means abandoning Liam to his fate."

Noah's determination burned brighter as he responded staunchly, "Well then, let's hope that doesn't happen. I promised Liam I would save him, and that is a promise I intend to keep."

With a confused shake of her head, Serena expressed her concern over her grandson's unwavering focus on this apparent stranger. "I do not understand why you have decided he is so important, nor do I comprehend this bond you seem to share with him. I know you are a kind person, Noah, but Liam cannot jeopardize our ultimate goal and safety. We must reach our allies in Elnoth."

Noah felt torn between his emotions and the gravity of their mission. "I know it's hard to understand, Grandmother," he replied sincerely. "But Liam is not just a random stranger to me. The light brought us together, and I feel inextricably linked to him. He will play a role in what is to come, of that I am certain. I cannot simply abandon him now, especially when he is in need."

Serena's expression softened slightly, acknowledging her grandson's heartfelt connection. However, she maintained her resolve to stay focused even as she lay back to rest. "I understand that you care for him," she said gently. "But we must prioritize the greater cause. The fate of the kingdom relies on us, and we cannot let personal feelings get in the way."

Liam's expression darkened at her dismissive words, but he held his tongue for the moment. Pushing aside his frustration, he took a deep breath and focused on preparing for their river journey.

The tension between them hung heavy in the air, as unspoken emotions simmered beneath the surface. Though hurt by her seeming disregard, he knew that now was not the time to further a discussion. Their mission loomed large, and he could not afford to let personal conflicts distract him from the greater purpose.

Resolutely, he gathered the necessary supplies and efficiently crafted a small raft using stout branches from the nearby trees. His hands worked skillfully, a testament to his resourcefulness and dedication. But the memory of their dispute gnawed at him even as he toiled away. Keeping his emotions in check, Noah refused to let them spill over and hinder their progress. The silence between his grandmother and himself was heavy with unspoken thoughts and unexpressed feelings, each silently grappling with their own inner turmoil.

As the preparations neared completion, he glanced briefly at Serena as she rested on her uninjured side, sensing her conflicted emotions as well. Although he knew that her stern demeanor stemmed from concern, it still stung to feel misunderstood. Yet, he couldn't afford to let this rift widen further.

Taking a deep breath, he made a conscious effort to approach his grandmother. He wanted them to find a way to bridge the gap between their viewpoints and emotions. His grandmother did not know the depth of his bond with Liam, nor the attraction he felt towards him. He was not sure if he was ready to discuss his feelings yet so she would not know that Liam meant something to him. To her he was just another person who needed help in a sea of people crying for help.

The river journey ahead would not only test their physical endurance but would also challenge the strength of their bond. As the sun dipped below the horizon, painting the sky with shades of crimson and gold, he hoped that the journey ahead would both lead them closer to their destination and bring them closer to understanding one another.

Chapter 15:
The River

The next morning, Serena's recovery was much improved. The continued application of medicinal poultices through the previous day and the night had done their work. As the sun burned away the night's mists, Noah loaded the raft with all of their belongings and materials, ensuring they were safely bound to the raft itself. The responsibility of their safety weighed heavily on his shoulders, but he refused to falter. The river was their chance to leave behind the hardships of the road, and to reach Liam in time to rescue him from the sorcerers.

Noah gently carried his grandmother onto the raft, settling her comfortably on bedding cushioned underneath with fragrant leaves. He made sure her dressings stayed dry and that her position wouldn't aggravate her injury as they embarked on their river journey. Having observed the benefits of the herbal bandages, Noah was optimistic that the additional time for rest would expedite her healing, considering the week-long journey on the river would require her to remain reclined.

The moment had arrived, and as Noah pushed the raft into the water, his heart raced with anticipation and trepidation. The sturdy raft had been crafted simply, born from the urgency to escape and survive. It would fulfill its purpose as their only lifeline to a safer destination as long as they exercised caution while navigating obstacles on the river.

The current swiftly embraced the raft, and he gripped the makeshift oars firmly. He was ready to steer them through the potentially treacherous currents of the dark waters that held their own secrets and dangers. Their journey would be risky enough and Noah sincerely hoped that his grandmother's tales of Zefra's monsters proved to be unfounded.

After steering the raft safely through the faster currents into the calmer centre, Noah shifted to stable kneeling position, trading the oars for a long pole that he used to guide the raft along the currents, keeping it firmly centered in the river. Although the current was slow and gentle at this juncture, Noah suspected they would encounter sections where the pole would prove indispensable for guiding the raft away from potential hazards. His attentiveness and foresight were crucial, ensuring their safe passage along the river's unpredictable path.

Relief washed over Noah, allowing him to finally relax. A pleased smile graced his lips as he stole a glance at his grandmother, who returned the warm gesture. Settling in, they let the gentle embrace of the current guide the raft on its onward journey. Noah's burden of constant navigation had eased; from this point on, the river's natural flow would chart their course. A sense of liberation filled him as they meandered towards the great river Alrun, anticipating their imminent arrival at the vast expanse of the Albian Sea. Their interim destination, the coastal city of Rankier, lay on the Albian Sea's shore. So long as everything went to plan, their destination to the city would take approximately 10 days.

As the raft glided along, Noah was consumed by thoughts of Liam. Worry for his safety gnawed at him, knowing the peril Liam faced. Memories of their intimate moments lingered in his thoughts—the imprint of Liam's lips against his, tongues mating in an open-mouthed kiss, ignited a fire of passion within him. A soft grin danced across Noah's face as he relished the memory of Liam's alluring presence and firm body pressed against his own. The river journey became a moving backdrop to the vivid memories of their shared moments, and Noah's heart yearned for the day they would be united in physical form.

*****

As Serena rested, she felt sense of pride watching her hardworking grandson in action. Throughout their arduous journey, his perseverance and dedication had shone brightly, reinforcing the qualities she had always admired in him. His attentive care for her comfort, meticulously tending to her wound dressing throughout the day, touched her heart deeply.

Amidst the journey, they exchanged polite conversation while admiring the surrounding landmarks and geological wonders. Serena noticed moments when Noah fell silent, a telltale smile playing on his lips—a smile she had witnessed before, but only in connection to one person. Her heart filled with concern as she grew certain that her grandson held deep feelings for the boy they were on their way to rescue, Liam.

Though she wished for nothing more than her grandson's happiness, Serena couldn't dismiss the grave implications. Noah was the heir to the throne, and she knew all too well the responsibilities and challenges that came with such a position. Love between two men was forbidden in their society, and the prospect of an heir produced through such a union was impossible. The weight of the kingdom's expectations weighed heavily; Noah's reign would be threatened if he couldn't swiftly secure an heir.

The significance of the royal bloodline loomed large, making adoption an impossible option for Noah. The continuation of their divine gift, bestowed by the gods, was of utmost importance for the future of their dynasty. While an adopted child would be embraced as part of the family in every way except blood, they would not inherit the sacred gift and, therefore, could not be considered a legitimate heir to the throne.

Placing an adopted child on the throne would lead to certain disaster, both for the child and the House of Earpa's dynasty. The divine connection would be severed, threatening the future stability and prosperity of Kirenth. The responsibility of maintaining the gods' gift demanded the preservation of the bloodline, creating an unyielding barrier for any other path to the throne. It was a harsh reality that left Serena's heart torn for her grandson and the unavoidable constraints of their divine heritage. The delicate balance between his heart's desires and his duty to the kingdom seemed like an insurmountable challenge. Amidst her reflections, an audacious idea crossed her mind—a marriage of convenience with the Wood-Elves.

The prospect of such an alliance held potential for Noah for he would fulfill his fatherly duty and produce an heir, securing the lineage's future while still finding happiness. Although unconventional dalliances were met with disapproval, historical accounts of past kings forming close relationships with same-sex friends, even in the intimate confines of their bedchambers, had been documented. Serena considered the possibility that this unorthodox alliance with the Wood-Elves might offer her grandson the happiness he sought while safeguarding the prosperity of the empire.

Yet, the implications of such a decision extended beyond personal fulfillment. Infusing Elven blood into their lineage could bestow significant advantages upon their dynasty. The Wood-Elves' magical heritage had been known to extend lifespans and enhance the potential for magical abilities. Throughout their history, many heirs had demonstrated a natural inclination for magic, with some possessing the gift of seers while others displayed prowess as mages. This affinity for magic often flourished when the bloodline received an infusion of Elven ancestry.

The prospect of a half-Elven child ascended beyond personal happiness—it held the potential to fortify the throne, amplifying their strength and magical potential. It was a thought that ignited Serena's hope for the future, blending the promise of love and prosperity for Noah and the family dynasty.

Such a decision carried weighty consequences, yet she couldn't dismiss the possibilities it held. Ultimately, the choices that lay ahead rested with Noah, and she could only hope that he would find a path that would bring him joy and fulfillment, while ensuring the prosperity and continuity of the throne he was destined to inherit.

*****

After several days, they had made substantial progress along the river. The current had pushed them beyond their initial projections by over 20 miles, drawing them closer to the river Alrun, a promising sign that they were on the right path. However, looming ahead like a haunting specter was their last and most daunting obstacle: Zefra.

The name alone sent shivers down their spines, a reminder of the malevolent past that cloaked the city's ruins. As they approached, the air thickened with an ominous energy, warning of the darkness that lay ahead. Noah and Serena exchanged solemn glances as they felt the potent energy of the mage spells as they passed through them. It was a strong warning of what was to come.

The tales of Zefra's cursed past filled them with a mix of trepidation and determination. Every mile they took toward the forsaken city brought them closer to their destination, but it also brought them closer to confronting the horrors that had plagued their ancestors.

Their surroundings grew eerily quiet as they ventured nearer to the ruins, the sounds of nature fading into a haunting silence. The very atmosphere seemed to pulse with an ancient malevolence, as if the very land itself mourned the dark history that had unfolded within those forsaken walls.

As they approached the city's outskirts, they could see remnants of once-grand structures, now reduced to mere shadows of their former glory. Crumbling buildings and overgrown pathways bore witness to the passage of time, yet they also served as a stark reminder of the evil that had befallen this place.

Noah's grip on the makeshift raft tightened as he steeled himself for what lay ahead. Every instinct told him to turn back, to flee from the evil that seemed to seep from the ruins. But he knew that this was the final test they had to overcome, the ultimate trial on their quest to save his friend and fulfill their greater mission.

Serena braced herself for what awaited them in the heart of Zefra, knowing that their determination would be put to the ultimate test. She offered up a silent prayer that they would emerge unscathed, both physically and emotionally.

As Noah scanned the skies, his heart sank further with each passing moment. There was no sign of life, no birds soaring above or any other living creature in sight. The eerie silence that enveloped the city's ruins raised the hair on the back of his neck.

The once vibrant city now lay desolate and abandoned, exuding an air of sorrow. The fishing lines that had once yielded sustenance and hope, now dangled still and silent, mirroring the city's lifeless state. The only sign of life was the struggling and sickly plant growth that stubbornly clung to existence amidst the decay. It seemed that nature herself had turned her back on this forsaken place.

Noah couldn't shake the feeling that they were trespassing on forbidden ground. Unseen eyes watching their every move caused him to draw out his bow in readiness as he wondered if the echoes of the past still reverberated through its crumbling walls. Even the river, which had been their companion throughout the journey, now felt like a solemn witness to the darkness that lurked within Zefra.

Serena, too, felt the weight of the silence and the absence of life. It was as if the very essence of the city had been drained away, leaving behind a dark, empty husk. She exchanged a speaking glance with Noah, their shared apprehension palpable.

As their raft floated further into the heart of the city, the sensation of being watched intensified, sending shivers down their spines. The unseen eyes seemed to regard them with an intensity that fueled their unease.

Noah's grip on his bow tightened, his instincts on high alert. With a quick and fluid motion, he drew an arrow from his quiver and notched it to the bowstring, readying himself for any potential threat. Every fiber of his being responded viscerally to the unseen peril, and he was determined to protect himself and his grandmother.

Serena clutched her staff with white knuckles, seeking solace in its familiar presence. The cool touch of the wood against her palm was a reassuring reminder of her connection to her magical abilities. Her heart raced with each passing moment, her heart filled with fear and determination. Based on the circumstances, she felt that her control over her gift was not as strong as she would have liked, but the urgency of the situation left her with no choice but to try. She was ready to attempt to call on the winds for aid if needed but the winds were capricious, and her command over them was far from perfect. She hoped they would lend their assistance in their time of dire need. In the eerie silence, Serena focused her thoughts, reaching out with a silent plea to the elemental forces around her. The air around her responded, carrying a faint whisper of her power. She had to stay calm, her mind clear and focused, to successfully channel her gift.

A piercing shriek sliced through the eerie silence, causing both Noah and Serena to snap to attention. It reverberated against the empty ruins, echoing off the crumbling walls and sending waves of chills over them both. The source of the cry remained hidden in the shadows, its origin masked by the darkness.

Noah's heart pounded in his chest as he stood up, feet spread in a solid stance, his bow firmly grasped in his hands. Every fiber of his being primed for action as he scanned the surroundings, trying to discern the location of the disturbing sound.

Serena's magic coiled tightly within her, ready for whatever lay ahead. She once again exchanged a glance with Noah, their eyes glinting with steely determination. They had come too far to falter now, and they couldn't let fear paralyze them.

In the distance, amid the haunting echoes of that awful cry, a flicker of movement caught Noah's attention. He narrowed his eyes, trying to make out the shape in the shadows. There, amidst the remnants of a once-grand building, a figure emerged, silhouetted against the dim light that filtered through the ruins.

It was unlike anything they had seen before, a grotesque and monstrous being with twisted features and jet-black limbs that seemed to glisten under the sunlight. Its eyes glowed with an unnatural light, and its elongated limbs moved with an otherworldly grace. The creature emitted another guttural cry as it drew nearer.

Noah's instincts told him to react swiftly but Serena held out her hand, silently urging him to stay his arrow. She took a deep breath, her focus on the winds, her gift intertwining with the forces of nature around her.

As the creature closed in on them, Serena summoned her magic, attempting to channel the winds to their aid. The air around them stirred with her efforts, a soft breeze brushing against their skin. She silently hoped that the winds would heed her call and provide the advantage they needed.

The creature paused momentarily, its eerie gaze fixed on them. For an instant, time seemed to freeze, the weight of the encounter pressing upon all three of them. In that charged moment, Noah and Serena deeply felt their unspoken trust in each other, lending them each strength.

As the creature's unnatural form suddenly lunged towards them with alarming speed, Noah's instincts took over. He swiftly released an arrow into the air, aiming to take down the approaching monstrosity before it could reach them. His heart pounded, every second feeling like an eternity as the arrow streaked towards its target.

The arrow struck true, finding its mark with deadly precision. However, to Noah's horror, the creature seemed unfazed by the hit. It let out a guttural snarl, its glowing eyes fixated on them with an unsettling intensity.

With his heart pounding in his chest, Noah took a split-second to assess the situation. The ten feet between them and the shore felt like an impossibly minute chasm in the face of the creature's swift approach. He knew that they had to act quickly if they were to have any chance of surviving this nightmarish encounter. With no time to waste, he quickly notched another arrow, drawing the bowstring back with steady hands.

Serena's command over the winds proved to be their saving grace once more. As the creature lunged towards them, the wind shifted, guiding Noah's arrow with unerring precision to find its mark, embedding deep within the creature's eye socket. The beast let out a guttural howl of pain, recoiling in agony. Its claws scraped against the edge of the raft, missing Noah's chest by a hair's breadth.

Noah's heart pounded in his ears as he saw the creature stagger back, momentarily stunned by the blow. He took the opportunity to push the raft further away from the shoreline, increasing the distance between them and the creature.

Serena watched the scene unfold with horror. She knew that they had to keep moving, to stay one step ahead of the relentless monstrosity that pursued them.

"Row, Noah! Row as fast as you can!" she urged him vehemently. "We need to get out of here!"

With adrenaline coursing through his veins, Noah seized the oars and began rowing with all his strength. The raft surged forward, propelled by his desperate efforts.

The creature let out another bloodcurdling cry, its remaining eye locked on their retreating raft as it gave chase with inhuman speed, making it a relentless pursuer.

As they navigated the narrow waterway, Noah rowed with all his might, sweat dripping down his brow as he pushed their makeshift raft to its limits. Serena stood beside him, her staff held firmly, ready to channel her magic if needed. The hauntingly foul ruins of Zefra closed in around them but they pressed forward, their bond providing them the strength to face the darkness that lay ahead.

With the creature stalking them from the shore, their only hope of survival was to outmaneuver it and find a safe haven beyond the limits of the haunted city. Their journey through Zefra had turned into a desperate race for their lives, a battle against time and evil.

Noah stole a backward glance at the pursuing creature and locked with the monster, dread trickled through him at what he saw in those eyes. It was not just the primal hunger of a beast, but a cunning intelligence that struck terror in his soul.

It was as if he was looking into the eyes of a fearsomely vile strategist, a creature that not only hungered for their flesh but took pleasure in the torment it could inflict. The creature's gaze bore into his very being, sending a surge of primal fear through his veins.

The raft rocked with each powerful push of the pole, but Noah knew they had to do more to escape the relentless predator behind them. "Grandmother, we can't keep going this pace forever!" he called out urgently. "We need to find a way to lose it!"

Serena acknowledged the grim reality of his words. The narrow waterway they were navigating left them with no viable escape route, and the ancient ruins seemed to conspire against them, offering no place to hide from the relentless creature that hunted them. Despite her fear, her mind raced for any possible strategy they could employ. She knew that their best chance was to be prepared for any attack the creature might launch and to do everything they could to keep it from reaching the raft again.

"You're right but we need to keep pushing forward, even if it feels like there's no escape," she said with determination. "We must anticipate its next move and do everything in our power to protect ourselves."

As they floated deeper through the haunting ruins, the creature's presence remained ever-present, a lurking darkness that threatened to pounce at any moment. Suddenly, the waterway widened, revealing an open area amidst the ruins. It was unsettling, as if the city itself had designed this area as a trap. The raft drifted into the open water, leaving them exposed and vulnerable.

Just as Serena and Noah braced themselves for the creature's next move, the air around them grew charged with an unnatural energy. The winds that had aided them before now seemed to turn against them, as if corrupted by the malevolence of Zefra's ruins.

Without warning, the creature emerged from the shadows, now flanked by several others. Its horrid eyes fixated on them once more, it let out a bloodcurdling cry that echoed through the ruins.

Noah's grip on the oar tightened even more as he prepared for the imminent attack. Serena lay beside him, her mind focused on using her magic to aid their defense. As the fiendish being lunged towards them, Noah's instincts took over. With a swift and agile movement, he steered the raft away from the open space, seeking the cover of the ruins' debris.

"Grandmother, now!" Noah called out, urging her to use her magic to distract the creature.

Serena summoned the winds once more, her magic mingling with the corrupted energy of Zefra. The winds howled with an otherworldly force, as the light and dark battled for control of the elements, creating a chaotic whirlwind that surrounded the creatures.

Momentarily disoriented, the creatures faltered, giving Noah and

Serena a brief reprieve to steer the raft towards a narrower passage, seeking shelter from the pursuit of the creatures.

As the raft entered the narrow passage, Serena's heart pounded in her chest, she was ready to use her powers repeatedly and at any cost. She would rest once they moved far away from this city of horror. Their encounter with the creature had taught them that they were no match for its strength and cunning. But in the darkness of Zefra, they clung to each other, knowing that their only hope was to face this malignant evil with unwavering resolve.

*****

Exhausted and relieved, the pair finally reached the edge of the city's boundaries. It seemed like they had finally lost the evil beings that hunted them but the lingering feeling of being watched remained. The haunting cries of the monsters still echoed in their ears, a constant reminder of the disease that had infected the forsaken city. Their desperate flight on the river had felt like an eternity. They had played a dangerous game of cat and mouse with the relentlessly pursuing monsters but Serena's command over the winds had proved invaluable, continually thwarting the creatures' attempts to reach the raft.

Under the fading light of the setting sun, the river led them under a large stone bridge that had somehow withstood the decay of time. The bridge stood as a testament to the city's past grandeur, but it now served as a gloomy reminder of its downfall.

As they began to pass under the bridge, their eyes continued to dart to every shadow, ears attuned to any hint of movement. Once under the shelter of the heavy stone arches, they felt a brief sense of relief from the merciless pursuit. However, Noah's blood ran cold when he saw the monster perched upon the other side of the bridge, waiting for them. The relentless creature had caught up with them once again.

Beside him, Serena's expression mirrored his alarm. Her eyes widened with fear as she attempted to call upon the winds once more, only to find her powers depleted and unresponsive. The connection she had relied on for so long had faded, leaving them helpless and vulnerable.

"No…" Serena whispered, her voice barely audible. She tried again, her hands trembling as she reached out to the winds, but they remained stubbornly still.

As the creature leapt from the bridge, Noah took a deep breath and pushed aside his own fear. He felt a surge of power welling up inside him, a whispering voice in his mind guided his every move. He swiftly drew his sword toward the monster and a torrent of lightning burst forth from the tip of the blade. It crackled with electricity, and Noah's eyes glowed a powerful blue hue as sparks showered the monstrous creature.

The lightning struck the creature with a force that sent it sprawling backward, its monstrous form convulsing. The deafening crackle of electricity filled the air, drowning out the haunting cries of the creature. With a fierce determination, Noah continued his onslaught, channeling the energy within him with every strike of his blade. The creature struggled to regain its footing, but it was no match for the unleashed power of lightning.

Serena watched in wonder, unsure of what had come over Noah, but knowing that he was tapping into something extraordinary. The raw power he wielded was both impressive and unsettling, but there was no denying its effectiveness against the underworldly being.

As the battle raged on, Noah's connection to the powers surged, guided by some unseen force. The whispering voice inside him urged him on, filling him with a sense of purpose and confidence. The lightning danced around him, a display of elemental prowess that left Serena in awe. Her grandson had tapped into something extraordinary, something beyond their understanding, and she could only watch in amazed trepidation.

Finally, with one last powerful strike, lightning engulfed the creature with a blinding burst of energy. The creature let out a final, anguished cry before succumbing to the overwhelming power. Its body trembled, then went still and its form began to dissolve, melting into the ground and dissolving in puddles of black acid which steamed and boiled before disappearing.

The electric blue of Noah's eyes faded as the power inside him subsided. He stood there, breathing heavily, head hanging and sweat dripping from the tips of his hair. Adrenaline coursed through his veins like fire across a drought-riddled field. The silence that followed was deafening, broken only by the crackle of dying sparks and his breaths.

Serena struggled to rise from her pallet and approached him cautiously, concern etched on her face. "Noah, what was that?" she asked with awe and uncertainty.

He looked at her through sweat-slick locks of hair, still catching his breath. "I don't know," he replied honestly. "Something inside me… it took over. I felt a connection to the power, like it was guiding me."

Serena nodded, awestruck by the display she had witnessed. "We will discuss this later. For now, we must make haste to get out of the city."

Noah nodded in agreement, feeling the aftereffects of his power and the resulting exhaustion clawing at him. He persevered to channel the remainder of his flagging energy into guiding the raft out of the city. They passed through the ancient mage spells that kept the creatures confined within and outsiders at bay with relief, grateful for the safety it provided them.

As they moved further away from Zefra, the oppressive malevolence that had plagued the city's ruins now felt like a distant memory. Noah glanced back at the city, the dark silhouette of its ruins against the now moonlit sky. He could hear the haunting cries of the surviving monsters echoing in the distance. The sight of the creatures writhing and thrashing on the bridge, screaming and screeching in defiance was a chilling reminder of the horrors they had faced.

"We made it," Serena exclaimed, exhaustion evident in the slight slur in her voice. "We're finally out of that cursed city."

Noah nodded, still grappling with the aftermath of his fight. "Yes, and I hope we never have to return," he replied quietly, his eyes still fixed on the distant ruins. "Zefra's secrets are better left undisturbed."

As they put more distance between themselves and the forsaken city, the atmosphere lightened, and the sounds of the wilderness returned. The rustling of leaves and the gentle flow of the river were a welcome change from the haunting silence of Zefra. With each moment, the sense of renewal and hope grew. Their journey was far from over, but they had faced one of their greatest challenges yet and emerged victorious.

As the sky gradually lightened, they found a safe spot to rest, far away from the blackness that was Zefra. The night had been long and filled with danger, but they were grateful for the new day and the chance to continue their quest.

Chapter 16:
Rankier

After another week on the river, Noah and Serena finally laid eyes on Rankier—the sorcerer's city - in the distance. Noah lifted his gaze to the awe-inspiring city walls that graced the horizon. They were adorned by colossal structures and seemingly endless crenelations stretching as far as the eye could see, it truly was a formidable site.

The river journey had been challenging, and the haunting ruins of Zefra had been particularly harrowing for the two of them. However, the tribulations were well worth it, for the latter part of their expedition had been a delightfully relaxing cruise along the majestic Alrun river. As they floated downstream, Noah marveled at the river's transformation. With each passing mile, it swelled in size, its flow fortified by converging tributaries. The landscape shifted around them, and Noah found joy in watching the serene beauty that surrounded their vessel.

The culmination of their river odyssey brought them to the edge of the Albian Sea, where the waters stretched endlessly, meeting with the distant horizon. They spent a day cautiously hugging the picturesque coastline, trying to avoid the treacherous and choppy seas that lurked further offshore.

Their trusty raft, a solidly constructed vessel that had served them well on the river, soon proved its limitations on the tumultuous sea. The crashing waves and powerful swells threatened to overwhelm it if they ventured further into the open sea. Thankfully, they remained close to the safe embrace of the shore.

They were fortunate to encounter no adversaries outside of Zefra, providing an exhausted Serena with precious time to recuperate. The ordeal with the Zefra monsters had taken a toll on her, causing setbacks in her healing. Despite not being fully recovered, she had made considerable progress, enough to walk short distances when they shored up for the nights, and regain some of her mobility. Yet even with the fortifying rest, she was not well enough to join Noah in his mission to infiltrate the city.

Their previous argument over Liam, although still remembered by both, had eased over the weeks and for the time being they allowed the issue to rest. Discord over the issue would not help them accomplish their goal, so they both tactfully avoided the topic for the moment.

As night descended, Noah navigated their way to the destination under the veil of darkness, carefully evading detection from merchant and military vessels in the bustling harbor. Beaching their raft on a secluded strip of sand, they remained inconspicuous amidst the sea of activities surrounding the city. An overwhelming sense of relief rolled through Noah as his feet touched solid ground once more and he breathed a deep sigh.

Their shrewdness led them to select a copse of trees, strategically distant from the city, as their campsite. The dense foliage created natural concealment, shielding them from prying eyes and potential threats. The shelter of the trees also provided a comforting sense of safety as they braced themselves for the imminent challenges that awaited them in the heart of the city.

Sitting close to the small campfire to warm themselves and dry their clothing, Noah and Serena partook in a quiet meal, their minds deep in contemplation of their next moves.

Serena broke the silence, "I think the best way to move around the city undetected is to procure one of the sorcerer's cloaks. With it, you can assume the appearance of a sorcerer and navigate the city without raising suspicion."

Noah considered Serena's point, "You're right," he conceded, "though finding a sorcerer's cloak won't be a simple task. They won't be lying around for us to pick up, that's for sure."

He leaned in closer to the fire, deep in thought, and then a spark of an idea lit up his eyes. "There might be a way," he exclaimed. "The city's outskirts are known to have travelers passing through. Some of them might be sorcerers or associated with them. If we keep our eyes open and seize the right opportunity, we might be able to discreetly relieve one of them of their cloak."

Seeing the potential in his plan, Serena nodded, "But it's a risky venture," she cautioned. "You'll have to be incredibly subtle and ensure you don't draw any attention to yourself. The last thing we need is to attract unwanted trouble."

"Yes," Noah agreed, "that's why we must be patient and wait for the perfect moment. Once I find the best mark, I can tail them discreetly and then strike."

Fully aware of the limitations her injury imposed on their mission, Serena nodded. "I won't be able to accompany you, so you'll need to exercise utmost caution once you're inside the city," she responded, concern evident in her voice.

As Noah continued to ponder the challenge of entering the city, another idea materialized in his mind. "What if I smuggled myself into one of the carts or carriages entering the city?" he suggested, excitement in his eyes.

"That just might work," Serena replied. "If you can find a way to conceal yourself cleverly, the guards might overlook your presence during their inspections. It's worth a shot, but either option had substantial risks."

With the meal concluded and a plan laid out, they exchanged a few soft words before bidding each other "goodnight" and retreating to their respective bedrolls. The campfire continued to cast a warm glow, its gentle crackling and popping adding a soothing rhythm to the nocturnal sounds that enveloped them.

As he lay under the stars, Noah's mind still buzzed with the upcoming challenges. A blend of excitement, fear, hope, and longing settled in his chest. He was excited to infiltrate the city, but afraid of being caught and the consequences of it. Hope burgeoned in his heart at the thought of finally meeting Liam in the flesh, and longing sang in his blood for when they would be able to hold each other close and explore their relationship further. Liam dominated his thoughts as his eyes drifted closed, the image of his beloved enveloping him in a comforting embrace painted a vivid picture behind his eyelids. The night sounds, the rustling leaves, and the distant calls of night creatures served as a gentle lullaby, easing him into a peaceful slumber.

*****

The next morning, as a gentle glow began to lighten the land, Noah bid his grandmother farewell and ventured towards the heavily rutted dirt road that led to the city. In the pre-dawn hours, the road remained quiet, soon to be disrupted with the influx of bustling activity.

In his mind's eye, he visualized carriages carrying wealthy merchants and esteemed sorcerers, their attendants scurrying about, preparing for the day's transactions. Alongside them, the wood carts of local farmers and diligent laborers would roll in, laden with their bountiful wares destined for the city's markets.

Noah's heart raced with anticipation as he contemplated his daring plan. He aimed to stealthily slip onto the back of a carriage, taking advantage of the preoccupations of its occupants to conceal himself within their midst. Once inside the city, he would seize an opportunity to pilfer the crucial garb of a sorcerer.

His desire for a peaceful and inconspicuous entry was driven not only by practicality but also by the yearning to avoid unnecessary violence. It wasn't that he was opposed to violence when necessary, but the idea of needlessly taking a life made him feel queasy. He knew that a trail of chaos would also leave a visible path of where they had been, which would in turn allow for them to be easily tracked. An elegant and subtle approach was the key to accomplishing this daring rescue.

The bushes growing directly beside the road provided excellent concealment, the foliage enveloped him like a protective cloak, as he waited for the best opportunity to move. He had chosen his hiding spot wisely, ensuring that his presence would go undetected by the causal eye.

The slowly rising sun painted the landscape with soft gold and pink hues, casting long shadows that stretched across the uneven road as Noah focused his thoughts, channeling his determination and resolve. He knew the risks were high, and the stakes even higher, but the thought of reuniting with Liam and accomplishing their mission kept him steadfast.

Time seemed to slow as he waited, every second feeling like an eternity. The road remained relatively quiet, but it would soon come alive with the bustling activity of the city's awakening.

The rumbling sounds of an opulently appointed carriage drew near, Noah's heart skipped a beat as he evaluated the opportunity it presented. The lavish display of gold and gem inlays testified to the wealth and status of its occupant, undoubtedly a powerful sorcerer. Through the carriage window, Noah saw that the sorcerer was engrossed in a large tome, seemingly oblivious to the world outside.

Atop the carriage, a vigilant horseman guided the majestic vehicle forward, flanked by two guards armed with swords and crossbows, watchful for any signs of potential danger. Noah assessed the situation quickly, weighing the risk against the reward. He knew that attempting to board this particular carriage would be too perilous. The guards' alertness, the lack of easy hiding spots, and the potential consequences of being caught outweighed any potential benefit.

With his decision made, Noah remained concealed within the bushes, his heart racing, and allowed the carriage to pass. As the coach disappeared down the road, he took a moment to gather his thoughts. Taking big risks for an uncertain chance was not the best option and he was prepared to bide his time. He would wait for a more favorable opportunity to present itself, one that would be both discreet and safe.

Shortly afterward, the anticipated opportunity materialized. In the distance, the faint sound of a cart's wheels drew near, accompanied by a man's jovial whistling and off-key singing. An elderly farmer was at the reins of a ramshackle wooden cart, cheerfully transporting a load of wheat that was destined for the mill inside the city.

Noah crouched low, anticipation electrifying his muscles as he gauged the perfect moment. With precision timing, he swiftly emerged from the undergrowth and silently glided into the rear of the card just as it cleared the bushes, concealing himself within the bundles of wheat. The farmer, lost in his own merry tune, remained oblivious to the sequence of movements unfolding behind him.

Settling himself amidst the golden wheat, Noah realized this would be a very uncomfortable ride. The cart jerked and bounced along the uneven and rutted roads causing his backside to bounce vigorously and jarringly against the hard wooden boards. Adding to his discomfort, the telltale rustling and high-pitched squeaks of mice scurrying through the wheat sheaves settled around him. Determined to overcome the situation, he steeled himself and settled in, suppressing his reactions and emotions as he counted the minutes until he could take his leave of the cart.

*****

Shaking himself with disgust, Noah quickly brushed off the remnants of the straw and wheat that clung to him from the back of the cart. After what felt like an eternity, he'd heard the cart pass through the city gates, waited a reasonable time before allowing himself to peek out over the edge and, when the time seemed right, he'd quietly leapt from it and flung himself discreetly into a dark alleyway.

Having tidied himself, Noah paused to assess his surroundings and discovered that he stood on the outskirts of a cobblestone square, flanked by merchants energetically peddling their wares. Adjacent to him, the cart that had conveyed him into the city rested alongside a nearby wall, a silent sentinel to his clandestine journey. A tavern entrance stood in proximity, where the farmer, his temporary and unknowing accomplice, had vanished inside to quench his thirst.

An abundance of sorcerers were in the square, their presence both conspicuous and influential, as they effortlessly occupied a significant portion of the area, exerting a palpable sway over the city's affairs. Observing the sorcerous milieu, Noah made a deliberate choice to enter the tavern, opting to use this interlude to strategize his next move.

Stepping into the dimly lit establishment, Noah encountered an ambiance steeped in shadows, the air thick with drifting, dreamlike tendrils of smoke. In one corner, a group of sorcerers congregated, their silhouettes softened by the haze of a shared hookah session, engaged in hushed conversations that seemed to weave spells of their own.

Contrasting the mysterious gathering, several vacant tables were scattered along the opposite corner, while a compact bar counter, presided over by a barkeep diligently polishing glasses, occupied the rear space. Along the opposing wall, discreet booths with drawn curtains offered an oasis of seclusion, inviting patrons to withdraw into their own private realms amidst the tavern's mystique.

Noah approached the weathered barkeep, his movements relaxed as he exchanged a few coins for a pint of ale. Accepting the frothy drink with a nod of gratitude, he shifted his gaze to a nearby booth occupied by a solitary sorcerer who appeared unmistakably inebriated. A captive of excessive libations, his form swayed precariously as a testament to the telltale signs of overindulgence. An idea began to take shape in Noah's mind, fueled by the prospect of the sorcerer's imminent descent into unconsciousness. Perhaps the sorcerer's inebriated state would give him the opportunity to acquire the clothing he needed to make his way into the tower.

Noah pushed himself from the bar, and pasted a genial grin across his mobile mouth as he ambled toward the befuddled sorcerer. Exuding an air of friendly warmth, he reached the inebriated figure and spoke with a cheerful lilt, "Greetings, friend. Would you mind if I joined you for a moment?" His tone was light and inviting, a veneer of conviviality masking his underlying intentions.

"Go ahead and do whatever you like," the sorcerer retorted, his hand dismissively fluttering through the air.

"Much appreciated," Noah responded with a friendly nod, seizing upon the sorcerer's casual acquiescence. He eased himself into the booth across from the man and settled in with an air of relaxed camaraderie. His smile remained affable as he prepared to execute the next phase of his plan.

Leaning forward slightly, Noah maintained the facade of genuine interest. "It's not my business but I couldn't help but notice all the way from bar over yonder that something might be troubling you. Now I'm not a mind healer, but I have been known to be a good listener from time to time. Care to share what's weighing on your mind?"

Blurry eyes met Noah's as sorcerer downed another substantial gulp of ale before his speech flowed, heavy with slurs. "Y'know," he began, his voice betraying the effects of his drink, "ish 'bout a girl, you shee? Belinda, she's like the ocean, beaut'ful wit eyesh sho fine. Loved 'er da' momen' I first shaw 'er, I did. But 'er father – he ain't keen on ush bein' wed."

Meeting the sorcerer's gaze with empathy, Noah observed the man's actions before his slurred words reached his ears. "Ah, it seems matters of the heart trouble you," he responded, concern vividly painted on his face. "Belinda, a name as enchanting as her eyes, it seems. Love has a way of weaving its intricate threads, doesn't it?" He maintained his façade as he encouraged the sorcerer to tell him more. "But why, my friend, does her father withhold his blessings for your union? You seem like such a decent and fine man."

The sorcerer rambled on, blissfully unaware of Noah's feigned demeanor. As his narrative spilled forth, his words became increasingly muddled, echoing the progression of his intoxication. Noah played his role flawlessly, interjecting with well-timed murmurs of empathy, stoking the conversational flames as required.

With calm subtlety, Noah drew the curtains of the booth closed to veil them in privacy. The dim illumination within the alcove seemed to cocoon their secret exchange from prying eyes, allowing Noah's plan to succeed. A triumphant grin spread across Noah's features as the sorcerer succumbed to the inevitable embrace of slumber, head thumping heavily on the table between them. His resonant snores punctuated the air within the booth as Noah saw the opening he needed.

Swiftly moving across the table, Noah maneuvered the sorcerer out of his cape and most of his clothing. Donning the garments quickly, he found they fit him well, if a bit large. As a ruse, they would suffice to see him undetected into Liam's cell. The challenge then would be to escape the city with Liam, and he hadn't quite worked out that part yet.

Sliding out of the booth, he drew the curtains tightly closed concealing the sleeping, almost naked sorcerer from plain sight. Considering his inebriated state, the man would remain unconscious for several hours, giving Noah time to find Liam and escape the city, however he didn't want someone to stumble upon the man in the interim.

With an artful imitation of the sorcerer's speech, Noah jested with the barkeep, feigning the sorcerer's tone and demeanor, "Kid can't hold his ale, can he?" A casual quip that aligned seamlessly with his fabricated role. Without missing a beat, he sauntered out of the tavern, his movements calculated to avoid drawing undue attention.

Now cloaked in his borrowed identity, Noah drew closer to the citadel. His path intersected with a growing tide of foot traffic, the urban pulse quickening with every step. As the streets passed, the number of common folk gradually gave way to an increasing number of sorcerers who traversed the thoroughfares with an air of authority, their conversations an intricate tapestry woven from the threads of arcane knowledge and ambition. Each step closer to the citadel heightened Noah's awareness of his surroundings, intensifying the gravity of his mission within the heart of this arcane stronghold.

The vendors that dotted the thoroughfare in this area of the city now catered exclusively to the demands of sorcery. Cauldrons of various sizes and shapes were proudly displayed, their metallic surfaces gleaming in the ambient light. Jars of exotic ingredients lined the stalls, their vibrant hues enticing passersby to explore the potential of their alchemical concoctions. Among the wares, an array of magical accouterments beckoned, each item a potential key to unlocking the boundless mysteries of the arcane arts.

Despite the inherent peril, an undeniable curiosity tugged at Noah. His attention was ensnared by an exquisite sight – a dagger resplendent with gems, its captivating radiance commanding attention from its prominent placement in the stall. The pull was irresistible, and he found himself compelled to pause and admire its beauty. The dagger spoke to something within him, something that responded to it as the gems began to glow in his presence.

As he approached the weapon, a sage figure emerged from the periphery, his presence like a sentinel of the arcane. The man's darkened skin told tales of a life lived, his weathered visage a canvas painted with wrinkles like the pages of an ancient tome. The bold testament of a scar etched across one eyelid and cheekbone, his intense gaze bore into Noah. His eyes – one a deep, earthy brown, the other a peculiar silvery gray were filled with mystical knowledge.

"You diverge from the rest," the man intoned, his voice an incantation of shadows and intrigue.

Perplexed, Noah furrowed his brow in curiosity. "I'm sorry, I don't quite understand. What do you mean?" he inquired in confusion.

"Your tale is written in the stars, your destiny will be momentous" the man continued, disregarding his question. "The dagger calls to you even now, for it was forged by the same powers that enable your own."

A shiver coursed down Noah's spine, a visceral reaction to the man's cryptic utterance. Instinctively, he drew back, his apprehension evident. The stranger seemed to discern the truth that lay beneath the surface, his words disconcertingly familiar as they struck a chord within him. "I'm not sure what you're getting at," Noah responded, his voice firm with insistence, a facade that masked the internal turmoil.

"Perhaps I am the one stuck in one place," the man replied, a cryptic smile gracing his lips. "But you, young Noah, your journey has just begun. Much lies ahead, and the road stretches far before you." His eyes held a spark of enigmatic understanding, as if he held secrets that spanned eons.

"How… how do you know my name?" Noah whispered in alarm and disbelief.

"In the same manner I sense the dagger is beckoning to you. Its creator was graced by the divine, much as you are," the man responded, a deliberate gesture guiding Noah's attention back towards the captivating dagger. "Embrace it, and you shall find it a steadfast companion, attuned to your very essence."

Noah's hand trembled as he tentatively extended his fingertips to the hilt of the blade. An involuntary gasp escaped his lips, as an otherworldly current coursed through his veins upon contact. In that pivotal instant, an alien consciousness brushed against the edges of his mind, a fusion of ethereal energies intertwining with his own. The presence blazed with a righteous fervor as its metaphysical tendrils unfurled through his thoughts. It was an intimate examination of his very essence.

Time seemed to suspend, the world around him fading into insignificance as he became the sole focus of this divine scrutiny. Then, a realization dawned upon Noah – a verdict had been reached. A surge of awe and humility coursed through him as the presence, with an air of finality, deemed him worthy of its sanctified benediction. The presence felt familiar, much like his experience in the fortune teller's tent when he was but ten years old.

Noah's awareness snapped back to the present, his gaze re-focusing on the man who stood before him, a shrewd observer of his encounter with the dagger. "Indeed, my intuition is well-placed; you possess the potential for remarkable feats," the man declared.

Leaning into the weight of his words, the man's tone became somber and emphatic. "Yet, heed my words, young Noah. As you venture forth, remain vigilant and attuned to the currents of betrayal. It can emerge from the unlikeliest of sources, a venom hidden within familiar faces." The man's cautionary advice hung in the air like a dark and pointed reminder.

"Claim the blade and depart; our paths will intersect anew when fate deems it so. Seek me out upon her arrival with the crown," the man pronounced, his words brimming with an air of preordained finality. With that, he pivoted away, his form disappearing into the depths of his stall, swallowed by the curtain of mysterious wares that concealed his presence.

Noah stood frozen, a mask of incredulity on his face, as the man vanished into the obscure depths of the stall. Time hung suspended for a breathless moment, the weight of the encounter sinking in. With a shake of his head, Noah dispelled the daze that held him in thrall, his mind whirling with thoughts that would be reflected upon at another time.

Hurriedly, he concealed the dagger within the folds of his cloak, its newfound energy a reassuring secret against his chest as he turned away towards the citadel's entrance, its imposing architecture casting a menacing silhouette against the sky.

The citadel was protected by a formidable defense, an imposing bastion bristling with vigilant sentinels who prowled its ramparts and thoroughfares. Armed soldiers, their watchful eyes like vigilant hawks, maintained a ceaseless vigil along the towering walls and imposing gateways. The sole ingress and egress, a solitary drawbridge, hung suspended over the yawning abyss of a foreboding moat, a precarious link to the heart of the stronghold.

Noah advanced toward the drawbridge with determination coursing through his veins. Yet, his progress was abruptly halted by the formidable presence of two towering sentinels with imposing steel pikes that barred his passage. One of the guards addressed Noah with stern suspicion. "State your business here. You're a stranger to these halls," he intoned, his gaze unyielding and unwavering.

His companion chimed in with a nasal voice, mirroring the sentiment. "Indeed, you're not a face we recognize." His skepticism was openly displayed as they stood united in their scrutiny of Noah's presence.

Noah's resolve wavered for an instant, but then a resolute determination surged within him, empowering him to speak with an air of feigned authority. "And why should I divulge my purpose to mere guards?" he retorted, his voice carrying a veneer of confidence. "I am, in fact, among the esteemed ranks of the King's elite sorcerers, a fact that should suffice for your inquiries."

The grizzled guard's lips curled into a disdainful sneer as he shot back a retort. "A sorcerer, eh? You're hardly old enough to be one, aren't you? I'd wager you're naught but a lowly commoner, much like myself, dressed in a costume trying to skulk your way in and lay hands on something you've no right to." His skeptical words dripped derision; a challenge flung at Noah's proclamation.

"Aye, a sly pilferer, I'd bet," the guard with the weasel-like countenance chimed in, his tone laced with mockery.

A theatrical sigh escaped Noah's lips, masking his inner turmoil as he grappled with his fear. Fueled by a surge of desperation, he summoned every ounce of his latent power, his hand raised with fervent intent. With an almost imperceptible motion, a ball of fire manifested, its radiant glow dancing with an ethereal brilliance that illuminated his palm. The warmth it radiated was tangible, an intense heat rippling in harmonious cadence with his apprehension.

"Shall we persist with this charade?" Noah challenged; his voice now laced with daring defiance. He allowed the fire to writhe and dance, a vivid display of his untapped potential. The guards, taken aback by the mesmerizing spectacle, visibly paled, their bravado quelled by the flames that seemed to heed his very command.

The gruff guard's defiance crumbled before the blazing spectacle, his posture humbling as he sank to his knees. "Forgive us, your Lordship," he uttered with contrition, his voice heavy with deference. The weight of his error hung palpably in the air.

His companion, the weasel-faced guard, quickly followed suit, his tone similarly remorseful. "Indeed, it was our duty, your Lordship. We meant no offense nor disrespect," he added, his words a conciliatory echo of the guard's sincere apology.

Allowing the flames to gradually dissipate, Noah's gesture mirrored his acquiescence. He nodded in acknowledgment, his features softening as he addressed the guards with an air of understanding. "No harm done, gentlemen," he replied, his tone a measured blend of reassurance and camaraderie. "You fulfilled your duties admirably. Just remember, let's avoid any hindrances to myself in the times to come, shall we?" His words carried a touch of light-hearted jest, extending an olive branch that hinted at future interactions between them.

"Indeed, your Lordship," both guards chimed in unison, their voices carrying a palpable sense of relief.

"Excellent," Noah affirmed with a confident nod, his bearing steadfast as he strode across the drawbridge and through the imposing gate. His posture exuded an aura of regal authority, effectively warding off any further challenges from the guards who dared not cross him.

Maintaining his dignified stride, Noah traversed the citadel's inner sanctum, his countenance a portrait of poised assurance. He projected an image of a noble lord, a visage that served as both his protection and his passage. He searched the castle's interior looking for a brief respite, a momentary haven where he could lower the facade he had so artfully constructed.

Upon discovering an unoccupied chamber, Noah surrendered to the fatigue that coursed through him, collapsing onto the cool floor. Each breath was a labored effort, punctuated by the lingering tendrils of panic that threatened to undermine his composure. The toll exacted by his display of power was palpable, a cost he had no choice but to conceal beneath the facade he had so painstakingly crafted. His reserves had been stretched to their limit, the mask of unwavering confidence hiding the strain that was wearing him down.

As he lay there, the weight of how far he had come lay heavily on his shoulders. Had the guards pushed him even a fraction further, the delicate equilibrium he had maintained might have shattered. His control, a fragile thread stretched to its limits, could have unraveled, revealing the extent of his vulnerability.

Amidst the jumble of his thoughts, his inner child had relished the exhilarating rush in the deception he had orchestrated. Yet, the gravity of the true stakes weighed heavily upon him, any discovery of his true identity would mark the swift and irrevocable termination of his very life. He understood the stakes with crystalline clarity – any misstep, any deviation from his charade, and the delicate tapestry of his plan would unravel, leaving the three of them in extreme jeopardy.

Having gathered his composure, Noah reassembling the mask of authority he had donned earlier. Rising with renewed purpose, he buried the remnants of his fatigue, and emerged from the chamber. His footsteps echoed through the castle's corridors as he embarked on an unknown trajectory, aiming upwards to reach whichever tower Liam was held in. He didn't know the layout of the castle, but he would find Liam no matter how long it took.

Chapter 17:

Rescue

Tower after tower, Noah ascended and descended countless flights of stairs in his relentless quest for Liam, yet his efforts bore no fruit. A pervasive weariness enveloped him, his energy sapped by what seemed an endless odyssey within the castle's confounding depths. The citadel, an intricate puzzle of stone and shadow, thwarted his every attempt to unravel its enigmatic layout.

It felt as though the very fabric of the castle conspired against him, its passageways and staircases transforming into an ever-shifting maze. His steps had become a dance of futility, intricately choreographed to lead him further from his goal. Despondency loomed in his thoughts, casting doubt upon his resolve as the chances of finding Liam dimmed like a flickering candle in the face of encroaching darkness.

Time, his ally turned adversary, now raced against him. The threat of discovery grew more palpable with each fleeting moment he spent searching the towers without any sense of direction. His friend's fate hung in the balance. Hope, a fragile ember threatened by the gusts of uncertainty, waned as Noah recognized the delicate precipice upon which he stood.

"Come on, there must be a clue in this castle. I can't have many towers left to search!" Noah muttered to himself in frustration, his brow furrowed in exasperation. "If only there was some way to locate him, or even a map of this labyrinthine castle to guide me."

Noah stood silently brooding, his thoughts a tempest of vexation. Then, as if in answer to his fervent plea, a subtle sensation brushed against the recesses of his mind. The feeling deepened, its presence insistent. His gaze darted downward, drawn to the dagger that had been bestowed upon him beyond the citadel's gates. A revelation emerged as he withdrew the weapon from his cloak, his eyes widening in astonishment.

Embedded within the dagger's pommel, a gem pulsed with an inner radiance, casting ethereal luminance around Noah. Anticipation unfurled within him, as if the blade itself approved of his acknowledgment, an unspoken rapport established between them.

Noah regarded the dagger with a mixture of incredulity and determination. "Can you guide me to Liam?" he inquired, a wry smile tugging at the corner of his lips, his words voiced aloud to the silent companion that had unexpectedly revealed its latent power.

In response to his query, the gem within the dagger pulsed twice in silent affirmation. Noah's heart quickened in tandem with the gem's response, a shared purpose reverberating in his consciousness.

Without further ado, a palpable force stirred to life from within the dagger and tugged at him with an insistent urgency. Its presence was a magnetic pull, guiding him through the castle's intricate corridors with an uncanny purpose. The blade was unwavering, almost impatient in its persistence. It propelled Noah forward as if it possessed a will of its own. The stairs became a blur as the dagger led the way, its pull so potent that it was as if he was merely a secondary passenger on an ethereal journey.

Despite the surreal experience, Noah could not help but marvel at the connection the enchanted blade had forged with him. As they continued further in their venture, he clung to this newfound beacon of hope, driven by the assurance that Liam's salvation was finally within reach.

After what felt like an eternity of being led through a winding labyrinth, the compelling force came to an abrupt halt. Noah's breath hitched, his heart racing in tandem with the sudden cessation of movement. As he took in his surroundings, his eyes lit upon a carpeted corridor that bore a striking resemblance to those he had traversed earlier. Yet, a subtle difference set this passageway apart —five solid wooden doors, each one with its own small viewing hole, lined the corridor in a disciplined formation.

Noah nervously approached the first door, anticipation thrumming under his skin, his gaze fixed on the small viewing hole. As he peered within, his heart sank at the sight of an empty room. He repeated this routine at each successive door along the corridor, finding each one devoid of any sign of life.

As Noah stood before the last door, he whispered fervently, "Please be in here," and held his breath in a silent plea as he looked through the viewing hole. His heart pounded against his ribs, a frenetic rhythm that underscored the gravity of the moment, and then a surge of relief washed over him as he laid eyes upon Liam. A smile tugged at Noah's lips, the elation at finally locating Liam bringing tears to his eyes that he quickly dashed away.

The locked portal stubbornly resisted his initial attempts to open it, a reminder of the strength of the fortress that held his lover captive. The key to opening it was nowhere to be seen and he hadn't the time to search for it. Yet, his determination would not be quelled as an idea formed in his mind to summon the power of his flames.

Noah channeled his concentration, focusing on the wellspring of his power. The air crackled with energy as a tongue of fire materialized at his command to engulf the iron lock on the door. Intense heat radiated from the metal, casting distorted shadows on the walls as the lock succumbed to the inferno's embrace, its once-solid form liquefying under the onslaught of Noah's untapped potential.

The weight of maintaining his concentration bore down on Noah's shoulders, his very being pushed to its very limits. Each flicker of intense heat, an embodiment of his resolute purpose, tested his endurance to its utmost. Though his strength and control wavered under the unforgiving pressure, his determination remained steadfast and unyielding, his spirit an unwavering flame that ignited his will.

Finally, Noah's dedication with his power broke the lock. The acrid scent of melted metal and scorched wood permeated the air, a sensory testament to his mastery over the inferno he had summoned. With a resounding clang, the last vestiges of the iron lock relinquished their grip upon the door and tumbled to the floor.

Breathless and battling the encroaching tide of exhaustion, Noah tiredly pulled open the cell door and moved toward the still slumbering Liam. He reached out and gently shook his friend with tender urgency. In a whirlwind of motion, Liam erupted from the bed, a primal instinct propelling him to react with immediate and unyielding strength.

Noah found his feet swept out from under him as he was forcefully thrown to the cold, unforgiving floor, his world turned upside down in a heartbeat. With a gracefully savage move, Liam shifted to straddle his chest, knees pinning his arms to the floor, fist poised to strike, terror and unrestrained anger painted across his features.

Noah's desperate plea pierced the air, his voice held a mixture of urgency and pain. "Stop, Liam! It's me, Noah!" he implored, his voice raw and unsteady.

Liam's eyes flared with the spark of recognition, the curtain of rage lifting to reveal the true person beneath the frenzied assault. Astonishment and gratitude played across his features, emotions that found voice in his trembling words. "Oh my gods, you actually came for me," he whispered, his voice raw with emotion.

Driven by his overwhelming emotions, Liam's eyes glistened with unshed tears. He extended a trembling hand to touch Noah's cheek and shifted to lay his head upon Noah's chest in relief. The rhythmic cadence of a heartbeat echoed against his ear, a steady reassurance amid the tempest that had ravaged his soul. And then, as if a dam had burst, Liam's composure crumbled as Noah's arms wrapped around him, and he surrendered his emotions into a wave of cathartic tears.

Sobs wracked Liam's form, the pent-up anguish, rage and fear finding release in the solace of Noah's tight embrace. Noah's arms became a sanctuary of unwavering support, his voice issuing soothing sounds, a tender lullaby of comfort that melded with the rhythm of Liam's tears.

In this intimate moment, within the confines of his broken prison cell, Liam allowed himself to be vulnerable, to let go of the burden that had been weighing on his heart. Noah held him, a steadfast anchor in the storm, their bond unbreakable and the flicker of love between them growing.

*****

Once the storm of Liam's release had subsided, the two friends nestled together in tranquil silence, their connection stronger than ever. It was within this hushed interlude that Noah showed him the dagger and began to recount his arduous journey, from the moment of their separation to the daring feat of infiltrating the heart of the castle.

As Noah spoke, Liam's gaze remained fixed upon him, an expression of awe lighting up his features. The tale of the dagger, a vessel of unexpected power, seemed to captivate his imagination, a spark of wonder that danced within his eyes as he held it in his hands.

"I can't feel anything from it," Liam murmured and extended the dagger back to Noah, hilt first. Despite this revelation, genuine gratitude radiated from him, a silent acknowledgment of Noah's unwavering loyalty. He offered a soft smile, a gesture that spoke volumes even as words eluded them.

In the wake of Noah's narrative, a charged silence enveloped them, their unspoken emotions hanging heavy in the air. In a sudden and unexpected gesture, Liam leaned to bridge the gap between them with a tender touch of his lips against Noah's. It was a kiss that resonated with feeling, an unspoken connection that transcended any spoken words.

As their lips fused together, emotions surged between them, a passionate current that ignited their senses. Noah instinctively pulled Liam closer, his arms banding to align their bodies in an intimate embrace that dissolved the space between them. Lips parted as their kiss deepened, tongues entwined as their longing for each other seeped together from their very beings.

A soft moan of pleasure escaped Liam's throat and echoed through the space they occupied. In this stolen moment, the world around them seemed to fade, leaving only the palpable presence of their burgeoning love and the intensity of their connection.

Breaking their kiss, Liam sought to convey a depth of gratitude that words alone could not define. He gazed deeply into Noah's eyes, his own brimming with love, desire and passion. Each flicker of his lashes, every beat of his heart, spoke of the profound appreciation he felt for this man who had dared to risk everything to rescue him.

"Thank you for coming to rescue me," he breathed, his words a heartfelt acknowledgment of Noah's courage and devotion.

Noah's lips curved into a playful smile, a glint of mischief dancing in his eyes. "Anytime, especially if the reward is another kiss," he quipped. The atmosphere between them shifted, the weight of emotions lifted as they shared the lighthearted exchange.

However, the levity soon gave way to a more serious demeanor as the gravity of their situation pressed upon them once more. With a resolute look, Noah rose and lifted Liam up to his feet.

"We need to leave before they come and find that you're missing," Noah's voice was steady despite the urgency that thrummed beneath his words. "Do you know the way out from here?"

Liam shook his head, his expression full of frustration. "No, I was always blindfolded when they took me from this cell. This castle seems to go on forever," he confessed, a hint of helplessness in his tone.

"No worries, we can use the dagger. I'm sure it will help us find our way out," Noah replied as he lifted the dagger. Its intricate design caught the light as he addressed it with a quiet intensity. "Help guide us out safely," he implored, his words an earnest plea. In that moment, the dagger pulsed with a renewed energy, its gem-encrusted hilt glowing softly in response to Noah's request.

The gentle glow illuminated their path, casting a soft radiance on the walls as it guided them through the maze of corridors. Their footsteps echoed quietly in a steady rhythm that underscored their cautious progress as they descended from the tower.

Looking around them, Noah's voice broke the quietude of the halls. "Does it seem unusual to you that we haven't run into anyone yet?" he inquired. The absence of any sign of life within the castle's walls was beginning to weigh on him, raising questions about the nature of their surroundings.

Liam nodded, his own unease showing in his expression. "It does," he admitted. "This castle houses a multitude of the King's sorcerers. We should have crossed paths with some of them by now." A note of uncertainty entered his tone as he continued. "Perhaps they're occupied with something urgent? Or there's another reason they're not out and about."

"Whatever the reason is, let's hope we don't find them all at once." Noah said.

A wry smile touched Liam's lips as he nodded in agreement. "Definitely hoping for that," he replied, his voice laced with a mix of humor and caution.

The dagger continued to lead them on, their journey now marked by a descent that brought the sprawling cityscape beneath the citadel into view through the windows they passed. With each step, their progress was a tangible reminder that their escape was drawing nearer.

The corridor led them to an expansive landing, providing a brief respite from the winding staircases and intricate passages. As they stood to the side of the entrance to a grand hall, the distinct sound of a harsh and gravelly voice echoed from within. Noah quickly motioned for silence, his finger to his lips, as he eased himself into the room. Liam followed closely; their movements synchronized in stealth.

Within the grand hall, shadows painted a tapestry of intrigue upon the walls, enhancing the air of mystery that hung over the setting before them. From their concealed position at the rear of the room, Noah and Liam were granted an unobserved vantage point, allowing them to witness the unfolding scene unnoticed.

As their eyes adjusted to the dim lighting, the full scope of the situation revealed itself. The vast hall was filled with a sea of sorcerers, seated in hushed anticipation and all eyes fixed upon a stage that commanded their attention. The atmosphere was charged with an electric energy, the audience's collective focus drawn to the figure who held the stage.

The main speaker, an older man dressed in the robes of a sorcerer, stood at the forefront. At first glance, it seemed that he would appear unremarkable within a crowd, his benign countenance a deceptive veil. Yet, closer inspection revealed something that set him apart from others. The left half of his face bore the cruel legacy of a hideous scar, an embodiment of his dark past. The veins on that side of his face were prominent amidst the scar tissue, coursing with inky shadows and dark miasma, tracing intricate web-like patterns up towards his entirely black left eye.

Noah and Liam exchanged glances, their expressions curious and uneasy. The man was frightening, and both felt unsafe in his presence. Liam reached for Noah's hand, gripping it tightly for reassurance.

The figure upon the stage raised a commanding hand, and a stifling hush descended upon the room as if all sound had been devoured by an unseen abyss. Shadows seemed to converge around him, shrouding him in foreboding darkness. His voice emerged from the silence, a whisper that slithered through the air like a venomous serpent, sending a chill down their spines.

"Welcome, brethren," the man's words drifted forth, each syllable laden with an unsettling malevolence. His eyes, an abyss of darkness, locked onto his audience, his presence radiated evil like a storm cloud poised to unleash its fury.

"How long has it been since we last convened?" his voice rasped, the question hinting at the secrets and horrors that had transpired in the interim. The room, captive to his every utterance, remained suspended in an eerie silence, as if time itself had been ensnared within the grasp of his chilling proclamation.

"Too long, indeed," the man's voice slithered forth, laced with anticipation and dark purpose. His chilling gaze pierced through the air, seeming to strip away the facade of normalcy that had shrouded the room.

"Yet, fret not," he continued, his tone dripping with malevolent assurance, "for the King's command has reached my ears as a Herald of

Doom." The sibilant words, draped in an ominous veil, resonated like a dire prophecy of impending doom.

"Word has unfurled its wings, whispering tales of the heir's impending vulnerability. Soon, he shall waltz unwittingly into our clutches." A cruel smile danced upon his lips; his eyes gleamed with twisted satisfaction as he delivered the harrowing news like a venomous promise.

"When the stars align, we shall ensnare him and extinguish his pitiful existence, along with that of his frail grandmother, and in so doing end this rebellion," he declared, his tone like a death knell ringing through the air. The room seemed to shiver in response to the malevolence that emanated from his very being.

With a fervent intensity, he continued, his voice swelling with vehemence, "The King's decree echoes through the corridors of our fate. We are summoned to assemble, to amass our might and march upon the Elven domains. No longer shall their defiance be tolerated, for their treachery is laid bare." His proclamation held a dark energy that seemed to infect the very air around them.

"Collaborators with the enemy, they scheme to shelter the usurpers and orchestrate our King's demise," he hissed with venomous disdain. "But we, the King's most loyal, shall not yield. We shall rise as a tempest of vengeance and obliterate their delusions." The edges of his lips curled into a feral snarl, revealing pointed teeth that gleamed in the dim light like a predator's deadly maw.

In that moment, the room seemed to pulse with malefic intent as the man's words painted a vivid picture of the impending horror soon to be visited upon the Elves. The chilling revelation was etched upon the very fabric of Liam and Noah's souls, a stark reminder that the forces of darkness were poised to unleash an unrelenting storm upon the world.

A chorus of sinister elation surged through the hall from the congregation, an ominous symphony of jubilation that seemed to rise from the very depths of the vacuum of their souls. The sorcerers, their faces twisted in a macabre ecstasy, erupted from their seats with a chilling cacophony of cheers.

"Gratitude, my brethren," the man's voice echoed through the chamber. His words seemed to cascade like shards of ice, each slippery word laced with a fervor that mirrored the twisted enthusiasm of the crowd.

"The hour approaches when the King shall stand triumphant, liberated from the clutches of Elven folly," he proclaimed, his voice carrying the weight of zealous anticipation. A sense of finality hung in the air, a prelude to the impending climax of their dark ambitions. With an air of ominous ceremony, the man directed their attention to a grim spectacle that materialized beside him – a pool of inky blackness that seemed to writhe and pulse with a life of its own. Its unsettling presence seemed to distort the very fabric of reality, casting an eerie pall over the room.

"Our pact with the denizens of the abyss has borne bountiful fruit," he declared, his words ringing with a sinister pride. "From their infernal embrace, we have absorbed unparalleled might, a force that shall propel us to the pinnacle of supremacy."

A maniacal intensity consumed his visage as he beckoned them closer to the abyssal pool, his eyes aflame with a fanatical zeal. "Now, dear brethren, the final step awaits us – a leap of unwavering faith, a communion that shall bestow upon us power beyond measure. Embrace the abyss, intertwine your essence with the primordial demonic darkness, and become vessels of unparalleled strength, fit to serve the King's will."

The applause of the sorcerers morphed into a macabre procession towards the dark pool. With eerie uniformity, they filed forward, an unbroken line of devotees drawn inexorably towards the Chief Sorcerer. His cackles rang out like a haunting dirge as he reveled in his malevolent orchestration, a discordant melody that echoed the eerie cadence of the approaching ritual.

Noah's heart pounded as he watched in horrified fascination. The pool of inky blackness beckoned like a hungry maw, its form shifting and writhing with a malefic energy. As the sorcerers entered its depths, the liquid responded with an unsettling vitality, its tendrils reaching out hungrily to embrace them. They vanished into the depths, disappearing from sight only to reemerge moments later.

The transformation was undeniable, their once-familiar forms now tainted by an otherworldly darkness. The dark miasma coursed through their veins like a sinister poison, etching a grotesque tableau upon their flesh. The air grew thick with an unsettling aura, as though the very fabric of reality recoiled from the abhorrent communion unfolding before them.

Noah's heart clenched as he beheld the gruesome metamorphosis. Limbs contorted, flesh twisted, and appendages sprouted like grotesque blooms from their bodies. Some emerged bearing monstrous deformities, their forms warped beyond recognition, their very essence irreversibly altered by the malevolent communion. It was a grotesque and unholy union that wrought an irreparable fracture upon their humanity.

As they observed the nightmarish spectacle, Noah and Liam exchanged a wordless glance, their horror mirrored in each other's eyes. The grotesque transformation unfolding before them was a grim testament to the depths of darkness that these sorcerers were willing to embrace. Having seen and heard enough, Noah subtly signaled to Liam, guiding them towards the opposite end of the hall with calculated stealth. They slipped away, shadows in the sea of fervent devotees, moving with a silent urgency.

Staying within the shadows of the room, their soft footfalls concealed their escape from the chamber of horrors. At last, the door beckoned, a portal to freedom that promised respite from the evil they had borne witness to. Noah's hand met the cool metal of the door handle, and with a steady twist, they stepped out of the nightmare and into the dimly lit corridor beyond.

Time was of the essence, and they did not pause to catch their breath. Noah led the way, his footsteps swift and sure, the dagger guiding them through the tangled passages of the citadel. Their escape was quick, drawing them closer to the entrance and the promise of freedom.

Finally, the imposing gates of the citadel loomed before them, a threshold between captivity and liberty. Noah released Liam's hand, locking his gaze onto the two guards stationed there. With a nod, he communicated his authority, invoking the same confidence that had paved his path into the castle. The guards, recognizing him, offered a respectful acknowledgment, unwitting allies in their escape.

As they crossed the threshold of the citadel, the weight of their harrowing journey began to lift. The square lay before them, bathed in the pale glow of moonlight, a stark contrast to the darkness they had left behind. Noah reached for Liam's hand and tightened his grip in silent reassurance. They had triumphed against the odds, and swiftly leaving the square, they rushed to get to the city gates, and away from the sorcerer's stronghold.

As they moved through the streets by the tavern, Noah's lips twitched with suppressed amusement. The image of the befuddled sorcerer, disheveled and caught in the aftermath of Noah's ruse, danced before his mind's eye. The memory carried a certain satisfaction, a playful victory that lightened the weight of their recent trials.

The tavern, once a fleeting scene of his deception, now held a comical tableau as the sorcerer, still wearing naught but his undergarments, was escorted out with a mixture of indignation and confusion. Noah stifled a snort of laughter that threatened to escape him. The juxtaposition of the sorcerer's once-authoritative demeanor with his current state of undress was quite entertaining to behold.

As they reached the city gate, their pace did not slow and with a final glance over their shoulders, Noah and Liam stepped beyond the threshold, their footfalls carrying them out onto the marshes that surrounded the city.

The fenlands stretched before them, a vast expanse of rugged terrain and murky waters. The air was heavy with the earthy scent of damp vegetation, a stark contrast to the city's stifling atmosphere. The ground beneath their feet was uneven, and soaking wet moss clung to their feet as they trod through it.

They finally slowed their rapid pace, stopping to rest in a dry patch beside a large sycamore tree.

"Now that we're free, how do you suppose we'll warn the Elves?" Liam's impatience and concern was evident in his voice.

"I'm not sure, but speed is crucial. Our initial plan was to rescue you and proceed on foot. However, at that pace, we might not reach the Elven Kingdoms before the King's armies do," Noah replied, his expression clouded as he pondered the challenge at hand.

"If the Elves aren't alerted, their cities will crumble under a sorcerer assault. We witnessed those corrupted sorcerers – if they're set loose, they'll lay waste to the forests and the concealed cities," Liam exclaimed in distress as he recalled the haunting image of the disfigured sorcerers.

"I know, Liam," Noah responded soothingly, recognizing the onset of panic. "We will find a solution, don't worry." His gaze shifted to something on the horizon beyond the city walls. "Didn't you mention your father is a wealthy and reputable merchant?"

Liam nodded, seeking comfort as he nestled beside Noah, his head finding its natural resting place on Noah's shoulder. "Yes, he commands a fleet of trading ships that sail the vast seas. He's also a staunch supporter of the King, likely because our family's wealth owes much to that allegiance."

"Is it possible that he has ships docked there, ones we could perhaps… commandeer?" Noah's lips curled into a self-assured grin.

Liam paused, momentarily taken aback, before a smirk spread across his face, and he burst into laughter. "Well, indeed he does. We have quite a selection at our disposal."

Noah joined in the laughter. "I believe we've stumbled upon our answer. Let's go get ourselves a ship!"

Chapter 18:
Open Waters

Noah and Liam made their way to their chosen vessel, selected from among the ships owned by Liam's father and anchored in the bustling port. The ship was sturdy, its wooden beams gleaming under the sunlight, its sails tightly secured with well-knotted fabric. Diligent maintenance was evident in every detail. It was middling in size, neither overly large yet not too small, offering a robust and roomy feel that could be efficiently managed by a modest crew of sailors.

"You there!" Liam's voice carried an air of authority as he pointed at a rugged sailor engrossed in tending to the deck of the vessel. The sailor halted his work, pivoting to meet Liam's gaze, his eyes widening in recognition.

"I be Harbin, your Lordship. How may I assist you?" he replied with a sailor's twang, deference and curiosity in his voice.

"Get the ship ready for sail. I've orders from my father; we must depart immediately." Liam said, still acting the part of a wealthy nobleman.

"Right away, we'll set the sails immediately and should be ready to depart in fifteen minutes, sir!" Harbin's response was prompt and respectful, and he wasted no time in hurrying off to initiate the necessary preparations.

Liam turned back to face Noah, who was gawking at the performance and the way the sailor had swiftly taken his orders.

"Who in the world is your father? You said wealthy, but that man looked at you like you were actual royalty!" Noah asked, flabbergasted.

Liam chuckled bitterly. "My father may not wear a crown, but he knows how to command respect. He's a shrewd businessman, and his connections reach far and wide. Let's just say he has a way of making people take notice. He is also a right bastard for trying to gift me to the King" Liam said, his voice turning spiteful at the thought of his father.

Noah noticed Liam's face turning sour. "Well, he might be a good businessman but he's an absolute idiot for what he tried to do to you," he said reassuringly. "Let's get loaded up onto the ship, shall we?"

Quickly distracted from his inner turmoil, Liam's enthusiasm was palpable as he eagerly nodded and flashed a bright smile, beckoning Noah to step onto the ship. They ascended the sturdy stairs leading to the ship's helm, where Liam's gaze was immediately drawn to an array of controls. His fingers traced the contours of the ship's wheel, his eyes alighting on a set of intricate dials mounted to the polished wood railing.

"Marvelous luck befalls us! This vessel is one of the spirit ships my father invested in several years past," Liam declared, his voice vibrating with an infectious sense of excitement.

"A spirit ship?" Noah inquired, his curiosity piqued.

"Yes, they're incredibly rare! It's a ship that has had its hull beams interwoven with mystical threads that are entwined with the spirits of deceased mermaids. Its grace upon the waves surpasses all others, carrying it swifter than the wind itself. And, even in the tumultuous heart of a tempest, it will stand unwavering, a bastion against the fury of the elements. Spirit ships have emerged unscathed from the strongest of gales and squalls."

"With this ship's speed, we stand a good chance of outpacing the

King's sorcerers and delivering the warning to the Elven kingdoms before their arrival," Noah replied, his back against the railing.

"It does appear that way," Liam agreed, stepping closer to rest against Noah, who warmly enveloped him in his embrace.

Harbin approached with purpose, ascending the sturdy stairs and positioning himself skillfully behind the ship's wheel. "All set and ready to sail! Where shall we be heading, Young Master?" he inquired, his eagerness evident in his tone.

"We have another passenger to pick up just down the way, and then we're off to Elnoth," Liam declared. "Noah here will guide you to our passenger; you'll follow his orders as if they were my own," he commanded with confidence.

*****

With Harbin skillfully at the ship's helm, which Noah discovered was named the Scimitar, they anchored a short distance from the shore alongside the makeshift raft he had made for himself and his grandmother. Serena's astonishment was palpable when she saw Noah returning with Harbin, and her amazement only deepened when she beheld the waiting vessel, Liam's smile radiant as he stood proudly at the helm to welcome her.

Once on board, they swiftly acclimated to their new surroundings, moving past the initial awkward introductions. Serena, still in the process of recovery, had made herself comfortable in a cabin below deck. Despite the ship's relatively modest appearance from the outside, its interior surprised them with its ample space. Another well-appointed cabin awaited them, complete with enough room for Noah and Liam to share. Inside, the cabin housed two separate bunks positioned closely, prompting a knowing exchange of glances between Noah and Liam.

Harbin, displaying his rugged seafaring spirit, chose to rest above deck. A hammock was slung up near the helm, granting him an optimal vantage point to monitor the ship's course and make necessary adjustments. He playfully quipped about Noah's fair skin when they extended the offer of sharing the bunk below deck, explaining that he preferred spending his days beneath the open sky while at sea. "It's better for my old bones to rest under the stars at sea, Young Masters," he declared with a hearty chuckle and a toothy grin.

With the group comfortably settled, the ship gracefully glided onto the Albian Sea. The iridescent waters danced under the rising sun casting shimmering reflections all around. The Scimitar sliced through the waves as its sails billowed in the wind's embrace. Dolphins frolicked near the ship's bow, adding a touch of playfulness and life to their voyage.

Harbin charted a course, referring to a weathered sea map, and determined a northeastern direction. The ship's route would lead it across the expanse of the Albian Sea until it intersected with the Duras River, which would then guide them to the vast Northern Ocean. Following the coastline, they would pass by the Elven city of Falnir before eventually arriving at Elnoth. Given the ship's renowned speed, Harbin confidently estimated that the voyage would take no more than a week.

The salty ocean breeze was revitalizing, and Noah often found himself leaning against the bow's sturdy wooden railings, absorbing the brisk gusts and filling his lungs. This was his first time on a ship, let alone at sea, and the experience awakened a newfound sense of excitement within him. The sensation was akin to a rebirth under the embrace of the ocean sun, the rhythmic lapping of the waves against the ship's hull a serene passage of time.

Liam would often join him, and together, they would spend hours engrossed in conversations that flowed effortlessly. Laughter and light-hearted jests peppered their exchanges. The days spent aboard the Scimitar allowed them to delve into each other's histories, forging a deeper connection. Liam eagerly recounted tales of his upbringing and his life before the clutches of the Sorcerer's keep. In return, Noah spoke about his life with his grandmother, recounting the struggles they had overcome and the precious moments of happiness they had cherished together.

Noah also revealed the truth of his family dynasty, a facet of his life that he had not previously divulged in their previous interactions. Liam's initial surprise was palpable, yet he swiftly embraced Noah's history as part of the person he had come to deeply care for. Liam's heart remained steadfast, holding love for the person Noah was, irrespective of his ancestry. Acknowledging that their relationship might face additional challenges due to this revelation, Liam chose to set aside those complexities for the time being. Instead, he focused on cherishing the moments they spent together on the Scimitar, relishing their connection and reveling in the shared experiences that were strengthening their bond.

Serena's presence added a layer of wisdom and comfort to their journey. Even as she rested and recovered, her watchful eyes caught the subtle changes in Noah and Liam's interactions when she came above deck for some sun and fresh air. She recognized the blossoming affection between them and the genuine happiness they found in each other's company. It brought a warm smile to her lips, knowing that they were forging a deep connection that transcended the challenges they faced. She shared knowing glances with Harbin, both of them silently bearing witness to the love that was growing stronger with every passing moment.

*****

"Young love, t'is a sight to behold, eh? I've not been young for quite some time myself, but I can remember what it felt like," Harbin remarked in passing, as Serena walked by heading to her cabin after one of their meals.

"It is, as do I. Young love makes fools of us all, though I wouldn't trade my memories of it for anything," Serena chuckled, her eyes shining with nostalgia. "Although I fear they don't understand the ramifications of the path they're treading. They will each have destinies and obligations to uphold for their family's sake."

"Ah, well now, no one ever said that young love had to make sense, did they?"

Serena chuckled, acknowledging the truth in his words. "I haven't the heart to break it up, nor to make Noah unhappy at the same time."

Harbin shrugged back, smiling jovially. "Then don't. Let the boys be, and see what may come."

155

"Indeed," Serena agreed, her gaze drifting towards the deck where Noah and Liam were engrossed in a lively conversation. "Perhaps they'll find a way to navigate their paths together, despite the challenges ahead."

Harbin nodded knowingly. "Sometimes, love finds its own way, like a current in the sea. We can steer our ships, but the tides have a will of their own."

Serena smiled at the metaphor, appreciating Harbin's wisdom. "You're right, Harbin. And who are we to stand in the way of the tides?"

"Naught but mere mortals you and I." Harbin said laughing, before turning away to tend to the ship.

Serena lingered for a moment longer, contemplating the significance of Harbin's words. Despite his humble background, there was undeniable wisdom in what he had said. She shook her head, a mixture of resignation and determination in her expression. If Noah were any ordinary young man, she would encourage him to pursue his happiness without reservation. But his path was marked by a greater purpose, one that required sacrifices beyond personal contentment. A kingdom's fate hung in the balance, and that called for a level of commitment that surpassed individual desires.

With a sigh, Serena retreated to her cabin, her heart heavy with the weight of her knowledge and the decisions that lay ahead. The sea continued its rhythmic dance against the ship's hull, a soothing backdrop to the complex emotions swirling within the hearts of the passengers aboard the Scimitar. As the ship sailed on towards its destination, the future remained uncertain, yet filled with the promise of adventure, love, and the pursuit of a greater purpose.

Chapter 19:

Fun Below Decks

Noah eased into bed, and Liam turned to curl up against his side, draping his arm across his chest to stroke the soft skin of his shoulder. Since they had settled into the cabin, they had swiftly reconfigured the sleeping arrangements. They both felt the need to nurture their growing connection, both physically and emotionally, so they pushed their two beds together. Their intimacy had deepened and, as they wordlessly agreed to pace themselves, their bodies became more acquainted with each other in tender moments they shared. However, as their feelings deepened, the magnetic pull between them became irresistible. The need to succumb to their desires, doing to each other what they instinctively knew would bring pleasure, finally took over.

Now Noah's fingers danced across Liam's back, mapping the contours of tendons and muscles in a gesture that conveyed both affection and longing. The journey of his fingers swept lower, exploring the tempting dip of his spine with a ticklish flicker, then slipping under the fabric of Liam's undergarments to cup and knead a firm, taut buttock with his whole hand. The press and pull sensation elicited a shiver of pleasure from Liam, who arched into the caress in response. His leg shifted restlessly across Noah's thigh as his cock, slowly hardening in response to the erotic massage, rubbed against Noah's growing erection. His lips sought the curve of Noah's strong neck trailing soft, heated kisses to the tender spot where it met the shoulder.

Their moans and sighs mingled in the sultry air of the darkened cabin as Liam's lips and tongue marked a wet path along Noah's skin, the tender touch igniting a fire that begged to be quenched. Noah savored the sensation of the heated suction of Liam's mouth and tilted his head to offer easier access as lips slid further down his chest. Spreading his thighs to allow their cocks to come into closer contact, he groaned at the sensation of their underclothes, the thinnest barrier, rasping against his tumescent penis with each shift of Liam's leg.

In a voice that held a potent blend of desire and vulnerability, Noah confessed the depths of his yearning. "I want you," he moaned, his hot gaze locked onto Liam's pliant form resting atop his chest, bared emotions shimmering in his eyes.

Liam looked up from his diligent ministrations to Noah's erect nipples, his eyes heavy with lust and longing. "Then take me; I'm yours."

Noah didn't hesitate. Rolling over, Liam now beneath him, he swiftly stripped Liam of his drawers and then removed his own, tossing them to the side to land in a disheveled pile by their bed. Sitting back on his haunches, he took a moment to stare with wonder and admiration at the male beauty stretched out before him. He reached down and spread Liam's legs, his hands settling firmly on the back of his knees, bringing them up and out, rolling Liam's hips up so that he could look his fill, ignoring Liam's blushes. His cock throbbed as he ogled the feast laid out before him, watching the dark rosette as it winked at him invitingly and the luscious dick presented to him lengthen further. Without warning, his control snapped, and he swooped forward to devour the little hole. Lips opened wide to allow as much access as possible, the flat of his tongue rasped repeatedly with greedy swipes along the sensitive skin before worming its way into the little orifice. Liam shrieked with surprise and lust, spots of red high on his cheekbones as his fingers immediately tangled in Noah's hair to hold him in place so that he could gyrate against his lover's mouth.

After the initial stab of hunger for his lover was sated, Noah settled in to take his time, exploring as he laved his tongue from crack to scrotum, leaving nothing untouched except for the dripping cock. Liam would have to earn a blow job later, he thought wickedly. Drunk on the scent of sex rising from Liam's stiffened dick, he took each of his balls into the hot, wet cavern of his mouth to suck and test them with tongue and lips and teeth. In the dark of their cabin, the sounds of Liam's moans grew louder with each moment, his turgid manhood strained for release, just one more lick would send him over the brink but as if by instinct, Noah pulled back and with a sharp bite on the tender skin where hip met leg, he looked up between Liam's twitching thighs.

"Oh no you don't. Not yet," he growled, lust expanding his pupils to swallow the blue of his eyes. Blowing on the wet skin he had just attended to, Noah curbed his lover's imminent release and then settled himself in the cradle of Liam's body. Their erections rubbed together, causing friction as they kissed sloppily and with desperate desire. Liam slid his hand down, wiggling it between their sealed bodies to grasp Noah's firm cock finding it already slick with their mingled precum. His grip tightened as he slid his hand down the long shaft, right to the base, his fingers barely meeting around the girth. Feeling Noah sigh into his mouth, he stroked him from root to tip and back in a swift hard jerk and was rewarded with a dribble of more precum and a groan as Noah shifted ever so slightly to give Liam's hand more room. He relaxed his grip and set to steadily glide his hand up and down the long, incredibly thick shaft teasingly. His fingers drifted to smooth the liquid seeping from the slit at the top of the hard mushroom head down to the root and back up to collect more. This time, his fingertips slithered under the head, to the sensitive spot just beneath to press and rub.

"Gods that feels good" Noah whimpered, leaning back on his haunches to let Liam sit up.

Liam shifted to his stomach to face Noah's crotch, his ass slightly up in the air as his spread knees supported him and slid his tongue along the steadily leaking erection in front of him. He ran his tongue slowly around Noah's cock head, collecting the juices there and swallowing with a hum. The flat of his tongue followed the path that his fingers had taken and rubbed delicately along the sensitive underside of the head, chuckling at Noah curses of pleasure above him. Shifting further down, he opened his mouth, tongue out, teeth covered, and took his cockhead fully. Then in one slick move, with lips stretched taut by the girth, he swallowed the thick length to the root, nose nestled into the base of Noah's abdomen. Curly pubic hair tickled his nose as he swallowed, the movement constricting Noah's cock that was firmly lodged in his throat. A strangled whimper burst from Noah's lips while the musky flavor of his lover's manhood filled Liam's mouth.

Aroused beyond measure at the erotic act he was performing, Liam pulled back to the tip of Noah's cock and then swallowed it again and held it deeply, his tongue fluttering and throat constricting. On the third pass, he changed tactics and began bobbing his head up and down sucking on the long thick cock like a child would a candy stick while Noah leaned back to give him better access to his treasure. Noah wailed out a breath, hands twisted into Liam's hair, guiding his plunging head up and down. As his tongue twisted and snaked around Noah's cock, the sounds of Liam's erotic services inflaming their need for each other.

Noah was in paradise; he had never felt anything like this in his virginal life. His own hands, although capable and lubricated with oils, had never been able to give him such pleasure. The feel of his lover's hot, wet mouth and tight throat were indescribable, sending him into a delirium of lust. He released one hand from Liam's hair and reached forward to slide his hand between the ass cheeks presented in front of him, his fingers fondled the dark little rosette exposed to the air. This forward motion caused Liam to impale himself on Noah's cock, cutting off his breath. They froze like this for a moment and then Noah reached around to gather some of Liam's precum on his fingers, He then slid his hand back to his lover's asshole, all the while keeping Liam's mouth firmly mounted to his cock, nose pressed against his pubic hair. His fingers played and pressed against the tight hole, eventually causing it to open slightly and allow him to penetrate to the first knuckle. Although pliant,

Liam's body began to spasm from lack of air and Noah reluctantly released his prize to pull Liam off his cock. Drool and precum stringing from his chin, Liam gazed at Noah with watery, worshipful eyes. As he swiped the back of his hand across his mouth, Noah pulled him forward and kissed him violently.

He flipped Liam over, positioning him head down, ass up. His knees stretched as far apart as possible, chest and shoulders flush against the bedclothes, ass cheeks as high as possible and spread wide, exposed to a single pair of ravenous eyes. Noah moved forward, positioning his thick, hard cock between Liam's firm cheeks, rubbing and tapping it against the tight little entrance found there. To his joy, it expanded and contracted like a hungry mouth at his attention. Leaning down, whispered, "This is mine, isn't it?" His hot breath brushing along Liam's ear causing him to shiver in anticipation.

"It's all yours, I am all yours." Liam groaned in the throes of passion, his ass pushing back against the hard instrument pressed against him.

Resolved to make his lover scream with fulfillment, Noah shifted to squeeze Liam's thighs together, straddled his closed knees, and then pushed his cock down between them to rub their dicks together. Hands on Liam's shoulders holding him in place, he shifted his hips back and forth to masturbate them against each other using their precum as a lubricant and Liam's thighs like a vise. Liam, a captive audience of one, turned his head to look down his body for a first-hand erotic view of hide-and-go-seek that made his mouth water. Noah then pulled his cock back, pushed Liam's knees apart again, grabbed an ass cheek in each hand to lift and spread them as far as he could. Gazing at the display for a moment, he leaned forward to lick softly at the twitching orifice located there with the flat of his tongue, his nose buried at the top of Liam's crack.

Liam keened loudly in pleasure, his voice singing out in the hushed stillness of the room, satisfying Noah with its thready whimpers and moans. The feeling of Noah's hot tongue teasing and licking at his tight hole made stars shoot behind Liam's eyelids. He gasped as Noah's tongue plunged into his anus without warning, a tongue that became more insistent, pushing in harder and faster making him buck in pleasure as it slipped further and further inside, each wet plunge making him more malleable. A finger joined the tongue in his ass and Liam groaned as he pushed back in ecstasy, hands clutching the sheets in a twisted grip of agonizing rapture. After a few minutes, two fingers entered his anus, pistoning in and out with a force that had him shrieking and writhing with desire, his own hand moving to jerk his cock in time to the thrashing. The two fingers scissored inside of him, stretching his poor little rosette to the point of pain, bringing repeated throaty moans from his mouth with every thrust.

Finally, Noah pulled his fingers from their erotic work and moved away. Liam exhaled a frustrated breath at the absence of Noah's presence inside him. "Please don't stop, fuck me" he begged, his ass presented enticingly, his cock dripping onto the sheets, fingers loosely encircling it.

Noah moved to the side of the bed and pulled a vial of oil from the table there. He presented it to Liam and commanded, "Oil me and do it well." Liam shifted to his elbows to desperately grasp the vial. From this position of supplication, he filled his palms with the oil, hastily spreading it onto the cock bobbing in front of his face. His tongue swiped out to lick at the sensitive slit as he completed his task.

Tossing the empty vial aside, Noah shifted behind Liam and placed his cock into position, pressing it firmly but slowly against the tight pucker. As he felt the resistance of Liam's dank hole give way, he watched in awe as his cock stretched the ring of flesh, disappearing inch by inch.

"Oh fuck, fuck! Gods you're huge, it hurts so good." Liam cried, as he felt his virgin anus being forcibly stretched open by Noah's long thick cock.

"Just a little more, it's almost all the way in, baby" Noah muttered. Sweat forming at his temples, he positioned his hands firmly on Liam's hips holding him tightly in place as he continued his relentless conquest. Finally, Noah bottomed out, feeling his tight balls rest snugly against Liam's perinium, cock deeply buried inside that deliciously tight hole. He paused a moment to allow the muscles of his lover's ass to accommodate his girth, growing more aroused as Liam moaned and cried and writhed at the pleasure-pain of being impaled.

"Make love to me. Stretch my ass wide and fill me with your cum"

Liam begged breathlessly a few moments later, looking at Noah over his shoulder and pushing back.

Noah smiled and began moving slowly, withdrawing and then plunging his cock gently yet deeper inside with every thrust. Soon he was pulling nearly all the way out before slamming back in again and again. Liam moaned and squirmed, his own cock fisted in his hand, arousing Noah further as he began fucking him in earnest, getting rougher and rougher. They both grunted and groaned at the force of their fucking, the slapping of balls against balls joining in to create a symphony of sex that echoed around the room. Suddenly Noah stopped, buried deep inside Liam and leaned forward to kiss the back of his sweaty neck.

"Roll over and lift your knees for me" He grated, his voice rough with unspent passion as he pulled his incredibly rock-hard cock out of Liam's ass and watched as the hole slowly closed, swollen and ready for more. Liam scrambled to obey and quickly lifted his legs, gripping his knees wide, spread and eager for penetration.

Without preamble, Noah shoved himself back into Liam, his thrusts forceful and steady. Their eyes locked as his driving motions came harder and faster, his need more urgent. He grabbed at Liam's knees and rolled his hips further allow for deeper penetration and to watch his own glistening cock hammering in and out of his lover. It was an erotic sight, made doubly so as he saw Liam cruelly twist his own nipples, his voice shredding the air around them with pleasured cries.

An incoherent mess of words and emotions tumbled from Liam's mouth at each push of Noah's thick dick. His insides felt stretched and torn and swollen, the pleasure of Noah's taking of his virginity pushing his mind into a tangle of emotions. His own dick was steadily leaking precum, ropes of it oozing out with every penetrating thrust that stretched him further. As Noah's huge cock pushed and rubbed against something deep inside him, rays of pleasure shot inside Liam's mind. He was close to shooting his load, a pressure building up inside him that he couldn't hold back much longer.

"Give me your seed, I need you to cum inside me" A desperately aroused Liam moaned, begging for the culmination of their lovemaking. His hand fisted his own length, fucking it as hard as Noah reamed his ass. He wanted to feel the hot jets of cum deep inside as his lover marked him.

Noah, skating on the edge of blinding fulfillment himself, nodded once and doubled his movements, his cock hammering in and out of Liam's tightly stretched entrance with uncoordinated, forceful jerks. His balls slapped lewdly against Liam's ass, the moans and ragged cries of their lovemaking filling the cabin as they both reached the point of no return.

With a great cry, Noah felt tingles race up his spine as he shoved his expanding cock as far as he could inside Liam and held himself there, shooting his seed deep inside his lover's rectum as he reached his orgasm. With the feel of Noah's cum spurting inside him, the hot, forceful jets unerringly hitting that wonderfully sensitive spot, Liam felt intense rapture break and roll through his body. He fisted his cock one last time, strangling it as ropes of his own seed shot over his chest, hitting his neck, his face and the bedding around him, his orgasm left him breathless as he felt the Noah's twitching cock release the last jets of hot cum deep inside him.

Knees weak with pleasure, Noah collapsed on top of Liam, still buried inside his tight hole and gasping for air. He slowly licked the cum from Liam's neck as he nuzzled his head there. His mouth trailing to the dips in Liam's collarbone that held additional wells of jism, he tongued the spots clean and stretched down to kiss the distended nipples reddened by Liam's own cruel fingers. Liam slowly lowered his legs and wrapped them about the back of Noah's, tightening them under his butt cheeks and locking his ankles to hold him in place, sealing them together as their cocks softened. They both began to laugh breathlessly as they felt their bodies rub and twitch against one another creating more sensual sensations.

After a few moments in which they gathered their bearings, Noah shifted to pull his now flaccid penis out of Liam and settled onto the bed beside him. He rolled Liam over and tenderly petted the swollen and oozing rosette that he had just reamed into fulfillment. Reaching for a soft damp cloth, his fingers were gentle as he massaged and cleaned Liam's abused posterior. That done, he kissed it gently, nuzzling it in gratitude and licking away a few stray drops of his own seed. He tossed the cloth aside and rolled to pull Liam into a comfortable position, resting full bodied onto his chest, Noah's legs spread to cradle Liam in the shelter of his embrace. In the gentle quiet that enveloped them, they breathed in the same rhythm. Noah's gaze remained fixed on Liam, who traced his fingers along the contours of Noah's chest, playfully entwining them in the soft curls of his chest hair.

Breaking the tranquil hush, Noah's voice filled the air, curiosity lacing his words, "What's on your mind?"

Liam's lips curled into a tender smile, his eyes locked onto Noah's. "I'm thinking that I want to experience every day like this," Liam replied, his gaze unwavering, emotion shining in his expression.

"I know," Noah replied with a warm grin, the air between them heavy with unspoken emotions. But the potential for a different existence wasn't far from their thoughts. "Things are simple on the ship; we can just be ourselves. But I'm aware that will change once we arrive in the Elven realm," Noah confessed wistfully. He felt Liam's body tense against him, the destination looming on their horizon would be laden with unknown challenges.

Liam's concern was etched across his features as he spoke, "Will our relationship still be the same when you're there, and your grandmother is pushing politics down your throat?"

After a brief pause, Noah replied, his voice gentle and earnest. "Liam, no matter the circumstances, my feelings for you won't change. Yes, my grandmother will undoubtedly have her own agendas, especially in the Elven realm. She'll aim for alliances and positions of influence, but I promise you this: I won't let anything come between us. Your safety and happiness are as important to me as my own."

Liam's eyes softened as he listened to Noah's reassuring words. He intertwined his fingers with Noah's, a gesture of unity and trust. "I believe you, Noah. And I'll be right there by your side, facing whatever challenges come our way. You're my partner, remember?"

Noah smiled, his heart warming at Liam's unwavering support. "You're right, I'll be right by your side."

With their fingers still entwined, they lay there in the dim light of the cabin, the gentle rocking of the ship beneath them. The motion of the ship lulled them both to sleep, still wrapped together naked in a warm embrace.

Part 3

Chapter 20:
The Tempest

Noah and Liam strolled onto the deck, their fingers entwined as they emerged from their cabin. The night before had been profound, deepening their connection and solidifying their physical attraction to each other. They carried themselves with a newfound confidence, their bond strengthened.

Harbin manned the ship's helm, diligently mapping their route to navigate around the nearby sandbars where the Duras River converged with the Great Northern Ocean. He welcomed the boys with a friendly grin and a knowing wink, causing them both to blush, realizing that he was privy to more than they intended to reveal.

"How goes the course Harbin?" Noah asked, hoping to distract the man.

"It goes well thus far, Young Master," Harbin replied, before pointing to the horizon. "We've not long until we've navigated this river, and we reach the Ocean. I'm a wee bit concerned about those clouds in the horizon though; I fear they may be indicators of a storm coming in."

"Oh, should we be concerned?" Liam asked, stepping up.

"No, t'is nothing the Scimitar can't handle. These ships are built tough, and she's weathered many a gale in her time. That being said, you may want to let your grandmother know so she can settle down below for it. The deck shan't be a fun place to be during the storm."

Noah nodded and headed down below to warn Serena of the impending storm. Meanwhile, Liam stayed behind, sharing a companionable silence with Harbin.

"Do you think you'll require assistance with the ship during the storm?" Liam inquired cautiously.

"Aye, I'll need both you and Master Noah above deck with me. If the winds come in too strong, they might rip the ship's sails apart. I don't fancy us being stuck at sea as we try and sew them back together."

"Of course, Harbin. We'll be there to help," Liam replied, determined to be of assistance to this loyal seaman. "We'll do whatever it takes to keep the ship safe and on course."

"Good boys, the both of you. We'll get you through this no worries and get some calluses on those hands of yours while we're at it!" Harbin exclaimed, laughing.

Noah returned with Serena, who wanted to confirm preparations for the storm. She was calm yet concerned, realizing the potential dangers they might face. "Thank you for letting us know, Harbin. Is there anything I can do to help? It's good to be prepared," she said, acknowledging his consideration before heading back to her cabin to make her own preparations. Assured that the young men would help Harbin above deck.

Finally reaching the ocean, they saw the storm clouds grow closer as the wind began to pick up, causing the ship to rock gently on the waves. The sea turned choppy and restless, and the sky darkened as thunder rumbled in the distance.

Liam, Noah, and Harbin worked together to secure the ship, tightening ropes, adjusting sails, and ensuring everything was in place. The rain began to fall in heavy drops, quickly drenching them. Despite the challenging conditions, there was a sense of camaraderie and determination among the three as they battled the elements to keep the ship afloat.

As the storm intensified, lightning streaked across the sky, illuminating the turbulent waters below. The waves grew higher, crashing against the ship's sides with force. The Scimitar creaked and groaned under the strain, but the crew remained steadfast, knowing that they needed to weather the storm together. The ship itself seemed to thrum with power, resisting the pull of the ocean currents and straining against the winds. Noah sensed the spirit of the ship crying out, defying the elements as it pushed onward.

Hours passed, the storm showing no signs of easing yet they continued their with efforts. Liam and Noah exchanged glances, their hands clasping briefly in a reassuring gesture before they returned to their tasks. Strangely, the power of the storm became more potent by the minute.

Harbin's previously calm demeanor shifted, revealing his genuine concern. "I've naught seen a storm this furious 'fore; it's as if the tempest is driven by something otherworldly."

Noah's eyes narrowed as he contemplated the implications, his heart sinking at the thought. As if confirming their suspicions, all three men lifted their heads as a visceral scream erupted from the heart of the storm. A moment later Serena burst out from below deck, her expression one of panic, having heard the haunting sound through the ship's solid wooden structure.

"What was that?" She screamed into the howling wind.

Just then, a bolt of lightning struck the ocean, revealing a cluster of towering rocks jutting dramatically from the water's surface. As the Scimitar battled through the storm, drawing closer to the treacherous formation, the outlines of Sea Nymphs perched upon the rocky spires came into view, their figures illuminated by the flashes of lightning. What greeted the eye was an abomination of nature.

The Sea Nymphs emerged from the darkness, their once alluring forms twisted into grotesque shapes that sent a shiver down Serena's spine. In the intermittent bursts of lightning, she caught a horrifying glimpse of their disfigured bodies. Their once enchanting allure had given way to a perverse corruption, features now marred by a black, writhing miasma that seemed to infect their very essence. Their eyes, once the color of the sea, now glowed with an eerie crimson hue, radiating a terrifying ethereal malevolence.

"It's the same corruption that turned the King's sorcerers," Noah yelled over the roaring storm, his voice tense with realization. Liam met his gaze with equal dread, understanding the dire implications of the spreading evil.

"The release of such malevolence would spell doom for mankind; we cannot permit this corruption to spread any further," Serena replied determinedly even though her voice trembled with fear.

As if hearing them, the Nymphs began to descend from their rocks and disappeared into the ocean. They watched as the Nymphs approached the ship, their glowing eyes visible from above the water.

"Harbin, do we have weapons onboard? I think we're going to need them!" Noah cried, turning to the sailor who frozen in shock.

"Indeed we do, Young Master. There's a stash of weapons in the storage below deck," Harbin replied, snapping out of his shock and springing into action. "We'll arm ourselves and defend the ship with all we've got."

Noah turned toward Liam. "You should go below decks with my grandmother; I don't want you getting hurt."

Liam glared back defiantly. "Where you go, I go. We fight together."

Noah's expression softened, touched by Liam's determination. He nodded, realizing that Liam was too stubborn to be bargained with, even in the face of danger. "Alright, let's gather the weapons and defend this ship together."

"I'll be here as well. Perhaps I can use the winds to our advantage. They could speed us through the storm and away from these monstrosities." Serena said primly.

Noah nodded as Serena swiftly ascended the stairs to the fo'c'sle, positioning herself well in front of the ship's helm in a defensive stance. Harbin emerged, bearing a collection of steel-tipped harpoons and spears from the ship's hold, and efficiently distributed the weapons among them.

Noah and Liam assumed defensive positions on the port side, while Harbin positioned himself near the starboard. They braced themselves as the nymphs drew nearer, with the Scimitar's enchanted spirit skillfully navigating the storm's currents and waves on their behalf as they fended off their assailants.

Noah sensed the approaching corruption before he even saw its source. The foul presence lingered in the air, a tangible malevolence that heralded the emergence of the corrupted nymphs. With a vicious leap, one emerged from the sea, landing on the ship's deck with a sickening thud. Its toothy grin revealed pointed fangs as it lunged at Noah with claws extended, its form contorted by the twisting darkness within it.

In a swift and coordinated motion, Noah and Liam raised their spears, striking the nymph in unison. The steel-tipped weapons pierced its corrupted flesh, releasing a torrent of black miasma. The nymph writhed in agony, its body contorting as the corruption seeped from its wounds, before falling back into the ocean.

From behind them, the sounds of Harbin's battle with another nymph echoed. Curiosity getting the better of him, Noah turned his head to check on the seasoned sailor's progress. To his relief, Harbin seemed to be handling himself well in the fight, his weathered demeanor disguising his determination. With a powerful thrust, Harbin hurled his harpoon with precision, impaling a nymph in mid-air just as it attempted to launch itself onto the ship's deck.

"Ye won't be claimin' this old sailor today!" Harbin's voice carried on the wind, his mad laughter mingling with the storm's fury.

At the ship's helm, Serena's mastery over the elements was evident. She harnessed the power of the wind, channeling it into the ship's sails with remarkable finesse. Her control amplified the ship's speed, propelling them further away from the approaching monsters. The Scimitar responded to her command like an eager puppy, cutting through the tumultuous waves as she guided them to safety.

Noah's attention was yanked away as he heard Liam's anguished cry. Whipping around, his heart clenched at the sight: Liam was pinned against the ship's mast, a pike driven into the solid wood, with a nymph desperately pulling itself along the length of the weapon. The pike was embedded in the creature's twisted flesh, and it writhed in a frenzied dance, swiping at Liam with its claws.

In that agonizing moment, time seemed to stretch. Noah's heart pounded as he witnessed a claw descending, slicing into Liam's arm and drawing blood. Anguish and fury surged within him, his protective instincts overwhelming. With an outstretched arm, Noah brought forth a surge of power, a tempestuous gust of wind transforming into a violent force. The wind tore into the nymph, tearing it apart and propelling its remains violently into the sea, a considerable distance away.

Serena's gasp of shock echoed in the stormy air as she witnessed Noah's emerging power. Noah, however, was consumed by his concern for Liam. Ignoring Serena's reaction, he rushed to Liam's side. Liam was sprawled on the ship's deck, visibly shaken and in pain, cradling his wounded arm where the nymph's claws had torn into his skin.

"Are you alright?" Noah asked, worried.

"I'll be fine" Liam grimaced, getting to his feet while wrapping his arm with a piece of cloth he grabbed from the nearby decking.

"We have to put an end to this soon; I don't think my grandmother can maintain this much longer," Noah exclaimed, his gaze shifting worriedly towards Serena, who appeared increasingly fatigued as the force of the wind began to wane.

The nymphs circled the ship, and as if hearing this they swarmed it again. Several of them clung to the starboard side, their screams of fury piercing the air. Harbin fought valiantly, but the sheer numbers overwhelmed him. He roared in defiance, harpoon and spear in hand, striking down nymphs left and right. However, for every monster he defeated, two more seemed to take its place. Slowly but surely, he was being pushed back towards the ship's center. Blood began to stain his shirt, as various claws found their mark.

Noah and Liam were facing a similar onslaught. Dozens of monsters emerged from the sea, charging at them with frenzied aggression. Despite their efforts, they found themselves overwhelmed and were forced to retreat towards the ship's center, where the battle was now converging. The situation grew increasingly dire as the winds finally failed, and Serena was unable to muster any more power to drive the Scimitar forward.

The ship's spirit seemed to react to the chaos, its displeasure palpable as it bucked against the onslaught of monstrous attackers. It strained against the current and the lack of wind, managing to propel itself forward through sheer determination, yet even with its efforts, it couldn't outrun the relentless creatures.

The sea began to churn ominously, giving birth to a maelstrom. The ship proved feeble against the forceful pull, gradually succumbing to the swirling vortex as the water whipped into a frenzied funnel. Amidst this turmoil, the nymphs seemed to revel, their eerie chatter rising in macabre pleasure.

A colossal tentacled monster emerged from the depths of the vortex with a deafening roar, its massive jaws snapping hungrily at the air. Positioned at the heart of the maelstrom, the creature's writhing tentacles churned the waters, fueling the vortex's pull. These appendages bore the same taint of demonic miasma, twisting and contorting in unnatural ways. Irresistibly, the ship was drawn toward the center, the monster's rage increasing as the vessel neared its monstrous grasp.

Noah's heart clenched as he gazed at Liam, who clung to his side in a mixture of fear and helplessness. The monsters on deck emitted eerie chittering sounds, their delight evident as they anticipated their grim victory. Harbin stood by their side, still battling against the odds, but even he could feel the futility of their efforts. Serena had pushed herself to the brink, fighting against the storm's onslaught until her strength finally gave out, and she collapsed in a heap of exhaustion on the wooden deck.

Noah's emotions were a mix of detachment and simmering rage as he observed the sinister anticipation in the eyes of the demonic creatures. "Get down and stay down," he yelled, his tone commanding, his gaze shifting between Liam and Harbin.

Raising both hands, Noah surrendered to the surge of power within him as he relinquished his control. He ascended into the air, a sense of detachment enveloping him as he felt like a passenger in his own body. The ethereal force gripped him, casting a crimson hue over his surroundings. Flames materialized all around him, engulfing his body and incinerating the remnants of his tattered clothing.

"By the Gods," Harbin exclaimed in shock as he dropped to the ship's deck beside Liam, utterly astonished by the awe-inspiring display of elemental power.

With a simple gesture, a ring of fire formed around the Scimitar, closing in tightly. The monstrous creatures let out agonized shrieks as the flames came into contact with them for it burned with an otherworldly white heat. The flames consumed them in an instant, reducing their forms to ash that fell upon the ship's deck and into the roiling seas. The air was filled with their anguished cries, only to be silenced as their existence was obliterated.

The remaining creatures in the water made desperate attempts to escape the fiery onslaught, but Noah's power proved unrelenting. As he extinguished the flames, his eyes blazed a brilliant blue, reminiscent of the ocean itself. With a mere motion of his hands, the water around the creatures seemed to solidify, rising into the air in the form of suspended bubbles. Helpless, the creatures writhed within these watery prisons until Noah's control over the water became absolute, causing it to freeze into solid blocks of ice. Their struggles ceased as their life force faded away, trapped within the icy tombs that had become their final resting place.

With the nymphs handled, the force controlling Noah turned and faced the monster at the center of the maelstrom. It lashed out at the ship, a tentacle smashing against one of the solid masts and snapping it sending slivers of lumber across the ship and into the air. Noah's form didn't tremble or react, reaching out with both hands as he harnessed his elemental powers once more.

Beneath the churning waves, the ocean floor convulsed as towering stone columns emerged from its depths. These colossal pillars swiftly encircled the monstrous entity, seeking to subdue its thrashing form. The monster's frenzied struggles were met with unyielding dominance, as the columns shattered, they gave way to fresh ones that rose in their place. Amidst this tumult, sharp stone spikes emerged from the water like harpoons, impaling the creature and rendering it immobile. Noah's eyes burned with righteous anger, his intent clear as he commanded the very earth itself to restrain and punish the demonic entity.

A colossal sphere of searing flames materialized above the ensnared monster, and its defiant cries echoed through the air as Noah directed the fiery barrage. Numerous smaller spheres of fire followed suit, descending upon the creature like celestial meteors. Upon impact, the flames devoured its flesh, inciting anguished shrieks that reverberated across the sea. Unstoppable, Noah continued to command the barrage, each fireball further wreaking destruction on the entity as it writhed and burned. The surrounding waters churned and boiled from the infernal heat.

At last, the monstrous entity met its end and dissipated into oblivion. Its once-frenzied limbs fell to ash, and the maelstrom gradually subsided. The storm immediately began to abate, the waves calming and the torrential rain gradually relenting. The turmoil receded, unveiling the aftermath of the struggle — the lifeless forms of the defeated monsters floating amidst the lingering traces of blood and miasma in the water.

Noah's form descended from the air, his legs wobbling on the deck as the immense power retreated, leaving him drained and exhausted. He collapsed onto the ship's deck, and Liam rushed over, cradling Noah's head in his lap, his tears mingling with the remnants of rain.

"Is it over now?" Noah's voice trembled as he spoke, his eyes half-lidded from the exertion.

"Yes, you did it. Rest now, I've got you," Liam whispered, his voice breaking with emotion. Harbin joined them, placing a comforting hand on Liam's shoulder.

"We'll take it from here, Young Master," Harbin said, a newfound respect in his eyes as he surveyed the scene of their victory. He stepped away, his gaze shifting to Serena, who still lay unconscious by the ship's helm. With a concerned expression, he moved towards her to ensure her safety and well-being.

Noah's body finally gave in to the overwhelming exhaustion. His eyelids grew heavy, and he felt himself slipping into the comforting embrace of sleep, the tumultuous events fading away as his consciousness drifted into the realm of dreams.

Chapter 21:
After the Storm

L iam's restless footsteps echoed on the deck, his worry palpable in the air. Harbin and Serena observed him with empathy, aware of the turmoil brewing within him.

"Two days… it feels like an eternity," Liam muttered, his voice laced with frustration. "Why hasn't he woken up?"

Harbin leaned against the ship's railing, his gaze distant yet thoughtful. "He's been through somethin' extraordinary, lad. It takes time for the body and soul to recover from such exertion, and the forces he wielded."

Serena nodded in agreement, her voice gentle. "Remember, he displayed an immense power that no one in the family's history has ever mustered. It's possible that he's in a deep restorative state."

Liam's eyes remained fixed on the spot where the cabin was beneath their feet, where Noah lay unconscious. "I know, but I just wish there was a way to help him."

Harbin rested a hand on Liam's shoulder. "Sometimes, all we can do is wait. He'll wake when he's ready."

Liam's shoulders slumped with a sigh, "I suppose you're right… I just want him to be okay."

"Noah will be alright Liam. We just need to give him time." Serena said comfortingly, moving to hug the young man who so clearly loved her grandson.

"You're right, Serena," Liam replied, his voice wavering with his emotions. "I just… I've never felt this helpless before."

Serena held him close, her voice gentle as she whispered, "Love makes us vulnerable, Liam. But it also gives us strength."

Liam's grip on Serena tightened for a moment, feeling gratitude for her wisdom. "Thank you."

Harbin nodded in agreement, his expression supportive. "She's right, lad. We're all here, and Noah's a strong one. He'll pull through."

Liam nodded, stepping from Serena's comforting embrace. "I'm going to go and sit with him. I feel like I need to be there for him in case he wakes up."

Harbin and Serena observed Liam's departure, their gaze following him as he descended the stairs. A companionable silence settled between them. After a moment, Harbin broke the silence, a mischievous grin on his weathered face. "So, should I be addressing you as Empress now?"

Serena chuckled at his playful tone, shaking her head with a knowing smile. "Those days are far behind me." Harbin's laughter joined hers, the sound mingling with the salt-kissed breeze that swept across the ship's deck.

"Aye, yet you once were the Empress, and the lad below decks is the heir to the throne," Harbin remarked, his tone growing more serious.

Serena looked at him, her eyes curious and cautious. "Are you considering revealing our identities?"

Harbin shook his head, his weathered features thoughtful. "No, I've no intention of meddling in matters that don't concern me. Besides, I've no desire to draw the ire of either of you. I'd rather not find myself looking like one of those monsters we faced yesterday."

Serena's lips curved into a wry smile. "A prudent choice, indeed."

"Besides, I've taken a liking to the pair of you. Adventure like this wasn't something I expected in my old age," Harbin continued, his laughter carrying across the water.

"If you believe this has been an adventure so far, brace yourself. There's much more ahead of us, and a lot to accomplish. Noah has a destiny, and he'll need support on this journey," Serena said, her gaze carrying weight.

"And you're hoping I'll be among those supporters?" Harbin responded, his tone indicating he comprehended the unspoken request. Serena silently nodded.

"Well, you'll have my aid. Can't say how much it's worth, given I'm just a weathered old sailor," Harbin replied with a grin.

*****

Liam restlessly occupied the chair beside the bed, his patience wearing thin as he stood vigil for Noah's awakening. During the first day of Noah's slumber, Liam had brushed it off as mere exhaustion from the exertion of his arcane powers. However, as the second day neared its end, anxiety had taken over. A deep worry gnawed at him – the fear that Noah might not rouse from his sleep, leaving Liam alone in a world growing ever more perilous.

Liam's voice was a soft murmur as he spoke to the sleeping Noah. "You know, if you hadn't arrived when you did, I don't think I'd be alive today." He let out a soft sigh, as he confided to the unconscious form of his love. "I had a plan to end things before they could hand me over to the King, and I would've done it too. I wasn't going to be his plaything." The weight of his words hung in the air.

"But then you showed up and changed everything," Liam's voice held a wealth of emotion. A soft chuckle escaped him. "I thought you were a figment of my imagination, like some Prince Charming come to rescue me from a tower. It felt unreal, too good to be true. And then, not only that, but you fell in love with me." His voice wavered as he continued, emotions clogging his throat. "For almost my entire life, I've been seen as the son of a wealthy merchant, nothing more. People have always seen my father's status, not me. They grovel in his presence, and I've felt invisible. But you, you see me for who I truly am, beyond those expectations. And now, it's as if you're slipping away, and you won't wake up." Tears welled up and trailed down his cheeks, his voice cracking with vulnerability, "I need you to wake up, because without you, I'm back to being alone."

Unable to help himself, Liam slid into the bed beside Noah, his head finding a resting place on Noah's chest. Even though Noah remained unconscious, the physical closeness provided him with comfort,. Noah's heart continued to beat steadily and strongly; the only calming influence Liam had in this moment.

Liam started as he felt Noah's arms enfold him, looking up he watched Noah's eyes open blearily.

"You're not alone, and you're not going to be alone so long as you're with me," Noah said, his voice still hoarse with sleep.

"You're awake!" Liam exclaimed, sitting up quickly and passionately kissing him. "You must need water and food! I should go get it" he rambled excitedly. With a gentle smile, Noah's arms pulled him back down, snugly holding him as they shared a deeply intimate moment.

"Yes, I'm awake, no I don't need any water or food," he whispered softly, his voice still laced with drowsiness. "Your story, your presence, it brought me back. In my solitude, I found you, and you've given me a connection I never knew was missing. Growing up with just my grandmother, it was good but often lonely even though she's been my anchor all my life. Having you here now has brought a new light and warmth that I never thought I'd find." He leaned in, their lips meeting in a tender kiss that spoke volumes of their shared emotions.

Liam sighed contentedly, nestling his head back onto Noah's chest as they shared a tranquil moment of togetherness.

"So what did I miss?" Noah's voice broke the silence, shifting the conversation's focus.

"You've been asleep for nearly three days, since the monsters attacked," Liam explained, his words carrying a mix of relief and concern. "We've been working to repair the ship and clean up the aftermath. We had to find a sheltered bay and cut down a tree to replace the mast that was destroyed by that leviathan." His tone was eager, glad to have Noah back and ready to catch him up on what had transpired while he was unconscious.

"It's strange," Noah began, his expression troubled. "I have these fragments of memory, like shattered pieces of a mirror, but the complete picture is missing. It's as if I'm a spectator in my own body when that power takes over. I can't control it, and it's terrifying to think about what I might become." He looked at Liam, his eyes seeking understanding. "But having you by my side, knowing that you accept me despite all this… it gives me hope that I won't be consumed by whatever the power is."

Liam listened attentively, his fingers tracing abstract patterns on Noah's chest as he spoke. "It must be frightening, to feel like you're not in control of your own actions," Liam empathized softly. "But you were able to protect us and defeat those monsters. If you hadn't done that, we would all be dead right now. That's something to be proud of, even if you don't remember every detail." He looked up at Noah with reassuring eyes.

"As long as this power doesn't harm the ones I love, I'm glad it's a part of me. According to my grandmother, it's a gift bestowed by the Gods to our lineage. If that's true, I can only hope their intentions are good," Noah mused, his eyes reflecting his hope and uncertainty.

Liam nodded, but said with determination, "We'll figure it out, Noah. We'll find a way to control it, to harness its potential without letting it control you completely. And if it truly was given by the Gods, then they must have intended it for a reason. We'll use it to protect those we love and to make a difference in this world." He reached out and held Noah's hand, giving it a reassuring squeeze.

"In the meantime, I think I have an idea of how I can cheer you up…" Liam said, a smirk growing on his face.

Noah raised an eyebrow, intrigued. "Oh really? And what might that idea be?" he asked, a playful glint in his eyes.

"You'll find out soon enough," Liam responded with a grin, his hands trailing down Noah's body as he playfully uncovered them from beneath the sheets.

Noah's lips curled into a mischievous smile as he watched Liam's movements. "I'm definitely looking forward to it," he murmured, anticipation evident in his voice.

Liam smiled as he reached Noah's groin and pulled Noah's undergarments down to his thick thighs, exposing his flaccid cock. Leaning down, he nuzzled into it breathing in Noah's musky scent. He opened his mouth, tongue darting out to tease the tip of Noah's dick, then drawing the whole of it in his hot mouth. Instantly his sensitive cock responded and began to harden.

Liam leaned back laughing softly, amused by the sight of Noah's instant arousal. He shifted to take Noah's rapidly growing cock back into his mouth, swirling his tongue around the sensitive glans and down the shaft. As he did, he felt it growing instantly larger in his mouth, the mushroom head hitting the back of his throat with surprising quickness. Fighting his gag reflex, Liam relaxed his throat and pushed his head down further, feeling Noah's long fat cock slide down deep as he did. He stayed there, impaled on his love's turgid length and swallowed as his tongue rubbed the underside of the head.

"Oh fuck, you're so good at this" Noah moaned above him, as his hands threaded through Liam's hair holding him in place on his cock, fighting the need to savagely fuck his face.

Liam's stretched lips twitched in a smile, unable to reply as his mouth was full of Noah's delicious meat. His hand slid under Noah's balls to cup and squeeze gently, fingers then shifting to delicately probe at his anus and Noah accommodated him by spreading his legs further. All the while, his head bobbed up and down, gagging a little as his uvula was tickled but he forged on, plunging his mouth onto Noah's cock until his neck ached, then settling it into his throat again to swirl his tongue around the shaft. Quickening his pace once more while rubbing and pressing in on that dark little bud, his wet slurping sounds mingled with Noah's frantic grunts of pleasure.

Liam felt Noah's balls tighten as he neared orgasm and pulled back. He released Noah's thick man-meat with a loud pop, saliva and precum coating it in a glistening sheen. He stood from the bed and hurriedly shed his clothing to climb on top of Noah. He attempted to position himself above Noah's long erect prick but Noah stayed him and said, "turn around on your hands and knees. I want to eat that ass while you suck me some more with that gifted mouth."

Grinning, Liam quickly obeyed, turning and presenting himself while he once again gobbled down Noah's turgid length. In turn, Noah reached up and spread Liam's ass, then pulled him down to sit on his face, his tongue a pointed instrument with which to penetrate that winking eye. Without ceremony, he slid the thumb of each hand into the dank hole alongside his tongue to stretch the ring of muscle mercilessly. Guiding Liam's ass up, he watched as he added his index fingers to continue opening Liam up. In the meantime, he held onto his control as Liam did his best to swallow him whole.

After several pleasurable minutes in which only moans and erotic sounds issued forth, Liam pulled away and turned to swiftly straddle Noah again. He leaned down and passionately kissed him, each tasting themselves on the other's lips. Noah stared in awe at Liam's gloriously naked form above him as Liam murmured, "Don't move, let me do all the work."

Noah nodded eagerly, and Liam adjusted his position so his aching hole was resting on the tip of Noah's saliva-slick cock. Bearing down slowly, he forced his tight hole to expand around Noah's hard member, bouncing slightly to help ease the sting of the tight ring of muscle that resisted at first, until finally giving into the inevitable. Despite having been prepared by Noah's attentions, he still felt the sting of pleasure-pain as his tight asshole was stretched wide open. Biting his lip, he held back moans as that huge tool sank deeper and deeper inside him, forcing its way past the tight muscles.

Noah held still, allowing Liam to control the pace. He watched in fascination as Liam struggled to take all of him and resisted the urge to buck up and shove his cock deep inside Liam's ass. The sight of Liam's sweaty form leaning in front of him as he impaled himself on his cock was beautiful, and Noah couldn't help but reach down to grasp onto Liam's own substantial cock. As Liam inched his way further onto his prick, Noah slid his hand along Liam's shaft making Liam moan and sigh in pleasure at the dual sensation of being penetrated and played with at the same time.

Finally, Liam felt his ass settle on Noah's lap, it was a glorious feeling of being stuffed to the brink. Noah's balls were trapped against his own thighs and the back of Liam's tight hole, his thick cock bounced and quivered deep inside Liam whose insides stretched to accommodate the girth.

Giving himself only a moment to adjust to the feeling of fullness, Liam began to bounce up and down, riding Noah's cock like a horse, feeling it gliding in and out of his anus with every frenetic bounce. His thighs trembled as he used Noah's cock like a stud, and he moaned as he strained his ass to take it in deeper and with more force. He increased his pace, bouncing up and down on Noah's cock with more violence, the initial pain he'd felt as he'd taken Noah's cock had long since turned to pleasure, and he wanted Noah's cock to push and press against that spot inside him which made him see stars.

Beneath him, Noah began to thrust, unable to hold himself back any longer. His arousal at the sight of Liam bouncing up and down and his cock disappearing into his lover's asshole had been too much to handle. He swiftly reached up and grabbed Liam's hips as he thrusted upward slamming his cock into Liam's man-cunt. With each thrust Liam cried out above him, and his cock steadily leaked a clear stream of precum onto Noah's abdomen.

"Fuck, oh please! Please! Don't stop. Fuck me harder, make me bleed," Liam cried in pleasure, as he pitched forward against Noah's chest.

Noah eagerly fucked him faster, savagely pounding his cock up into Liam's ass like a battering ram. Liam moaned and whined incoherently into his chest, each brutal thrust bouncing him forcefully upward, his dick sliding tightly against Noah's sweaty abdomen and driving him further to the edge of oblivion and release. Noah felt the pressure building up inside his spine and knew it was just a matter of moments until he would reach his orgasm as well.

"Where do you want it?" He asked, panting for breath as he continued sledgehammering his expanding meat into Liam's swollen and aching asshole.

"Inside me, fill me up with your hot cum." Liam begged, hands clamped onto Noah's chest bracing himself.

"I can't hold it anymore, I need to shoot" Noah roared, thrusting ferociously upward one final time as he clamped Liam down firmly on his cock. Jets of his hot seed shot deep inside Liam's distended hole, once again hitting that sweet spot that catapulted Liam over the edge. Liam cried out in pleasure, his own cock spewing seed on Noah's abdomen in waves.

Weak with his release, he collapsed back onto Noah's chest coating himself in his own cum. Too weak to move, he just lay there as the feeling of his release overwhelmed him. Noah continued thrusting gently into him, shooting every last bit of seed inside him before finally stopping.

Still joined together, Noah wrapped his arms around Liam, savoring the warmth of his body and the basking in the sheen of their sweat. He absorbed the moment, feeling Liam's heart beating rapidly and the rise and fall of his chest against his own.

"I love you" Noah said simply, gazing down at Liam.

"I love you too," Liam replied with a soft smile, his eyes locked onto Noah's in joy.

Chapter 22:

Elven Realms

In the wake of the ensorcelled tempest and the monstrous attack, the sea had regained its tranquility. Several days had passed, and their voyage continued without any further hindrance or storms. This period was dedicated to repairing the ship, meticulously erasing scorch marks from the wood caused by Noah's elemental display and restoring it to its former gleaming state.

The ship itself seemed to respond with appreciation and contentment, its spirit resonating with joy as it sensed the repairs taking place and the attentive care being lavished upon it. Their journey gained momentum, the ship seeming eager to resume its course now that the repairs were complete.

Noah approached Harbin, who was stationed near the ship's helm, carefully studying the ship's map. Harbin looked up with a friendly smile as Noah approached. "Well, hello there, Young Master. How are you feeling?"

Noah's cheeks tinged with a hint of embarrassment at the continued concern the others showed for his well-being, even after several days of recovery. "I'm well, thank you," he replied. He gestured toward the sea map that had captured Harbin's attention. "How is our course?" Noah inquired, his interest in their journey evident in his voice.

"Ah, we've not far now until we pass by the Elven city of Falnir," Harbin replied, his tone disgusted as he mentioned the city.

Noah picked up on the change in Harbin's demeanor and his reaction to Falnir. Concern creased his brow as he questioned, "Is there something wrong with Falnir? You seem to have an aversion for it."

"All sailors have a dislike for Falnir. The Elves there are wretched, and you can't trust 'em further than you can throw 'em. I docked there once when I was a young man on my first merchantman voyage, and they robbed us blind. The ship was damaged in a gale, and we had to stop and ask for aid. They took everything of value from the ship, charged extortionate amounts, and nearly bankrupted the vessel's owners. The Elven folk may be known to be fair and kind, but the ones in Falnir are different. You'd do best to avoid 'em yourselves, they're a dishonorable lot entirely," Harbin warned, his voice laced with bitterness and disdain.

"Noted, my grandmother seems to have the same view of them as well," Noah responded evenly.

"My father agreed with your opinion, Harbin. He refused to have any dealings with them whatsoever and had a company-wide policy that none of our ships were to dock there under any circumstances," Liam chimed in as he came up from the deck below.

"Aye! 'Tis why I joined up and came aboard this vessel," Harbin laughed heartily.

The hours drifted by as the Scimitar gracefully sailed along the picturesque coastline. Serena had settled into a comfortable chair set up on deck, engrossed in a book she had found in her cabin. She had recovered quite well from the wounds she had suffered as well as the toll from commanding the winds. Meanwhile, Noah and Liam engaged in a friendly game of chess at a small table they had placed nearby. Harbin, ever attentive to the ship's course, stood firmly behind the ship's wheel, occasionally breaking into a merry tune while he guided their vessel.

"Ha, checkmate! I finally got you! It only took 5 rounds, but I finally won!" Noah exclaimed excitedly, getting up and doing a little celebratory dance to mark his victory over Liam.

"Did you actually win though, or did I just let you win out of pity?" Liam asked, his tone playful.

Noah halted abruptly, his eyes widening in realization. "No, you wouldn't be that devious. Wait, would you?"

Liam met Noah's gaze with a sly smile. "Wouldn't I?" he replied, his tone dripping with playful mischief.

Serena let out a snort of laughter from her chair behind them, and Noah turned to look at her with an expression of mock betrayal. He could clearly see the amusement in her eyes at his dilemma.

Harbin playfully chimed in, "Ah, young love! The battles on the chessboard are just as fierce as the ones against sea monsters, it seems."

Noah managed to regain his composure, shaking his head and laughing. "Well, at least I can still claim victory, even if it was with a little help."

Liam grinned and leaned in, whispering, "Just remember, my strategic mind might have let you win this time, but next time, I'll make you work for it."

The banter continued as the ship sailed on, a light-hearted atmosphere enveloping them all. This atmosphere was cut short though, as Harbin announced they would shortly be passing Falnir on the port side. Noah and Liam moved the railing along the port, and Serena joined them shortly afterward.

They were met with a grim sight as the ship ventured further, the once vibrant green forest now thinning and decaying. The air grew oppressive, laden with an eerie pollution that seemed to seep into their very beings and made their lungs feel heavy. The ship's passage revealed a sinister scene: voracious machines mercilessly mowing down trees, while sickly, pallid Elves worked in fields, cultivating a crop that seemed to suck the energy from everything around it.

The Elves appeared to be afflicted by a grotesque infection, their skin marred by a diseased corruption that seemed to devour their flesh. The horrified gazes of the shipmates fixed upon an Elf who stumbled into the path of the tree-felling machines, yet no cries of alarm or concern emanated from the ranks of others. The other Elves seemed to either not notice or not care to stop and help their comrade.

As they neared Falnir, the city loomed like a sickened specter in the distance. The once graceful structures now exuded an unhealthy aura, coated in a heavy layer of soot. Tall chimneys spewed forth thick plumes of acrid smoke, darkening the sky. The waters flowed murky and tainted, choked by refuse and oily residues. Lifeless fish floated on the surface; their existence extinguished by the suffocating grip of industrial pollution.

"Something is gravely amiss; this is not the Falnir I remember," Serena said, her voice quivering with alarm.

"Indeed, Falnir might not have been a fond memory for me, but this is a distortion far beyond what I recall," Harbin agreed, his tone grave.

"The Elves derive their vitality from their harmony with nature, yet this city appears to be a direct contradiction to that principle. How can such a stark deviation exist?" Noah questioned, the scene conflicting with the teachings he had received from his grandmother over the years.

"It defies reason. It might provide some insight into the condition of the Elves we observed toiling in the fields, but the underlying mystery is why this aberration has come to pass," Serena remarked.

"I think I know what is going on," Liam's finger pointed towards a massive industrial pipe extending into the ocean as they sailed past the city's filthy harbor. With a grim expression, Noah followed his gaze and felt a sinking feeling in his gut as he recognized the black, noxious liquid miasma streaming out from the pipe. The resemblance between this miasma and the corruption that had consumed the King's sorcerers was undeniable. The Elves were producing this toxic substance in alarming quantities and dumping it directly into the ocean, killing or perverting everything it touched.

Noah paled as understanding dawned upon him. "This is how it happened. This miasma is contaminating everything with disease and decay, destroying the environment. The Elves are falling ill under its influence, and the natural world is perishing."

Spoke with desperation, her eyes reflecting the weight of the revelation. "The only plausible conclusion is that the city has succumbed to the King's control. Our hopes for allies now rest solely on Elnoth and Vardrun."

"It's not just about the land. If this city continues to release that toxic liquid, the entire sea will suffer the same fate. Something must be done to stop them. We've witnessed what it did to those sea nymphs, but now imagine the entire ocean becoming a breeding ground for those monstrous creatures!" Liam spoke, his voice filled with dread.

Noah shuddered in response, moving closer to Liam and holding onto him tightly. "I'd rather not imagine that."

"Nor I," Harbin said from the helm, steering the ship away from the city. As they sailed further away, the air gradually cleared, and Falnir faded into the horizon behind them.

"Once we reach Elnoth, this will certainly give us much to discuss with Queen Efaldrin," Serena said, sitting back down.

"Queen Efaldrin?" Noah asked.

"Yes, Queen Efaldrin is the leader of Elnoth. Her husband passed away over a century ago, and she has been ruling the city in his stead until their heir comes of age. Elves don't reach maturity until they're two hundred and fifty years old. The last time I saw the heir to the throne, he was celebrating his eighty-fifth birthday," Serena mused openly, reminiscing about past visits to Elnoth during more prosperous times.

"Does the Queen have other family members?" Noah asked.

"Yes, she also has a daughter who would be around two hundred years old by now. I'm sure once we reach the city, they'll be celebrating her name day," Serena replied, a distant look in her eyes as she recalled her earlier plans to arrange a marriage between Noah and the Queen's daughter. Reflecting on the events of their voyage and the strong relationship Noah had developed with Liam, she realized that her plans to betroth him might be more challenging to fulfill than she had initially thought.

Liam remained quiet by Noah's side, his gaze fixed on Serena with an air of understanding. She could sense that he had an inkling that she had plans for Noah's marriage, but until she openly shared her intentions, he would hold his silence. Despite that, she was aware that Noah would likely acquiesce to her plan if she framed it as vital for their survival.

Even though Noah was deeply in love with Liam, Serena was determined to ensure that he would fulfill his duties to his legacy and destiny.

*****

Noah and Liam stood on the deck, nervousness washing over them as they observed the graceful spires and majestic towers in the distance drawing nearer. In the week that had elapsed after passing by Falnir, they had remained close, but the apprehension among them all had heightened as the ship sailed closer to Elnoth. As they finally reached the Elven city, the young men realized that their lives were on the brink of a significant transformation.

Serena, adorned in elegant and formal attire, approached the young men. Her insistence had led to both Liam and Noah also donning similarly formal garments, the clothes seeming slightly awkward on Liam due to their original sizing for Noah.

"You will both need to be on your best behavior," Serena commanded with a stern tone, her gaze alternating between Noah and Liam. "I will request an audience with the Queen, and Noah, you must embody the demeanor of an heir to the throne. Liam, during our time here, you are to be Noah's manservant and nothing more. It's imperative that our connection remains hidden. The revelation of your relationship could jeopardize any chance of forming an alliance."

Liam's face contorted with suppressed anger at Serena's decree, but he chose to bite his lip and reluctantly nodded in agreement. While he understood the importance of the situation, he knew that a conversation needed to be had with both Serena and Noah about this matter. He couldn't bear to suppress his feelings or hide his love for Noah, and he was determined to ensure his voice was heard.

Noah's response was a nod, his emotions swirling in a mix of anxiety and frustration. While he shared Liam's unease about concealing their relationship, the urgency of their current circumstances left little room for debate. As the city's docks came into view, he found himself preoccupied with the impending encounter and the weight of his responsibilities. He reached out, and gave Liam's hand a quick squeeze for reassurance, before releasing it and settling into a more regal demeanor as well.

Noah's reassuring touch provided a small measure of comfort to Liam, who reciprocated the squeeze with a faint smile despite his inner turmoil. With a deep breath, they composed themselves and adopted the poised demeanor befitting their roles. As the ship approached the docks of Elnoth, their hearts raced, knowing that the path ahead was uncertain for them.

Under Harbin's skillful guidance, the ship was docked smoothly, its ropes secured to the pier. The Elven harbormaster, a middle-aged elf with a gentle countenance, engaged in conversation with Harbin. As Serena's intention for a royal audience was conveyed, the harbormaster's brows lifted in a subtle show of surprise. He studied the group, his eyes lingering on their attire and Serena's dignified posture. Then, his gaze settled on Noah, a thoughtful look crossing his features. With a confirming nod, he swiftly dashed away to deliver the message to the palace.

After a short while, Harbin returned to the ship and approached Serena. "The harbormaster has dispatched a messenger to the palace. Once they receive the news, an escort will be arranged to take you to the Queen, provided she chooses to grant you an audience."

"Thank you, Harbin," Serena acknowledged. She then turned her attention to him, her expression turning concerned. "Will you be alright overseeing the ship in our absence?"

"Aye, fear not. I'll ensure the Scimitar is well taken care of. Our stores will be replenished, and I've enough funds from the company to cover any expenses we may have," Harbin reassured her with a nod.

With a nod of gratitude, Serena turned her attention back to Noah and Liam. "Remember, once we meet with the Queen, you both must maintain the facade. Noah, your future is at stake, and Liam, I understand your frustration, but our priority now is securing an alliance."

Noah and Liam exchanged a glance of unspoken understanding. They both knew the gravity of the situation and the importance of their roles in this delicate political dance.

Time passed with excruciating slowness as they awaited the harbormaster's return with news from the palace. The weight of their circumstances bore down heavily on them all, the outcome of this meeting carrying immense significance. The Scimitar, though their sanctuary, couldn't guarantee safe harboring in the face of potential political turmoil. Their options were narrowing, the uncertainty of their future looming over them.

As they waited, Serena's thoughts turned to the dwarves of Gazdun, residing in the distant northern mountains. The dwarves had historically remained detached from the affairs of other nations, preferring to maintain their neutrality. The likelihood of receiving aid from them, if Elnoth would not assist, was uncertain at best. Their journey had led them to Elnoth, yet Serena hadn't dedicated much consideration to what lay beyond this point. While she had devised plans and political strategies, the reality could now diverge significantly from her expectations.

Finally, after what seemed like an eternity, carriage with an armed guard of fourteen made its way towards the harbor. Ten soldiers, their armor a radiant silver that caught and gleamed in the sunlight led the way. Three warriors, wielding large and polished blades, marched behind an imposing Elven Commander. His long, silver-white hair was tied back in a ponytail, and his eyes were as sharp as his facial features that could have been carved from stone, adding to his formidable presence.

The soldiers halted on the wooden pier and stepped to the side. The Commander, flanked by the warriors, advanced towards them, stepping onto the Scimitar. He bowed slightly, his demeanor formal and respectful, as he addressed Serena. "Empress, Elnoth extends its welcome to you. Queen Efaldrin is prepared to receive you in the court today. My men and I are tasked with escorting you and guaranteeing your safety during your stay in our city," the Commander's voice was stern and firm, his words measured and precise.

"We are grateful for your hospitality. Might we inquire about your name, Commander?" Serena inquired respectfully.

"Apologies, Empress. I am Commander Novath, the Commander-General of the Queen's Armed Regiments," Novath replied with a formal nod.

"We are delighted to make your acquaintance," Serena said with regal formality, gesturing toward Noah.

"Allow me to introduce my grandson and heir to the throne, Noah Rostropovich, the first of his name."

"Honored, Your Majesty," Novath responded, bowing respectfully to Noah, his gaze lingering on Liam with an assessing look.

Noah acknowledged with a nod. "Thank you. This is Liam, my most trusted confidant and loyal servant," he stated, gesturing toward Liam, who offered a respectful nod to the Commander.

"Welcome to you both," Commander Novath replied, before turning back to Serena.

"The Queen awaits your presence. Please accompany us and we will send for your belongings," Commander Novath stated formally.

With a nod from Serena, the three of them followed the Commander's lead, walking behind him as he guided them away from the docks and toward a waiting horse-drawn carriage that gleamed with intricate gold and gem decorations. Taking their seats inside, they settled themselves as Novath and his men formed a protective perimeter around the carriage. The journey through the city's streets began, the carriage smoothly making its way with an air of regal elegance.

Noah allowed himself a moment of relaxation inside the privacy of the carriage, his eyes wide as he gazed at the breathtaking cityscape around them. Unlike the bleakness of Falnir, Elnoth exuded beauty and grandeur. The Elven architecture was a masterpiece of intricate design, seamlessly blending with the natural world. Towering trees grew in forms that defied nature's logic yet seemed perfectly at home.

"The elves have a unique bond with the trees here. They shape them to their needs through their songs, creating living structures that harmonize with nature. No trees are cut down, and every building you'll see in the city is a living entity," Serena explained, noticing Noah's amazed expression.

"What about weapons? How do they forge them, if they require wood?" Liam asked, curious.

"They sing to the trees, and in return, the trees offer them branches and wood to shape. The elves hold a deep reverence for nature, and they consider the trees to be sacred. They would never allow harm to befall their life-giving companions," Serena elaborated.

"It's beautiful" Noah said, feeling breathless at the nature surrounding them, even in the center of the elves' largest city and realm.

"It truly is," Serena agreed, her own admiration evident in her tone. "Elnoth has always been known for its exquisite blend of nature and architecture. It's a testament to the Elves' deep respect for the world around them."

As Noah observed the elves in the city's streets, he was captivated by their graceful presence. The contrast between these healthy, vibrant elves and the ones they had witnessed in Falnir was stark and unsettling. These elves exuded an aura of vitality and connection to their surroundings. Their luminous eyes and radiant hair reflected the harmony they shared with nature, creating an atmosphere of ethereal beauty in the city.

In contrast to the rugged and stern demeanor of the men he had encountered, the elves exhibited an innate, otherworldly beauty that appeared to be woven into their very essence. This natural allure set them apart from humans and conveyed a grace and elegance that was uniquely their own. The Elven women were even more captivating, with long tresses of flowing hair that glimmered under the sunlight. Their skin, a lighter shade of green, was adorned with iridescent freckles that added to their ethereal charm.

As the carriage gradually slowed to a stop, nearing the Queen's palace, the group inside started to reposition themselves in preparation to disembark. Commander Novath opened the carriage door, and with Serena gracefully leading the way, they stepped out onto the palace grounds. Noah and Liam followed closely behind, maintaining an air of respectful anticipation.

The palace before them was a sight to behold, constructed from the massive trunks of colossal trees that reached hundreds of feet into the sky. Towering spires made of living wood soared upwards, adorned with intricate arches and artistic fountains that graced the surroundings. The grandeur of the palace was undeniable, exuding both elegance and authority. It was evident that its inhabitants lacked nothing, and the Elven Queen's influence and affluence were palpable.

As they entered the palace courtyard, servants and guards bustled about, offering respectful bows as they passed. The thrum of anticipation filled their chests as they made their way towards the opulent audience chamber where the Queen awaited them.

As they approached the imposing doors of the audience chamber, adorned with the intricate image of the Elven crown—a depiction of two trees with their branches entwined, graced by the radiant sun filtering through the foliage—Novath addressed Serena.

"Here is where we part ways. I must offer a word of caution, if you'll allow me. The Queen's health has been ailing, and her mental state might not be as you remember. I beseech you to approach her with kindness. She holds great affection among our people, and any offense against her would not sit well with them. The court's eyes will be upon you, and your conversation with her will undoubtedly become known throughout the city before long," Novath added, his tone emphasizing the potential gravity of their interaction.

"I understand." Serena replied gracefully. "Thank you for the warning, and your discretion."

With a nod, Novath gestured toward the doors. "May your audience be fruitful and beneficial to both Elnoth and your kingdom. Please proceed."

Serena nodded in return, and with a final deep breath, she stepped forward to enter the grand audience chamber, her heart heavy with the weight of the impending conversation. Noah and Liam followed her, their expressions a mixture of curiosity and trepidation as they walked into the heart of Elnoth's power.

Chapter 23:
The Court

As Serena stepped forward with Noah and Liam following in her wake, noise in the chamber hushed with an almost reverent anticipation. The courtiers lining the walls fixed their gazes upon them, their eyes assessing and measuring every aspect of their presence.

The grandeur of the hall itself was awe-inspiring, adorned with intricate paintings depicting the rich history of Elnoth. At its focal point stood a magnificent golden throne, positioned before a carved wooden mural portraying the Elven creation myth—a monumental tree that stretched into the heavens, Elves ascending its branches toward the gods.

Seated on the throne was an Elven woman of regal stature, radiating an inner luminosity that set her apart from her kin. Her golden-white hair cascaded elegantly, her skin bore a faint green hue, and her yellow eyes seemed to hold both wisdom and sadness. A gentle smile graced her lips as she rose from her throne, approaching Serena with a warmth that contrasted the weight of her memories.

"Welcome, Serena. It is a joyous surprise to see you alive after the tragic uprising of the usurper," the Queen spoke with a blend of fondness and sorrow, her voice echoing in the chamber.

"Thank you, Efaldrin. It is indeed a privilege to return to your court and this exquisite realm," Serena responded with genuine appreciation.

As the conversation turned to the companions Serena had brought with her, the Queen's gaze shifted toward Noah, her curiosity evident. Serena introduced him with a gentle smile, "This is my grandson and heir, Noah Rostropovich, the first of his name. He has accompanied me to your esteemed court."

"Your grace," Noah said, offering a respectful bow to the Queen.

"Such impeccable manners you possess, unlike your father. He was quite the rascal back in the days when I used to visit Spriting! He even dared to play pranks on me when he was just a child," the Queen recounted with a laugh, her memories of those playful times lighting up her eyes.

Noah chuckled softly, his tension easing as he felt a connection to his father through the Queen's stories. "Though I never had the chance to meet him, it warms my heart to hear these stories. I would be honored if you would share more tales about my father with me."

The Queen's smile softened as she looked at Noah. "Of course, dear child. I would be delighted to share stories about your father with you later. He was a spirited and mischievous young man, full of life and vigor. There are many tales I could tell, and it warms my heart to see a glimpse of him in you."

The Queen's attention shifted to Liam, her gaze focused on him. "And this must be Liam, son of Harvey Brandt, the renowned merchant of Spriting."

Liam was taken aback, momentarily lost for words at being addressed by the Elven Queen herself. "Y…yes, your majesty," he stammered, still in disbelief.

"I thought as much; your reaction confirms my theory. It was quite clear when the guards reported the arrival of three individuals, accompanied by the Scimitar no less. That vessel is renowned even within our lands, and rumors of your disappearance from Rankier Castle and the simultaneous theft of the ship had reached our ears. It appears we now have the answers to the who, what, and where of this tale," the Queen remarked astutely, a wry smile playing on her lips.

"I rescued him," Noah interjected, only to stop as Serena shot him a sharp glance.

"Ah, so this sounds like quite the intriguing tale," the Queen purred, her curiosity piqued.

"Efaldrin, might we find a more private setting for our conversation?" Serena asked pointedly, her gaze shifting to the crowd of onlookers who were hanging on to every word exchanged between them and their Queen.

"Ah, indeed, we shall," the Queen replied, acknowledging the courtier's overly curious gaze. "Come, let us adjourn to my private lounge. There, we can delve into your journey and catch up on all that has transpired since our last encounter."

Efaldrin motioned for one of her courtiers to approach. "Fetch my daughter, Enwa, and inform her to join us in my private lounge."

The courtier offered a respectful nod and swiftly turned to carry out the Queen's command.

"Shall we?" Efaldrin inquired, gracefully guiding them out of the hall and into a softly lit corridor branching off from the main audience chamber. "You know, I've always detested that chamber – far too formal for my liking. I can't fathom why my late husband insisted on its construction. I can hardly bear to be in there for too long," she chatted, her regal gown trailing behind her as she moved swiftly through the hallway.

"Ah, here we are. This will be much more suitable," she declared with a composed demeanor, opening the door to reveal a snug private lounge embellished with plush chairs, inviting them to settle in comfort. Efaldrin gracefully eased into a chair, while the others positioned themselves to face her. A servant arrived with tea, and a tranquil hush enveloped them as the tea was served.

In the midst of the tea service, Efaldrin's daughter, Enwa, entered the room discreetly. Taking a seat beside her mother, she settled in and observed the conversation unfolding before her. Noah's gaze rested on

Enwa, taking note of her fair complexion that mirrored her mother's. She possessed a slightly shorter stature than her mother, and she had a more approachable, less imposing demeanor. Kindness emanated from her, but there was also an underlying air of unhappiness that Noah couldn't help but sense.

Once they were alone, Efaldrin commenced the conversation. "Now then, start from the beginning and tell me what happened. As I mentioned, we had been informed that you and your family had met your end during the usurper's uprising."

"My son and daughter in law, yes. They perished fighting the usurper in the palace. However, Noah's mother was able to smuggle him out of the city safely before that." Serena said. She continued, explaining the long story of their escape from the city, how she had raised Noah, and the life they'd had.

Efaldrin maintained a thoughtful silence, offering sympathetic sounds at appropriate moments, yet her gaze retained its sharp calculation. Once Serena had recounted her story, the Queen spoke, her tone conveying both empathy and astuteness. "You have faced much adversity, my dear. The years have indeed been unkind. Which leads me to my next inquiry: why have you ventured here? You must be aware that I lack the power to reinstate you on the throne. While you are certainly welcome to find refuge within these walls, I doubt that living in such a state of limbo would satisfy you."

"I had never intended to bring Noah here. As you can recall, the years following the usurper's rise were riddled with turmoil and violence. I couldn't guarantee the safety of a baby within your court during those times, so I opted to remain in exile, far from the capital," Serena replied earnestly, before elaborating. "However, that plan shifted after Noah unexpectedly had his first vision, and the elements forewarned us of impending danger."

Efaldrin leaned forward in her seat, her interest piqued. "A vision, you say? How intriguing. I do recall your lineage's history of having prophetic visions, and they've often proven accurate. Noah, would you share with me what you saw?"

Noah cleared his throat, not expecting to be called upon. "The vision was fragmented, not entirely clear. I saw war and death, fires consuming cities, and a malevolent force spreading across the world. A woman screamed in anguish, experiencing a profound loss, while a man consumed by evil laughed maniacally as he wrought the suffering."

Elfadrin remained silent for a moment, absorbing his words. "An ominous omen indeed, though not much to base a decision on," she conceded. "Surely, that alone wouldn't have been enough to prompt you to leave your safe haven."

Serena added her perspective. "Individually, perhaps not. However, the elements intervened, delivering a warning of impending evil. They revealed the usurper forming an alliance with malevolence, a demon taking hold of him completely. The wind carried glimpses of a potential future, one where we fled only to meet our doom at his hands, as he unleashed a horde of monsters upon the world."

Efaldrin's demeanor grew tense at the mention of monsters, her expression turning cold. "This is deeply concerning. Information from the capital has been limited, but what we've heard suggests the mobilization of armies and the King's sorcerers preparing for some nefarious event. Court rumors speak of the King's sudden fits of rage and his obsession with violence. It's even been said that he killed three men with his bare hands when his breakfast was served cold one day," Efaldrin mused aloud. "I initially dismissed these reports as mere gossip, but your vision and the warning you've received lend a more ominous perspective to these events."

Noah's voice grew more intense as he recounted their encounters. "Indeed, the reports of monsters are not mere rumors. In the Ceredor Pass, we came across a corrupted soldier—a grotesque creature that seemed to have lost all semblance of humanity. We barely escaped its clutches.

"Moreover," he continued, his tone weighted with concern, "while in Rankier, Liam and I witnessed a disturbing ritual. The King's sorcerers submerged themselves in a black miasma, emerging transformed and infected with malevolent energies. The King's chief sorcerer openly spoke of forming an alliance with infernal powers and preparing for war against the Elves."

The room grew heavy with tension as Noah's words settled like rocks in a pond. The gravity of their situation was undeniable, and it was evident that the Elven kingdom was facing a threat unlike anything they had encountered before.

Efaldrin's eyes widened with alarm as Noah recounted their encounters with the corrupted soldier and the King's sorcerers. She leaned forward, her expression grave. "These are dire tidings indeed. Corrupted soldiers, sorcerers making pacts with infernal powers… It appears that the King's descent into darkness is deeper than we had feared. Your visions and experiences align with the disturbing changes we've heard about from the capital."

She sighed, her gaze thoughtful. "It's clear that the situation is far more dangerous than I had anticipated and that the realm is on the brink of an unprecedented catastrophe. Tell me, what do you propose we do in the face of this impending threat?"

"We must unite the Elven realms. For too long, the three cities have been divided and embroiled in internal conflicts. You know the wisdom in my words," Serena stated, her tone carrying an air of conviction as Efaldrin visibly hesitated.

"Elnoth stands strong on its own, we do not require the assistance of other Elven realms to maintain our power," Efaldrin retorted, her annoyance evident as she responded to Serena's proposition.

"Against a conventional army, undoubtedly. Your people are known for their strength and unity. However, when facing the hordes of demonic monsters that have been unleashed, I fear that even Elnoth may struggle to survive," Serena replied with earnest concern, her voice carrying the weight of her words.

"Let's imagine I agree to your proposal, and we unite the Elven Realms as one, combining the strength of Elnoth, Vardrun, and Falnir. Are you implying that we should then march on Spriting and wage a war to reclaim your throne? This is not a conflict of our making, and while we have been allies in the past, it does not necessarily mean we will step into the role of warriors for your cause," Efaldrin stated pointedly, her eyes fixed on Serena.

"War is a force that can be thrust upon us regardless of our desires, and it is the responsibility of the Elven Realms to determine their course of action," Noah interjected, adding his perspective. "My grandmother is offering her insights and wisdom based on the experiences we've gathered during our journey. And considering what we witnessed from the Scimitar, I am inclined to believe that Falnir may no longer be a viable option."

Enwa's voice rang out with clear concern, "What do you mean Falnir is no longer an option?" she asked, her sudden words hanging in the air with a sense of urgency, a hushed silence enveloping the room. Efaldrin's eyes held a weariness that mirrored her daughter's concern as the mention of Falnir seemed to cast a shadow over the room.

"When we passed by Falnir, it was evident that the city was in decline. The Elves we observed appeared afflicted, as if their vitality was decaying outward. Mechanical devices were ruthlessly felling the once-thick forests surrounding the city," Noah explained, his phrasing measured. "Enormous chimneys spewed pollution over the city, and a sewage pipe poured the same tainted miasma that the King's sorcerers employed for their unholy pact into the city's harbor and water sources. The city's demise is unmistakable, and its inhabitants are suffering the same fate. Whatever force is at play here, it is causing widespread destruction, and I fear there might be no salvation for them."

Enwa's eyes widened in shock and disbelief, while Efaldrin's gaze turned distant as she processed the grim details Noah revealed about Falnir's dire state. "Mother, you must summon Helion back immediately!" Enwa exclaimed, rising to her feet with urgency and imploring her mother to take action.

"Helion?" Noah asked.

Enwa turned her gaze back to Noah, her voice filled with urgency. "My younger brother, Helion, holds the title of the heir to Elnoth. He embarked on a journey to Falnir three moons ago to negotiate a new trade treaty between our cities. However, there has been no word from him since he departed. This silence is unlike him, and I have grown increasingly concerned about his well-being."

"If that is indeed the case, then Helion is in grave peril," Serena remarked, her gaze locked with Efaldrin's, who appeared to have aged visibly under the weight of the revelation.

"I believe it would be best for us to have some private time to discuss this further," Efaldrin said, rising from her seat, visibly shaken. "The guards outside will show you to your guest chambers where you can rest and freshen up for tonight's feast. We can resume our discussions at a later time when I have had the opportunity to reflect on all that has been revealed."

"We are grateful for your hospitality, Efaldrin," Serena said, standing up from her seat, with Noah and Liam promptly following suit.

They made their way out of the room, the guards at the door guiding them to a luxurious wing of the palace where two spacious private rooms awaited them. An adjoining smaller room was designated for a servant. The two main rooms converged in a common area with a blazing fire already ablaze in the hearth. Thoughtfully arranged seating surrounded the fire, creating an inviting and cozy atmosphere.

Noah and Liam made their way into the room with the smaller adjoining servant chamber, upholding their pretense, though Liam had no intention of sleeping apart from Noah. Meanwhile, Serena settled into the other room, placing her meager belongings on the spacious bed. Later, the three reconvened in the central common area, gathering to discuss their day.

"How do you think that went?" Noah inquired, his expression anxious as he looked at Serena. "Something feels amiss. The Efaldrin I remember would have reacted more strongly; the news we shared about the infernal alliance should have provoked a greater response. I worry that age or other factors might be influencing her, or there might be more happening behind the scenes," Serena replied thoughtfully. "Should we be worried for our safety?" Liam questioned, his concern evident as he held onto Noah's arm, seeking reassurance.

Serena shook her head. "No, as long as this city stands, the Elves will ensure our safety. Efaldrin has offered us sanctuary within the city's walls, and she will uphold her word. The people of Elnoth are known for their honor and integrity."

"So, what should we do then? We don't seem to have convinced Efaldrin, and she seems hesitant to do anything in our favor," Noah said, frustrated by the Elven Queen's inaction.

"We need to be patient and cautious," Serena replied, her expression serious. "Efaldrin may need time to process everything we've shared. Meanwhile, we should gather more information about what's truly happening in Falnir and the extent of the King's alliance with infernal powers. We also need to find out more about Enwa's missing brother, Helion. There might be pieces of the puzzle we're missing, and we must tread carefully to avoid making any hasty decisions."

"You understand the Elves better than anyone," Noah conceded, acknowledging Serena's expertise.

"I do," Serena agreed with a laugh. "In the meantime, let's freshen up for the feast tonight. We'll likely be in the spotlight. I'm sure the Elves have prepared appropriate attire in your rooms already," she added, before rising and departing to her own chambers.

*****

Noah and Liam made their way to Noah's assigned chambers, both impressed by the lavishness and comfort provided by the Elves. The linens were of the finest quality, velvety to the touch, and the bedding promised a restful night's sleep. Noah's chamber boasted a spacious bathing area, seamlessly integrated into the floor, featuring magically charmed taps that dispensed both hot and cold water for a soothing bath. Alongside, an array of scents and fragrant soaps had been thoughtfully arranged for his use.

Noah and Liam undressed without hesitation, the intimacy between them making such moments natural and easy. They stepped into the bathing area together, the warm water rising to envelop them in comfort. With an intimacy born of their connection, Liam leaned back into Noah's touch. Noah had picked up one of the fragrant soaps, and his hands moved with care as he lathered and cleansed Liam's back, his touch a soothing balm against the fatigue of their journey. The water, initially clear, soon took on the evidence of their travels, growing cloudy as it carried away the accumulated grime. As Noah's fingers massaged through Liam's hair and over his skin, a sigh of contentment escaped

Liam's lips.

"I could get used to this," Liam murmured, resting against Noah after having the soap washed from his body and hair.

Noah laughed lightly. "So could I. My turn now."

He turned about, and Liam assumed his position behind him. Taking the soap into his hands, Liam carefully lathered it before applying it to Noah's back, his fingers gliding over the contours of Noah's hard body. The touch was both intimate and soothing, Liam's hands traced patterns across Noah's abdomen, pectoral muscles, and across his scalp, evoking soft, involuntary moans of pleasure from Noah. The closeness they shared was a welcome respite from the outside world and the troubles they'd encountered on their way.

With both of them clean, Noah reclined back with Liam resting on his chest facing him. They lay in the warm bath, quietly enjoying the comfort of the water and the intimate moment they had to themselves. They'd had little chance for the privacy of a bath while on the road or onboard the Scimitar, and the ability to close themselves away in Noah's chamber was refreshing. This now was their moment to be together, and to enjoy each other away from potential interruptions.

"You cut quite the figure today," Liam said softly.

"Well, I couldn't really help it, could I? They were expecting the heir to the throne, and I didn't want to think about the consequences if I hadn't played the part."

"You definitely played it well. Honestly, it was quite arousing," Liam confessed, a shy blush painting his cheeks.

Noah's lips curled into a playful grin, his gaze appreciating Liam's nude form. "Is that so? So my authoritative demeanor got you all worked up?"

Liam's heart raced, and he nodded, his blush deepening as he met Noah's gaze.

"Well then, this could be quite interesting," Noah mused, a playful chuckle escaping him as he fixed an intent gaze on Liam's exposed form. A noticeable warmth stirred within him.

Liam's breath hitched, his arousal heightened by Noah's suggestive words and the hungry look in his eyes. "Is that what you desire, my

Lord?"

Noah lowered his head, his lips claiming Liam's with a surge of passion. Their tongues danced in a heated kiss, leaving Liam both exhilarated and breathless as Noah pulled away, leaving him yearning for more. "Yes, you are what I desire" Noah breathed into Liam's ear, sending shivers down his spine.

Liam shifted with a splash to straddle Noah's lap, rubbing their erections together, the warm water adding a layer of sensuality to their play. The friction between the two of them caused them both to hiss and sigh in pleasure. Liam kissed Noah back deeply, wrapping his arms around his neck as Noah's hands roamed his body freely, tweaking his nipples with a firm hand and running fingers through his hair to tug his head further back for another deep, hot kiss.

Reaching down into the water, Liam's hand wrapped around Noah's long firm erection, gliding up and down his shaft and further to cup and fondle his balls. Noah moaned in appreciation, his eyes burning into Liam's, challenging him to continue.

Liam reached over, grabbing a vat of body oil that had been set by the fragrant soap, and poured a generous quantity onto his hand. He immersed his hand in the water, the oil resisting the water's pull, and spread the slippery liquid along Noah's wet cock making it slick.

Lifting up, Liam turned to raise his ass out of the water and awkwardly poured the more of the oil along his crack in a silent invitation. Noah reached out and slid his fingers along the valley between his lover's buttocks, oiling his hand as he caressed the slick skin. His two middle fingers sank into the dusky hole he found there with ease. Soon a third finger joined the game and then a fourth as Liam moaned and whined with lust. Watching his thick fingers slide in and out of Liam's tight ass, stretching it for his monster cock, almost had Noah coming right then but he tamped his reaction down, banking the fire in anticipation of ecstasy of that juicy ass gripping his cock. Pulling his fingers from their dark haven, he turned Liam to face him and kissed him with savage intensity.

Liam lifted himself and positioned his tight ass over Noah's cock. Easing himself down in the warm water, he stifled a moan as he felt the tight ring of muscle stretch further and expand as Noah's fat head popped inside him. Liam leaned forward, resting his head against Noah's, feeling his insides stretch as he sank further down on Noah's girthy cock.

"Ugh, you're so deep," Liam moaned, as he finally felt Noah's dick bottom out inside him. He rested for a moment, tenderly kissing Noah, wiggling his hips closer as his tight man-cunt adjusted to the invasion.

"Do you like feeling your future King deep inside your guts?" Noah asked, voice gruff with lust.

"Mhmm, yes I do. It feels so good, having my King's cock buried inside me" Liam responded, fully entranced by Noah's lust-filled voice.

Noah bucked upward suddenly, causing Liam to swear and moan in pleasure at the feeling of Noah's cock somehow sinking even deeper inside him. Not giving him time to adjust, Noah began to thrust upward, hands tightly gripping a rounded buttock in each hand, he lifted Liam into the air with the impact of his every forceful thrust of his cock plunging deep inside him.

Liam in turn lifted himself up, slamming back down and impaling himself deeper on Noah's cock in tandem with Noah's thrusts.

"Oh fuck, your ass is so tight," Noah moaned in pleasure, his hands tightly clawed onto Liam's ass cheeks as he rode him, the water sloshing around them. His fingers crept inward to feel the place where they joined, sneaking their slippery way in alongside Noah's massive cock, stretching Liam open even more. He now had four middle fingers, two from each hand of his King, and a cock buried in his anus. Those fingers guided his movements as he sobbed and choked on the painful pleasure washing through him.

Liam's head was thrown back, eyes closed in intermingled pain and pleasure at the feeling of Noah's cock plunging deeper inside him, a cock that slid against the fingers that held him open for the reaming. With every thrust upward from Noah's hips, he guided Liam's violent downward descent. Each thrust caused a moan to escape from Liam and a curse from Noah, the feelings of pleasure intensifying thrust by thrust. Noah's cock hit the point inside him which made him feel dizzy, and he wanted it to hit harder. He opened his eyes, looking to meet Noah's lust-filled gaze. "Fuck me harder, rearrange my guts like a King" he said, voice filled with challenge.

Noah smiled savagely, quickly pulling Liam off of his cock who yelped at the sudden sensation. Flipping him around, Noah pinned Liam against the edge of the bath, kicked his knees apart and quickly hammered his cock back inside Liam's tight ass. Liam sobbed in pleasure at the full stretching, burning feeling, as Noah's cock pushed firmly up against his sensitive prostate. Each brutal thrust caused Liam's hard cock to leak a string of precum. Noah used Liam's ass like a cum-bucket and teased his prostate with every deep stroke in.

With one hand clamped on Liam's shoulder and the other digging into his hip to hold him in place, and Liam tightly gripping onto the edges of the bath, Noah furiously pounded his expanding dick into Liam. He watched as his cock plunged in and out, pace frantic, as his balls slapping against Liam's ass in a fierce tempo. Liam's incoherent cries of pleasure mixed with jumbled words and prayers as Noah used his tight hole roughly.

Noah felt the pressure building up inside him, Liam's rippling asshole bringing him closer and closer to the edge of release with each thrust. His pace now a staccato rhythm, he felt his balls tighten, preparing to expel their treasure. "Oh shit, I'm going to cum. Get ready for my load."

Liam keened feeling Noah beginning to tense up as his orgasm neared. "Yes, fill my cunt up with your hot seed. I need your royal babies inside me!"

Noah roared as he reached his orgasm, ramming into Liam's hole, plunging his cock as deep as possible inside Liam's guts to, release jets of hot seed inside him. Noah held him in place, not allowing Liam to squirm away from the intense sensation of his thick cum coating his innards, and filling his guts.

The sensation proved too much and pushed Liam over the edge. His own load shot out of his cock, splattering up against the bath's edge and coating him in the sticky cum. The two remained locked together in ecstasy, both experiencing their orgasm simultaneously in a minute of sensual intimacy.

After a few moments, Noah pulled his softened cock out of Liam's sore hole, and slipped his four fingers inside, watching lazily as they easily pistoned in and out of the swollen and stretched orifice while his cum leaked out in dripping dribbles. He tried to scoop it up and push it back inside Liam's man-cunt but only succeeded in sliding all five fingers into him to the deepest knuckle. Testing the resistance, he pushed a little more, rotating his hand and spreading his fingers. Another time, he thought to himself while Liam moaned in lustful agony as his thoroughly abused ass was violated by his lover's hand. Noah slid his hand back and reached around saying, "Lick you King's fingers clean."

And Liam did.

Finally exhausted, Noah laid back against the edge of the bath and Liam dragged himself up to sit on his lap, resting his head on his shoulder. He glanced down and snorted, chuckling as he realized the mess they'd made.

"I think we're going to have to clean up again," he said wryly, looking over at Noah who smiled back bemusedly before joining in laughter.

*****

Within her secluded private chamber adorned with mystic tapestries, Efaldrin's restlessness knew no bounds. Beside her, her daughter Enwa remained composed, a portrait of patience against her mother's tempestuous emotions. An air of tension clung to the room, as the unwelcome tidings carried by their unforeseen visitors gnawed at Efaldrin's very core.

"Mother, I implore you, find solace in stillness," Enwa's voice carried a note of exasperation, a plea to quell the tempest within Efaldrin's heart.

With a weary sigh, Efaldrin yielded to her daughter's counsel and lowered herself onto a regal seat. Casting a sidelong glance at Enwa, she saw the concern and the unyielding determination in her gaze. Such traits, Efaldrin mused, were a poignant reflection of the father who had etched his boldness upon their lineage. Even when it vexed her, she couldn't help but acknowledge the pride she felt for her firstborn. For in Enwa pulsed the fiery spirit that kindled her father's legacy.

"Forgive me, my child," Efaldrin's voice trembled with the weight of her fears. "The words they bore have stirred a tempest within me. T'is news that threatens not only Helion, my cherished son, but also the very mantle of power that shrouds Elnoth's throne."

"Helion shall return, of this I hold unwavering certainty," Enwa's words flowed like a gentle stream, an elixir of solace meant to calm the storm in her mother's soul.

"He must, for should he falter, our claim to the throne shall crumble like ancient ruins," Efaldrin's voice wavered, bearing the weight of weary resignation. "As an unwed ruler, the mantle cannot pass to you, and the sands of time hasten their descent. I sense it in my very bones and the whispers of my flesh—the ageless ache that bespeaks the approaching twilight. I yearn for the embrace of closure, to reunite with my departed consort upon the Trestos, the sacred bough linking our world to the beyond."

Enwa's exclamation resounded with a mixture of shock and anguish, cutting through the chamber's still air. "Mother, you mustn't utter such words! Your path in this realm remains unwoven, your tapestry far from complete. The tapestry of your destiny yet holds numerous threads waiting to be woven into the grand design. The news that has been delivered unto us signifies an hour when Elnoth hungers for its steadfast Queen to grace the throne, a beacon in these times of uncertainty."

Efaldrin's laughter echoed through the chamber in a blend of amusement and pride. Enwa's unwavering devotion was humbling. "Ah, my dear Enwa, your loyalty is a balm to my soul," she mused, a glint of appreciation lighting her eyes like stars in the night sky. "True it is that a day shall arrive when my shadow can no longer shield you. Should Helion's mantle of protection waver, I shall have to seek another guardian from the constellation of choices."

A pause, the air pregnant with the gravity of the moment, before Efaldrin continued, "Let our hearts unite in a fervent hope that Helion returns, his strength intact and his spirit unbroken. May these fears, which this old heart clings to, dissolve like morning mist in the embrace of the sun's first light."

"Very well, Mother," Enwa replied with a grace that mirrored her mother's own poise, her voice a gentle cadence that caressed the room before carrying her away from Efaldrin's chamber. As the door closed behind her, a veil of loneliness settled around Efaldrin, her thoughts like whispered secrets weaving through the air.

As Enwa stepped away from the closed door of her mother's chamber, the hushed corridor seemed to absorb her thoughts like a silent confidant. The weight of her brother's predicament bore down heavily upon her heart, its urgency a relentless drumbeat in her mind. Yet, another layer of unease had been woven into her thoughts by her mother's candid words.

The panic stirred by those words swirled within her, a whirlwind of emotions that wrestled with her deepest fears. Her mother, an ageless presence who had graced this world for millennia, had always been an unassailable beacon of strength. Through the tapestry of history, she had been the unwavering foundation when Enwa's father held the scepter of power, and it was her mother's unyielding spirit that guided their kingdom even after his passing.

Now, the realization that one day her mother might depart this realm sent tremors through Enwa's very being. Her mother's formidable presence had been both a security and a source of wisdom. To live a world without her was akin to imagining a sunless sky, a prospect that sent shivers down Enwa's spine.

Deeper still, Enwa's thoughts delved into the intricacies her mother's words had unveiled. The notion of finding another protector to stand in her brother's stead carried more weight than just ensuring her safety; it echoed with the subtle strains of a different kind of fate, one that might ultimately bind her in ways she had never envisioned.

Two centuries of her life had been lived in the uncharted expanse of freedom. Yet now, her mother's intentions loomed over her like gathering clouds. The idea of marriage, often spoken in hushed tones during courtly gatherings, whispered of a life that felt like gilded chains. If she were to wed, her future would be irrevocably tied to the realm's politics, her own aspirations overshadowed by the intricate dance of power and alliance.

Her mind painted vivid scenes of a future where her status would transform from a sovereign woman, filled with her own agency, to a symbolic figurehead, a validating presence beside a man who sat upon the throne. The very thought felt like a cage, her vibrant spirit trapped within the confines of duty and expectation. She was no naive maiden, ignorant of the games played in the corridors of power. Men would vie for her favor, not out of affection or love, but as a strategic maneuver to secure their grasp on her family's legacy.

Enwa's contemplation wandered to her feelings about the opposite sex, a territory that her thoughts navigated with a certain detachment. She found herself harboring a distaste for men, a sentiment that meandered through her mind like a distant river. In her eyes, the actions of men often seemed driven by impulses that clouded their judgment, a folly she found irksome.

She mused, absently, on the propensity of men to be swayed by their baser instincts, often thinking with the "wrong head," as the old saying went. Their motivations often seemed convoluted and veiled, their intentions less forthright. In stark contrast, Enwa perceived women to be more transparent in their motives, their dedication and authenticity shining through like a beacon in the night.

Reflecting further, her thoughts spun around the realm of intimate connections. She held a quiet conviction that women, as lovers, brought a depth of understanding and tenderness that was often elusive in relationships with men. Her experiences had led her to a realization — that men often approached intimacy with a selfishness that belied their grandiose gestures. This insight had guided her choices, and over time, she had embraced women as her partners of choice, drawn to the sincerity and profound connection she found in their embrace.

As Enwa entered her chambers, a different atmosphere enveloped her. The air held a warmth that transcended the flickering candles casting soft, dancing shadows upon the ornate walls. Her presence was met by the graceful figure of Finnae, a lover whose presence exuded a certain allure that was more than physical. A gentle rustling signaled Finnae's rise from the luxurious silken sheets that adorned the ornate bed, and a slender glass of wine was extended toward Enwa.

Enwa's lips curved into a tender smile as she accepted the glass, her eyes locking with Finnae's in a silent exchange of affection. A soft, meaningful kiss was exchanged, a fleeting connection that spoke of familiarity and shared moments. It was a gesture that carried more depth than mere physicality, a language only known to them.

The glass held a deep red wine, its color reminiscent of the finest rubies. As the glass found its place in Enwa's hand, the rich aroma of the vintage reached her senses, a sensory indulgence to accompany the emotions swirling within her. It was as if the glass itself held whispers of shared stories, secrets told in sips and unspoken conversations.

"So, indulge me, what might your mother's thoughts be regarding these newcomers?" Finnae inquired, a spark of curiosity alighting in her tone. "The Court is alive with chatter and whispers about their arrival. I've heard it said that half the women within these hallowed halls are already plotting to capture the attention of the young man, Noah."

"Ah, my inquisitive Finnae," Enwa chuckled, the sound a melody that danced on the air. "You're well aware that the whispers within my mother's thoughts are bound to her alone. Her mind, like the deepest well of mystery, guards its secrets with the utmost care."

The laughter in Enwa's voice held a touch of playfulness, a testament to the familiarity they shared. The boundary between their personal lives and the realm's intricate politics was clear, a line they'd learned to tread with grace and understanding. It was a dance that echoed the delicate balance of their love and the external forces that sought to shape their paths.

Enwa's voice held a reflective quality as she began to unveil the impressions she had gathered about the newcomers. "Noah strikes me as a young man of gentle demeanor, his kindness and thoughtfulness evident in the way he carries himself. His grandmother, while bearing the weight of age, exudes a certain consideration that is unmistakable."

Pausing for a moment, Enwa chose her words carefully, aware of the delicate balance between sharing and safeguarding her mother's thoughts. "Their journey to our realm has not been without its hardships, and the omens they have brought with them have cast a shadow of concern upon my mother, the Queen."

"Ah, I understand now," Finnae replied, her expression adopting a thoughtful cast as Enwa's revelations unfolded. Concern knitted her brows, the depth of her care for Enwa evident in her eyes.

Enwa regarded her lover with a sense of appreciation, recognizing the genuine worry in Finnae's gaze. "Yes, the shadow extends to my thoughts as well," she confirmed softly, a touch of vulnerability in her admission.

With a deep breath, Enwa delved further into the intricate web of fears and potential outcomes. "My mother's concerns are not unfounded. The specter of her own mortality looms, and she senses the veil between this realm and the next drawing close. Helion's fate hangs in uncertainty, and should he not return from Falnir, the very foundation of our claim to the throne falters."

Enwa's voice carried the weight of the choices that lay ahead, her gaze fixed on Finnae's eyes. "In the wake of such a scenario, my mother would be left with no choice but to secure the dynasty's hold on power. Marrying me off to a suitor of great influence would be a strategic move, a safeguard against the upheaval that might follow her passing."

Finnae's response was carefully considered before being offered up. "In truth, so much hinges on these intricacies, but life seldom offers us certainties. The words we've exchanged could weave threads of possibility, or they might simply drift away like leaves upon the wind. Rest assured, my love, that dwelling on the future's uncertainty holds little merit."

Her voice held a soothing cadence, a testament to Finnae's ability to provide solace even in the midst of uncertainty. The offer that followed was both an invitation and a promise, its allure underscored by a persuasive charm.

"Now, let go of these somber musings and come to bed," Finnae's words carried an undertone of allure, a whisper that promised to whisk Enwa away from the weight of the world. "I am confident that I possess the skills to distract you from these shadowed thoughts, a the very least until the feast this eve."

A gentle smile brushed across Enwa's lips at Finnae's words, the promise of respite and solace resonating in her heart. The weight of her worries seemed to lighten ever so slightly in the wake of Finnae's soothing presence.

"You speak true, my love," Enwa conceded with gratitude. "The loom of fate weaves threads we cannot fully comprehend, and perhaps the uncertainties that hover are but shadows cast by what-ifs."

The pull of their private sanctuary and the promise of a distraction offered a balm to Enwa's thoughts. As she met Finnae's gaze, an understanding shimmered between them, a mutual recognition of the power they held to grant each other a respite from the complexities that surrounded them.

"Yes, let us turn our gaze from the darkness for now," Enwa agreed, a trace of playfulness infusing her words. "To the realm of shared moments and the comfort of each other's embrace."

They crossed the threshold from worry to the intimacy they nurtured together in the candlelit chamber that held the promise of a haven. A sanctuary where the tapestries of their emotions interwove, carrying them away into the refuge of each other's presence.

Chapter 24:
Dark Messenger

Noah, Liam, and Serena were welcomed into the palace's magnificent banquet hall, their gaze drawn upward to the intricate tapestries and masterful carvings that adorned the walls like living pieces of history. The grandeur of the hall was matched only by the vibrant energy that pulsed through it; a bustling symphony of Elven voices intertwined in conversation.

Amidst the opulence, a long table stood adorned with a rich array of dinnerware, a tableau waiting to be filled with the culinary delights the servants were rapidly ushering in. Steam rose from the platters, creating a tantalizing aroma as the dishes were placed meticulously along the table, a delicious mélange of flavors and colors coming together in harmony.

At the heart of it all, Efaldrin sat regally, her place at the head of the table as Queen. Seated beside her, Enwa was a poised presence. They were engaged in a conversation that made her mother laugh, her voice ringing clear as bells throughout the chamber.

As their arrival into the hall was noted, Efaldrin's graceful rise from her seat acted as a silent command, and the hum of conversation began to wane, respect weaving through the air like a whisper. The deference the Elven people gave to their Queen was palpable, a sign of the reverence that echoed through the court.

"Welcome, dear friends," Efaldrin's voice carried a warmth that enveloped the newcomers as she extended an inviting gesture. "Come, take your place by my side."

Noah, Liam, and Serena acknowledged the Queen's welcome and proceeded to find their places at the table. The echoes of Efaldrin's words reverberated throughout the hall, and the court members, who were already settled, shared warm smiles and exchanged greetings as the newcomers took their positions. Serena found herself occupying the seat nearest to Efaldrin, a proximity that carried a distinct aura of honor and respect. Beside her, Noah and Liam were situated next to Enwa, who greeted them with a polite smile as they approached.

Remaining standing, Efaldrin's gaze swept across her court, her presence commanding attention. Her voice, as it carried through the hall, held a regal tone that resonated with authority. "It is with immense gratitude that we welcome the return of our cherished friends," she addressed them all. "Understand that they are not only visitors but also kin to our realm, and as such, they deserve the same respect you would afford to me or my daughter."

The blend of warmth and firmness in Efaldrin's voice carried a weight that spoke of her inner strength. The proclamation she made wasn't merely a suggestion but a declaration of principle, a reminder of the expectation of the court's unity. Her words rippled through the hall, and the members of the court, in response to her powerful address, stilled visibly, absorbing the significance of her decree.

A moment of silence hung in the air, as if the weight of Efaldrin's words needed to settle within each heart. Then, as if responding to an unspoken cue, the room erupted in applause. The court members' hands came together in a resounding show of acknowledgment, an outward expression of their understanding and acceptance of the Queen's directive.

"Thank you, my dear friends," Efaldrin said graciously, in

appreciation for the court's response. Her words acted as a bridge, transforming the official moment of proclamation to a more relaxed atmosphere.

With an elegant gesture, Efaldrin signaled for the feast to commence, guiding the court members to partake in their meal. As the Queen took her own seat, the hum of conversation rekindled as elves began to chat and savor the delicacies before them. The banquet hall now buzzed with life and camaraderie, as the communal repast became the threads of a tapestry, woven between the court members and their honored guests.

"We are truly grateful for this opportunity to share this meal with you, Your Majesty," Noah's words bore a genuine politeness.

A gentle laugh escaped Efaldrin's lips, a sound that carried an air of approachability. "No need for formalities, Noah. Please, do call me Efaldrin," she responded, her voice light with warmth.

"Still, we are truly grateful for your warm reception," Serena spoke with sincerity. "The journey here was quite challenging, and the opportunity to finally have a warm bath and freshen up was nothing short of marvelous."

"Your gratitude warms my heart, Serena," Efaldrin replied, her gaze generous with understanding. "The road's challenges can be arduous, and the simple comforts of a warm bath can feel like a luxurious embrace after such journeys. I haven't journeyed in a long time, yet I can still keenly recall the discomfort of it. I'm delighted that we could provide you with a moment of respite."

Serena and Efaldrin continued their conversation, reminiscing over previous travels and adventures of their own, while Noah turned to speak with Enwa. Liam remained silent for the most part, quietly observing his surroundings and the conversations around him.

"Enwa, would that you tell me about yourself," Noah said courteously, sincerely wishing to learn more about the Queen's daughter.

"I'd be happy to," Enwa replied with a welcoming smile, appreciating Noah's interest in getting to know her better. "I've spent much of my life within the realm's boundaries, learning the intricacies of courtly matters and the responsibilities that come with them. But beyond that, I find joy in the arts, particularly music and literature. There's something enchanting about the way melodies can convey emotions, and words can transport you to different worlds."

Her gaze held a spark of curiosity, as she turned the conversation towards Noah. "And what of you, Noah? What passions and adventures have shaped your journey?"

Noah hesitated, as he'd never had the chance to develop his passions on the farmstead. His life had been borne through struggle, and they had been too busy putting food on the table to enjoy leisurely pastimes.

"I'm afraid to say that I don't have many hobbies or knowledge of the arts. We had little, so I spent much of my time working to provide food for us. I did enjoy my studies greatly though, there is nothing quite like digging into an immense scroll and absorbing the knowledge within," Noah replied, trying to hide his embarrassment at his lack of polish.

Enwa listened attentively, understanding and empathetic as he shared his experiences. She observed the hesitancy in Noah' honest response, reflecting on his life that had been defined by different circumstances.

"It sounds like your life has been a tapestry woven with its own set of challenges and aspirations," Enwa replied gently, her words devoid of judgment. "While you may not have had the luxury of pursuing hobbies or delving into the arts, your dedication to providing for your loved ones and your passion for learning are equally commendable."

Her smile was reassuring, seeking to alleviate any feelings of inadequacy that might have surfaced in Noah's heart. "Studying, especially when driven by curiosity and a thirst for knowledge, is a journey unto itself. The wisdom you've gleaned from those scrolls holds its own kind of richness."

Enwa's eyes lit up with genuine enthusiasm as an idea formed in her mind. "You know, we should definitely make time to explore the Grand Library together. It's a place that holds treasures beyond imagination. Scrolls and texts from ages past, some even dating back thousands of years, are stored there. And you might be interested to know that among those treasures, we possess some priceless pieces that were gifted to us by your own family."

"That sounds wonderful," Noah's excitement was palpable, his eagerness to delve into the library's treasures radiating from his words.

"Tomorrow it is, then, unless another obligation makes itself evident before then," Enwa's voice held a note of anticipation, as if she could already envision the two of them immersed in the library's world of knowledge.

As the topic shifted, Efaldrin and Serena's attention was drawn to the conversation, the mention of obligations sparking a practical consideration. Serena's voice took on a more formal tone, embodying the responsibility of her role. "Indeed, we have important matters to attend to. Noah, your training and refinement of skills will be crucial. Swordsmanship and control over your elemental powers will serve you well in our realm."

Commander Novath, positioned a few seats away, couldn't help but respond to the mention of sword-craft. His voice carried an air of authority, his dedication to his duty evident. "If it pleases my lady, I would be honored to guide Noah through his training. I believe there is much he can gain under my tutelage."

Noah's agreement was swift, his enthusiasm shining through. "I am truly grateful for the offer, Commander. I would gladly accept, pending my grandmother's approval."

Serena's response held a blend of gratitude and assurance, her words flowing gracefully as she acknowledged the significance of the training offer. "Your kindness is much appreciated, Commander Novath. The well-being and capabilities of my grandson hold great importance to me, and his ability to defend himself is of utmost concern."

Commander Novath's pledge was steadfast, his voice carrying a sense of conviction. "Rest assured, my lady, I shall dedicate myself to honing Noah's skills until he becomes a force to be reckoned with on the battlefield."

As the conversation shifted to the topic of magical training, Efaldrin's presence held an air of authority. Her words carried a sense of determination as she revealed her plans. "For your magical training, Noah, I have a particular mage in mind, one whose expertise is unparalleled within our realm. He may be wary and reluctant to teach strangers, but I have no doubt that he will not deny my request. He will be the one to guide you."

"Your support means a great deal, Efaldrin," Noah expressed his gratitude sincerely. He then turned his attention to Commander Novath, his request considered and deliberate. "Commander Novath, would it be possible for my companion, Liam, to partake in the training too? He's always by my side, and it's crucial that he can provide protection for both of us should the need arise."

Commander Novath's agreement came promptly, reflecting his commitment to empowerment and defense. "Absolutely, I'm more than willing to offer training to anyone who seeks to learn how to safeguard themselves and others."

"Wonderful, I'm glad that is settled," Efaldrin stated, ushering this portion of the conversation to a close.

A subtle exchange passed between Liam and Noah, a silent "thank you" conveyed through glances and unspoken gestures. It was a moment of connection that resonated deeply between them. Beneath the table, Noah's hand found Liam's, their fingers entwining in a reassuring squeeze, hidden from the eyes of others.

Unbeknownst to them, Enwa's observant gaze had caught the flicker of their interaction. Her curiosity was piqued, an intrigued arch of her eyebrow revealing her awareness of the private exchange. She chose to catalog it for the moment, however at some point would need to bring it up with Noah. Perhaps they had more in common than she had originally thought.

Enwa's thoughts were interrupted as a messenger ran into the court, approaching the Queen and kneeling before addressing her.

"Your Majesty," a messenger burst into the hall, breathless from haste. "An envoy from King Vladimir has arrived. He requests an immediate audience with you."

Efaldrin's gaze shifted, her attention drawn to the messenger's urgent words. The unexpected arrival of an envoy from a neighboring realm seemed to ripple through the atmosphere, casting a sense of intrigue and anticipation over the scene.

"It seems news of your arrival has already reached Spriting," Efaldrin's voice held a measured tone, her words directed at Noah and Serena. "Rest assured, this changes little within the realm of Elnoth. King

Vladimir's influence holds no sway here."

With a decisive nod, Efaldrin addressed the messenger's request. "Allow the envoy entry to deliver his message. Once that is done, make haste in sending him on his way. I hold no wish to entertain one of Vladimir's emissaries within my realm longer than necessary."

"At once, milady," the messenger responded, hastening to convey the message to the guards.

After a brief moment, the imposing doors of the chamber creaked open, revealing the entrance of the King's emissary. The figure that emerged was nothing short of grotesque and twisted, an embodiment of darkness that sent a shiver down the spines of all. Serena, Liam and Noah's instincts flared, and they sprang to their feet in alarm. The man's skin writhed with an inky black miasma, a familiar and unsettling presence that they recognized all too well.

His attire appeared to be fashioned from an unnatural organic material, pulsating with a malicious life of its own. Slimy tendrils slithered across his form, befouling the air around him. As the envoy advanced toward the Queen, an unsettling wickedness radiated from his very being, silencing conversation in the court to an eerie hush.

Commander Novath, ever vigilant, had already risen from his seat and moved closer to the Queen. His hand hovered near the pommel of his sword, poised to defend her at a moment's notice. From seemingly nowhere, several soldiers materialized, forming a protective circle around the Queen and Enwa. Their expressions were a mixture of revulsion and unease, their eyes locked onto the approaching envoy.

In this tense moment, the court was poised for action, their readiness for defense mirrored by the palpable sense of repulsion that hung in the air as the envoy closed in on the Queen.

"Your Majesty," the envoy's voice grated like jagged stones, his words dripping with spite. "The King has commanded that you yield the false claimants to my custody, or he shall lead his forces to march upon your realm."

Efaldrin's response was swift, her noble demeanor unaffected by the envoy's venomous words. Rising from her seat, her presence radiated a chilling fury that stood against the man's foul aura. "I have no intention of complying with such demands. The usurper holds no place nor power within my realm and has no right whatsoever to command me. You can tell him to crawl back into the hole from whence he came."

"I suspected as much," the envoy's reply was laden with sinister anticipation. "I advised the King that your response would be unfavorable to such a demand. Yet, I would offer you counsel to tread carefully, for the safety of your kin may be at stake."

The envoy's words oozed with evil, foreboding hanging heavily in the air. As the tension in the chamber escalated, it was a confrontation between opposing forces of unyielding strength, a battle of words that hinted at the storm to come.

"You dare to threaten my family," Efaldrin's voice cut through the air like icy steel, her words a manifestation of her smoldering anger. The fire in her eyes burned with intensity, her resolve unyielding in the face of the envoy's veiled and ominous words.

The envoy's evil snicker echoed through the very air of the chamber, sending shivers down the spines of all who were present. His sinister tone seemed to crawl beneath the skin, a haunting presence that left no one untouched.

"Perhaps a token from the King himself will sway your resolve," the envoy's words were laden with a dark promise. With deliberate intent, he reached into the folds of his clothing, his slimy tendrils retracting to allow him access to a sizeable object concealed within. Wrapped in coarse fabric, he tossed the item toward the Queen, a move that set Commander Novath and the surrounding soldiers into swift motion.

Commander Novath's protective instincts sprang into action. Swift as a striking serpent, he positioned himself between the Queen and the incoming object, catching it with deft precision before it could make contact with her person. The soldiers tightened their guard, weapons drawn, bellies in, eyes watchful.

"Open it, and witness the hollowness of my King's threats," the envoy's words dripped with a chilling challenge. The atmosphere in the chamber seemed to constrict, every eye focused on the object in the Commander's grasp. The tension hung thick in the air, tangible and ripe with disquiet and foreboding.

Upon Efaldrin's nod, Commander Novath proceeded to carefully unwrap the fabric that enshrouded the mysterious object. As the coarse fabric fell away, revealing the contents within, his features contorted into a grimace of distress and horror. Quickly, he stepped away from the Queen, placing the object onto a nearby table, distancing it from her.

A collective gasp of shock rippled through the court as their eyes fell upon the gruesome sight before them. The severed head of Helion, the Queen's son and heir was before them. The eyes of the rotting head gleamed with an otherworldly, silvery hue, the skin pallid and mottled in death. The air seemed to grow heavy with the weight of the macabre revelation that cast a pall over the chamber. The court members exchanged horrified glances, their shock mingling with a growing sense of horror as the envoy's malevolent message became painfully clear.

Enwa's scream pierced the air, a raw and guttural cry of anguish and grief. Her heart-wrenching recognition reverberated through the chamber, her exclamations a mournful declaration that cut through the shock like a blade. Tears streamed down her face, her pain echoing the depths of her loss as she gazed upon the head of her departed brother.

Efaldrin, her regal composure shattered, appeared frozen in a moment of incomprehensible devastation. Her eyes were fixed upon the gruesome sight before her, her features contorted with horror and grief. Tears welled in her eyes, tracing silent paths down her cheeks as she absorbed the reality of her son's death.

Enwa's heart-wrenching cry acted as a catalyst, sparking Efaldrin into action. Her voice trembled with grief and steely determination, and her gaze shifted to Commander Novath. The command she uttered was a resolute pronouncement, a merging of a mother's anguish and the unshakable sense of responsibility that came with her role as a ruler. "Put an end to him and deliver his remains to his companions at the city's gates, piece by piece."

"With all my heart, my Queen," Novath's response was laced with fierce determination, his own memories of the young man he had once trained as a warrior reflected in his eyes. His sword was drawn with a fluid motion, the steel hissing as it bade farewell to the scabbard and gleamed in the dim light of the chamber. Simultaneously, the soldiers, their expressions a mixture of grief and unwavering resolve, converged upon the envoy with a shared purpose. Their eyes held a fiery intensity, the flames of vengeance and justice dancing within them.

"So, it is death you seek then, and the end of your line. So mote it be," the emissary said, each word echoing with a finality.

The envoy's eyes shuttered closed, a prelude to the unleashing of a malevolent power that sprang forth from him. The writhing tendrils that had adorned his clothing erupted with a surge of force, slamming into the soldiers like a malicious force of nature. The impact was fierce, the soldiers knocked aside with unsettling ease, their bodies propelled like leaves caught in a fierce wind.

Commander Novath's battle cry reverberated through the chaos, his sword arcing through the air with a determined strike. The blade sliced through the tendrils with a sickening screech, the sound ringing like a defiant bell. Yet, for each tendril that was severed, two more emerged to fill the void, an onslaught that drove Novath backward with growing urgency.

The commander's alarmed shout rang out, directed at Noah, Liam, and Serena as he valiantly fought against the relentless tide. His gaze bore into them with urgency. "Protect the Queen! Take her and run! I'll hold this abomination back!" The court around them scattered in a desperate scramble for safety, leaving a chaotic scene in their wake.

Noah immediately turned to Liam and his grandmother. "Lead Efaldrin and Enwa to our chambers. It's the last place they'd expect. I'll stay and face this menace." He ordered them urgently.

Liam's gaze locked on Noah as he reluctantly agreed. "You better return in one piece, or I'll make sure to finish the job myself."

Serena's resolute nod echoed Liam's sentiment. "Liam's right, and I'll be right there with him."

They swiftly guided Efaldrin and Enwa down the corridor, their steps quick and purposeful as they retreated to the safety of their designated wing within the palace.

*****

Noah's attention was riveted on the unfolding battle as he strategized his movements. He quickly realized that Novath's struggle was nearing its end. Watching the relentless monster efficiently drive Commander Novath into a tight corner of the chamber in order to gain the upper hand ignited a fierce determination within his chest.

Drawing from the wellspring of power within him, Noah reached for the essence of the elements that resided there. Yet, despite his efforts, he struggled to grasp the familiar warmth of the light that had aided him before. Panic rose within him as he faltered, his control over his abilities wavering in this critical moment.

As desperation took hold, Noah made a swift decision. Reaching down, he seized a fallen soldier's blade, its cold steel a tangible extension of his resolve. Springing into action, he attacked the monster from behind, his movements driven by sword-craft skills learned from his grandmother along their journey.

The unexpected assault caused the creature to falter, its attention momentarily diverted. Noah's actions provided Commander Novath the opening he needed, allowing him to unleash a counterattack against the relentless foe. The combined efforts of Noah and Novath began to turn the tide, driving the monster back as Liam and Novath worked in tandem to sever its tendrils.

Commander Novath gave a rallying cry, his encouragement a powerful force that galvanized their efforts. "Keep at it! We can force it to retreat!"

Noah responded with steadfast determination. "We need to corner it, then strike together to end it!" The battle raged on, as they made steady progress and pushed the monster into a corner.

Their efforts bore fruit, the tide of battle gradually shifting in their favor. But as the momentum tilted in their direction, a sudden twist of fate turned the situation dire once again. Commander Novath's misstep, caused by debris on the floor, proved to be a fatal moment of vulnerability. A tendril struck his temple, knocking him unconscious and leaving Noah to face the relentless monster alone.

Noah's heart raced as the reality of his situation sank in. He now stood alone against the creature, his only ally incapacitated. His gaze narrowed as he watched the monster withdraw a long, gleaming blade from its tendrils. The blade's sharp point glinted ominously in the dim light.

The creature's menacing words cut through the air like a blade. Its intent was chillingly clear as it hissed, "With this blade, I shall cut out your heart and present it to my King."

Noah's instincts urged him to take action even as fear coursed through him. He stood at the precipice of a life-or-death struggle, his own survival hinging on his ability to face this nightmarish foe with courage and ingenuity. He steeled himself for the impending battle that would determine the fate of not only himself but also his family and lover.

With a savage, powerful motion, the monster's blade lashed out, clashing violently against Noah's sword. The impact reverberated through the chamber to shake the very air. To Noah's shock, the creature's blade sliced effortlessly through his own weapon, as if it were little more than paper. A gasp escaped him, his disbelief and vulnerability evident in his widened eyes.

Reacting swiftly, Noah leapt backward, his heart pounding with shock and desperation. His mind raced, searching for a solution, any potential weapon he could wield against this formidable adversary. Yet, before he could find his footing, the monster closed in, its satisfaction evident in the twisted grin that formed on its grotesque visage.

As panic clawed at him, Noah's hands grasped for whatever debris lay at his feet. He hurled the fragments toward the creature in a desperate bid to stave off the impending danger. But the monster's tendrils moved with an uncanny precision, swatting aside the makeshift projectiles with disdainful ease, as if they were mere nuisances to be dismissed.

Noah's breaths came in rapid, shallow bursts as he tried to keep his wits about him, his mind racing to find a way out of this dire confrontation. His heart pounded in his chest as his back met the unforgiving wall, his escape route cut off and his last line of defense shattered. With Novath incapacitated and the once-proud Elven soldiers now fallen, the grim reality of his situation engulfed him. He was cornered, his chances of survival dwindling rapidly.

In his mind's eye, he saw the faces of his loved ones: his grandmother, Liam, and all those he held dear. Closing his eyes, he prepared to face his fate, his thoughts filled with regret for promises unfulfilled and the future that had been snatched away from him. Yet, amid the darkness that threatened to consume him, a faint but unmistakable pull tugged at his consciousness.

It was a sensation he recognized, a mental signature he had encountered before—the dagger he had acquired in Rankier. Hope sparked anew within him as he followed the familiar tug, retrieving the dagger that he had kept close for safekeeping.

As the blade came into his hand, a renewed determination surged through him to face the monstrous creature with the dagger. The creature's taunting laughter only fueled his determination, his grip on the blade steady and true. "That tiny blade will do you no good; I will kill you and all those whom you love. Your hearts will be delivered to the King for his pleasure."

With grim focus, Noah met the creature's gaze, his voice steady despite the fear that gnawed at him. "This might not kill you, but you shall not harm anyone else I care about."

In this climactic moment, Noah grasped the dagger not only as a weapon but as a conduit for his unyielding spirit. The struggle between opposing forces—light and darkness, good and evil—unfolded in a crescendo of tension.

As Noah's declaration resounded in the chamber, an unexpected response emanated from the dagger. A resonating trill sounded in his mind, a response that sent a jolt of surprise through him. He watched in awe as the dagger transformed, shifting and changing before his very eyes. The he handle broadened to fit his hand, the blade extended and morphed into black obsidian, its surface gleaming and emitting an aura of latent power.

Where the monster's blade emanated malevolence and wickedness, Noah's newfound sword radiated righteous fury and unwavering goodness. The transformation was more than physical; it carried with it the embodiment of his determination, his will to protect and his commitment to standing against the encroaching darkness.

With the sword in hand, Noah stood ready to face the creature that had threatened his world. The chamber's air crackled with tension, the battle now a clash of not only physical strength but also that of opposing forces. A battle cry on his lips, Noah launched himself into action. His blade clashed against the monster's weapon with a deafening resonance that echoed through the chamber. To the creature's astonishment, Noah's transformed sword sliced through its blade as if it were butter, the metal dissolving as if exposed to a corrosive acid. In that moment, fear crossed the monster's contorted face, a rare glimpse of vulnerability in its wickedness. A furious roar erupted from its throat as it responded by launching its tendrils in a desperate attempt to lash out at Noah.

Yet, as the tendrils reached him, Noah's blade pulsed with radiant light. The tendrils withered and disintegrated upon contact as the monster's agonized screams reverberated through the chamber. Emboldened by his newfound power, Noah pressed his advantage, relentlessly driving the creature back. The radiance of the blade seemed to intensify, a beacon of righteous strength that matched his growing confidence.

Cornered and without escape, the monster lashed out one last time, its desperation palpable. But Noah's precision and speed were unmatched. He delivered a decisive strike, plunging his blade into the creature's form with ferocity. The sword cleaved through its arms and then, with a gut-churning squelch, decapitated the monster. The headless body crumpled to the floor, releasing a sickening miasma that began to ooze and spread.

With the battle won, Noah's sword seemed to resonate with his intentions. He pointed it toward the oozing miasma, a palpable connection forming between him and the weapon. Flames erupted from the blade of the sword, a righteous fire that was ignited through a fierce determination. The flames engulfed the miasma, scorching it away in a cleansing inferno. As the evil presence dissipated, the chamber was left in silence, the air heavy with the aftermath of a battle that had tested the very boundaries of light and darkness.

"By the Gods," a voice murmured behind him. Noah turned, his heart still racing from the intense battle, to find Novath standing behind him, his eyes wide with astonishment and awe. The commander's gaze was fixed upon Noah and the blade he held, its radiant power still emanating with an otherworldly glow.

"Novath, I didn't know if you'd wake." Noah said, his voice a mix of relief and exhaustion. Gesturing to his sword, he explained, "The sword came to me in Rankier, though as a small, jeweled dagger. Now it has transformed into a mighty blade."

Novath's eyes still held confusion, yet he nodded in understanding. "What will you call it? Every mighty blade needs a name to match."

Noah paused to think for a moment, weighing the significance of the blade and its purpose. Then, with resolute certainty, he declared. "Justice. This blade will serve justice upon the evil forces of this world, and so shall it be named Justice as well."

A trill resonated in Noah's mind, the blade's approval evident in its response. The name held meaning, a declaration of purpose and a vow to stand against the malevolent darkness that threatened their realm. As Noah stood there, the blade named Justice in his hand, he felt a profound connection—a partnership forged in the crucible of adversity, a symbol of hope and strength that would guide him in the battles yet to come.

Chapter 25:
Political Alliances

The aftermath of the emissary's attack on the Queen and her companions echoed through Elnoth and its Court, shattering the once-held belief that the Elves were insulated from the world's conflicts. The very foundations of their serene existence had been shaken. The near-fatal assault on their Queen served as a grim reminder that even their realm was not impervious to the tides of darkness sweeping across the land.

The entry of the malevolent monster and the ease with which it had dispatched some of the most formidable warriors of Elnoth left an indelible mark on the collective consciousness. The Elves, who had long regarded themselves as distant observers of the world's turmoil, now faced the harsh truth that they too could be swept into its throes.

Efandril and Enwa withdrew from the Court's gaze, cloaked in mourning for a full week as they oversaw the solemn funeral rites performed for Helion. A pall of sorrow cloaked the Court itself, their spirits heavy with the weight of loss. The incident had left an indelible scar on their hearts, a reminder of the fragility of life and the suddenness with which it could be extinguished.

As for the Queen, she emerged from the ordeal deeply shaken. The loss of her son and heir only exacerbated her concerns about the safety of her daughter and the stability of their claim to the throne. The incident had starkly illuminated the vulnerability of their realm, prompting her to confront the pressing need to fortify the defenses of Elnoth and ensure the security of her lineage.

Serena and Efandril found comfort within the confines of the Queen's chambers, where they could discuss the harrowing events that had unfolded in the safety of private conversation.

"I am sorry for your loss, Efandril," Serena spoke with a deep empathy, her voice carrying the weight of her own grief as well. "I too have experienced the anguish of losing a son, and I understand the depth of pain you are enduring."

Tears glistened in Efandril's eyes as she looked at Serena, the shared understanding between them forging a bond in the midst of their sorrow. Their losses, though from different circumstances, united them in the common thread of maternal grief.

I worry for Enwa now," Efandril confided, her voice filled with concern and apprehension. "With Helion gone, it feels as though everything we had hoped for is slipping away. Enwa may be burdened with the responsibility of the throne, a role that was meant for her brother."

Serena nodded, her expression understanding. "It is a heavy weight to bear, especially in such trying times. The loss of a rightful heir can send ripples of uncertainty throughout the realm."

Efandril's gaze grew distant, her thoughts mired in the complexities of succession. "Without Helion, Enwa's path may change. She may need to find a husband who can stand with her and ensure the stability of the throne. The future we envisioned is now uncertain."

Serena reached out and placed a comforting hand on Efandril's. "The future is unwritten, my friend. Even in the face of tragedy, new paths can emerge. Enwa is strong, and she has allies in Court who will support her."

Efandril nodded somberly, her expression reflecting a sense of resignation. "You are right. The Court will not easily accept an unwed Queen on the throne. My own ascent to power after my husband's passing was a unique circumstance, one that will not extend to Enwa."

Serena's gaze held both understanding and concern. "The traditions of succession can be rigid, especially in times of uncertainty. It seems that Enwa's path has been altered in ways that could not have been foreseen."

Efandril's shoulders sagged as the weight of the situation settled upon her. "Enwa deserves better than this burden, especially after the tragedy we have endured. And yet, the realm's stability must come first."

Reassurance filled Serena's voice as she declared. "Enwa has the spirit and strength to face these challenges. We must find a way to secure the future of Elnoth while also honoring her choices."

"The only way to secure Enwa's claim is to find a suitor who is her match," Efandril stated thoughtfully, her words carrying a weight of both duty and concern.

Serena nodded, her expression serious. "Indeed. A partner who can stand by her side, provide support, and share the burden of leadership."

Efandril's gaze grew distant as she considered the options. "We must seek someone who not only holds power and influence but also possesses the qualities that will earn the Court's respect. They must be virtuous, kind, generous, and strong."

Serena's voice was gentle as she added, "And someone who can understand Enwa's strengths and complement her weaknesses. Someone she can see as a friend."

Efandril sat in deep contemplation, her thoughts weaving a web of possibilities. After a moment, she looked up, determination in her eyes. "Noah. He is the only one I believe I can trust with my daughter's future. His actions during his time here have proven his loyalty, and his defeat of the monster showcased his strength and courage. The Court already views him as a virtuous defender of the realm, making the prospect of a betrothal to my daughter a reasonable consideration."

Serena listened intently, nodding in agreement outwardly, but inwardly her heart sank at the implications. She was acutely aware of Noah's feelings for Liam, and the thought of orchestrating a marriage for political gain weighed heavily on her conscience. "You have a valid point. Noah's character and actions have undoubtedly earned him respect, and his commitment to the welfare of Elnoth is undeniable."

Efandril's expression softened as she continued, "Enwa deserves a partner who can stand beside her as an equal, and Noah possesses the qualities to fulfill that role."

Serena's voice held a note of encouragement, hiding her misgivings. "He has proven his commitment to the realm, and if he and Enwa share a mutual understanding, it could be a powerful alliance."

Efaldrin regarded Serena with a solemn expression. "Would you be open to considering a marriage proposal that could unite our realms? Should Noah agree, he would become the King of Elnoth, a position that would grant him undisputed leadership over the Elven domains. With the combined strength of our forests, we could harness our magic and power to confront the usurper, eradicating the demonic threat and restoring his rightful place. Noah would rule over a united land, encompassing all except the realm of the dwarves."

Serena's expression grew solemn as she recognized the weight of the Queen's proposal. "I would indeed accept this arrangement, although my heart aches for Noah. In so doing, I would withhold from him the privilege of marrying for love. I granted my own son that choice, and he brought forth a strong heir to carry on our lineage."

Efaldrin's determination remained undeterred. "Enwa will also accept this path, just as I believe Noah will. They both understand the gravity of their destinies and the greater good they must serve. Even if their initial connection is born of duty, time may nurture a deeper affection between them.

"In addition, the offspring of this union will carry the noble blood of the Elves," Efaldrin added, her gaze fixed on Serena. "They will enjoy extended lifespans, robust health, and the heightened power that flows through their veins." The Queen's words underscored the potential benefits that a union between their two worlds could bring, emphasizing the long-term advantages of their decision.

Serena let out a heavy sigh, a weight settling upon her shoulders as she made the difficult choice that would shape Noah's destiny into a loveless marriage. "Very well," she conceded, a sense of resignation in her voice. "Prepare the contract, and I will affix my signature to it. Let our two dynasties be united through this union, using their marriage to bring stability to our realm." The gravity of her decision hung in the air, a sacrifice for the greater good of their lands.

*****

Enwa's laughter resonated through the palace corridors as she, Noah, and Liam returned from a pleasant afternoon spent in the Grand Library. The respite from the weight of her brother's passing and her duties in the Court had been a welcome reprieve, and the company of the two men had proven to be a delightful diversion. Noah's passion for knowledge had been evident from the moment they entered the library, and Enwa had found herself engaged and intrigued by their discussions.

In Noah and Liam, she had discovered kindred spirits, friends who offered support in the midst of her sorrow. There was no romantic spark between them, and she respected the bond Noah shared with Liam. Just as she had Finnae, Liam served as a loyal companion to Noah, and they both understood her need for companionship and distraction amidst the turmoil that had befallen her family and Elnoth.

As they spent time together, Noah's chambers became a haven where they could engage in thoughtful conversations, play games like chess, and share moments of laughter. Enwa noticed the unspoken affection between Noah and Liam, a love that was evident in their banter and the way their eyes met. Though they tried to conceal their love, it was plain to her eyes. She found their dynamic heartwarming, the deep connection they shared shining through the facade they presented to others.

Enwa felt a sense of gratitude for the friendship she had gained with Noah and Liam, appreciating their ability to uplift her spirits and provide a temporary escape from the responsibilities that weighed heavily upon her shoulders. Enwa's heartfelt gratitude filled her heart as they walked, passing by the entrance to her mother's private chambers on their way to Noah's quarters. Her words carried a sincerity that reflected the comfort and support she had found in their company during the past week.

"Noah, Liam," she began, her voice soft and appreciative, "I cannot express how much your companionship has meant to me in these difficult times. Your presence and friendship have helped lift my spirits and provide solace when I needed it the most."

She turned to them with a warm smile, her eyes reflecting her genuine feelings. "I consider myself fortunate to have both of you by my side, even if it's just for a short while. Thank you for being there for me."

Both directed open gazes toward her, their eyes reflecting genuine warmth.

"We were glad to be of assistance. After all, we are your friends, yes?" Noah's words carried sincerity, while Liam's eager nod beside him affirmed their shared sentiment.

Enwa's heart swelled at their genuine response, and a soft smile graced her lips. The bond of friendship they had formed was evident in their words and expressions.

"You truly are," she replied, a mixture of appreciation and fondness in her voice. "And I am grateful to have friends like you who are willing to stand by me during challenging times."

"I'm delighted to witness your peaceful coexistence and friendship," Efaldrin remarked, stepping out of her chambers with Serena trailing behind. The contrite expression on Serena's face caught Noah's attention, triggering a sense of concern within him.

"Mother, this is a surprise," Enwa expressed, clearly taken aback.

"Dear daughter, join me. Noah and Liam, you as well. There's a matter of importance we need to address," Efaldrin spoke with a grave tone, signaling the seriousness of the situation.

Serena nodded behind her. "Come Noah, this is important."

Noah nodded reluctantly, following Efaldrin and Enwa back into the chambers with Liam close behind him. He felt nervous, sensing that something vital had been decided without him.

Efaldrin turned to address them both, her own nervousness apparent in her eyes. Noah could see the weariness in the Queen's demeanor, and the grief that was still evident.

"There is no easy way to say this my dears so I shall not mince words. Serena and I have made an agreement and have signed a contract of betrothal. In order to secure Enwa's claim to the throne of Elnoth and to provide Noah with the strength he will need to reclaim his own birthright, you are to be married as quickly as possible," Efaldrin said bluntly, expecting resistance from her daughter.

Serena nodded, affirming Efaldrin's words. "Noah, please understand the weight of this decision. It's not taken lightly, but it is essential for the stability of our realms." Noah stood there, stunned and speechless for a moment. He exchanged a glance with Liam, who appeared shell shocked and frozen in place.

Enwa spoke first, overcoming her own astonishment. "Mother, you cannot do this. I should be allowed to wed whomever I choose; you promised me this!"

Efaldrin interrupted her, her voice sharp and unyielding. "That was before we lost Helion! Now I must ensure you have a throne to sit on. Noah is the only man I would trust to protect you when I am gone; the other suitors will want you for their own gain. You have an obligation to the throne and the realm, Enwa."

Noah found his voice amidst the turmoil. "Grandmother, you cannot expect this of me. You allowed my father to marry for love; why am I not allowed that same privilege?"

Serena felt the weight of her years in that moment, the burdens of responsibility and the implications of their decision. She understood Noah's unhappiness and the conflict within him. "Those were different times, and the reality is that we need this alliance as much as they need it. Without Elnoth, we would be dead right now. You need a throne to command, and Elnoth has the strength to help you regain your birthright," Serena said, her voice steady with the weight of her own duty. "Moreover, they are our traditional allies. Enwa will give you children blessed with the strength and the long-life of the Elven people. This union will strengthen our lineage."

"You cannot be serious," Noah said in disbelief.

"I am, and you will comply. You have a duty to your family, and to me. You and Enwa will be married, and you will honor my wishes," Serena ordered, her voice cutting through the room like a razor. Inside, she ached at the pain she saw crossing Noah's face, even as he yielded to her demand and his duty to the empire.

"Very well, I will acquiesce though I do not agree with this," Noah replied, his lips tight and his voice cold.

Liam looked at Noah in disbelief, his eyes welling up with tears as he felt the sting of betrayal pierce his heart like a dagger. "Excuse me," he said shortly, leaving the room as his tears flowed freely.

"Liam, wait," Noah cried out, his voice filled with urgency as he glanced over his shoulder. Then, turning his attention back to Efaldrin and Serena, he spoke with a cutting tone, "Excuse me, I need to go speak with him. I trust you do not need me here, as you've both already decided my destiny for me?"

"You may go," Efaldrin said, her voice somber, as Serena nodded behind her in agreement.

"I'm sorry it had to be this way, Noah," Serena murmured.

"Me too," Noah replied with a heavy sigh, his expression a mix of resignation and inner turmoil. With a last glance at the two queens, he turned and hurried after Liam, his heart heavy with the weight of the choices that had been made for him.

"I will go with him, he at least understands the anguish you are both putting us through," Enwa said, her voice laced with anger and frustration. She followed after Noah and Liam, her steps quick and determined, leaving Efaldrin and Serena behind to contend with the aftermath of their decisions.

Serena turned to Efaldrin, a heavy sigh escaping her lips. "Well, that could have gone better."

Efaldrin nodded wearily, sinking into a nearby seat as if the weight of the world rested upon her shoulders. "Undoubtedly, though they will forgive us. With age comes wisdom, and one day they too will see the wisdom we have employed here today."

Serena sighed, a mixture of resignation and hope in her voice. "One can only hope, my friend."

*****

Noah hurriedly followed Liam back to their chambers, entering to find Liam sitting on his bed, tears streaming down his face. Without hesitation, Noah approached him, sitting down beside him and pulling him into a tight embrace. Liam buried his face in Noah's chest, his sobs shaking his entire frame as he clung to him.

"I am sorry, I was not expecting this to happen," Noah said sadly.

Liam tried to hold his sobs back, his chest still spasming as he felt Noah's warm arms wrapped around him. "It's not your fault, I should have known this was going to happen."

Noah held Liam even closer, his own heart heavy with guilt and regret. "I wish there was something I could have done to prevent this. I never wanted to hurt you like this."

Liam shook his head, his voice muffled against Noah's chest. "It is not your fault, Noah. It's… the circumstances, the politics. We both knew this could happen."

Noah gently stroked Liam's back, his fingers tracing soothing patterns as they clung to each other in the midst of their shared pain. "I love you, Liam. No matter what happens, that will never change."

Liam looked up, his eyes meeting Noah's with a mixture of sadness and affection. "I love you too, Noah. I just… I cannot stand the thought of losing you."

Noah kissed the top of Liam's head, his own eyes welling with tears. "We will find a way through this, Liam. We'll face whatever challenges come our way, together."

Enwa's sudden entrance into the room startled Noah and Liam, causing them to quickly pull apart, composing themselves with alacrity. She began to speak, her voice carrying a mix of emotions. "I apologize if I am intruding, but I needed to talk to both of you. I am aware of your relationship."

The young men shared a quick, worried glance, uncertain of where the conversation was headed. Enwa's next words surprised them both. Her voice softened as she continued, "It's quite obvious, really. You two certainly think you are subtle, and maybe to others you were, but it was apparent right from the start. However, I want you to know that it does not change anything. While we might be bound by this arranged marriage, it does not mean we have to pretend to be something we are not. Do you understand what I am saying? I have Finnae, and I am not looking for a romantic connection with you, Noah."

Both Noah and Liam let out a breath they did not realize they were holding. Noah spoke, his voice filled with gratitude, "Enwa, I cannot express how much it means to us that you understand. And that you have your own love."

Liam nodded in agreement, a relieved smile forming on his lips. "Thank you, Enwa. Speaking from the heart, your understanding and acceptance makes this situation much easier to bear."

Enwa returned their smiles warmly. "We are all trying to make the best of this. Let's find a way to navigate this arrangement without causing unnecessary pain. Together, we can make this work. I see Noah as a friend, and nothing more. This is a political alliance, and we can all play the part, while still being with the ones we love."

Trying to find the best strategy with their next move, Noah spoke up. "So, how do we plan to handle this publicly? Should we keep Liam and Finnae hidden from the Court?"

Liam added, "I would prefer not to be kept in the shadows like a dirty little secret, if that works for everyone."

Enwa chuckled at Liam's comment. "Oh, I agree with Liam. We should not have to hide our relationships. It might make things even more complicated if we try to keep secrets. As for the Court, we can present ourselves as allies and friends, a necessary relationship, but not necessarily a romantic couple. It would not be the first royal marriage to be like that in this Court."

Noah nodded in agreement. "That makes sense. It is important that we maintain a united front, even if it is not the conventional form of unity that is usually expected."

Liam added, "And if anyone has the audacity to ask about our relationships, we shall simply say that they are separate from our duty-bound arrangement."

Noah frowned, a thought crossing his mind. "What about the matter of children? Surely, they shall expect us to start a family soon after the wedding?"

Enwa hesitated, reflecting on her thoughts for a moment before responding. "Yes, we will need to have children to secure the line. I do not relish the idea of being intimate with you any more than you do with me. We shall have to tackle that issue when the time comes. But we will not proceed if Liam and Finnae are not comfortable with it."

Liam considered the situation, trying to be pragmatic. "The idea of Noah being with you like that makes me uncomfortable, but if it is necessary for him to have heirs, I agree that we will address it when it becomes a reality. For now, let us leave that topic for later."

Enwa smiled appreciatively at both of them. "I am glad we are on the same page. We shall navigate this together, and hopefully, in time, we can turn this alliance into something positive for all of us."

Noah and Liam both nodded back in agreement, relieved that the forced marriage would not destroy their own relationship. The future would be difficult, yet this at least gave them a chance to still be together.

*****

The news of their betrothal and impending marriage was announced the following morning in the Court, with the Queen proudly declaring their relationship and the agreement that had been reached. While some members of the Court remained skeptical, most applauded the decision, seeing it as a prudent one. Noah's reputation for his deeds had garnered him political favor within the Court, and many who might have opposed the union for their own gain found themselves outnumbered by public sentiment.

With the announcement made, word quickly spread throughout the realm. Wedding preparations went into full swing, and the tentative date for their wedding was set during the Elven festival of Erlathan, a celebration of the creation of the universe and the world, four weeks away. Courtiers and Courtesans alike spread the word, touting it as a positive development for the nation, as the ascendancy of the world would align with the union of the two dynasties.

Amidst the bustling wedding preparations, under the watchful eyes of the Queen and Serena, Noah and Liam delved into their training with renewed dedication. Noah's proficiency in swordsmanship quickly garnered him praise from Commander Novath, who was impressed by the swift progress he demonstrated during their training sessions. Serena's lessons along their journey to Elnoth, in addition to Noah's practical experience gained fighting their opponents, had given him a solid foundation to expand upon.

Liam, too, managed to earn Novath's admiration. His formal training and natural skill with a blade were evident, thanks to the education he had received from his father's tutors. Novath saw the potential in both Noah and Liam and devised rigorous training sessions that often pitted them against each other. These bouts left them fatigued yet invigorated, as they found both challenge and camaraderie in pushing each other to their limits. Both of them were naturally competitive, and this physical competition drove them to compete furiously in a friendly battle of wills.

*****

Efandril had also fulfilled her commitment to aid Noah in honing his magical skills. Following the conclusion of the funeral rites for Helion and her mourning period, she guided Noah to a secluded glen nestled deep within the woods, far from the protective walls of Elnoth. There, a modest wooden hut had seamlessly merged with the grand trees of the area, surrounded by a small field through which a gentle stream meandered. As they arrived, Efandril knocked on the door, and a venerable Elven man emerged, his slim form radiating an air of wisdom and respect as he greeted the Queen.

Noah studied the man before him, observing his tall and slender frame. The Elf's golden-white hair, a hallmark of his people, cascaded gracefully over his shoulders, and his pale green skin complemented the vibrant hue of his emerald eyes, which seemed to emit a subtle luminescence in the sunlight. Clad in the intricate attire crafted by the skilled hands of the Elven weavers, he effortlessly melded with the natural environment. However, beneath his unassuming appearance, an air of authority and mastery emanated, leaving no doubt about his strength and poise.

"Norodiir, please allow me to introduce Noah. He is the intended spouse of my daughter, Enwa, and the exiled heir of the Kingdom of Kirenth," Efandril explained, motioning towards Noah who offered a respectful bow to the elder Elf.

"I am honored to make your acquaintance," Norodiir responded, reciprocating the bow. "In what way may I be of service, my Queen?"

"Noah requires instruction in the arcane arts," Efandril stated succinctly. "He possesses an innate magical ability that requires refinement, particularly if he is to safeguard my daughter and the throne."

Norodiir stilled, before making a negative motion. "I am sorry your majesty, I will not be able to teach him. I do not take on students and have not shared my knowledge."

Efandril's nostrils flared, her demeanor became imposing. "In this, I must insist you teach him. Your Queen demands it of you."

Norodiir paused, his expression unwavering. "I apologize, Your Majesty, but my decision stands. I have not taken on students after the incident. It is truly best my knowledge go to the grave with me."

If possible, Efandril's posture straightened further, her voice snapping with authority. "Consider this an order, Norodiir. You will teach him. His abilities hold immense significance for the security of our realm," she decreed, her voice firm. As her tone softened, her expression mirrored empathy. "I recognize your reservations, and I would not make such a demand if the situation did not demand it."

Norodiir's gaze flickered, torn between loyalty to his Queen and his long-standing principles. After a moment of internal deliberation, he sighed, his resolve softening. "Very well, Your Majesty. I will make an exception and provide guidance to Noah."

The Queen departed, leaving Noah alone with Norodiir. The elder Elf turned to regard him in silence, his gaze assessing and meditative. After a few moments, Norodiir spoke, his voice firm and probing. "Tell me, what do you understand about magic?"

Noah remained quiet, allowing the weight of the question to settle. He then responded, his tone steady. "I know only what I've witnessed through my abilities. My powers seem to emerge in moments of crisis, and I can manipulate various elements – fire, earth, wind, and water. My grandmother claims it is a gift bestowed by the gods, a hereditary trait in our lineage."

Norodiir's expression held a hint of surprise as he absorbed Noah's words. "And can you wield these elements at your will, under your control?"

Noah shook his head. "No, not at will. It is more a response to dire situations. During our journey here, when all seemed lost, I managed to harness these abilities, but it was not a conscious choice. I couldn't draw on them when the monster attacked during the Queen's feast."

Norodiir paused for a moment, as if deliberating something, then gave a nod as if finding what he sought in Noah's response. "Very well," he said, motioning for Noah to follow him into the depths of the forest.

The elder Elf led Noah through the dense woods, where the towering trees intertwined to create a lush canopy. The sounds of nature surrounded them, the playful sounds of squirrels and the melodies of birds echoing through the air. After a short while, they arrived at a clearing nestled among the trees, where two large boulders rested. Norodiir settled himself on one of the boulders, indicating for Noah to take a seat on the other.

"Magic is the manipulation of the underlying forces of the universe," Norodiir explained, adopting a lecturing tone as he began to share his knowledge. "While not everyone possesses this power, everyone can sense its presence. As mages, we can tap into this power temporarily and shape these forces to our will."

Noah listened intently, absorbing Norodiir's words. "So, can magic be used to create objects?"

Norodiir shook his head. "No, magic does not create things from nothing. It allows us to influence the elements and channel their natural tendencies to shape objects, but it cannot conjure something out of thin air."

"So, when I drew upon the elements to create fireballs, were those elements already present and could be transformed into fireballs?"

"Yes, precisely," Norodiir confirmed. "When you summoned those fireballs, you tapped into the existing heat and air, causing them to combust and create the flames. It was your intent and need that guided the elements to manifest in that way. Your mind unconsciously directed the magic, and the elements answered your call."

Noah's eyes brightened as he began to grasp the concept. "So, it's about understanding the elements and channeling them through intent?"

Norodiir nodded approvingly. "Exactly. To become a skilled mage, you must learn to understand the nature of the elements and how they interact. It is not just about raw power, but about finesse, control, and the alignment of your will with the forces of the universe."

Noah pondered that for a moment, ceding that the logic of it aligned with his experience. The times he'd been in control of the power, he had drawn on what he wanted and it seemed as if the elements manifested automatically. Though, it did not answer the feeling of loss of control he experienced.

"There have been times where I have lost control of myself, and it has felt like someone or something else is controlling me," Noah said hesitantly, expressing his concern about his lack of control to his teacher.

Norodiir looked alarmed at Noah's statement. "A situation like that implies outside interference, either divine or infernal. A mage is always in control of their powers; to lose control is to endanger others around you," he said, his gaze growing distant as he lost himself in a memory.

"Have you ever experienced anything you could not explain? A loss of control such as this, or visions you have received?" Norodiir asked, after a few moments.

Noah nodded and recounted the visions he had received, starting with the encounter at the harvest festival he'd had as a child. He elaborated further, explaining his dreams that had triggered their fleeing the farm, meeting Liam, and the times he'd used his power while on their journey. Norodiir merely nodded, asking probing questions for further details, yet making no comment apart from that until Noah's tale was complete.

He took a few moments to analyze the information he had heard before commenting. "Your grandmother's assertion about god-given magic may be correct. Your encounter as a child seems to imply there is some divine intervention in your life, and the times that power has entered your life confirm that. This god intervened to ensure you rescued Liam, which marks him as an important person in your life, and this same power has intervened to save you from the infernal forces at play in this world. Your magic reeks of destiny."

"Is that a favorable omen?" Noah inquired anxiously.

"It can be, but it also carries potential challenges. When granted by a benevolent deity, it often becomes a force for good, harnessed to benefit others. Yet, there are also trickster gods, capricious beings who may bestow powers for the sake of amusement or to sow chaos across the realm," Norodiir replied, his demeanor darkening as he spoke of trickster gods.

"Then there are infernal forces—demons. They forge pacts with magicians and sorcerers, those who dare to meddle with powers beyond mortal grasp. These agreements might appear innocuous at first, but over time, they corrode one's essence. Those who descend into the abyss of infernal pacts invariably lose their souls, transmuting into monstrous entities eventually," Norodiir explained, his voice heavy with the gravity of mentioning demonic compacts.

Noah gasped with recognition, the events he'd watched unfold with Liam in the Tower of the Priors now making more sense. "This is what I watched in Rankier!"

Norodiir inclined his head, acknowledging Noah's realization. "Indeed, the machinations of higher powers and the influence of magic can intertwine in intricate and often treacherous ways. The threads of destiny are complex and understanding them requires careful observation and guidance. Those fools made a deal with dark forces, trading their souls for fleeting power."

"What will happen to them?" Noah asked.

"At first, though physically deformed, their lives will continue normally. They will find they have more magical power, more latent abilities which manifest, and more control over the powers they previously had. Then, an insidious voice will begin to manifest within their minds, gnawing away at their presence, until it overtakes their bodies. Once it has done this, they will become vessels for the demons they made their bargains with. The demons will roam this land, wreaking havoc upon humanity and mortals alike," Norodiir said, his voice growing darker with each word.

Noah remained silent, his mind consumed by worry as he recalled the number of the King's sorcerers that had entered the pool in Rankier. If each of those men became demons and were unleashed on this world, chaos would ensue. His memories of the demon hybrid progenies in Zefra were enough to make him shudder in fear, knowing that the actual demons themselves would roam the world freely was too much.

"I need to learn everything you can teach me," Noah said firmly, voice filled with urgency. "A demon army will soon be unleashed upon the earth, and I think this is why the gods have chosen me as their vessel. I need to understand how to use my powers, as only then will I be able to protect those I love and the kingdoms."

Norodiir smiled grimly and nodded. "Well then, let's begin."

Noah's initiation into the world of magic unfolded with mental exercises, Norodiir guided him to regain his mental composure and concentrate on maintaining a clear mind, free of distractions. He led Noah through the currents, teaching him how to sense his surroundings within his mind and feel the elements both within and around him.

The task was more challenging than Noah anticipated. Amidst the backdrop of animal life and ambient noise, distinguishing the elements proved perplexing. It felt almost maddening as he grappled with distinguishing external sensations perceived by his ears from the inner sensations he believed he should feel within his mind.

As the sun began its descent, signaling the end of the day, Norodiir indicated that their session was concluded. Noah felt discouraged, acutely aware of his perceived failure.

"Do not lose hope. It often takes time for individuals to attune themselves to the elements. Had you succeeded today, it would have been an impressive feat," Norodiir advised, his tone encouraging despite Noah's setback. "Return tomorrow at noon, and we shall continue."

The subsequent weeks were a flurry of training for Liam and Noah.

Each morning, they engaged in challenging exercises under Novath's guidance. Novath, always inventive, devised increasingly adventurous ways to push their limits. The afternoons were dedicated to individual pursuits: Noah delved into magic with Norodiir, while Liam honed his combat skills and strategic thinking.

The days were arduous, the training sessions demanding, and by day's end, their bodies were left weary and fatigued. But with perseverance came progress.

Then, on the eve of the royal wedding, a breakthrough arrived for Noah. With Norodiir's guidance, he had spent what felt like an eternity on a rock, striving to harness and direct the elements around him. Amidst the mental effort, he discovered a subtle thread—a resonance that harmonized with the world's essence when all else was muted.

Seizing the thread in his mind's grip, Noah tugged at it, his eyes widening as a sudden gust of wind upended him from his rocky perch. He landed on the ground with an undignified yelp. Norodiir chuckled warmly, rising to assist him.

As Noah got to his feet, he couldn't suppress his elation. "Did you see that? I did it!"

Norodiir nodded, approval shining in his eyes. "Indeed, you've uncovered the connection with the elements. Now that you've established it, summoning it in the future will become second nature. You've taken your first steps towards mastering your magic."

"Let me attempt it again," Noah requested, his features tense with concentration as he reached out for the mental thread. As Norodiir had suggested, this time it felt more accessible, and Noah held onto it tightly while visualizing his desired outcome. To his exhilaration, a small sphere of water lifted from a nearby creek and drifted towards him. Thrilled by his success, Noah was about to turn and share his achievement with Norodiir when an unexpected splash of cold water drenched him.

With a chuckle, Norodiir's voice carried a tone of amusement. "And that is the consequence of losing focus while manipulating magic."

Noah shivered from the lingering chill of the water that had drenched him from head to toe. He listened intently to Norodiir's guidance, the calm and instructive tone of the elder Elf helping him regain focus. He nodded, determined to succeed this time.

As he reached out for the mental thread once again, a warm and flickering flame materialized in his hand. The heat radiating from the flame was a stark contrast to the cold water that had drenched him, and he felt his clothing slowly drying as the water evaporated under the flame's warmth.

Norodiir's encouraging words pushed Noah to further extend his control. He carefully maneuvered the flame away from his body, directing it towards a pile of kindling nearby. Sweat formed on his brow as he concentrated, pushing his magical abilities as much as he could. The flame hovered above the kindling, waiting patiently as Noah strained to maintain control.

As Norodiir praised his progress and instructed him to release the flame, Noah complied. The flame descended onto the pile of kindling, igniting it and transforming it into a warm, smokeless fire. Norodiir joined him, sitting down in front of the fire with an amiable smile.

"Wonderful," Norodiir complimented. "Now, how about we enjoy some dinner?"

Chapter 26:
Murder

Noah entered his chambers to find Liam resting on the bed, engrossed in a book borrowed from the Grand Library. With a comfortable smile, he joined Liam, settling in and resting his head on Liam's shoulder.

Curious, Noah asked, "What are you reading?"

Liam looked up from the pages, his eyes lighting up. "It is the tale of the Elven explorer Finlayel and his journeys beyond our realm. They say he discovered vast continents across the seas and encountered enormous sea monsters on his voyages."

Noah nodded, intrigued. "Sounds fascinating. I'll have to give it a read once you're done. Guess what? I managed to control the elements today." Excitement filled Noah's voice, his pride was evident.

Liam's expression lit with pleasure. "That's incredible news!" He leaned in, capturing Noah's lips in a tender kiss, celebrating this achievement together. Noah instinctively responded, eagerly kissing back deeply, pressing himself firmly against Liam's warm body.

Noah's arms encircled Liam, his touch filled with desire as he started to peel away Liam's clothing. Liam responded with eagerness, moving with a graceful fluidity that allowed Noah to uncover his heated skin. Simultaneously, Liam's hands moved to Noah's clothing, the anticipation evident in his actions as he removed each layer with a sense of urgency.

Finally, both were kneeling naked on the bed and they stared at one another hungrily. Noah's erection was in its full glory, his cock already leaking with arousal. As he devoured his lover's body with his eyes, Liam's skin flushed red with blood, his desire high at the sight of Noah's lust for him.

Liam swooped in to make the first move. Leaning down, he took Noah's thick cock in his mouth, lapping greedily at the juices that leaked from it. Noah sighed in pleasure as Liam's warm mouth enveloped his member, tongue lapping along the shaft and sensitive tip.

"Gods, that feels amazing," Noah said, looking down at the top of Liam's head bobbing up and down on his cock. His own hands fisting at his thighs.

Liam took Noah's praise as encouragement, and he began eagerly dipping his head up and down Noah's long shaft. With each descent, he lowered his head further down until he felt Noah's cock sliding deep into his throat. Fighting his gag reflex as tears formed in his eyes, he held it there and then used his tongue to massage around the shaft making Noah groan in pleasure in above him.

Liam began plunging his head up and down, steadily throat fucking himself on Noah's phallus. While his pace was slow at first, relishing the taste of Noah's cock, quickly he picked up his speed as his arousal overwhelmed his patience. With each dip of his head, Noah became harder and longer, his moans more urgent. Noah unclenched his fingers to thread them through Liam's hair lovingly, watching with dazed, lust-filled eyes as Liam repeatedly took his cock deep into his throat.

Finally, Noah pulled Liam up from his cock by his hair. Breathlessly yanking Liam's head back and unfazed by the strings of saliva and precum clinging to his chin, he devoured his lips with an open-mouthed kiss, his tongue swept in to slide along teeth and gums before dueling with Liam's tongue. Leaving him gasping for air, Noah flipped his lover around to position him on all fours. Hand fisting in Liam's hair again to keep him in position, Noah ordered, "Spread your ass for me. Show me the cunt I'm going to violate."

Using one hand to spread open his ass cheeks, Liam hissed out a moan as his cock leaked a stream of precum at the dirty words. His other hand moved to his dribbling dick to stroke it hard. The unexpected stinging slap on his other cheek caused him to yelp and jerk forward, his neck arching painfully, scalp smarting from the hair pull as Noah held steady.

"Did I say to use only one hand? Use both hands." Noah's words came out hoarse with lust, "Spread them wide and arch your back so that I can see everything, you filthy little boy."

Liam's eyes rolled back in frenzied excitement as Noah's grip on his hair yanked his head back even further, stretching his neck while pushing his shoulders down. His hand immediately released his penis to reach back and cup the ass cheek that was blessed with a burning red handprint. He sobbed as he lifted and spread his buttocks, widening his stance and shifting his hips higher in offering.

"Beautiful, so fucking beautiful and all mine," Noah breathed in admiration. His free hand reverently brushed against Liam's tight hole, then his finger flicked hard against it to watch it twitch and contract. Liam jerked forward again in surprise and squealed, only to be yanked abruptly back again, his hair being used like reins on a horse. The deceptively gentle petting of his anus continued, yet he was now on guard, breath hitching as he waited for another stinging caress.

Loving that he kept Liam guessing, Noah released Liam's hair to let his head drop to the luxurious bedding and then shifted down to bury his face as tightly as he could into that incredible ass crack. His hot tongue eagerly lapped at Liam's tight hole, pushing in deeply on first penetration. His hands reached around and under Liam to grasp his nipples, twisting them cruelly to earn a strangled scream and copious amounts of precum for his efforts. His palms then soothed the tortured little nubbins, pressing and massaging only to pinch them viciously again while he tongue-fucked Liam's dank man-cunt.

Liam moaned a constant stream of gibberish, overwhelmed by

pleasure as he rocked on his lover's tongue. He pushed back to attain deeper penetration, wanting to be stretched and spread open as much as possible. Each push of Noah's tongue drove Liam into the pillows, his nipples on fire from the tenderly stern attention of strong fingers.

Noah lifted his head and pulled back to reveal Liam's sopping wet hole that quivered with anticipation. He reached to the side table for a vial of oil and poured it into the valley of Liam's ass. Liam remained pliant, moaning and shifting as he felt the cool liquid run along his crack and drip from his scrotum, his hands diligently holding himself open and presented to his lover. Noah murmured his approval as he doused his fingers, set the vial aside and without warning pushed his two middle fingers deep inside Liam's tight hole, riding them deep to their full length. He then immediately set a pounding, squelching rhythm that had Liam sobbing in ecstasy. Soon a third and then fourth finger joined the game and Noah watched in fascination as his thick fingers disappeared deeply into the tight ring of flesh only to reappear as he savagely scissored them to stretch Liam's burning rectum, preparing him for his monster cock.

Removing his fingers, he watched in appreciation as Liam's now swollen hole gaped slightly and then closed to wink in invitation. Unable to control himself any longer, he positioned his long fat cock against Liam's anus and meeting no resistance from the relaxed ring of muscles guarding Liam's asshole, he battered his way inside to immediately bottom out. Liam cried out in ecstatic pain, the feeling of his tight man-cunt being stretched open almost too much with the force of that first thrust.

Noah's mammoth cock pulled out completely and then pushed deep inside him again, pressing against pressure points that triggered euphoria. Liam felt the head rubbing firmly against his prostate, making him see stars and bite his lip at the sensation. Already insensate, he raised his ass higher in the air giving Noah full access to desecrate and use it.

Noah pulled out completely and bottomed out repeatedly, watching as his cock stretched the ring of muscle to sink in and hit a depth that made Liam moan in pain and pleasure, his balls slapping obscenely against Liam's scrotum. Hands still dutifully holding his ass open, Liam shifted to look back at his lover and saw lust and desire darken Noah's face.

"Please Noah, fuck me harder, ravage my pussy," Liam begged, biting out moans of pleasure as he felt Noah harden further within him at his pleading.

Noah responded, his hips moving rhythmically as his cock began plunging in and out of Liam's hole. As his head brushed up against Liam's prostate repeatedly, strings of precum dripped steadily onto the bed beneath him. The room echoed with the mingled sounds of hot, sweaty body parts slapping together, Liam's mewling sobs and Noah's steady grunts.

Noah felt the familiar tingles, knowing his orgasm was near. "I'm coming deep inside my pussy; get ready for it," he grunted out each word, as his thrusts picked up at a feverish pounding pace, pushing him closer to the edge.

Liam mewled in anticipation. "Yes, give me your seed, fill me up with it."

With one final groan Noah hammered his cock firmly into Liam's stretched hole, his expanding cock spurting long ropes of his cum deep inside Liam's guts, filling him up with his hot juice. Liam whimpered, the feeling of Noah's hot seed filling his insides triggering his own orgasm making him jizz out onto the bed beneath him.

Noah kept them positioned this way for a few moments, holding Liam firmly in place as his cock twitched and jerked and spewed his seed deep inside, painting his guts with man-jam. Liam whimpered and whined, his tight hole spasming around Noah's member. Finally, weak in the knees, Liam collapsed onto the bed, with Noah following him to lay on top of him.

Both gasping for breath, with Noah still buried deep inside Liam's juicy pit, they stayed there for several minutes. Shifting to pull out of Liam, Noah sat back on his haunches and fingered Liam's dripping hole. It was distended and red and raw and so gorgeous that he leaned forward to kiss it, tonguing his own cum out then leaning forward and kiss Liam, feeding him his seed.

Finally exhausted, he fell back onto the bed and drew Liam up to his chest, draping him over his body. Liam settled in, legs on the outsides of

Noah's thick thighs, to relish the warmth of Noah's body, feeling safe and loved in his arms. Noah's hands smoothed down Liam's back and into the valley of his ass, spreading the cheeks and teasing the abused little orifice with six fingers, using his own cum to help stretch it open even more. Liam moaned passively and rubbed against him in weary thrusts, letting him do whatever he wanted with his exploited rectum. After a time, Noah slowly withdrew his hands one at a time and brought them to Liam's mouth. Obediently, Liam opened up, tongue out and lovingly sucked each finger clean.

"Are you worried about tomorrow?" Liam's voice broke the tranquil silence that surrounded them.

Noah considered the question, his gaze drifting towards the horizon outside the chamber's window before he replied. "Yes and no. I understand the reasons behind it, the weight it carries for our realms. But it's also hard, knowing that even after the ceremony, it's you who truly has my heart."

Liam's eyes met Noah's, understanding and sadness in his gaze. "I understand the politics of it all, the duty we both have. Yet, emotions don't always follow logic. My heart rebels at the idea of you being with someone else."

Noah sighed, his fingers absently tracing patterns on the smooth skin of Liam's back. "Believe me, this wasn't my dream either. But it's a reality thrust upon us. I wish there was another way."

Liam's expression turned even more melancholy, his voice tinged with vulnerability. "And what about me? What role do I play in this, in your life? Will I be the one who stands by you, loving you from the shadows while you play the part of a happily married King?"

"I…I don't know Liam. If I could marry you, I would, you know this. But I can't, I have a part to play. If it makes you unhappy, and although it would break my heart, then perhaps we would be better off separating. Maybe if I gave you distance from me, you could heal. Maybe you would find another man, one who could please you more than I do and love you better. They could give you what you deserve," Noah replied, heart aching as the words left his lips.

Liam looked at Noah, his eyes wide with surprise and hurt. "You're suggesting we end things between us?" His voice quivered, revealing the depth of his emotions.

"No, Liam, I am not suggesting that; I don't want that at all," Noah hurried to clarify, his fingers reaching out to gently touch Liam's cheek. "I can't imagine my life without you. But I also cannot bear to see you in pain because of me."

Tears welled up in Liam's eyes, his voice choked with emotion. "Noah, you are not just a passing fancy to me. I don't want anyone else. I want you, all of you. Even if it means sharing you with the world, with Enwa, and with your future children."

Noah's heart clenched at Liam's words, his own eyes shimmering with unshed tears. "I do not want to lose you either, Liam. But this path we're on is complicated and painful. I want you to be happy, to find someone who can give you the life you deserve."

Liam took a shaky breath, his gaze unwavering as he spoke softly. "You are the one I want, Noah. I'll take whatever part of you I can have, even if it's not all of you. I will be by your side, even if I have to do it in secret, even if it means pretending. Because I love you."

Noah's resolve wavered, his heart aching as he realized the depth of Liam's feelings. "And I love you, Liam. More than I ever thought possible. But I don't want you to sacrifice your happiness for me."

Liam shook his head, a determined glint in his eyes. "Being with you is my happiness, Noah. Don't push me away. Let's find a way to make this work, even if the world sees us differently. Our love is worth it."

Noah's hand tightened on Liam's cheek, his gaze intense and full of raw emotion. "You're right. Our love is worth fighting for. I'll find a way to make this right, to keep you by my side."

Liam's lips curved into a small, watery smile. "That's all I want, Noah. To be with you, no matter the challenges."

Noah leaned in, capturing Liam's lips in a passionate kiss, sealing their promise to each other amidst the uncertainty that lay ahead.

*****

Efandril found peace in the quiet of her chambers, the weight of the day's responsibilities and preparations finally settling. Her chambermaid's oversight in leaving the window open had allowed a cool night breeze to infiltrate, and she took a moment to close it, ensuring her rest would be undisturbed. The hours had stretched long, marked by the culmination of final arrangements for Enwa's upcoming wedding. The coordination and fine-tuning alongside Serena had been demanding, but they had managed to address every detail. Efandril's determination was resolute; her daughter's union with Noah must unfold seamlessly.

As she prepared for bed, Efandril's mind wandered through the whirlwind of preparations that had consumed the past few weeks. The wedding arrangements had indeed been hurried, an outcome she deemed necessary following the untimely death of her beloved son, Helion. The urgency was palpable, driven by the need to secure Enwa's position in the wake of the tragedy. The potential threats to her daughter's claim to the throne loomed, and the weight of that responsibility had guided Efandril's decisions.

Despite the haste, she found a measure of contentment in the match she had orchestrated. Noah, the chosen suitor, bore a noble lineage and possessed strength that could safeguard Enwa. Efandril acknowledged that there was an undercurrent of attraction between Noah and Liam, yet she firmly believed that matters of the heart could be set aside in service of their duty to the realm. Just as Enwa cherished her affection for Finnae, Efandril held confidence that Enwa and Noah would find a way to balance their personal desires with the stability of the kingdom. In her heart, she hoped that their shared understanding of duty would guide them toward a harmonious union, even in the midst of their own private yearnings.

Efandril's mind remained immersed in her contemplations, oblivious to the silent presence that emerged from the shadows behind her. A shrouded figure, clad in the depths of darkness, made his way into her chamber. His form was concealed in black attire, a mask of obsidian paint veiling his features. Twin daggers adorned his hips, glinting with the promise of lethal intent. This was an assassin, a master of the deadly arts, deployed when outcomes demanded certainty.

Her heart pounding, Efandril's gaze finally met the reflection of the intruder in her chamber's mirror. Panic surged within her, but her reaction was belated. As she moved to arm herself, grasping for a concealed blade she had stashed for these very moments, the assassin was already in motion. Swiftly, he bridged the distance between them, his blades finding their mark with deadly precision as her throat was slashed open.

A strangled gasp escaped Efandril's lips, her hands instinctively reaching to stem the flow of her own lifeblood. Warm crimson seeped through her trembling fingers, staining her attire a vivid scarlet. Her strength wavered, and she sank to her knees, the world swimming before her eyes. In the mirror's reflection, she watched the shadowed figure melt back into the embrace of darkness, retreating through the window she had sealed only moments before.

As life's tendrils slipped away, Efandril's mind was consumed by thoughts of her daughter, Enwa. A powerful surge of maternal love pulsed through her weakening form, a final farewell sent through the ethereal threads of connection. The tears welled in her eyes, merging with the rivulets of blood. A silent goodbye was whispered in her mind, a last projection of her affection. With her husband's memory echoing softly in her thoughts, Efandril surrendered to the inevitable. Her eyes closed, the world faded, and she embraced the unknown with the anticipation of reunion with him on the boughs of the Trestos, the sacred tree to the afterlife.

*****

Enwa's world shattered as a chilling mental touch jolted her from her slumber. It was a sensation both intimate and terrifying, a connection to her mother that transcended the physical realm. The tendrils of death's approach were unmistakable, conveyed through their unspoken bond. Gasping, Enwa sat upright, her heart racing in sync with the drumbeat of dread in her chest.

The urgency of the moment spurred her into action. She sprang out of bed, a whirlwind of movement and purpose. The world around her seemed to blur as she navigated the corridors of the palace, her steps guided by instinct and desperation. At her command, a guard was dispatched to summon Commander Novath, while another was dispatched to alert Noah and Liam, the only people she knew she could trust in this harrowing hour.

Moments later, Enwa arrived at her mother's private chambers, Novath's presence a somber reassurance at her side. His grave expression mirrored the gravity of the situation. They shared a silent understanding, a union of purpose in the face of impending tragedy.

Novath took the lead, his armor-clad figure a bulwark against the unknown horrors that awaited within. Enwa followed, her breath caught in her throat as the chamber's door swung open to reveal a scene of unspeakable anguish.

There, bathed in a pool of crimson, lay her mother's lifeless form. Enwa's eyes widened in shock and horror, her breath hitching as grief collided with the shock. The blade, untouched and unused, rested beside the lifeless body like a cruel mockery of the failed protection it had offered.

The room felt stifling, the air heavy with the scent of death, steeped in sorrow and unspoken questions. Enwa's hands trembled as she covered her mouth, unable to look away from the devastating tableau before her. Commander Novath's presence was a grounding force at her side, his strength lending her a measure of stability in this maelstrom of emotions.

Enwa's voice trembled with a mix of anguish and anger as she demanded answers. "How did this happen?"

The weight of her mother's death pressed upon her, suffocating her like a heavy shroud. She struggled to contain the tempest of emotions brewing within her, knowing that unraveling now would only hinder her ability to uncover the truth.

Novath's analytical gaze swept over the scene, his experience and training allowing him to maintain a semblance of composure even amidst the harrowing circumstances. Kneeling by the Queen's lifeless form, he assessed the grisly aftermath of the assassination.

"Her throat has been cut, an assassin must have been waiting for her in her rooms and slipped out once the deed was done," he said, voice filled with sorrow while his eyes burned with a need for vengeance. "There is a note here, laying by your mother's side, bearing the symbol of the Jade Dawn. They are an assassin's guild, one which guarantees results and exacts a high price for it. Whomever wanted this done paid a fortune."

Her heart ached as he spoke the words she dreaded hearing. The Queen, her mother, had been murdered in the sanctity of her own chambers, a place meant to be safe and private. Enwa's tears flowed freely as she confronted the stark reality of the loss. Yet, amidst her grief, a fierce determination ignited within her—a determination to unearth the responsible party and bring them to justice.

Her eyes shifted to the note he mentioned, the symbol of the Jade Dawn glinting ominously in the dim light. It was a name she had heard whispered in the shadows, a name synonymous with fear and death. Her mother's death had been orchestrated by a cold and calculated hand, a truth that gnawed at Enwa's core.

Fury mixed with sorrow in Novath's eyes, a reflection of the storm of emotions that raged within Enwa herself. They shared an unspoken resolve, a commitment to unravel this conspiracy and avenge the Queen's murder.

Clutching the edge of a nearby table for support, Enwa wiped her tears away with a determined gesture. "We will hunt down this assassin's guild, this Jade Dawn. They will not escape justice for what they've done." Her voice held a quiet intensity, a vow made in the shadow of her mother's lifeless body.

Novath nodded in agreement, his gaze unwavering. "We will bring them to justice, Your Highness. I will marshal every resource at my disposal to track down these killers and ensure that they pay for their heinous crime."

"Thank you, Novath. See to it that our other guests are safe as well." Enwa replied, cradling herself with her arms, trying to fight back the grief that threatened to overwhelm her.

Novath bowed his head in acknowledgment, his commitment to his duty and his loyalty to Enwa unwavering. "Of course, Your Highness. I will ensure their safety and initiate a thorough investigation immediately."

He turned to leave the chamber, his footsteps echoing down the corridor as he went to execute his orders. Enwa remained in the room, her heart heavy with sorrow and determination. She couldn't change the past, but she could shape the future, and in that moment, she vowed to honor her mother's memory by bringing justice to those responsible for her death.

With a heavy sigh, Enwa approached her mother's lifeless form, gently closing her eyes and whispering a final farewell. The room felt colder now, a chilling reminder of the darkness that had infiltrated their midst. As Enwa's tears fell, a quiet resolve burned in her eyes—a resolve to stand strong, seek the truth, and ensure that her realm remained unshaken amidst the storms that threatened to tear it apart.

*****

Noah was abruptly roused from his sleep by an urgent knocking that reverberated through his chamber. With a swift movement, he got out of the bed where Liam still slept, his features relaxed after their earlier activities. Noah quickly donned his robe and retrieved his sword, Justice, before answering the insistent summons at the door.

As he swung the door open, a palace guard stood there with an expression of urgency etched across his face. The guard delivered his message promptly, "My lord, is everything well?"

Concern furrowed Noah's brow as he responded, "Yes, we are fine. Why do you ask?"

The guard's urgency was evident as he explained, "There has been an attack on the Queen. I've been sent to check on you and Lady Serena. Would you come with me to assess the situation?"

Noah's heart clenched at the news, his mind racing with thoughts of the Queen's safety. He exchanged a brief glance with Liam, who was now awake and alert, fully understanding the gravity of the situation. In moments like these, their connection was unspoken but profound.

Nodding to the guard, Noah and Liam swiftly dressed, ensuring they were prepared for whatever awaited them. As they followed the guard through the palace's corridors, Noah's thoughts were filled with concern for Enwa and the unfolding events.

The urgency in the air was palpable as Noah, Liam, and the guard reached Serena's chambers. The muffled sounds of a struggle emanated from within, accompanied by a sharp cry of pain that sent chills down their spines. Without a second thought, Noah's instincts kicked in, and he burst through the door with a powerful kick, his heart racing with worry.

Inside the room, chaos reigned. A man stood menacingly over Serena, her figure sprawled on the floor, blood seeping from a deep wound in her abdomen where a sinister blade was embedded. Even in her injured state, Serena fought back with fierce determination, her own blade buried in her assailant's chest. The man, however, refused to relent, determined to carry out his deadly mission.

With their entry, the man's attention briefly shifted, providing Serena a momentary respite. Sensing the urgency of the situation, he lunged forward, his remaining blade aimed at Serena with lethal intent. But Noah was swift to react, driven by a potent mix of fear and anger.

Noah's emotions surged as he harnessed the newfound connection he had with the elements. In a fluid motion, he gestured upward, his mind focused and his will commanding the wind. Responding to his call, the air around him stirred and then obeyed, enveloping the assailant and halting his advance. The man was lifted off the ground, suspended like a puppet on invisible strings, before being forcefully slammed against the nearby wall.

The impact was jarring, and the man's body crumpled against the hard wooden surface. Noah's control over the wind held him pinned, rendering him helpless and incapacitated. The room fell silent except for the labored breaths of the wounded and the eerie whistling of the wind that had been summoned to their aid.

Empowered by his growing mastery of his abilities, Noah wasted no time as he rushed to Serena's side, his heart pounding with a mixture of anxiety and determination. The scene before him was dire – Serena lay on the ground, her wound bleeding steadily, grimly staining the floor in a pool of red. Gritting his teeth, Noah's focus sharpened as he delicately extracted the wicked blade from her abdomen, causing her to cry out in pain as the blood flow intensified.

Liam, ever the supportive presence, cradled Serena's head in his hands, offering comfort amidst the chaos. With urgency, Noah applied pressure to the wound, his brows furrowing as he assessed the severity of the situation. The minutes ticked away, each one crucial as Serena's strength waned and she faded before him.

Noah's command cut to the nearby guard cut the tension. "Go for help; we need a healer immediately!"

Just as the situation seemed to spiral out of control, Commander Novath and a contingent of guards arrived on the scene. Concern etched on their faces, they bore witness to Serena's condition, their hearts heavy with worry.

A sense of urgency gripped Noah, time was of the essence and waiting for a healer to arrive might be a luxury they couldn't afford. His eyes met Serena's, a silent exchange of understanding passing between them. Noah steeled himself, knowing the pain he was about to inflict upon her.

"No choice… need to cauterize… stop bleeding," Noah muttered, more to himself than anyone else. His voice was resolute, his decision made. Gently retracting his hand, he focused his power, summoning flames to his fingertips. He held his hand over Serena's wound, the flames dancing with an intensity that matched the turmoil in his heart.

Serena's cry of pain pierced the air, mingling with the scent of burning flesh. Her body tensed against the searing heat, and Liam's grip tightened on her as he murmured soothing words. Noah's concentration was unbroken, the flames carefully applied, their purpose clear. The heat scorched the wound, cauterizing the injured vessels and halting the dangerous flow of blood.

The room was heavy with tension as the process unfolded, Serena's pain etched onto her features. But as Noah surveyed his work, his chest tightened with relief. The bleeding had ceased, and though the wound would scar, the immediate threat had been quelled.

With his task complete, Noah released his hold on the flames, letting them dissipate. He met Liam's gaze, finding gratitude and concern there. The bond between them, tested by turmoil, remained unbroken. Serena's shallow breaths filled the room, a reminder of her fragile state, but for now, they had managed to stave off the worst outcome as the blood flow had stopped.

As Noah's relief transformed into a fresh wave of dread, his heart sank like a stone in his chest. His eyes widened in horror as he beheld Serena's once-pale veins now marred by the ominous spread of dark poison, its insidious advance mercilessly heading towards her heart. Panic threatened to consume him, but he clenched his fists, determination mingling with the terror coursing through him.

The chilling sound of the assassin's chuckle sent a surge of rage through Noah's veins, a red haze of anger clouding his vision. He pivoted towards the source of the sinister sound, his voice a dangerous growl as he demanded answers, his fury a tangible force. "What did you do?" he bellowed, his voice laced with a raw intensity that mirrored the storm within him.

The assassin's weakened coughs were punctuated by gory splatters of blood, his body betraying the consequences of his own actions. In the face of Noah's wrath, the assassin's amusement remained unabated, his dark demeanor contrasting starkly with the gravity of the situation. With a voice as venomous as a serpent's bite, he revealed the sinister truth. "T'is the devil's kiss. There is naught that will save her now."

Noah's entire being trembled with fury and despair, his heart aching as he stared at Serena's weakening form. Every fiber of his being screamed for vengeance against the assassin responsible for this vile act. He took a step closer, his gaze locked onto the dying assassin's form. "You'll pay for this," he vowed, his voice a chilling whisper.

A chorus of approaching footsteps echoed in the chamber, the guards who had accompanied Noah now closing in on the assassin. Commander Novath's presence loomed, his face a mask of grim determination as he surveyed the scene. "Secure him, he will tell us who paid him to do this atrocity," Novath ordered, his voice holding a promise of justice.

A final, mirthless laugh escaped the assassin's lips, the chilling sound a haunting echo in the room as he bit down on something concealed within his mouth. Noah's eyes widened in alarm as he watched the scene unfold, dread settling over him like a suffocating fog.

Foam erupted from the assassin's lips, a grotesque display of his body's violent reaction. His complexion rapidly drained of color, leaving his features a sickly shade of ashen gray. The unfolding events played out in cruel slow motion before Noah's disbelieving eyes, and a knot of despair tightened in his chest.

The assassin's body convulsed in its death throes, his final moments marked by a brutal struggle as life relinquished its grip on him. Noah's heart pounded like a war drum, a mixture of horror and grim realization settling heavily upon him. The assassin's scheme had reached its gruesome conclusion, and there was no stopping the inevitable.

As the last breath of life escaped the assassin, his body went limp, crumpling to the floor in a final, irreversible slumber. The wind that had held him aloft dispersed, its once powerful grip now finding only empty an husk. Noah stood frozen, his chest heaving as he tried to process the macabre tableau before him.

His attention quickly returned to Serena, his fingers trembling as he gingerly touched her pale cheek. His heart ached at the unfairness of it all, the cruel twist of fate that had threatened to tear her from him. Grief and determination intertwined within him, and he met her fading gaze with his own fierce resolve.

Serena's lips parted weakly, her voice a fragile whisper laden with pain. "Noah…"

"I'm here," he replied, his voice a brittle attempt at comfort. He gripped her hand tightly, his presence a steady anchor amidst the chaos surrounding them. The turmoil in his eyes mirrored the storm of emotions in his heart.

"Look after Enwa; she'll need your protection more than ever. And Liam, keep him safe," Serena managed, her voice weak from the encroaching darkness. "I wish I could have done better for both you and Liam. The realm required your union, for stability and order," she continued, her words fading into the feeble whispers of her fading breath.

"Don't blame yourself, Grandmother," Noah's voice trembled as he tried to offer comfort, tears slipping down his cheeks. The weight of impending loss settled heavily on his shoulders, and he struggled to contain his grief. "Please hold on, Grandmother. The healers will be here soon; they can save you."

Serena's pale lips curved into a faint, bittersweet smile. She reached out a feeble hand to touch Noah's cheek. "My dear Noah, you've always been a source of strength. Remember, sometimes sacrifices are necessary for the greater good."

Noah's heart ached as he held her frail hand against his cheek. "I understand, Grandmother. But right now, my heart aches for you."

Liam stood by, his eyes glistening with unshed tears. He took Serena's other hand, holding it gently, his voice cracking. "You've shown us love and wisdom. We'll honor your memory, I promise."

Serena's eyelids grew heavy, her breathing shallower with each passing moment. Her gaze shifted between Noah and Liam, serenity spreading across her features. "My time draws near... But your journey, yours is just beginning..."

As her voice faded into silence, her grip on their hands weakened, and her body seemed to relax. The room fell into a heavy silence, and grief hung in the air like a veil. Noah's tears flowed freely, and Liam's shoulders trembled with sorrow. Noah's anguished cry reverberated through the chamber as he collapsed onto Serena's lifeless form. He held her with a desperation born of grief, clinging to the last remnant of his family. His tears flowed freely, his sorrow a torrential storm that matched the turmoil in his heart.

Liam stood beside him, his own tears falling as he placed a comforting hand on Noah's shoulder. There were no words that could assuage this pain, no gestures that could mend what was broken. Together, they shared in their profound loss, the weight of it binding them even closer.

Commander Novath and the guards respectfully maintained a somber distance, their heads bowed in honor of the fallen Empress. Serena's presence had been a beacon of strength, wisdom, and guidance. Her absence left a void that could never truly be filled.

Chapter 27:
Ascension

The next morning arrived, casting its pale light upon Enwa, Noah, and Liam as they gathered in private with Commander Novath. The weight of the previous night's tragedy still clung to them, a heavy shroud of sorrow and loss that none could escape. For Enwa, Noah, and Liam, it was the ache of losing loved ones, while for Novath, it was the bitter taste of failure that gnawed at him.

"We cannot proceed with the wedding after what transpired last night," Enwa declared, her voice tremulous with the lingering emotions of grief.

Noah's answer came swift and sad, his eyes carrying the telltale signs of someone who had spent the night in tears. "Is postponing the wedding is the appropriate course of action?" he asked, his voice carrying a weight that mirrored the heaviness in his heart.

Liam said sorrowfully. "It wouldn't be right to celebrate while our hearts are burdened with this loss."

Novath's demeanor reflected the weight of the circumstances they found themselves in. "I would normally be inclined to agree, Your Majesty" he began, his voice coloured with understanding and reluctance. "However, I fear that postponement might not be a viable option. The Court is already aware of last night's events, and some may interpret it as a sign of vulnerability. To halt the wedding now could be seen as an opportunity for our enemies to exploit."

Enwa, Noah, and Liam exchanged uneasy glances, their thoughts racing as they grappled with the conflicting emotions of grief and duty. Enwa's brows furrowed, her heart torn between honoring her mother's memory and safeguarding the stability her union with Noah would bring. Noah clenched his fists, frustration and sorrow warring within him, while Liam's eyes bore a mixture of sympathy and determination.

"Are you suggesting that we proceed with the wedding as if nothing has happened?" Enwa's voice wavered with disbelief and indignation.

Novath's expression softened, his compassionate gaze locking onto Enwa's. "I'm suggesting that we find a way to honor your mother's memory while also showing strength in the face of adversity. We can acknowledge the tragedy that has occurred, pay our respects, and then proceed with the wedding as a testament to the unity that the realm needs now more than ever."

Enwa's lips pressed together, she glanced at Noah and Liam, seeking their input, and found understanding and support in their expressions.

"It will not be easy Enwa, but logically, Novath has a point," Noah replied as he wiped tears from his tired eyes. "We can use this occasion to demonstrate our resilience, to show that despite the hardships, we stand strong together."

Liam also nodded, his gaze steady as he met Enwa's eyes. "We can honor your mother's memory in our own way, while also sending a message to our adversaries that we won't be deterred by their attempts to sow chaos."

Enwa's shoulders sagged with the weight of the decision before her, but she understood what they meant, they could not afford to show weakness. With a heavy sigh, she nodded her agreement. "Very well, we'll proceed with the wedding. But we will find a way to honor my mother's memory and ensure that her sacrifice is not in vain."

*****

The wedding took place in the elevated embrace of the mountains, nestled within the Elven sacred enclave known as Ilvalon. Perched atop the zenith of the tallest peak, Ilvalon was revered as a place where Elves could aspire to touch the heavens. The journey to Ilvalon was a passage along cobblestone paths that wound through the dense woods, the towering trees standing sentinel over the winding trail.

Noah and Enwa stepped onto the path, adorned in regal attire befitting their positions. Noah donned a suit crafted from lavish fabrics that sparkled in the dappling sunlight filtering through the trees. Enwa graced the path in an elegant gown, its material as ethereal as air, yet radiant under the gentle illumination. A resplendent necklace of diamonds adorned her neck, culminating in a magnificent emerald at its heart.Perched atop her head was a graceful silvery-gold tiara, perfectly nestled within her hair.

As they made their way along the path, Elves lined its sides, offering their well wishes and praise. However, the atmosphere was more solemn than celebratory. Many of the Elves nodded respectfully, tears glistening in their eyes as they mourned the loss of their beloved Queen.

Novath, Liam, and Finnae followed closely behind, acting as their escort and members of the wedding party in lieu of Efaldrin and Serena. A contingent of ten Elven soldiers formed an honor guard, discreetly interspersed among the well-wishers and common folk along the path. Given the recent assassinations, no risks were being taken, and the presence of the guards ensured an added layer of security.

As they proceeded through the forest, Enwa and Noah walked hand in hand, surrounded by the somber procession. The trees appeared to acknowledge the significance of the occasion, some seemingly bowing in reverence as they passed, showering the path with a cascade of fallen leaves that danced gracefully through the air.

Noah stole a moment to look back at Liam, their eyes meeting in a silent exchange. Liam's nod conveyed his support and understanding, his expression a mix of tension and affection. They both knew that this day would be particularly difficult for Liam, given his feelings for Noah, but he remained steadfast in his commitment to stand by him. They were trapped in this intricate political dance with no easy way out.

Finnae maintained her composed demeanor, her expression carefully neutral. Concealed beneath her calm exterior, Enwa could discern the undercurrent of discontent and unhappiness. Despite her ability to hide her emotions, Enwa could see the weight of the situation on Finnae's shoulders. They too were ensnared in circumstances beyond their control, forced to navigate a complex web of politics. Enwa found solace in the fact that Finnae had someone who understood her feelings in Liam, providing a sense of companionship in the midst of the turmoil.

Upon reaching the summit of the mountain, they stepped out from the sheltering canopy of trees and were greeted by a breathtaking scene. At the summit's crest, a grand spectacle unfolded before them. Positioned at the forefront of a sweeping staircase meticulously chiseled into the mountainside, a colossal stone obelisk loomed over an elevated platform. Adorning this platform was an intricately painted depiction of Qyana, the revered Elven deity and the embodiment of the world's mother. Standing an impressive twenty feet in height, the painting appeared to possess a lifelike essence, its depiction of Qyana seeming to come alive within the confines of the stone.

Situated on the elevated platform, a carefully chosen assembly of Court members awaited their arrival. Although Noah was unfamiliar with the majority of them, a few individuals stood out from the crowd. Among them, Norodiir caught his gaze and offered a reassuring smile. This sight provided Noah with a sense of comfort, knowing that amidst the sea of unfamiliar faces he would soon be responsible for, at least one of his mentors was present to witness this pivotal moment.

Atop the platform, positioned beneath the grand depiction of Qyana, a high priestess awaited their arrival. She was draped in a long, flowing gown of pristine white, which seemed to radiate an inner glow. Despite the marks of age on her face, her beauty remained intact, and her eyes exuded warmth and hospitality. As Enwa and Noah ascended to the platform, the priestess extended her greetings to them and the gathering spectators, her words resonating with a sense of reverence and grace.

"Welcome, esteemed witnesses, to this most remarkable occasion," her voice resounded with a gentle authority, captivating the assembled attendees and silencing them. "In ordinary times, this would be a celebration of joy, a union of two souls into one harmonious bond. However, today bears a different tone," she continued, taking a brief pause to collect her thoughts. "We find ourselves in mourning, lamenting the departure of Efandril, our revered mother-Queen, and the Empress Serena, whose wisdom exceeded her years and whose friendship was a beacon to our people. Their memories shall forever linger, and our hearts ache in the wake of their absence."

The assembled gathering remained hushed, touched by the priestess's words. Enwa's emotions were visibly stirred, tears streaming down her cheeks as she remembered her mother and the pain of her loss. Noah extended his hand, gently gripping her arm to offer solace and strength. Liam and Finnae moved closer, their presence a silent yet powerful reassurance, as they placed their hands on Enwa's shoulders, supporting her through the poignant moment.

The priestess's words carried on, allowing the crowd a moment to absorb the gravity of her statements. "Nevertheless, this remains a time for celebration. Today, we unite two souls as one and forge an unbreakable bond. We rejoice in the union of Noah, the final heir of House Earpa, destined to rule the Kingdom of Kirenth, and Enwa, the last descendant of House Eedwull, heir to the illustrious Elven realm of Elnoth. Through this union, we intertwine these noble houses for all eternity, reaffirming the enduring connections of friendship and love between our peoples."

The Priestess turned her attention to Noah, her gaze steady. "Noah, do you accept this proposal of marriage with a sincere heart and a clear mind? Are you ready to embrace the responsibilities it entails, and do you pledge to safeguard and cherish Enwa for all time?"

Noah's internal battle between his love for Liam and his duty played out across his features, a moment of hesitation visible. But then, a sense of acceptance settled upon him. "I do," he answered, his voice carrying the weight of his commitment.

"And Enwa, do you vow to stand by Noah's side with unwavering support and love? Will you ensure the continuation and fortification of his legacy, providing him the strength necessary to triumph over any challenges?" the Priestess inquired, directing her gaze towards Enwa.

Enwa also paused, her gaze shifting towards Finnae, who returned her stare with defiance. With the weight of her decision evident in her gaze, Enwa finally answered, "I do."

The Priestess smiled, her expression radiating warmth and approval. "With my blessing, I pronounce this union. May you both thrive in the light of Qyana." Her words resonated through the gathering, and the spectators offered their polite cheers and applause for the couple's union.

The depiction of Qyana radiated down upon Noah and Enwa, and to the astonishment of the crowd, she materialized from the painting, stepping out with a warm, golden glow. She materialized over the wedding, her form adjusting to their height. Her presence silenced all noise, the world seeming to hold its breath as she approached Noah and Enwa. The crowd fell to their knees in devotion, the High Priestess dropping down prostrating herself to Qyana, the mother deity of all.

Qyana extended her hand, enveloping Noah and Enwa's hands within her grasp, her benevolent warmth permeating their bodies. Enwa's tears flowed as she felt the maternal love within that touch, feeling a connection to her mother that transcended the physical realm. For Noah, astonishment washed over him as the warmth evoked memories of his grandmother. Vivid recollections of their shared moments from his childhood surged through his mind, as if Qyana herself was reliving those cherished experiences alongside him.

Qyana regarded them both with a sense of approval that transcended words, her gaze conveying a deep understanding of their experiences. Her gentle voice carried a soothing comfort as she addressed them within their minds, acknowledging the pain they had endured.

"You have both known profound suffering, my dear children, enduring losses that cut deep," Qyana spoke, her tone tender and caring, her presence embracing their grief. "Life's fairness often eludes us, yet the challenges ahead are not yet over. Stay steadfast in your bond, and in the love you hold for those dear to you. In a world tainted by darkness, your unity is a beacon of hope. Though this union may not be one born of passionate love, it is graced by my blessing. The Father has already granted his

approval to one of you, and his endorsement remains unwavering, strengthened by your actions."

Qyana gently withdrew, letting go of Enwa and Noah's hands, leaving them with a sense of both emptiness and fulfillment. The residue of her love remained, a radiant energy coursing through them, soothing their sorrow and offering a glimmer of solace. Qyana directed her attention to Liam and Finnae, reaching out to clasp their hands in her ethereal embrace.

"You both have sacrificed much for those you love. Stand by them still, through hardships, and endure with your love. Sacrifice is rewarded, and true love is worth every cost," Qyana's voice carried within their minds, resonating in the hearts of Liam and Finnae as her words held a weight of both encouragement and prophecy.

Having concluded her message, Qyana gracefully retreated, her form expanding to match the grandeur of the painting she had materialized from. She cast another gaze over the assembled crowd, a sweeping gesture of her hand initiating a profound transformation. Noah and Enwa suddenly found themselves cocooned in a radiant golden aura that radiated from their very beings. From within this luminous embrace, intricate coronets forged from mysterious metals, unfamiliar to both humankind and elves, manifested upon their brows with an otherworldly shimmer.

Upon the landing, a manifestation of regal splendor unfolded: two magnificent golden thrones emerged, their opulent grandeur equal in stature. Positioned nearby were two smaller yet equally exquisite thrones, adorned with an array of gems that emitted a celestial brilliance reminiscent of starlight.

Liam and Finnae, not exempt from the ethereal transformation, were also immersed in the radiant luminescence. Their previous attire underwent a metamorphosis into something otherworldly. The fabric itself seemed to emit an inner radiance, intricately woven with luminescent metals that caught and reflected the light. Adorning their brows were delicate tiaras, symbols of their honored positions as cherished companions to each heir.

With her message delivered, she disappeared back into the painting, resuming her prior appearance smiling benevolently above them all.

Noah and Enwa glanced at one another, still breathless from Qyana's embrace.

"Please, after you," Noah courteously gestured, indicating for Enwa to take her seat upon the right-hand throne. As she settled into her designated seat, Noah followed suit, occupying the left-hand throne. A profound silence enveloped the space as the divine light cast a gentle glow upon the assembled guests, a visual testament to the blessing they had received.

On the thrones adjacent to Noah and Enwa, Liam and Finnae took their positions, mirroring the unity displayed by the heirs. Hands joined and intertwined, Noah and Enwa firmly held the hands of Liam and Finnae, intertwining their fingers as an emblem of unbreakable connection, unity, and affection. The four figures, bathed in the radiant light, formed a tableau that resonated with both the divine and the earthly.

Amid the resounding horns that seemed to echo from the very heart of nature itself, Commander Novath stepped forward, his presence commanding the attention of all. With a powerful yet respectful tone, he declared, "All hail King Noah, the last heir of House Earpa, now the sovereign ruler of Kirenth and Elnoth. And hail Queen Enwa, heir of House Eedwull, now the reigning monarch of Elnoth and Kirenth. May their reign be prosperous and enduring, casting light upon these lands and realms for generations to come." His words resounded like a clarion call, carrying the weight of tradition and hope, and they were met with thunderous applause and cheers from the gathered crowd, rejoicing in the divine blessing and the promise of a new era under their united rule.

Amidst the cheering crowd and the weight of their newly bestowed titles, Noah's gaze flickered between Enwa and Liam, finding comfort in their presence. The squeeze of Enwa's hand and the reassuring smile from Liam provided him the strength he needed to face the challenges ahead. As the joyful celebrations continued around him, Noah's thoughts turned to the responsibilities that lay before him.

He knew that this moment marked not only a celebration of love and unity, but also the beginning of a battle against darkness that threatened to engulf their realm. The ominous shadow of the usurper and the malevolent forces that plagued their lands loomed large, reminding him that the journey ahead would be arduous. Noah was determined to rise to the occasion, to protect his people, and to fulfill his duty as king.

With his heart filled with resolve, Noah looked out over the crowd, his eyes ablaze with determination. This was just the first step in a journey of courage, sacrifice, and unwavering commitment. He was ready to face whatever challenges lay ahead, alongside those he loved, as they embarked on a path to secure the realm's future and bring light to the darkness that threatened their world.

This was just the beginning.

Epilogue:
Usurper

The messenger cautiously stepped into the King's chamber; the heavy curtains tightly drawn to barricade any intrusion of light. The room had become a sanctuary of darkness, mirroring the depths of the King's deteriorating sanity. The air within was thick with tension, and an unsettling energy seemed to hang in the air.

Navigating through the gloom, the messenger's heart raced as their eyes fell upon the disturbing remnants of the King's rage. Claw marks marred the once-pristine wooden headboard of the opulent four-poster bed, as if some feral creature had sought escape from its confines. The bedding lay shredded, torn apart as though by invisible hands possessed by a maddening fury.

As the messenger moved further into the chamber, they couldn't help but notice the details that whispered of the King's unraveling mind. Shadows seemed to writhe and contort in the corners, as if they harbored some evil presence. The air was heavy with an oppressive sense of foreboding that settled upon them like a suffocating shroud.

The messenger's heart pounded in their chest, each step fraught with unease. They had been summoned to deliver dire news, and were terrified of the reaction they would receive, their own life in mind. The once-grand chamber now exuded an aura of terror, a reflection of the turmoil that had consumed the King's soul.

Approaching the King's unnerving presence, the messenger's breath hitched as they beheld the scene before them. The King was ensconced in a pool of swirling black miasma, his labored breathing punctuating the eerie stillness that hung in the room. The very air seemed to shiver with an otherworldly energy, as if the chamber itself recoiled from the malevolence that now inhabited it.

Resisting the urge to shrink back, the messenger stood their ground, their heart pounding in their chest like a drumbeat of dread. The darkness seemed to seep into their bones, wrapping tendrils of unease around them. With bated breath, they awaited the King's acknowledgment, knowing that their presence in this unholy realm could tip the scales of his temperament.

At last, the King's voice shattered the heavy silence, cutting through the air like a blade. The messenger's spine tingled with an unsettling mixture of fear and anticipation, their very soul recoiling at the distorted duality of his tone. It was as if his words were a manifestation of the chaos that gripped his mind, an unholy symphony of torment.

"What is it? Speak."

With trepidation, the messenger delivered the news that had prompted their intrusion into this abyss of darkness. "Your Majesty, I bring news." The words tumbled from their lips, "The assassin failed to complete his mission. The Elf Queen was killed, along with the Empress-in-Exile, however they failed to kill the boy," they continued hesitant and shaken as they recounted the failure of the assassin's mission. The room seemed to absorb their words, the very walls echoing with the weight of the revelation.

The King stilled, as if having an internal conversation as his eyes went blank, before returning to the present and the messenger. "I see." He emerged from the pool naked, showing the unholy spread of the miasma through his deformed body.

The King stilled again, the voice inside his mind calming him. Its message was clear; now was not the time for panic. Deformed face composing itself, he regained control of his rage, as he dressed.

The King's demeanor shifted, his gaze momentarily distant as if engaged in an unseen dialogue within the depths of his tormented mind. Then, just as abruptly, he refocused on the messenger before him, his eyes devoid of emotion yet gleaming with an unsettling knowledge. His voice, when it resounded, held an eerie resonance, as though it emanated from the union of two distinct beings trapped within his form.

A shiver crept down the messenger's spine as they stared at the King. The very essence of the King seemed corrupted, a grotesque melding of flesh and darkness that defied the natural order. It was as if the malevolent force that had consumed him sought to reshape him into a vessel of chaos.

Without warning, the King's fury erupted, his arm contorting into a grotesque, living blade that cleaved through the air with a deadly precision. The messenger's head was severed from their body in an instant, their final gasp silenced by the macabre tableau that had just unfolded. Their lifeless form crumpled to the ground, a grim testament to the King's wrath and the terrifying capabilities he now possessed.

The chamber resonated with the echoes of the King's primal roar, the very walls quivering in response to his unbridled fury. His rage surged like a tempest, a storm of darkness that threatened to consume everything in its path. But as swiftly as the storm had arisen, it subsided, leaving behind a chilling calm that hung in the air like a shroud of dread.

As his rage abated, the King's voice reverberated through the chamber once more, its tone chillingly composed despite the violence that had just transpired.

"What now? The plan has failed, and the boy now commands Elnoth. With its forces, he will attack," the King bellowed, voice resonating with panic.

"Worry not, we shall kill the boy ourselves. Ready the army, it is time to march and end this. We shall spread my message through all the realms, and end this world. You will be the King forevermore, transcending death," the insidious voice

replied, echoing within the King's mind.

The King's demeanor shifted once again, his face regaining a semblance of composure as the voice within his mind asserted its influence. A sinister calm settled over him, and he began to dress, his form clothed in regal attire that contrasted starkly with the malevolent aura that enveloped him. His body seemed to revert to its earlier form, the twisted aberration hidden beneath the veneer of a king.

In this unholy sanctum, the King's descent into madness had reached a chilling zenith. His existence had become a mélange of darkness and power, and with every calculated move, he brought the realms closer to the brink of oblivion. The messenger's death was but a harbinger of the horrors to come, and the world trembled in anticipation of the malevolent forces that were now set in motion.

Author's Note

Thank you so much for reading my debut novel! I truly hope you enjoyed the first part of this story, and stay tuned for future releases in the near future. If you enjoyed the story, please feel free to leave an honest review on the site of your choice. Reviews greatly influence the reading decisions of others, and help independent authors stand out from the crowd.

For release updates, advanced reader signup opportunities, and more please subscribe to my newsletter at www.CGMacington.buzz.

Happy Reading!

C.G. Macington